"We need to kiss.

Angie knew exactly [...] Ryan until it felt right. As if [...] couple.

To get to a comfort level would take a considerable amount of kissing. And touching. Could she really handle that? If she blew this sting because of some ridiculous secret crush on an impossible man....

His hands squeezed her shoulders. "You're right."

His gaze locked on hers. "We have to get rid of this awkwardness between us, or risk the operation."

"I agree. Totally." She forced a smile, casually placed a palm on his chest, as if kissing him was no big deal, and hoped he didn't see her pulse leaping out of control.

This was it. The moment of truth.

He took a step. Stopped. "I'm getting a scotch."

Her whole body sagged in relief, but before she asked for a drink of her own, the stakes flashed through her mind.

So she grabbed Ryan's shoulders, pushed herself against his body and pulled him straight down into the kiss of her life....

Dear Reader,

We have exciting news! As I'm sure you've noticed, the Harlequin Blaze books you know and love have a brand-new look, starting this month. And it's *hot!* Don't you agree?

But don't worry—nothing else about the Blaze books has changed. You'll still find those unforgettable love stories with intrepid heroines, hot, hunky heroes and a double dose of sizzle!

Check out this month's red-hot reads....

I hope you're as pleased with our new look as we are. Drop by www.Harlequin.com or www.blazeauthors.com to let us know what you think.

Brenda Chin
Senior Editor
Harlequin Blaze

Lying in Bed

Jo Leigh

HARLEQUIN®
entertain, enrich, inspire™

Recycling programs
for this product may
not exist in your area.

ISBN-13: 978-0-373-79734-9

LYING IN BED

ABOUT THE AUTHOR

Jo Leigh is from Los Angeles and always thought she'd end up living in Manhattan. So how did she end up in Utah, in a tiny town with a terrible internet connection, being bossed around by a house full of rescued cats and dogs? What the heck, she says, predictability is boring. Jo has written more than forty novels for Harlequin Books. She can be contacted at joleigh@joleigh.com.

Books by Jo Leigh

To get the inside scoop on Harlequin Blaze and its talented writers, be sure to check out blazeauthors.com.

Other titles by this author available in ebook format.

Intimate at Last

Led by noted marriage counselors
Delilah and Ira Bridges, MS, MFT, LADC,
these five-day getaways focus on communication,
hidden issues, commitment, fun, friendship and
life-expanding new vistas in sensuality.

*Held in the beautiful Color Canyon Resort and Spa
located just 15 miles from the Las Vegas Strip.*

Sessions daily 10:00 A.M.–4:45 P.M.

Private Sessions Available

- Massage/Body Work
- Daily Wake-Up-Revitalized Power Yoga Sessions
- Tantric Massage In-Room Tutorials
- All Massages By Professionally Trained,
  Licensed Therapists

*Between the group sessions,
there are delightful "homeplay" assignments
to practice in the privacy of your room!*

Workshop Fee: $4500/couple
Includes all sessions and selected massages.
Hotel and most meals extra.

1

SPECIAL AGENT RYAN VAIL tossed the brochure on the bed. The amazingly comfortable-looking bed, which was a far cry from most of the rat holes he'd been stuck with on various FBI stings and stakeouts. The Color Canyon Resort and Spa was a decadent oasis in the middle of the Las Vegas desert built for people with cash to spend and a yen for excitement and being pampered.

Ryan settled against the headboard, the puffy comforter billowing around him. Straight ahead was a forty-two-inch flat-screen TV. There was a wing chair, a leather love seat, an extravagantly stocked minibar and, if he turned his head to the right, beyond the private patio was a view of a nice little courtyard with a pool and spa pool all in the shadow of the Spring Mountains. It might be February in the rest of the world, but in the Vegas desert it was a balmy seventy-two degrees with copious sunshine on the docket for the rest of the week.

He grinned, pulled out his cell phone and went right to speed dial text.

You're gonna die when you see the bathtub.

He hit Send, adjusted the pillow behind him and checked out his work stuff. Another email update on Delilah Bridges, one of the cotherapists in charge of this barbecue. Four people ran the Intimate At Last retreat weekends, all suspects in a major blackmail scheme. Unfortunately for them, they'd unwittingly targeted a friend of James Leonard, the Deputy Director of the FBI.

Ryan's phone rang, and he knew it was his partner without even looking. "Jeannie Foster. How's my favorite witness for the State?"

"Shut up, you bastard," she said, her voice echoey, as if she were speaking in a vast hall. Or a toilet stall.

Of course, he'd taken a picture of the big-enough-for-a-party whirlpool tub, which he promptly sent her. A moment later, the mother of two cursed him with her usual flair.

"I hate court. I hate lawyers. I hate judges. And don't even get me started on juries. Get me the hell out of here, Ryan."

"It should be over soon, right?"

"Probably around the time of the next ice age. Jesus, they love to hear themselves talk."

"In a few hours you'll forget all about them. This place is something else. If I'm going to be forced to sleep with you, I'm glad it's in this beauty of a bed. Which is actually more comfortable than mine at home."

Jeannie laughed. "It's not the bed, honey, it's all your extracurricular activity. I think you'd have to find a titanium mattress to keep up."

"You're hilarious."

"Nothing is hilarious today," she said. "You get the new updates on Delilah?"

"Yeah."

Her sigh was long and filled with frustration. "Interesting about her father and his criminal record, but dammit, still nothing usable. With all the data we've collected, you'd think we'd have uncovered something more viable."

"Everyone makes mistakes. But," he added, "I'm going to be such a perfect mark, they're gonna wet themselves waiting to get to me. We'll be out of here in a few days."

"I thought you said the accommodations were super deluxe?"

He grinned. This is why he liked his partner, despite the fact that she could be a stick in the mud, what with being married and a mom. She was quick…and needed a vacation as badly as he did after the intensity of the past two months preparing for this sting. "Right. Maybe it'll take the whole week."

"There we go. I have to get back to the torture chamber. I hear they're planning on using the rack next."

"Hey, I'm gonna sign off on this phone, but Ryan Ebsen's cell and laptop haven't finished charging. If there's a God, I should be asleep when you arrive, so don't wake me."

"Coming off another late night, Romeo?"

"None of your business. Go be a witness."

"I'll talk to you in the morning," she said, and then she was gone, and he was faced with the prospect of what to do with the rest of the afternoon.

It would be more fun to play craps or hang out in one of the casino bars, but from the moment he'd checked in, FBI Special Agent Ryan Vail was locked in a vault for the duration of his stay, replaced by the fictitious Ryan Ebsen. Husband of the equally fictitious Jeannie Ebsen. Son of Felicia and Bob from Reseda, California.

Ryan sifted through the file, studying the cover story he already knew inside and out. But when you pretended to be someone else, there was no such thing as too much prep. Ebsen was a regional manager for a business software firm. His lovely bride of nineteen months didn't work because she didn't need to. Not because he brought in enough money to live their extravagant life, but because she had a trust fund. A very hefty trust fund.

But Mrs. Ebsen had been spending a little too much time at the club lately with a very handsome tennis coach, which made Ryan itchy. He doubted they were sleeping together, but there was always a risk that if she started to feel as if the honeymoon was over, she could find solace in the tennis pro's arms. It had been Ryan Ebsen's idea to attend this couple's retreat week, where they would "Learn how to transition to the deeper, more meaningful stage of a committed relationship."

Mr. Ebsen, the scoundrel, really, really wanted to make the marriage work. He'd grown attached to their Brentwood home, the Manhattan pied-à-terre, his Ferrari, the first-class travel. He'd even decided to break things off with Roxanne, the gorgeous receptionist at his office. He was nothing if not serious about this intimacy crap.

He continued to read the email from his team in White Collar Crimes back in L.A. The first report of blackmail had come shortly after a weekend Intimate At Last retreat in Los Angeles, and since it dealt with some historic artwork and blackmail, the L.A. team had taken point on the investigation and now this sting operation. The Vegas office was up to speed, of course. No one wanted a turf war, but there was a time limit on this gig, because in a matter of weeks, the suspects were moving their base of operation to Cancún, Mexico.

So he was on the clock. Since the missus wasn't here, he'd unpack, take a swim, order room service, charge his equipment and himself. Far from the carnal night Jeannie imagined, he'd been up till dawn talking the Long Beach P.D. out of putting his old man in jail. The stubborn idiot had been drunk off his ass again, trying to pick a fight with a half-dozen marines. It was like dealing with a rebellious teenager, only his father was in his fifties.

So sleep tonight, and tomorrow, he and Jeannie would be the very picture of a cookie-cutter couple: powdered sugar on the outside, but filled with lots and lots to lose if a certain trust-fund wife found out about her philandering hubby.

After he'd checked out the room service menu, and thank God there was an expense account because, Jesus, the prices, he opened up his suitcase while he found the sports channel on the TV. His thoughts weren't on the scoreboards, however, but on the reason he needed this operation to succeed beyond all expectations. Deputy Director Leonard was looking to fill a staff position in his Washington, D.C., office. Ryan was a contender in a very narrow pool of candidates. And now that he was in the spotlight, he was going to make damn sure he was a shining star.

ANGIE WOLF SIGHED WHEN SHE heard the voices of the rest of the White Collar Crimes team coming in from their break on the outdoor patio. Damn, it seemed as if they'd left two minutes ago, not nearly enough time for her to breathe let alone hear herself think.

They were a great bunch: competent, dedicated and generally nice people with whom she got along well considering work colleagues were always a crapshoot. But the past two months had been brutal. She'd spent way too many hours in the office and right now she'd give anything to be alone, preferably on a ten-mile run with nothing more to worry about than beating her last record.

Even as she heard them close in on the bullpen, she stayed just as she was, legs stretched out in front of her, ankles crossed, one heel on her desk, leaning back in her chair as far as she could. The fresh air would've been nice, but two of the team members smoked and that she could do without.

"Hey, how come you didn't come out for the lifting of the Red Bulls?"

Angie smiled at Paula, another Special Agent who'd been in charge of the artwork aspect of the operation. The painting in question was a Reubens, stolen during World War II and recovered in the late 1990s. It was worth millions, and had been "gifted" to a New Mexico art gallery, which had then sold it to an anonymous private collector.

The transaction had been legal on the surface, but the granddaughter of the original owner was certain her grandfather had been blackmailed into giving away the family treasure. The Deputy Director of the FBI had been friends with the family since birth.

And now, if Angie's White Collar Crimes team had done their jobs right, the task force was days away from zeroing in on the blackmailers.

Angie realized Paula was still waiting for an answer. Break time was definitely over. "Haven't we spent enough quality time together? Two months of eighty- and ninety-hour weeks? I mean, come on."

Paula flopped into her chair and turned it so she faced Angie. "You can take a break when you're dead. Or tonight, when we go out for drinks. That one, you're not getting out of. We'll use force if necessary."

"You and what army?"

"Me, for one." It was Brad Pollinger, Angie's partner in the field. He was followed into the room by several other members of the group, all of whom cheerfully let her know that they weren't above using every dirty trick in the book to get her to join them.

"Fine. But I'm having exactly one beer." The bullpen was pretty full now, with only Fred MIA, but he was perennially late.

"Don't you have any fun?" Paula eyed Angie's sturdy

low-heeled pumps propped on the desk. Comfort won over fashion every time for Angie. "Ever?"

"I have plenty," she said, although her definition of fun leaned more heavily toward achievement than clubbing. Whether it was cutting a few seconds off her morning run or working on side projects that could get her to the next stage of her ten-year plan, she wasn't much of a party gal.

She'd always been a big believer in setting short-term goals that fed directly into long-term strategies. Even though she'd stopped being a competitive runner, she still kept up the discipline and used the skills she'd picked up as a kid to keep herself on task.

From the beginning of this assignment, she'd realized the potential. With her computer programming skills and familiarity with investigation protocols she could make a significant contribution. And she had.

Angie's new program had led to the revelation about Delilah Bridges's father, that he'd been arrested under an alias for robbery on four separate occasions. It wasn't much as far as real leads went, but it was still a piece of an ever-expanding puzzle. The broader the picture, the more likely the pieces that didn't appear to connect would suddenly come together.

She'd worked damn hard on coding that sucker, a search engine with such a sexy algorithm it had given the guys in Cyber Crimes nerdgasms.

It had also been noteworthy enough to put her in the running for the position with the Deputy Director in Washington D.C. She wanted that job, badly. It would be a huge feather in her cap, the kind of promotion that would set her apart from the crowd. And it would put her squarely in the arena of real power, where she intended to not just stay, but thrive.

"Jeannie's the one having all the fun," came a voice from three desks down. "Can you imagine pretending to be Ryan Vail's wife all week?"

Angie stared at Sally Singer, a normally sedate forensic accountant, checking to see if she was serious.

"Um, yeah, I think Jeannie wins this round," Paula said, laughing, and God, looking a little envious.

Were they crazy? Ryan Vail was a hell of an agent, but he was a player of epic proportions. Everyone knew about his exploits. And while he kept his personal life separate from his work life, he hadn't even tried to keep his reputation from spreading. Legend had it that he'd "entertained" four different Victoria's Secret models, although no one was clear if that had been at the same time or not.

She had to give it to him. His technique was subtle and effective. To her own mortification, his charm had almost worked on her. Admittedly it had been at a party and they'd both had too much to drink, but it still embarrassed her to think about it. Nothing would have come of it, though, because the last thing she wanted was to be another notch on Vail's belt.

"I think you guys are nuts. This week isn't going to be easy for either of them," Brad said as he rolled a quarter over the backs of his fingers in what he called a dexterity exercise, but was in truth his way of coping without cigarettes. "Sharing a bed? Intimacy exercises? I mean, what the hell would intimacy exercises even be?"

"Oh, brother. If you have to ask I feel sorry for your wife," Angie said, and the rest of the crew laughed.

God, she hoped that cut the conversation short because she knew exactly what the exercises would entail. Lots of touching, kissing, maybe even getting naked and she absolutely could not think about Ryan in that context. At least not at work.

"I should have been the one to go undercover with him," Paula said. "Seriously. I would've appreciated the experience so much more than Jeannie."

Brad's laugh was more about disbelief than amusement. "You have a boyfriend."

Paula gave them an innocent smile. "It's not cheating if you're doing it for a case. That's like vacation sex but you still get paid."

"Like hell it's not cheating," he said to more laughter, which said more about their long hours and how punchy they all were than it did about the quality of the humor. "Angie should've been the one to go undercover with Vail. No offense to Jeannie but you two would've looked more like the Ebsens."

Angie snorted, and not with any grace. "Me and Vail? Yeah, right."

Paula shrugged. "You know I hate agreeing with Brad, but I see what he's saying." She tilted her head, glancing at Angie's shoes again. "The right clothes and hair and you two would look as if you'd stepped off the cover of *In Style*."

Angie chuckled. No one else did. Was it conceivable they were teasing her because they knew about her *thing* for Ryan? No, not possible. She barely glanced at him when he was in the office. Absolutely no one knew. Except for Liz, and Liz didn't count. As her closest friend who also happened to be an FBI agent in the San Diego office, she knew almost everything about Angie. But certainly no one at work had an inkling that Angie might have thought about Ryan in a sexual context. A few times. "Shut up. All of you. As if I'd ever volunteer for an assignment with Vail."

"You liar," Paula said, a little louder than was appropriate in the bullpen. "I've seen you check out that ass. Everyone with a pulse has checked out that ass."

"I've got a pulse," Brian said. "Trust me. I have never—"

"I meant people who were into that kind of guy."

"I have," Sally said, raising her hand without a bit of

shame. "And Angie, my dear friend, as cool as you play it, I've seen you blush when he walks by."

"Probably because Vail had done something to blush about." Angie was terrified she'd start blushing right this minute. The subject needed to be changed, although it wouldn't hurt to make a definitive statement. "I mean, come on. To sleep in the same bed as him? To act like his wife? Palmer could've offered to pay off my car loan and no way in hell would I have—"

Assistant Director Gordon Palmer walked into the bull-pen, and Angie swung her feet off the desk. Everyone else in the room sat up straight, dropping the banter like hot coals. "We have a problem," he said, as if his demeanor hadn't already tipped them off.

Palmer was a good man, a fair boss and someone who had a knack for assigning the right agents to the right tasks, unlike several A.D.s she could mention. "Agent Foster is being held over in court. Indefinitely. We've been trying to get a postponement, but the judge won't budge."

Angie's chest tightened as if pressed by a vise. All their work, all the hours they'd spent putting this sting together.... This was the final Intimate At Last retreat being held in the United States.

"However," Palmer said, turning toward Angie with purpose. Had he overheard? Was this part of the joke? No, he wasn't the type. "There is one solution."

The pressure in her chest got so heavy she could hardly breathe. "Oh, my God."

"You're up to speed with every aspect of the case," Palmer said, making it very clear he was completely serious. "You helped build the cover stories. I feel certain that you can pull it off."

"Wouldn't Paula be a better choice?" she said, her voice

tight and her hands gripping her chair as if her life depended on it. "She was just saying…"

Paula shook her head, all business. "I don't know the cover, not like you do."

Palmer walked to Angie's desk. "I can't order you to do this," he said, softly now, for her ears only. "And there will be no negative repercussions if you aren't comfortable taking over the assignment. I realize it's a sensitive situation. No one's going to blame you for declining to step in."

The very thought of sleeping in the same bed as Ryan Vail made her skin tingle, made her want to hide under her desk. For all his colorful reputation, he would be a perfect gentleman, she had no doubt, but that didn't mean she could be a perfect lady. Knowing she'd never be with Ryan in real life had no effect whatsoever on what she did with him in her fantasies. The idea of actually sleeping with him… She felt sick with panic.

Taking her own idiotic issues out of the equation, there were several practical reasons to turn down the assignment. She might have helped with the cover stories, but she couldn't step directly into Jeannie's shoes.

However, she couldn't dismiss the short- and long-term benefits of saying yes. She didn't want to let down the team. And if she'd thought writing the search engine code would get her noticed, agreeing to the undercover work would put her front and center in the Deputy Director's radar.

She weighed the pros and cons: pretending to be Ryan's wife all week versus nailing the job in D.C.

She stood. "We don't have much time. Jeannie and I aren't close to the same size so I'll have to get a new wardrobe. We'll need to put my paperwork and computer cover in place faster than is humanly possible."

A.D. Palmer shook her hand. "Thank you, Wolf. Or should I say, Mrs. Ebsen."

2

HE WOKE TO THE BED DIPPING. For a few seconds, Ryan's adrenaline spiked until he remembered where he was. He groaned at the bright red numbers on the clock. "One a.m.? What the…?"

The rest of the question got lost in the dark, but it didn't matter, because Jeannie didn't answer. He didn't blame her, she must be exhausted. At least she hadn't turned on the lights. And he had asked her not to wake him. "You okay?"

She tugged sharply on the covers, pulling more of them to her side of the bed. But she didn't confirm or deny.

Ryan craned his neck until he could just make out her head on the pillow, her back to him, hunched and tight. Must have gotten stuck at the airport or something. If she didn't want to talk about it, fine.

He curled onto his side hoping to find the dream she'd interrupted. It had been nice. Smelled nice. He sighed as he closed his eyes, thinking vaguely that he'd been right that sharing a bed with her was no big deal. Especially when he considered what else was going to take place in the next few days.

It was amazingly quiet; they weren't in the hotel proper, but a separate group of bungalows that had their own locked gate, their own pools, even an exclusive bar. That's why the retreat cost an arm and a leg. So they could be near the secluded Namaste courtyard where the private couples retreat would take place. Too bad he had to work. This was the best vacation spot he'd been to in years.

He sighed as he let himself slip deeper and deeper into sleep…. The scent came back, a little like the beach and jasmine, low-key and sexy like—

His eyes flew open. His heart thudded as his pulse raced and it had to be the dream. The dream had gotten him confused. That's all. No need to panic. That was Jeannie next to him. For God's sake, who else would it be?

So why wasn't he turning around? Even in the dark, it would only take one look to know for sure and then he would cool his jets and go back to sleep. Undercover jitters. It happened. Not to him, but he'd heard tales. Nothing to see. No chance in hell the boss would do something insane like pull a switch at this stage of the game.

Moving slowly, not wanting to disturb her, Ryan twisted until he could see his bed partner. He hadn't used the blackout curtains because he never did—might have to see in the middle of the night. Like now. Just to check. Just to be certain.

He swallowed as his gaze went to the back of Jeannie's head. *Shit.* It was a trick of the moonlight. Jeannie's blond hair looked darker, that's all. And longer. He bent closer, grabbing his side of the mattress so he wouldn't tumble on top of her, then took a major sniff.

"What the—" Ryan sat up so fast the whole bed shook. His hand flailed in his search for the light switch, but even after he'd found it he didn't blink.

It wasn't Jeannie. The woman next to him. Wasn't. Jeannie. Jeannie smelled like baby powder and bananas. The woman next to him smelled exactly like…

She groaned and as she turned over, he whispered, "No, no, no, no."

Special Agent Angie Wolf glared back at him with red-rimmed eyes. She wasn't supposed to be here. In the bed. With him.

"Jeannie is being held over in court," she said, her voice as gruff as the hour. "They weren't able to get a postponement. If you'd answered your phone or picked up your messages, you would know that. Palmer asked me to take her place. I would prefer not to be here, but we really don't have a choice if we want to salvage the operation. Now, turn off the light and go back to sleep. Please."

It took him a minute to digest what she'd said. Eventually he nodded. "Okay."

She punched the pillow, looked once more in his general direction and said, "Oh, and if you wake me before eight, I'll kill you with my bare hands," then pulled the covers over her head while Ryan thought of five different reasons he should get up and go straight back to L.A.

That would end any chance he might have had for the D.C. job, but hey, he was a good agent. He could still rise to the top, even if he had to climb stairs instead of ride the elevator. Which would leave one of the other candidates to slip right into that sweet, sweet position working for the Deputy Director. For example, the woman sharing the goddamn bed.

What he couldn't do was pretend to be married to Angie Wolf. This operation was possible because Jeannie and him, they had seen each other in their underwear before. It had been funny. No embarrassment whatsoever. Hell, he was pals with her husband. He played with her kids. They were cool, him and Jeannie, no matter what cockamamie new-age tantric yoga tofu-covered bullshit they might have to sit through.

Angie Wolf was a whole different kettle of fish. She was hot, for one thing. Hot as in smokin' hot. Tall, lean, small up top, but on her it worked, and legs… Man, those runner's legs. Her dark hair was straight and thick and flowed half-way down her back, and he'd found himself too often star-ing into her cocoa-colored eyes.

Worse than that, he'd almost broken one of his cardinal rules because of her: he did not cross the line with any-one connected to the job. But at last year's Halloween party they'd come uncomfortably close. He'd been joking, sort of, but then there was this heat between them, and he'd realized that the fire had been smoldering for a long time, probably since they'd met. But A.D. Palmer had interrupted what had been dangerously close to a kiss and she'd stepped back. He'd laughed as if it was no big deal, as if his heart hadn't been beating a wicked drum solo in his chest or that he'd been half-hard just from the scent of her perfume. They'd kept their distance since. Sixteen months later they still had to be careful because the pull hadn't diminished one iota. At least not for him. She was kind of hard to gauge.

God, just a few hours ago, he'd been laughing about the Intimate At Last brochure. Body work. Couples massages. *Delightful homeplay assignments.* Shit. How was this sup-posed to work now?

Once the light was off, he stared into the shadows of the room. He wasn't about to fall asleep anytime tonight. Angie Wolf was going to be his wife. For a week. Holy hell.

THE FIRST THING ANGIE thought when she woke up was how surprised she was that she'd slept at all. She'd assumed shar-ing a bed with Vail would have kept her wide-awake for the entire night, but the exhaustion of the day had won out. At least the bed was big enough that they wouldn't have to touch. The thought of feeling his bed-warmed body brush against hers was enough to cause a surge of panic that woke her more efficiently than a cold shower.

"I'm ordering coffee," he said, shifting behind her. "You want?"

She exhaled as she remembered her role. Not the one as his wife, but as his partner. "Yeah, thanks."

The sound of the bedding rustling as he reached for the phone caused her muscles to tense and her jaw to tighten. So much for her resolve. She'd made a choice yesterday. She could have refused the assignment. As with everything worth having, and there was no doubt that the job in D.C. was, compromise and sacrifice came with the package.

No matter what her personal feelings were toward Ryan, her only task this week was to play his loving, entitled, slightly insecure wife so that Ryan became the perfect target for blackmail. The end. Nothing else mattered. Not sharing a bed, not the intimacy exercises they would participate in, not the inevitable touching. As long as they were both completely clear that no "optional" nudity was going to occur under any circumstances, they'd be fine.

Behind her, Ryan hung up the telephone, then the comforter shifted as he stood. Angie stayed frozen on her side just long enough for things to get really awkward. A quiet huff broke the silence and a moment later, the bathroom door closed.

She rolled onto her back and the way she relaxed told her just how tense she'd been. She hadn't moved all night. Good thing because she'd been so close to the edge she could have very easily fallen right on the floor.

A shower would help things immensely. Personal issues aside, yesterday had been a killer. She'd barely made it on the last flight to Vegas. Getting into character had been insanity. While she'd had to suffer a mani/pedi, two of the L.A. team had hit Rodeo Drive armed with her measurements and crossed fingers to pick up a complete designer wardrobe.

Underwear. Bras. Shoes. Earrings. She hadn't had someone buy her panties since she'd been twelve.

Her own style was business casual, built around the fact that she carried a Glock in a shoulder holster. She'd be more comfortable dressing up as a vampire than pulling off Prada or bebe.

The bathroom door opened, and there was Vail. Shirtless. Wearing UCLA Bruins sweats that hung low on his sharp-edged hips. Of course, he was sculpted like a professional athlete, a swimmer, damn him. Even worse, he had a Hollywood–handsome face to go with it. Dark hair, piercing green eyes, goddamn chiseled jaw. She let out a groan but immediately stretched, trying to make it seem natural, and not a reaction to the six-pack and the shoulders-to-hips ratio.

He tried to fight a grin, not very convincingly, then took a few more steps toward the big dresser. "The bathroom's all yours. I showered last night."

Angie threw the covers back and swung her legs over, determined to get her act together. What she needed was to talk to Liz, who couldn't have picked a worse time than yesterday to be incommunicado.

"You gonna sleep in your clothes every night?" Ryan asked. "I suppose it wouldn't blow the gig, but I imagine it won't be very comfortable."

"Yeah, no, it was late," she said, keeping her head down as she went to get her suitcase. Why wasn't the room bigger? Like the size of Montana? "At least the room's nice."

"So is the minibar."

She didn't look up at him. "I don't think the budget's going to cover twenty-dollar beers." The snick of the pull handle on her suitcase seemed alarmingly loud, but then everything since she'd agreed to this…situation had felt excessive.

To give Ryan credit, he was being extremely civil. She'd been worried he'd be in her face about the change in plans.

She'd also imagined him very, very pissed. But then, they were officially on the job, and working for the government made acceptance of the absurd a necessity.

Ryan was a good agent. He was dedicated. More than that, he was smart. He wasn't as concerned with rules and regs as the brass would like, but that wasn't a big deal, not to her. He got the job done. He could be pleasant. Nice, even. He'd never been anything but professional, even after they'd had that brief…misunderstanding at the Halloween party. Hell, he'd moved on without missing a beat.

It was as a man that he failed spectacularly.

No, that wasn't fair. He had different values than her own, that's all. It wasn't up to her to judge someone's sexual practices. If he wanted to sleep with the entire female population of Los Angeles, it was his own business.

She made sure she didn't look too anxious as she made her way to the bathroom, but slamming the door might have given him a clue. When the back of her head bumped the door she realized that she'd done nothing but behave like a child since she'd opened her eyes. Not moving, not looking at him, avoiding his touch. The man didn't actually have cooties, and she would eventually have to meet his gaze. Touch him. Act like a professional. Act like his loving wife.

The first thing she did was turn on the shower. The second thing was to pull her iPad out of her suitcase and turn it on to Skype.

Liz answered the call in seconds. "I got your message. What the hell have you gotten yourself into?" she asked, and Angie could see her redheaded friend perched at her breakfast counter, still wearing her Nike running gear. In front of her was a glass of orange juice and a bowl, probably oatmeal.

"I'm already in Vegas," Angie said, keeping her voice low. She didn't want Ryan to hear, God no. "With Ryan Vail."

"Holy crap, Angie. Did you not have a choice?"

"Yes and no. I mean, how could I tell Palmer I didn't want to step in? The whole case would've gone down the drain."

"What are you going to do?"

"The job."

"But…"

"I know!" Angie said. "God, why weren't you around yesterday? I have to sleep in the same bed with him."

"Oh, sweetie, that is the least of your worries. Do you know what tantric massages are like?"

Angie closed her eyes. "Stop it. That's not helpful."

"Well, I'm not sure what I can do from here." Liz lifted the iPad and brought it up until her face almost filled the screen. "You can do this. I know you can do this, because you are fierce and you are a woman to be reckoned with. Besides, Ryan isn't about to cross any lines with you. In fact, I'd bet a million he's going to go overboard to make sure nothing hinky could even be implied."

"I wish I could fit in a run," Angie said. "I'm exhausted, but I'm wired."

"Find time later. What do you have to do right now?"

Taking a deep breath, Angie let her friend's steady voice calm her down. "Shower. Dress like Angie Ebsen. Coordinate our stories so we don't contradict each other. Go to the first session. Introductions, filling in forms. Then lunch, and after that, there's some kind of bonding ritual. God, Liz, a *bonding ritual*."

"Don't think about anything past lunch. Introductions are a piece of cake. You know the backstory, you're expected to be nervous. You'll be fantastic." Liz smiled broadly, and damn if that didn't help, as well.

"Now go get clean, then put on your disguise. Break it down like your training schedule. I'll be in the field, but you can call me during the day. I shouldn't be late, though, so we can Skype tonight, okay?"

"Sounds good. Thanks."

"No problemo. Later."

The screen went dark, Angie clicked off the tablet and stepped into the shower in no time. She'd already solved her first problem. No way she could have lasted the week with people calling her Jeannie. Thankfully Brian had thought of a way out of that little mess. Angie would be her middle name, the one she preferred. The computer guys had woven it into all the paperwork and background references.

The story of the Ebsens would remain intact. Unfortunately the team had used a lot of Jeannie's personal history for Mrs. Ebsen's childhood, and because Jeannie and Ryan had known each other so long, no time had been wasted filling in all those details.

Now those blanks would, by necessity, have to be replaced with Angie's past. And Ryan needed to give her the Cliff's Notes version of his history, as well.

With the shower running, she stripped, grabbed her toiletries and used her time to visualize herself as Angie Ebsen. She imagined the way she'd carry herself as someone wealthy, who had high-level expectations about service and general conversation. She could see herself playing the part, she really could, up until the point where she had to act as though she was in love with Ryan.

God, this was going to be tricky. Even in her own head, all she could picture was the humiliation of that single horrifying moment if, no, not if...*when* Ryan figured out that she still wanted him. How he'd been the man in her fantasies for more nights than she cared to admit.

She stared down at the unbelievably expensive engagement and wedding rings on the third finger of her left hand. She was so screwed.

RYAN REALIZED HE'D BEEN staring at the bathroom door for a while and that he might want to move before Angie finished with her shower. He shook his head as he turned back to the dresser to get ready for their first day of marriage.

He supposed they'd have to talk about it now. *It* being the distance they'd been maintaining for over a year. The polite nods without eye contact, the apologies that followed accidental touches. Walking on eggshells like that at work had been bad enough, even though their jobs required minimal interaction. But behaving that way here would ruin the mission.

What they needed was to be all over each other. Just shy of obsessively on his part, a little less so on hers. Jeannie and he had been A-OK with that plan. They'd practiced until they'd been able to stop cracking up with each vaguely sexual touch. But with Angie he faced the opposite problem.

Every touch was sexual with nothing vague about it. Hell, the slightest brush of Angie's skin had caused a chain reaction that left him unsettled and heading toward hard. Thank God he wasn't a teenager anymore, or he'd have had to walk around the office with a textbook handy to cover himself. As it was, he always managed to make a quick exit or distract himself long enough to settle down, but that wouldn't be a viable option when they were in public here.

He pulled out a pair of khakis and a striped polo shirt, selected, along with the rest of his wardrobe, by a personal shopper who specialized in outfitting guys who made fifty times Ryan's yearly salary. Even his boxer briefs and socks were ridiculously expensive, and he paid attention to his clothes.

The sound of the shower registered and, of course, his brain went straight to a very detailed picture of Angie naked with water running down her chest, a drop hesitating on the edge of her rigid nipple, streaking down her stomach only to get caught in the trimmed thatch of dark hair that signaled the approach to his happy place. Never mind that he hadn't actually seen her naked. He had a good eye and could connect the dots.

And right there was the crux of the problem. The big, elephant-size problem.

In order to make the sting operation a success, they would have to break every boundary they'd very carefully set in place, consciously or not, at the risk of his libido overtaking his good sense.

Angie was not the kind of woman who would make exceptions for special circumstances. Even if they hadn't been colleagues, she wasn't his type of woman at all.

Physically? No question. She was a wet dream even when she wasn't in the shower. But he suspected she wanted someone she could count on. Someone who would be there for the long haul. A man who would be an excellent husband and father. A stand-up kind of guy to share her life with.

He wanted a woman who didn't particularly care who he was, as long as there was a bed and he could keep up his end of the bargain.

So not only were he and Angie required to mix business with pleasure for an entire week, they already knew that getting too close was playing with fire. Hell, all they'd done was consider, for like five minutes, hooking up, and they'd both backed off so fast they'd left skid marks.

This arrangement did not bode well. For either of them.

As soon as he was finished dressing, he speed-dialed Jeannie.

"I was going to call you."

Ryan sat on the edge of the bed, leaning his elbows on his knees. "How is this gonna work?"

"She can do it," Jeannie said, in her *I'm being serious* voice. "We spoke last night and she's completely committed to getting the job done. Just spend as much time as you can this morning going over your personal histories. Between the two of you, you'll make it happen. I doubt there's going to be anything heavy on the first day."

"We can still postpone this. A family emergency or something. Before they meet her."

Jeannie's silence had him wishing he'd kept that last thought to himself. She didn't know about the thing between him and Angie. Didn't need to. No one did.

"What's wrong with you?" Jeannie said finally. "Delaying could blow the whole sting. We've all worked too hard to get this far. Sometimes we've just got to roll with the punches. I figured you better than anyone could deal with that."

"I know, I know. You're right."

Again she hesitated. "Is there something you want to tell me?"

"Nope. Nothing. I'm good."

"Okay. You two look great together. You're the perfect bait. Hey, get the evidence we need to proceed and you can come on home. Easy as pie."

"Jeannie?"

"What?"

"You can shove that pie where the sun don't shine."

"Why, Ryan Vail, I never."

"Yes, you have."

Her laugh made him even sorrier she wasn't here. But their conversation told him he'd better get his act together fast. "The trial going okay?"

"Same crap, different day. I'm really sorry, kiddo. I would have been there if I could."

"I know."

"Call me tonight, let me know what I'm missing."

"If I can, I will." He disconnected, shoved his phone in his pocket, hoping like hell there would be nothing to tell. Ever. That he and Angie would pull this sting off with no hiccups, and then he'd be on his way to D.C. to a new job before he had to give her another thought.

A minute later he still hadn't moved and room service was at the door.

THE COFFEE WAS ALL SET OUT on the patio when Angie left the bathroom. Two laptops were open, one on the table which Ryan was staring at, the other on the dresser. That laptop had to be Ryan Ebsen's because the screen saver consisted of revolving pictures of Ferraris.

She debated unpacking, but she needed the caffeine too desperately to wait.

Outside, it was surprisingly warm for February in the high desert, and the view of the mountains was beautiful. Ryan had a large cheese Danish on his plate, but in front of her seat at the round glass table was a yogurt-and-fruit parfait with a bran muffin on the side. She stared at the breakfast, then looked up to meet Ryan's gaze, but only for a second. "What's this?"

"Sustenance." He poured her a cup of coffee, then put the carafe down.

"Thank you." Interesting that it was the exact breakfast she would have ordered for herself.

"You're welcome. Look," he said, meeting her gaze. "I believe what's required here is to barrel through all notions of propriety and just get down to how the hell we're going to pull this off."

Angie knew she was blushing, she could feel the heat rise on her cheeks. "Can I at least have a cup of coffee first?"

"Yeah," he said, easing up, at least somewhat. His posture was still stiff and he could only hold her gaze for a few seconds at a time.

She proceeded to put the cream in her coffee, to take a few moments as she sipped to catch the view and try to relax.

Ryan looked different in his Ebsen clothes. She'd never imagined him in khakis and a too-tailored-to-be-off-the-rack polo shirt. The suede bucks were the perfect touch to put him on the Street Style map on *GQ*. He'd always dressed sharply, but this change made him look rugged and elegant at the same time, and she'd better stop thinking about him in or out of clothes and get down to work.

After another big sip of almost hot enough coffee, she gave him a nod.

"Okay," he said. "Starting with registration, we're going to be the Ebsens to everyone at the hotel, so from this moment forward, we're in character. We won't be able to pull it off 24/7, but the more we practice, the easier it will get. Your part shouldn't be too tough. I'm playing a ruthless bastard, so you won't have to act much, at least not to start."

She flinched at his words until she saw the way his mouth quirked up. Joking, just joking. Everyone in the unit, including Ryan, kidded around, often with really black humor, and as of yesterday afternoon, it had never made her blink. Now, though... Pulling out a smile, she said, "I don't think you're a bastard. I think you're going to be very good at this."

After a questioning look he cleared his throat as he reached down beside his chair and brought up a thick file folder.

"All right, then," she said. "You want to go first?"

"Go first?"

"I need you to tell me as much as you can about the parts of your real life you used to fill in your cover background. We let you and Jeannie handle that aspect because she knows things about you that the rest of us on the team don't."

"Right." He paused, obviously thinking over what he wanted to make public and frowning as if he wanted to be anywhere but sitting across from her. "I, uh. Huh. Maybe we should... How about you tell me what you know about me and I'll confirm, deny, fill in."

Bad idea. Really, really bad. It would be just like her to say some idiotic thing she'd made up in her head about him. Or ask a question that had nothing to do with the sting. "That seems more complicated than it has to be. And frankly, confusing."

He looked out at the distant mountains. "I'm not trying to be evasive, but what Jeannie knows, she's learned over the last three years."

"I understand. She's your partner. Kind of like a wife in a way."

"A wife?" He laughed. "We're not that close."

"You know what I mean," she said, saw the fleeting panic in his face and considered that maybe he didn't. "Have you ever lived with a woman?"

"No." He seemed affronted. "No," he repeated, this time drawing out the word and meeting her eyes. "You?"

She started to shake her head but stopped herself. "Nope, never have lived with a woman. I was trying to get you to think in terms of what you'd expect a wife should know about you."

He rubbed his eyes, and murmured, "Maybe you should go first."

Dammit. Angie was going to have to take the lead on this and she'd been counting on following his example. "Okay," she said finally, reminding herself to be cool and act her age. "We have one shot at these people, so when I'm finished, you can ask me any questions you like. And then we'll discuss exactly how far we're willing to go to see this through to the end."

3

"I KNOW YOU BUILT Jeannie's tennis playing into the cover story, but I'm just okay at tennis so we'll have to be careful there. Running is my thing," Angie said, and Ryan nodded because he already knew that. "In fact, I run every morning and I plan to stick to my schedule while we're here." She paused. "Do you want to write some of this down?"

He shrugged. "I will when I need to. But I already knew you were a runner."

"Really?" she asked with a slight tilt of her head.

"Yeah, you know, that 10k you did in August?"

The head tilt was now accompanied by narrowed eyes. "I don't recall talking about that at work."

Ryan stared at her. Damn. There was a risk of getting too close to the line if he spoke to her about her runner's body. Hell, it was obvious that she was dedicated to the sport. He flashed back to the picture he'd envisioned of her in the shower and he grabbed a pen, then ducked inside the room for a moment to grab a blank piece of paper and cool himself down. By the time he returned to the table, he was fine. "I must've heard someone mention it, but yeah, I'll write it down."

She seemed to buy that answer and turned to gaze thoughtfully through the sliding-glass door. "I'm not exactly sure what kind of subjects are going to come up during the intimacy exercises, so I'm gonna cover a broad spectrum. Um, I don't like roses. Of any color. If a man were to—" Her gaze shot back to him. "You'd send me a simple fresh-cut mixed bouquet if you were to do that sort of thing. Nothing fancy and prearranged."

He took notes. Flowers. Shit, he wouldn't have thought of that, though he'd seen Jeannie buy carnations on the corner after work. He liked that Angie didn't care for fancy arrangements, although he couldn't imagine why it made any difference.

"Good Lord, how much can you write about flowers?"

He looked up. "Which one is your favorite?"

"Tulips, lilies, no, lilies remind me of funerals. Anything but roses and lilies."

"Got it."

"I don't drink much, because of the running. But I don't mind sour apple martinis or white Russians. I can't see Mrs. Ebsen throwing back a Miller."

Ryan smiled. "I don't think I'd marry anyone who didn't like beer."

"I didn't think you'd marry anyone for any reason."

"That's true," he admitted, returning his eyes to the paper. "Back to Mr. and Mrs. Ebsen. I know you like sports in general so let's get that squared away."

She nodded. "I cross train in mixed martial arts, a beach volleyball league and ballet, but I watch basketball. I'm not into football at all, or hockey, sorry. Baseball bores me to tears, so let's just stick with basketball. You do like basketball, right?"

"Not as much as hockey, but yeah, I'm a Lakers man." He'd bet his official Gretzky jersey that she already knew that. He'd won the office pool several times. Just like she'd known he was into hockey. He remembered a disagreement they'd had about Larry Bird that had taken place before the Halloween incident.

"Good," she said. "We met at a sports event, then. A championship game."

He pulled out his own phone and started punching keys. "The 2010 Finals, there was a fund-raiser in one of the owner's suites. How does that sound?"

She nodded and scribbled on the margin of her report. "Perfect."

"Why don't we make that our safety topic, then. I don't think anyone would question it. We're pretty athletic looking. Meanwhile, what are you going to do about your name?"

"Tell them I go by my middle name, Angie."

"That'll work." He looked up from his phone.

Angie rose and stretched over to reach the coffee carafe. After topping off his cup, she tended to her own. It was interesting seeing her dressed as Angie Ebsen. Her blouse was red with big sleeves but snug around the waist. Nice, but not nearly as great as the slim, black pants. Completely unlike anything she wore to the office.

He'd never thought much about how she neutralized her looks by the clothes she wore. As far as he could recall, she completely avoided anything that hugged her figure, which was a damn shame.

"My favorite extravagant restaurant in L.A. is Mellise, which is somewhere the Ebsens would go," she said, sitting again, and allowing him to relax. "Do you know it?"

"Yep, it wasn't far from where I grew up. What about Matsuhisa?"

"Never been, but I have been to Nobu. If anyone asks, we'll use Matsuhisa or Mellise, okay?" She sipped her own coffee, then took a bite of bran muffin. If her surprised smile was anything to go by, she liked it a lot.

"What else do people want to know when they first meet?" he asked, anxious about the time they had left before they had to report to the workshop. "No kids, so there's that."

Angie swallowed, then dabbed her lips with her napkin, drawing his gaze. "The cover story takes care of a lot. Where we live, no pets. My parents being filthy rich, me attending school abroad, which Angie Ebsen doesn't like to talk about. Simple."

He went back to his notes, afraid she'd caught him staring. "I can't think of anything else."

"No questions?"

He shook his head.

"Okay, now you fill me in."

Ryan looked up, the urge to get out of this strong, but he couldn't think of one reason she'd believe. He'd have to tell her what he could, and let her ask her questions. It wasn't as if his life was anything horrible, or even that much of a secret. He simply preferred to keep work and personal life separate. It was easier and cleaner to let his coworkers believe what they wanted. Some of which was actually true.

ANGIE COULD BE WRONG, but she got the feeling Ryan's hesitation was more about figuring out what not to say than how to fill her in on his life. He had to know she'd heard the stories. It wasn't as if anyone said anything terrible about him. On the contrary. Men seemed to be jealous, but not enough to make him a target, and the women she knew…well, they were mostly like Paula or Sally if they weren't happily married, like Jeannie.

Finally, after finishing off his Danish and the last of his coffee, he said, "I grew up in Santa Monica with my father. Don't know much about my mother. She left when I was a kid. No siblings. I don't have any other hobbies except sports, and yes, even though it's less convenient, I work out at Gold's."

"Oh, I'm sorry."

"It's not that big a deal. In a pinch I'll go to the FBI gym."

"I meant…about your—"

"That was no big deal, either. Anyway, I graduated from UCLA. We already talked restaurants, I run, but it's not my thing, and I play tennis occasionally. I prefer a pickup game, but what the hell."

"So if someone in the group asks us to double at tennis? Remember I'm only so-so."

"Then let's give that a pass. We'll need to be *on* every time we're in public. At least if we go to the casino, there's lots of distractions. The important bit is to get me into a situation where I can confess my sins. That'd probably be with Delilah or Ira. They're licensed and have to honor client confidentiality, but if the opportunity arises with the other two staff members, I'll jump on it. No telling who's involved in their scheme."

Angie nodded, trying to digest all the data Ryan had rushed through. No mother? Wow, that had to have been rough. But it might explain why he played the field as if his life depended on it.

"What about movies?" he asked.

"I'm in favor of them."

He rolled his eyes, which was a good thing, in her opinion. Things had grown a little tense. "Fine. Spoilsport. I liked *Date Night. Sin City. To Kill a Mockingbird. African Queen. Harold and Maude.*"

Ryan inhaled. "I saw one of those movies."

"Let me guess. *Sin City.*"

His eyes narrowed. "That was a trick, wasn't it? You didn't like *Sin City* at all."

"I have no idea what you're talking about."

"Yeah, right," he scoffed, but it was friendly. Nice. Getting closer to the comfortable ballpark.

"So what are your favorites?"

"I know you're expecting all the Bruce Lee and Chuck Norris movies that have ever been made, but that wouldn't be true."

"You don't like Bruce Lee and Chuck Norris?"

"Not *every* one of their movies, no."

"Seriously, guy flicks exclusively?" she asked.

"I've gotten misty over a film or two. I'm not that much of a stereotype."

"Misty, huh? Like when Shaun had to kill his mom in *Shaun of the Dead* or when Rose let DiCaprio go in *Titanic?*"

Ryan's eyes widened. "You liked *Shaun of the Dead?*"

Angie couldn't help laughing.

"What?" Ryan looked hurt. Actually hurt. "It's a classic."

She smiled very slowly. "I agree. But for the purposes of this exercise, you go with *Shaun,* I'll go with *Titanic.* It explains so much in so few words."

"You're mocking me. You shouldn't make fun of someone's taste in films."

"You're right." She pursed her lips, trying to keep the straight face she'd struggled to find. "So we won't even start with novels."

"Can I ask one thing, though?"

Angie nodded.

"Is it a genetic thing with women, *To Kill a Mockingbird?*"

"It's more a Gregory Peck thing, I think. Also, how incredible Atticus is with Scout." She thought for a moment. "But maybe it's genetic."

Ryan seemed satisfied with that, and for the next while they ran through a quick list of favorite foods, best vacations, mountains versus beaches and family pets.

At least the questions and answers had helped ease some

of her concerns. "You know, I agree that there's not going to be a lot of intrusive questions, not on the first day, but we want to set the tone accurately. The single most important thing about both of us is my family fortune. So let's get really clear about why the Ebsens are here. I don't know you've been cheating on me, but do I suspect? Jeannie said she hadn't decided yet, that she was going to take her cues once she spoke to the staff, but I'd like to hear your opinion."

Ryan looked pensive for a moment, and she hadn't noticed before but when he was thinking, he looked straight down, not to the right or left. Unusual. "I think it works better if you're a little suspicious, which will mean keeping me close. I also think that, for today at least, we act like happy lovers but not ridiculously so. We're nervous. Not sure what to expect. So we stick together, hold hands. Whisper a lot. Don't stand out from the crowd. We can always switch gears as we get more comfortable."

He took a look at his watch, then excused himself, closing himself behind the bathroom door. She knew he had his phone with him, and at his unexpected exit she wondered if he was ducking out to privately call Jeannie. Or maybe another woman. None of her business, she reminded herself, not in this room. Why couldn't she have been partnered with Brian? He would have been a nightmare, too, but in a totally different way. At least with Brian, there was no fear of being caught ogling like a lovesick teen.

While Angie polished off her yogurt she thought about what Ryan had said so she wouldn't end up blowing their cover in the first five minutes. With the notable exception of the attraction situation, she was actually getting a little revved about this sting and what they were about to do. It had been a while since she'd been assigned to the field, and though she loved her computers more than Paula loved her cats, there was an adrenaline rush with casework that went unmatched, even by winning a major race.

An undercover assignment called on skills that were rarely used in any other type of investigation. Which was terrifying, and also exciting, although it would have been even more thrilling if they could have made the actual bust, but that wasn't up for debate. Besides, the blackmail text likely wouldn't come until after the week was over.

As long as she kept the goal firmly in mind, she should be fine. Jeannie had offered her services as her coach, and Angie had promised she wouldn't hesitate to call if she felt out of her depth.

"We don't have much time left," Ryan said, coming back outside, and powering down his laptop. "You okay with everything so far?"

"Fine. Anything else you need me to know?"

He held up a hand as he put the computer into a hard case and locked it. After that was in the closet, along with the rest of the luggage, he went to the dummy laptop on the dresser. He pulled out his wallet and extracted a small rectangle of clear plastic, which he was able to attach to the monitor seconds before it closed. If anyone opened it, the card would slip out, but not be observed. Clever.

He turned back to her and she was caught off guard once more at how broad his shoulders looked in that polo shirt. She shook the thought away, angry that she'd even think such a thing.

"Tonight," Ryan said, all business, "we'll have a much better idea how to proceed. For now, we stick to small talk and distractions. If anyone asks something we're not sure about, we plead 'sore subject' and move on."

"Good." Angie put her hands on the armrests ready to go, but Ryan slipped into his chair and leaned forward, capturing her attention fully.

"As for how far I'm willing to go, I want to make it perfectly clear that I will do my utmost to avoid any delicate situations. If we get stuck, I'll keep in character, but I'll do my best not to make you uncomfortable."

She inhaled slowly. His declaration wasn't a surprise, but it was welcome, nonetheless. Even though she'd tried not to imagine situations in which they could be forced into that kind of intimacy, way too many had come to mind. The massages, of course, and what if they were the only two who didn't jump onto the clothing-optional bandwagon? Would that make them look suspicious? Would that scream undercover cops?

Regardless, none of that should matter. Awkward stuff always happened on undercover operations. It was part of the job. Still, it was going to be damn weird. After that Halloween incident, she'd told herself that there was no way in hell she and Ryan were ever going to see each other naked. This week, it would be a miracle if they could avoid it.

PURPLE WALLS AND PURPLE carpet made it very clear why they called the main workshop space the Lavender Room. The giant bean bags on the floor arranged in a big circle were pretty much what Ryan expected, or should he say dreaded.

"What's that frown for?" Angie asked.

"I thought bean bags went out in the early eighties. But instead, they just continued to grow. Those are huge." Ryan gave her the smile that terrible joke deserved, and it felt great when she grinned back. Picturing the two of them curled up together on the bulging bag of polystyrene pellets just became a little more comfortable. For about a minute.

Jesus. A whole week of foreplay and no main event.

What the hell was it going to take to get him to stop thinking about her as anything more than a fellow agent? His gaze moved from her smile to the red blouse to her thigh-hugging trousers. The outfit made everything worse. At work, in her nonfitted suits she wore sensible shoes with small heels. Something she could run in. Today, the heels on her sandals had to be five inches. She was tall without them, but standing next to him like this, their eyes were almost level, and he was six-one. There was no way he could fool his brain into seeing her as anything but stunning. Beyond tempting. Sexy.

"Six couples," she said.

He nodded, then turned away, checking out the rest of the room. Two exits, a bank of closed windows. The carpet was industrial, the tables in the back standard and there were two whiteboards, a blackboard and too many posters of greeting card couples on the walls.

The long tables with chairs had clipboards in front of each of twelve seats, along with the ubiquitous seminar water carafes and glasses.

"There's Delilah," Angie said, bringing Ryan's attention back to her. She nodded toward a tall, attractive woman walking up to the whiteboard. Delilah had blond hair that reached past her shoulders. A nicely proportioned body and a broad smile completed the very-professional package.

"Older than her brochure picture."

"Not by much," Angie said, and they were both speaking softly, moving slightly away from a couple who hovered nearby. "She's pretty."

"Damn relaxed."

"She would be. This is old hat for her."

Delilah wore dark slacks and a sensible button-down white shirt. She would have looked at home in any business setting, and that surprised him. "I pictured flowing robes and too many flowers."

"I guess they left that up to Ira," Angie said, scoping out the tall, slender male therapist who'd just walked in.

"An aloha shirt?" Ryan watched Ira Bridges approach Delilah and put his hand on the small of her back. His salt-and-pepper hair brushed against his shoulders. Garish flowers covered the pale, roomy shirt. Ryan wouldn't be surprised to find he wore a ankh necklace or an infinity bracelet. "Tell me he's not wearing flip-flops."

Angie leaned just enough to the left so she could tell. "He is."

Ryan sighed. "They're going to play that pan flute music, aren't they? I hate the pan flute."

Angie poked him in the side with her elbow, dislodging his train of thought. It didn't hurt at all. In fact, it was more of a gentle nudge but it had been enough to remind him that her skin was slightly tan and looked like silk.

He held his breath, afraid to move. She'd never have done that back in L.A. under any circumstances. Angie would have cleared her throat, turned toward him, said something, but she wouldn't have touched him like that. Angie Ebsen not only would, but should, and the touching would soon be a hell of a lot more intimate than an elbow to the ribs.

Another couple entered the room, which was what Angie had been alerting him to in the first place. He had no doubt he would learn more about these ten strangers than he wanted to. So he smiled as he cataloged his first impressions of the group. All of them were nervous and most of them held on to each other in some way because their partner was familiar and safe.

He reached with his left hand and found Angie's right. She jerked at the initial touch, but he didn't look at her. He kept his own slightly nervous smile on his face, and sure enough, she caught on and slipped her hand into his.

And he'd thought the elbow was memorable. God only knew what it was going to be like when they had to hug or kiss or he had to rub warm oil into her lush, lean body....

He cursed Jeannie and the entire legal system for putting

him in this ridiculous position, and then he cut that nonsense straight out because Ryan Ebsen would be sizing up the men in the room and checking out the wives. Special Agent Vail would be looking for the other two staff members, and sizing up Delilah and Ira.

Neither of them would have an elevated heart rate because he was holding Angie's hand.

"Come in, come in." Ira Bridges welcomed the newcomers as he headed for the door. Delilah had written: *Intimate relationships satisfy our universal need to belong and the need to be cared for* in a clean, easy to read cursive on the whiteboard.

"There are nametags on the end of the tables," Ira continued, his voice friendly, his smile wide and earnest. "Find a seat and please fill out the three-page questionnaire so we can get that out of the way. When you're finished, come into the center of the room and find a spot...on the floor." Ira beamed at the surprised murmur. "That's right. Surprise is a wonderful part of intimacy, and it's also a large part of this week, so keep on your toes."

Ryan leaned close to her ear and whispered, "I'm going to grab us seats."

She jerked sharply, caught off guard, her eyes wide and her lips parted. He wanted to apologize but as soon as she settled, he wanted to surprise her again.

"I'll get the nametags," she said, then hurried away, glancing back at him once.

He walked more sedately to his chosen seat then stared at the papers in front of him without seeing a word. The last time he remembered touching Angie on purpose had been a brush of fingers across the back of her hand. He'd wanted her then, but it had been at the party, and she'd been dressed as Scully, and though he'd never tell a soul living or dead, one of the main reasons he'd gone into the Bureau was because of Dana Scully and the *X-Files*.

Not the best thing to think about when there was so much on the line. The sting, the convictions, the promotion. After pouring himself a glass of ice water and downing half the drink in one go, Ryan started filling out the paperwork on the clipboard.

The first page looked like something he'd find at a doctor's office. Some overarching medical issues, which were easily dismissed, some personal info about family and work and hobbies and that kind of crap. Since they were using their own basic backgrounds, he was able to fill in the blanks in short order. He kept checking the still-open door, glad to have his mind occupied.

"Here." Angie dropped his nametag, already filled out, in front of him. When she sat, she shifted the chair closer to his.

He didn't acknowledge the tag, just slapped the sticky side to his shirt. Then he flipped to the second page of the questionnaire. "Shit," he said, under his breath.

"What?"

"Page two."

Angie checked out the material before she looked at him. "What's the problem?"

"You need to go first. Just make sure I can see your answers."

Her brow furrowed for a moment as she studied him, but she relaxed quickly with a nod. He went back and fiddled with page one while she attacked the intimacy portion of the opening challenge.

The first question alone had stopped him in his tracks.

I think of my partner lovingly many times a day.

He doubted he'd ever thought lovingly of anyone. Not that he didn't have good thoughts about people, especially about women, but lovingly? "What does that first question even mean?" he asked, keeping his voice low.

"We're in love," she said. "You'd think of me lovingly a lot."

Right. They were in love. If anything, he should go overboard on this questionnaire. Still, he'd take his cues from Angie, follow her lead. Make it appear that it was love with a background note of desperation, that brought them to this retreat, desperation with a mask of love that made them want to put in the effort. No sweat as a concept, but he hadn't really thought through the language issue.

Statement two was no better:

We feel warmth and connection at least twenty minutes a day.

Who the hell knew how many times they felt connected? He felt *connected* to the L.A. Kings hockey franchise, at least when they were winning, but that lasted the length of the game.

He leaned closer to Angie with a sigh. "This is gonna suck. Even if they don't play new-age CDs."

She snorted. Daintily. Whispered, "It'll be fine. Go with your instincts. Pretend they're asking about you and your personal trainer. Trust me, all the answers will make perfect sense."

He probably should have been insulted by that, but it actually made him laugh. He decided that when he was in doubt, he'd go with the opposite of his instincts, and he should be okay.

He glanced again at her paper, then stayed for a while, reading. Most of her responses were unsurprising given her backstory. The one about initiating sex equally made him blink. She'd given that a "Happens often." Good to know.

Confident that he now had the game down, he tackled his sheet, filling in the numbers for Ryan Ebsen, a man dedicated to keeping his wife and her checkbook. By the time he reached the end of the third page, he figured this thing with Angie was going to work out just fine.

Then she stood up, leaned over the table to grab another pen, and he got a load of her picture-perfect backside.

Nope. No. This thing with Angie was gonna kill him. Dead.

4

"THE FOOD WAS REALLY GOOD," Angie said, sipping her coffee from the back of the Blue Room. The group lunch hadn't been nearly the ordeal she'd stressed over, but there had certainly been moments.

The whole lot of them had walked the short distance from the Lavender Room, passing another group, all of them holding fruity umbrella drinks. Angie had been tempted to switch her allegiance, or at the very least call room service for a cocktail of her own. Especially after she got a load of the weird as hell layout of their new location.

The lunch tables had been set up in odd configurations: some were long family style, some round that could seat eight, a couple of them could accommodate four and only one table for two. There were more seats available than participants and each seat had a complete table setting.

Delilah had asked them all to sit. Anywhere they chose. With no more than a glance between them, she and Ryan went for the round table for eight where, for the most part, they'd eaten and listened to other people talk. The person to her right had been Luke, husband to Erica. Luke had spent the bulk of the meal's two courses telling her how he was only at this workshop because of Erica and how the whole point of intimacy was sex, and since they had sex pretty much every night, what was the point? He also mentioned the cost three or seven times.

Fortunately it hadn't been difficult for her to play her role. Primarily because Ryan had kept checking in with her. Not with words. With a look, a smile, a roll of his eyes. Each one a string between them, connecting, strengthening, woven together like a safety net. That tie relaxed her enough that she was able to answer the few questions asked without overthinking or stumbling.

The one time she'd tripped up was when she turned to find him staring across the table at Tonya Bridges, the yoga and tantric massage instructor. He'd looked riveted, interested. But then he'd turned back to the man to his left. Chris looked to be in his fifties. The two went on to discuss basketball until it was time for dessert and they'd all been "invited" to find different seats. Ryan had taken her by the sleeve and pulled her straight to the back of the room, to the table set for two where they hid like the bad kids during assembly as they watched the most confusing game of musical chairs ever.

"I think Ira's wearing patchouli oil," Ryan said as he fiddled with his linen napkin. He'd gotten coffee, nothing else, while she'd fixed herself a small plate of fruit. "Think he's actually old enough to be a hippie?"

Ryan wasn't looking at her, but that was okay because she was too busy scoping out the room to look at him. Their little table was situated close to the desserts. There were only three choices: a crème brûlée, a New York–style cheesecake, which was calling Angie's name, and a bowl of fresh fruit. She ate another piece of cantaloupe and decided the cheesecake had to be a billion times better. "Delilah hasn't had any work done I don't think," Angie said, pushing her grapes around. "Which makes me like her more, and also makes me question her involvement."

"What? Why?"

"They've been living in L.A. and Vegas for years. Plastic surgery is practically required by law for any woman over the age of forty."

He looked at her, clearly disbelieving. "That might be true for celebrities, but—"

"Ellen Fincher."

Ryan tossed the napkin all the way past the table, which Angie doubted he meant to do. "Get out."

Ellen was Palmer's administrative assistant. Angie knew for a fact she was forty-seven, because Angie had been at the birthday party. Ellen's present to herself had been eye lifts and some lipo. "Oh, I'm right."

"I'll take your word for it, but why does that make Delilah a more trustworthy person?"

"If she had a ton of illicit money, she'd probably have a nip or a tuck. She's pretty, but she's starting to droop. On the other hand, she could be saving every last penny for her dream retirement in Cancún."

"Or maybe she's just not that vain. You know—" Ryan stopped talking as Zach, the banker from Orange County, came by. Rachel, his wife, followed shortly thereafter, and all four of them chatted about how fantastic the food was until the couple wandered off.

Angie would have been fine with that if Zach hadn't been eating his damn cheesecake right in front of her. But after four bites she'd broken like a dime-store toy. "You want anything?"

Ryan shook his head staring once more at Tonya, who was sitting at one of the long tables, talking with two other couples.

Angie refilled her coffee, then said, "Screw it," even though no one was near enough to hear her, and picked up the biggest piece of cheesecake on the table. As she took her first bite, standing there like a heathen, she did a quick scan of the room. No one had left, even though they were perfectly free to do so. Marcus had cornered Olivia and Kyle. Delilah had both Paul and Natalie and Chris and Hannah.

Ryan watched Angie come back to the table. She sat down, both pleased and troubled that they were alone once more and murmured, "We're the only ones without a staff member."

"Yeah, I was thinking that we should probably move."

"Not near Marcus," she said after she'd swallowed another bite of the incredible cheesecake.

"We'll have to talk to him at some point."

"Not now. I spent five hours with him when you excused yourself after the main course."

He blinked at her. "I was not in the bathroom for five hours."

"My point exactly." She'd rarely run across anyone as beige as Marcus. Not simply his skin tone, his dishwater hair and his clothes, but his voice and his whole demeanor were so dull it was almost mesmerizing. He could put whole cities to sleep. "Now that I think about it, it's the perfect disguise."

"What's that?" Ryan's lips were already quirked up a hair, which made her throat tighten for a second.

"Being so boring people will do anything to avoid you."

Ryan's smile broadened. "How come I didn't know you were funny?"

That wasn't what she expected him to say. "I have no idea. And I don't think I am. Not funny funny. I'm intermittently amusing."

"You're under-the-radar funny. I imagine it would be very entertaining to sit next to you during bad movies."

"Now that I know your taste in films, that's never going to happen."

"Excuse me? *Shaun of the Dead.*"

"You said bad movies."

He laughed outright, and she hoped that Delilah and Ira were watching because this moment would convince anyone she and Ryan liked each other very, very much.

"ALL RIGHT, EVERYONE, are we ready?" Delilah glanced around at each couple, smiling serenely, until her gaze stopped on Ryan. "Is there a problem, Ryan?"

"Nope," he said, eyeing the bean bag chair. "None."

Problem was putting it mildly. This was exactly the nightmare he'd dreaded. Only worse. They hadn't been back in the Lavender Room for five minutes when the woman had described their very first bona fide intimacy exercise. Of course, it involved a bean bag chair. One chair. To be shared by him and Angie. At the same time. Hell. For a second he'd seriously thought about faking an allergic reaction to something he'd eaten at lunch. But Angie would know. Not to mention they were on the job.

"Come on, Ryan, move it," she whispered, her impatient voice edging toward panic.

He looked around, saw that all the other couples were in place, the husbands somewhere between lying and sitting, their wives cuddled on top of them. Slowly he lowered himself into the torture pit. Once he arranged himself as best he could he stared up at Angie, waiting for her to join him.

She hesitated, briefly met his eyes, then concentrated on her feet.

Ha. *Yeah, real easy, right?* He killed all hints of a satisfied smirk as he offered her his hand.

Ignoring it, she plopped down, none too gracefully, then swung a leg over him. He sucked in a breath, pretty sure she hadn't meant to hit him there.

"Um, sorry, if I—"

"Don't worry about it." His voice came out wrong, more like a fourteen-year-old going through the change.

He refused to say another word. Just laid there and let Angie do her thing. She'd figure out exactly how they were supposed to be situated. At least her knee had eliminated the possibility of his cock getting involved, so that was something.

"Is this supposed to be comfortable?" he asked, his lips very close to Angie's ear as she lay with her head on his shoulder.

"I have no idea." She adjusted again.

Every time she moved, Ryan tensed another notch. Delilah had asked for one partner to be "enveloped" by the other in order to listen to their heartbeat. First off, he didn't think Delilah knew what enveloped meant, but that wasn't the issue. Having Angie curl up in his arms? Touching him from shoulder to calf? Mother of—

"You're squeezing," Angie said.

"Huh?"

"My elbow. Tightly."

Ryan jerked his hand away, but it turned out to be a load-bearing hand and Angie slid down his chest until they reached a brand-new level of discomfort. Especially when her knee ended up on his inner thigh. Perilously near the first event.

"Oh, boy," she said.

He swallowed a moan.

Then she made things a hundred times worse by trying to scoot back up using that damned knee. Against his thigh. He bit his lip and most definitely did not whimper.

"Sorry, sorry."

He moved, too, attempting to keep his privates out of jeopardy while they struggled to get into position.

"That's wonderful," Delilah said from the front of the room. "Now that you're all settled, I want you to listen to the sounds of the rain forest and become aware of your breathing."

"Settled?" Ryan whispered. He hadn't known a whisper could be high-pitched. He didn't dare look around the whole room, but the couples in his line of sight looked as cozy as lovebirds. The bastards. "We're doing this wrong."

"What would you suggest?" Angie whispered back, her frustration making him feel a little better. "We don't fit on this thing."

"Everyone else fits. You have to relax."

"Me? You're as tense as a bowstring."

"If you'd just arrange yourself over me like—"

"I'm not a lap blanket."

Her knee moved again and he was running out of thigh. "Stop. Please." He wasn't above begging. "They're all waiting for us." He'd managed most of that sentence with his teeth clenched.

Angie lifted her head. "They're not all *settled*. Erica looks completely pissed at Luke, and Olivia's sitting on the carpet."

"Ira's doing something with the iPod player. Where's Delilah?" Ryan didn't particularly care, but maybe if he distracted Angie she'd stop moving.

"Must be at the front of the room. Come on. We can do this," Angie said. "We've just got to coordinate."

"That's what I've been trying to say." He took in a deep breath and let it go slowly. "I'm going to just lie here. I won't move an inch. All you have to do is get comfy. In fact, I won't even watch, that way I won't anticipate or react. Deal?"

She rested her head on his chest again. The warmth and weight of it made Ryan close his eyes before he'd planned on it.

"Deal," she said.

"Angie? One favor?"

"What?"

"Watch the knee."

His eyes weren't merely closed they were clenched. Which

did nothing to stop him from hearing her sharp, soft, "Oh. Sorry."

Ryan couldn't imagine how they must look to the therapists. To the blackmailers. Maybe it would help if he pretended it wasn't Angie crawling all over him, but Jeannie.

That was good, good, excellent, he could picture her hair and the stupid second earring on her right ear, but then Angie's scent caught him by surprise and Jeannie vanished like his humor.

Instead of throwing in the towel he pictured the woman he'd met at Bordello back in L.A. Terry, Mary, Carrie?

And there it was. Nothing magical, no, because his balls still ached, but he improved. Relaxed, at least to the point he wasn't going to snap his spinal cord. He pictured the short-haired brunette on her large four-poster bed. God, she'd been flexible. He'd been tempted to call her again, but hadn't.

When she'd wrapped her legs over his shoulders, head arching back on the pillow, he'd had to... How had the image in his head turned into Angie? When? Hell, even with the ache in his groin his cock was getting interested.

"That's the ticket," Delilah said softly from really close by.

Ryan's eyes opened to find her crouching next to their bean bag.

"I thought you two were going to need some special assistance but you worked it out. Don't worry that it took a few moments to find your comfort zone. Being in a group like this requires some new skills. Trust me, it gets easier."

Angie's head, which was now in its proper position on his chest, lifted. "I think we're good, but thanks for checking on us."

Delilah patted the side of the bag. "That's what we're here for." She rose, walked away until Ryan couldn't see her at all.

Angie had draped herself over him with her left hand on

his ribs, her front pressed to his side and her leg now safely thrown across his own.

As he put his hand gently on her shoulder her muscles seized beneath his palm, which caused him to go from uncomfortable to suicidal in seconds. With both of them stiff as statues, he grew hyperaware of every part that touched every other part.

"This position, curled around each other in total harmony, is home base," Delilah said, speaking to everyone now, her voice as calm as a summer breeze. "It's where you go when you need to feel safe. You can use this position in your own rooms or in here, any time you feel at all uncomfortable or restless. In fact, your homework for tonight is to recreate this position when you go to bed. Let your partner reassure you with their body, their breathing."

"Are you kidding me?" Angie said, her whisper quavering with panic.

"Well, shit," Ryan said, closing his eyes again, this time trying to pretend he was anywhere else on earth.

ANGIE SHOULD HAVE TOLD Ryan she'd meet him back at their room, rather than waiting for him outside the workshop space. Leaving without him would only add fuel to the fire. She doubted the afternoon session could have been more of a spectacular failure.

If Ryan was never approached by the blackmailer, she would be perfectly justified in blaming herself. She'd been more nervous lying in his arms than when she'd had sex for the first time. Okay, bad analogy. As if she wasn't having enough trouble keeping her thoughts on the assignment.

Some Special Agent she was. Rookies with one day on the job would have handled themselves better than she had.

Yet, she managed a smile as the other couples left the room. All of them were touching. Every single couple. Chris and Hannah held hands. Kyle and Olivia were so busy gazing into each other's eyes they almost walked into a pole. Paul had his arm around Natalie and before they reached the gate, he'd pulled her into a kiss that made Angie ache.

She and Ryan were nothing like them. They were awkward and self-conscious, and if anyone paid attention for more than five minutes they'd see there was no love between them. Worse, there was no familiarity and that's what was going to blow this whole sting out of the water.

She wanted to go for a run. At the very least, she wanted to talk to Liz. She'd understand, and she'd help Angie find some perspective.

Ryan, who'd been talking to Zach, finally made his way out the door wearing a smile that looked genuine. She thought of dessert in the Blue Room, of how nice that had been, and how the minute they'd had to fake real intimacy, they'd completely fallen apart. The irony was not lost on her that what they needed to get through a five-day-long intimacy workshop was a five-day-long intimacy workshop.

"Zach and Rachel asked us to join them for drinks in the casino tonight," he said when he rejoined her. "I said I'd let them know."

"We can sure talk about it."

Ryan kept walking into her personal space, and when his arm went over her shoulder, she did her damnedest not to react. But she could feel her jaw tense, her arms stiffen. With a conscious effort she relaxed and slid her arm around Ryan's waist. "Did they say what time? I'm ready for a drink right now."

The two of them walked down the winding pathway, between buildings and manicured lawns, everything oddly green for February, for a desert. "No specific time, and no pressure. It was an open invitation," Ryan said, his smile gone now that they were out of anyone's sight. "But I won't feel comfortable seeing anyone until we work a few things out."

She slowed her step. "I'm sorry," she said, at the exact time he said the same two words. Stopping completely, she looked at him. "Why are you sorry?"

He glanced around as if searching for the person Angie was talking to, or maybe just to avoid meeting her gaze. "I was incredibly out of character. No way you missed that."

"I was the one— I froze, I was awkward. Everything we'd talked about went out the window."

Ryan shook his head and got them moving again. "Okay, so we both sucked. What are we going to do about it?"

"Talk some more. Tell jokes. I don't know... Maybe talk about what we were like growing up?"

His brow furrowed. "That's... Let's think some more."

A waiter pushing a room service cart came at them, and Ryan tugged her onto the grass so the man could pass. He put both hands on her shoulders while they waited, and all the reasons she'd been horrible during the intimacy exercise rose to the surface in great neon letters, along with the very obvious solution.

The path clear once more, Angie covered Ryan's hands with her own, keeping him behind her. "We need to kiss," she said, knowing exactly what she was getting herself into. She'd have to put on the most durable armor in her mental wardrobe to pull this off. To kiss him until it felt right. Until it was as natural as breathing.

She tensed, waiting for his response. But he didn't say anything. Maybe he hadn't heard her. Probably a good thing, because the more she thought about it the more her belly clenched, and that wasn't helping at all.

To get to a comfort level would take a considerable amount of kissing. And touching. Could she really handle that? Of course she could... She had to, or risk disgracing herself, him, the entire team and the Bureau. The one thing she had on this job, no matter what, had been her self-confidence. If she blew this because of some ridiculous crush on an impossible man, she would lose far more than a job in D.C.

His hands squeezed her shoulders, sending an unwelcome shiver through her body. "You're right."

"About what?"

"Kissing."

The panic returned, stealing her breath and freezing her body. Thank God he was still behind her and she didn't have to look him in the eye.

He hesitated, then turned her around to face him. His gaze locked on hers, his hands settling on her waist. "We have to get rid of this awkwardness between us or we need to pack up and go home."

"I agree. Totally. Of course." She forced a smile, casually placed a palm on his chest, as if kissing him was no big deal, and hoped he didn't see her pulse leaping from the side of her neck. His heart rate wasn't exactly coasting on idle, so that helped.

"Jeannie and I did it."

"Did what?"

Ryan smiled, probably because her voice had climbed three octaves. "Practiced kissing."

"Really?"

"Yep, until we could do it without laughing."

"How long did it take?"

"Um, far longer than either of us liked."

"Ah." She cleared her throat. "We'd better get to the room, then."

"Yeah," he said, but he didn't move.

Someone else, a young woman clutching a book, passed them, but that's not why Angie hadn't lowered her hand.

"Just to be clear," he said, "we're talking about kissing, right? Just kissing?"

She felt a blush flower on her cheeks. "Yes. There's no reason for us to change any of the ground rules. Kissing. Touching. Until we're okay with it—" Her breath caught. "You and Jeannie, you didn't practice doing—"

"No. Jesus." Ryan loosened his grip. "No. No."

"Right. Of course not." Angie stepped back on the path, and took hold of his arm as they continued the trip to the room, reminding herself twice to ease her grasp. With every step she repeated her goal to shake this absurd *thing* for Ryan and shoved away all other thought.

When he had his card key out, breathing became an issue as her heart pounded faster and faster. This was it. The moment of truth.

As soon as the door closed behind Ryan, she turned, ready as she was going to get.

But Ryan wasn't even looking at her. He pulled out a slick gadget that looked a lot like a cell phone but was in fact a nifty little electronic sensor.

Angie couldn't decide if she was grateful that Ryan could still think about protocol or if she should be insulted. Given how close she was to an arrhythmia, she decided she would be grateful and use this moment as a reminder that this kissing business was exactly that: business.

Ryan walked the complete perimeter of the room using the scanner that was the most sophisticated frequency detector in the world, disappeared into the bathroom for a moment, then went to the dresser to make sure no one had tinkered with the Ebsen laptop. Finally he joined her by the door, and up close, she could see he wasn't quite as composed as she'd imagined. "I'm getting a scotch," he said, as if she'd needed more proof than the panic in his eyes.

Her whole body sagged in relief, but before she let herself

ask for a drink of her own, the stakes flashed through her mind like a sign from on high. She grabbed Ryan's shoulder, pushed herself against his body and pulled him straight down into the kiss of her life.

5

THE VELVET SHOCK OF HER mouth on his sent Ryan stumbling back against the wall. She'd caught him off guard, nearly knocked the air out of his lungs. But he caught on quickly, abandoning every thought but to read her cues and give her what she needed.

He touched the tops of her arms, and while she didn't exactly jerk completely away, her body stiffened with tension. However this ended, it had to begin with feeling comfortable and safe.

Keeping his hands gentle and his mouth closed, he consciously relaxed. It wasn't a piece of cake. The idea that he was kissing Angie was messing with him something fierce. All the carefully constructed barriers that had helped him keep his distance had been crumbling since last night, and together with the "safety" position and now this, he felt defenseless. But he couldn't simply let go and have at her. She wasn't a one-night stand. He knew Angie's last name, and a whole lot more, and he wasn't about to call the shots.

She pulled back from him, not away. Just enough to breathe for a minute. To whisper, "I don't know if I can do this."

"Course you can. We can. Use your imagination. Who's your favorite actor?"

"What?"

They were so close together that with every word came a soft gust of her breath. He recognized the scent of wintergreen breath mints. "Who's the hottest guy you can think of?"

The way she blushed was startling. She must really like whatever actor she was thinking of, but that wasn't the point. He didn't want her embarrassed. "All right. Forget that. Did you ever have an unrequited crush?"

Now she turned her head, and the tension of a minute ago had been nothing. What kind of a past did Angie have? "An ex-boyfriend?"

"Yes," she said, so excitedly he jumped. "I have an ex-boyfriend. From my first year of college."

Because she was looking at him again, Ryan forced down his grin. He risked squeezing her arms a little more tightly, and yeah, okay, now they were getting somewhere. She wasn't exactly in a Zenlike state of calm, but she was a hell of a lot better. "Close your eyes," he said, keeping his voice low and calm. "Picture…?"

"Steve."

"Steve," he repeated. "How you felt when he kissed you, and how good it was." He pulled her closer, waited until the little furrow on her forehead disappeared. Then he kissed her.

This time, her lips weren't pressed together so tightly air couldn't have escaped if it tried. Her hands, which had gripped his shirt so firmly she'd nearly ripped the seam, had softened, and the energy that had been coursing through her body had shifted from electrical fence to a strong buzz.

Then her tongue swept across his lower lip, just a tease, a taste of what came next, and oh, hell, in his quest to make things easier for her, he'd forgotten that he was the one actually kissing Angie.

He probably should have stopped things right there. All she'd have to do was keep imagining he was this safe and comfy ex from college. Instead, he moved his hands to her back, tilted his head until their mouths were a perfect fit and kissed her like he'd wanted to for a very long time.

ONE SECOND, IT WAS STEVE on her lips and it was all so simple. The next, she wanted to climb Ryan like a tree and never let go.

Her moan would have been embarrassing if she'd had any brain cells left, but what he was doing with his tongue and how his large hands were stroking her back as if he couldn't get enough had fried all her synapses, leaving her helpless to do anything but kiss him back.

Those hands of his had reached the curve just above her behind. He paused and it felt important to tell him to continue, which she did by thrusting her hips forward.

Message received, and good grief he grabbed each cheek, pulled her close and oh, he was clearly aroused. The more they rocked against each other the thicker and hotter his erection became.

Considering she was Kegel squeezing to beat the band and panting into his mouth as if she'd just finished a marathon, she couldn't exactly complain.

God, he could kiss. He should quit the FBI immediately and become a professional— She lurched back, so roughly they had to take a few steps to catch their balance. He'd let go of her, and she...she remembered who he was and who she was and, "Oh, my."

Ryan, still obviously hard and flustered, cleared his throat. His lips glistened. "Well, that wasn't too bad," he said.

A burst of laughter escaped before she could stop it.

"It wasn't," he said defensively. "For a first time, given the circumstances, we did okay. We learned some things."

Things? Like, say, that *he* was the hottest guy she could think of? That Ryan was her unrequited crush? As if more proof was needed, she'd practically dry-humped the guy into coming. She made a sound. A sort of croak. Definitely not a word. But she couldn't look at him. She turned around and stared at the wall.

He very sweetly didn't comment on it. "Listen," he said, "we're two healthy adults with fully functioning hormones. It would have been more surprising if we hadn't responded so, uh, enthusiastically."

"Is that what happened to you and Jeannie?"

"What?"

Angie spun back. "When you two kissed?"

"We didn't…" He shook his head. "No. It wasn't like that."

Well, that was good, because it would have been creepy if they had. "You know what? I'm really feeling tight from sitting so much all day. I think I'll go for a run."

"A run? I thought we were going to keep kissing until we felt comfortable."

"Yeah, that was the plan, but you're right. For a first time, we did great, and the next time we'll do better, and we're probably not going to have to kiss in front of anyone, anyway. So I might as well do a few miles…."

"What about drinks at the casino?"

"You should go. Tell them I was tired. Which is true. I am tired. Unless you think it's important for the case—"

"No," he said, before the last word had time to settle.

The urge to look down was so strong she thought something in her brain might actually break. At the thought, she glanced. Quickly. His erection was still there. She could only imagine the kind of self-discipline it took to speak to her so calmly.

"The only reason we'd go is to make our cover stronger," he said, "but I'm thinking we'll skip it tonight."

Angie made a break for it. She pulled open her drawer, nearly yanking it out of the dresser. But she got her running gear, including socks, after only three tries. "Great. I'll just—"

She hurried to the bathroom and closed the door behind her. All she could think about was getting out of this hotel room, pounding the pavement until she could figure this damn thing out. There had been a single moment when things had gone to hell. Before she came back to their room, back to the bed they shared, she vowed to find the line between kissing him as part of the job and kissing him as the fulfillment of her fantasies, and stick to the proper side.

RYAN HAD TRIED TO WATCH television, but he couldn't disconnect from kissing Angie. He'd thought taking care of himself in the shower would give him enough relief that he could think again, but he couldn't get any kind of distance.

She'd been gone half an hour. He supposed he could eat, but he should wait for her to come back because they were supposed to be in love and recommitting themselves to their marriage. They were supposed to be a lot of things— professionals, for one. Rational adults, another.

He clicked off the TV and almost threw the remote against the wall, but instead he grabbed his gym gear. After he'd changed, he left a note on the bed, then he and his towel headed for the fitness center. Like Angie, he thought better when he was doing something physical, and the hotel had a lot of decent equipment. He'd pass on the free weights, but the machines would give him a good sweat.

The path meandered, as did all paths in this resort, except for the one to the casino. It reminded him of how they set up grocery stores, forcing people to walk by the expensive ticket items in order to buy the milk. The casinos paid for everything in this town, and it never ceased to amaze him that those damn slot machines were in every gas station and supermarket.

As he rounded the curve of the fitness center building, he heard familiar voices. Tonya and Ira along with another couple, maybe Luke and Erica? Ryan was in no mood to join in what sounded like a jovial chat, so he stayed where he was, moving a little closer to the building where it was darker.

Eavesdropping was something of a relief. It was work related and he didn't have to be alone with his thoughts. There was Tonya pimping her early morning yoga workouts, and Luke inferring that it was somehow girly. Jesus, the man was a Neanderthal. Ryan gave Luke's marriage a year, tops.

Goodbyes came shortly after, and the three of them, everyone but Ira, walked right past Ryan, who decided to stay where he was until he could see what the therapist was up to. He'd probably left for his room, but Ryan gave it a minute, just in case.

"A fickle lady," Ira said, but his voice got soft at the end as he spoke into a cell phone. Doppler effect; he was walking. No, pacing, because there was more and his voice grew louder. "…dime to win. On the second, I want number four to win, six to place. Third, gimme two to win. Fifth, three to win."

Ryan moved closer to the edge of the building, keeping himself against the wall. He'd been to enough races to understand that Ira was placing bets on the horses, and that the dime he'd mentioned was a thousand dollars. So his bets for that particular track were in the five to six thousand dollar range.

"Yeah. Not tonight. Tomorrow, early. Seven-thirty. Okay."

Ira's voice had grown closer, and the last thing Ryan wanted was to be caught skulking. He hurried back to the path and moved forward with his head down, almost running into the man.

"Excuse me," Ira said, holding his hands out in front of him.

They would have touched if Ryan had taken one more step. Instead, Ryan did the pardon-me shuffle as he smiled. "Sorry about that."

"On your way to the fitness center?" Ira asked.

Ryan nodded. "Angie's catching a run, so I'm gonna grab a quick workout before dinner."

"Good for you. I should do more of that myself. But not now. Late for a private session."

Ryan nodded as the older man walked away, his steps quick, his hands fisted in his pockets. Why in hell would a man staying at a casino with a major sports book place bets with a bookie? Only one thing Ryan could think of, and that was secrecy. Ira wasn't playing for peanuts, but there was nothing in the intel already gathered that indicated he had a gambling problem.

That opened up a whole new arena to investigate. How was he financing his hobby? Did anyone else on the Intimate At Last team know he was a gambler? Was the blackmail his source of funds?

Ryan pulled his own cell phone out of his left pocket, double checking that it was his personal iPhone. Ryan Ebsen's cell was an older-model Nokia that was simpler to clone. He speed dialed Jeannie. It was afterhours, or almost, but that meant she'd be out of court. Probably at home having a great dinner with the family, not worrying about kissing people and inappropriate erections.

"What's up?"

"New information."

"Okay, wait a sec."

Ryan heard her yell for her husband although her voice

was muffled. There was a discussion that lasted so long he'd made it inside the gym and had staked out a private corner where he could see all entrances and exits. There were only three people in the place, and he didn't know any of them.

"I'm back," she said, finally.

"I forgot what I was going to tell you."

"Shut up. You try having a family and being a secret agent at the same time, then come bitch at me."

"Secret agent?"

"According to my children, yes."

"According to me, too, double-oh-seven and three-quarters. Listen, I overheard Ira Bridges making a bet to a bookie. I know Santa Anita's running, but the track doesn't matter. The fact that he was betting several thousand dollars was interesting, however."

"Really? Oh, that's good. That's very…motivational."

"My thoughts exactly. He was on the down-low making the call, no one else in sight. But that doesn't necessarily mean he's kept it secret. Suspicious, though. I think he's going to meet someone at seven-thirty tomorrow morning. It could be a phone call, but I doubt it. I'm gonna go running with Angie at seven, circle around his bungalow. See if we can't get eyes on the guy or a license plate."

"Don't get caught."

"Yeah, I needed that reminder, me being a rookie and all."

"What the hell's wrong with you?" She snorted. "Your job is to play the loving couple. Our best shot at nailing these bastards is you getting targeted. I'll get the info to Parker and the rest and see what they come up with."

"Good." He rubbed his temple. Naturally she was right. "Thanks."

"So how's it going with Angie?"

"What do you mean?"

Jeannie puffed some air at the receiver. "I mean, how's it going with Angie?"

Ryan opened his mouth, then closed it, editing his thoughts. "Fine," he said. "Fine."

The huff of air was replaced by a derisive laugh. He knew that laugh all too well. "What?"

"Took you a hell of a long time to get to fine, kiddo. What's going on?"

"Nothing. You know. All that touchy-feely crap. Ira wears an aloha shirt, okay? There are bean bag chairs."

"That's swell, but how's it going with Angie?"

"She's not you," he said, hating that it sounded a lot like the way her kids whined about going to bed. "I was ready for you."

The silence that came back at him wasn't the friendly kind. It made Ryan nervous, and he found himself pacing, but still sweeping his surroundings for anyone who could be listening in. He shouldn't have to explain his discomfort, not to Jeannie. She'd spent a lot of time ragging on him about how they were going to be his longest relationship, how with women, he was made of Teflon, sliding in then sliding out, no fuss, no muss. Jeannie understood that he wasn't built for romantic relationships. She didn't make him want things he shouldn't.

"It's the touchy-feely stuff, right?" she asked. "We figured there was going to be a lot of physical contact."

"We weren't wrong."

"Okay, so today you realized that this wasn't theoretical, that you're undercover as a married man. The way I see it, you have about three hours left to freak out about it, and then you'd better get your act together, Ryan. Seriously."

"I'm not freaking out."

"Yeah, you are. I can't say I blame you. If the situation were reversed, and they'd stuck me with any other guy on the team, I'd have been a mess. Privately. Because I would know that my feelings are the last thing on earth that matter for the rest of the week."

"Well, you're a damn saint, Jeannie."

"Fine, be pissed at me. Just remember that you're the one who wants Washington so badly. You're the one who's determined to play Ryan Ebsen down to his short hairs. You two are going to touch each other. A lot. You'll have to kiss a time or two. And you're sleeping next to her. If junior won't behave, you have exactly one option. You keep it in your pants. That's it. There's not a plan B or a deal you can work out. Everyone's counting on you. Because you're the man in the spotlight. If anything, you need to make it easier on Angie. She's taking one for the team, and don't get smart with me, because you know what I mean. It was brave of her to step into this part with zero prep."

He scraped his teeth over his lip, then put the phone down while he slugged the padded back of a weight machine. Then he put the cell to his ear again. "Well, hell, when you say it like *that*..."

"All righty, then. Where are you, in the fitness center?"

"Yeah." He heard the relief in her voice, and it made him more determined than ever to get his thoughts in line. "You know it's not about Angie, right? This would be a problem with anyone who isn't you."

Her pause told him he should've left well enough alone. "Yeah, I know. Look, my tribe is going to revolt if I don't give them sustenance. You, work out. Hard. Think whatever you need to, then get clear. Get focused. Eye on the prize, kiddo. Eye on the prize."

After a brief goodbye, he shoved his phone in the correct pocket, then went to the elliptical, set it for maximum resistance and started pumping. The key was control and focus.

He was better at that than anyone he knew. Completely capable of putting away any feelings he had for Angie Wolf while still giving the performance of his career. Dammit.

6

ANGIE SAT ON THE EDGE OF the whirlpool bathtub, the steam from her shower redolent with the cucumber scent of her body wash. Liz Copper was front and center on Angie's iPad. In the background was the interior of Liz's SUV and the ambient sounds were a random car horn or an airplane. Liz could have been halfway home by now instead of listening to Angie whine as she sat in the Bureau parking lot.

"Hey," Liz said, "I'm sorry, but I don't understand the problem."

"It's Ryan," Angie said, her jaw clenching with the need to be quiet. Ryan wasn't in their room, but that didn't mean he couldn't come back any second. "I completely forgot myself and what I needed to accomplish. *I* kissed him. *I'm* not supposed to do that. I'm supposed to be in character, not wanting to jump the guy I work with five days a week. For God's sake, Liz, you know how risky this part is, and we're on day one."

"Again," Liz said, so calmly Angie wanted to punch her. "I don't see the issue."

"Stop it. You're not dense."

"You are, apparently. Look, Angie, this is one week out of your life where your future depends on you acting as if you love the man you're supposed to be married to. The more the lines blur between you and your character, the more effective you're going to be at playing the part."

Angie's head reared back. "That's insane. And inappropriate. And...and wrong."

"Why?"

"Because when this week is over, I have to go back to L.A."

"Not for long. Look," Liz said, leaning closer, making her head look very big. "You're attracted to him. A lot. I was there at that Halloween party, remember? I saw the way you two looked at each other. So use it. Make it work in your favor."

"That's not right."

"Have I ever advocated using someone like that in real life? No. But in this case... Think of it as pulling a Ryan. Trust me, he'll be thrilled. At least until he finds out you're going to D.C. instead of him, but hey, all's fair when seeking promotions that will pull you up several rungs on your career ladder."

Angie sighed, her instincts battling for dominance. "Let me get this straight. Are you saying that I should seduce him? While on the job?"

Liz blinked a little. "I'm not saying you should. I'm suggesting that in this case, it wouldn't be a bad thing to go with the flow. He wants you, you want him, that's a fact. The only reason you two haven't already gotten together is because of the job. Well, now the job is to convince two marriage counselors that you're hot for each other. Think of it as method acting."

"There's something fundamentally flawed about what you're saying, I know there is."

"Kiss him again tonight. If it feels wrong to go farther,

stop. But if it goes to the next step, don't beat yourself up for it. That's all I'm saying."

If it had been anyone else, Angie would have already laughed off the idea and moved on. But Liz really did know her better than anyone else. She was protective of Angie. Had been since their first year in college. "Okay. I'll let you know what happens. But I have to get out of this bathroom. For all I know he's right outside the door."

"Good luck," Liz said, then she was gone, and Angie put away her tablet. Her gaze moved to her reflection as she went to the door. She'd dressed in Angie Ebsen's clothes, a sheer white camp shirt over a silk tank, with winter-white jeans, the russet belt the only color in the outfit. It would have looked better if she'd been more tan, but she didn't actually live the life of an heiress.

She did have to play one, though, so it didn't matter whether Ryan was on the other side of the door or not. Now, if she could only erase her entire conversation with Liz.... Instead, she set her shoulders and walked out, ready to face him, face whatever the night would hold, but thank goodness she was alone. Her gaze went to his note. No indication of what time he'd written it, but even if he had spelled it out she couldn't begin to guess when he'd return.

Her stomach rumbled. No wonder, it was coming up on eight. She figured they'd go to one of the hotel restaurants, be seen together, maybe find the others in the bar, after all. She'd put on makeup.

Unsure what to do now, she thought of cracking open the minibar. She still didn't think the Bureau would pick up the tab, but she did get a per diem.

At least the run had done her good. Of course, Liz's "Go for it" pep talk had undone most of Angie's calm. Thinking of seducing Ryan made her hyperventilate, but she could sit with the notion of seeing where things led. Being open to entertaining the idea that there could possibly be more than kissing between her and Ryan. Maybe.

She stared at the door, then at the fridge, then back at the door. It seemed ridiculous to wait for an unquantifiable time, and though she didn't like interrupting anyone's workout—tough. She got her cell, dialed Ryan's.

He answered as the door to their room opened, his voice echoed in twin spaces. "I suppose you're wondering where I am," he said, smiling at her.

Eye-rolling was becoming something of a reflex. "You didn't say."

He still had his phone to his ear as she put hers back in her purse. When she looked up again it was to find him eyeing her, but not cynically at all. His gaze hovered over her chest for a few seconds then moved slowly down until he reached her shoes, yet another ridiculously high pair of strappy nonsense. With her heart thudding and praying he wouldn't notice that she was utterly panicked, she found a smile that almost felt normal.

"They're impossible to run in," she said. "I'd break my ankle in five steps. I don't know why they insist on putting TV cops in these high-fashion things. It's absurd."

He let his phone hand drift down as looked up. "To be fair, they only do that to the female TV cops."

"Ha, ha."

"You do look damn nice in them," he said. His workout was all over him, and it was a good look. The sweat on his shirt reminded her of her own before she'd showered. The flush of his neck and face was pretty close to indecent. "Did the fitness center live up to the brochure?"

"Oh, yeah. You'd like it."

"I'll stop in sometime."

"Whoever picked out your wardrobe did a hell of a job,"

he said. "You could be about to step onto a yacht. Did you want to go meet the gang for drinks?"

"Dinner first would be nice. I'm starving."

He nodded and headed for the closet. "Give me five minutes. Oh, and I overheard Ira making some impressive wagers with a bookie."

"Really? Why a bookie?"

"My question exactly."

As he gathered his clothes, he filled her in, and by the time he'd reached the bathroom, they'd gone over a quick half-dozen possible explanations. "I'll call Parker," she said, grateful beyond measure that the conversation had turned to the case and that she could breathe again.

"I spoke to Jeannie, already. She'll take care of it."

"You told Jeannie?" Angie wasn't sure why that surprised her, but it did. There was no reason for him to hold on to the information until he talked to her, and yet there was a niggling pressure in Angie's chest that felt too much like jealousy.

Ryan nodded, completely casually, as he should. "I'll be right out. Why don't you look over the menus, decide where you'd like to eat."

The only thing good about this brand-new overwhelming awkwardness that had taken up every available cell in Angie's brain was that she no longer felt weird about the kissing.

God, this assignment was going to kill her. The only way to survive would be to take it one second at a time, be present, stop projecting. They had a new lead, and who knew what else they'd find out next?

She just had to make sure she was in bed early enough to get some decent sleep. Then actually get to sleep. In the morning she planned on running. Then she was going to attend the morning yoga session, try to bond with Tonya. At the very least, the two of them shared a body consciousness that if played right, could lead to conversations outside the purview of the intimacy retreat.

Big stuff, all of it. She really did need to sleep. And to disregard all thoughts of Liz's idiotic suggestion.

"I THINK WE SHOULDN'T even try to find Ira with his bookie," Angie said.

Ryan stared at the big red 1:43 a.m. on the nightstand clock. It was hard to miss, lying on his side, facing away from Angie. "No?"

"We've been here one day," she said. "Give it time."

It wasn't exactly easy to hear her, as she was lying on her side, facing away from him. And the way her words were slightly muffled, he assumed she had her mouth smooshed on her pillow. The same mouth he'd kissed a few hours ago. He had to stop obsessing about that. Twice he'd gotten hung up on studying her lips and lost track of the conversation. "I keep thinking we need to do more."

"Tonight was good," Angie said, as if she was trying to convince him. "With Marcus in the restaurant, and then Tonya at the bar."

"Yeah. But not for long enough, and honestly I couldn't tell if they were being friendly or milking us for info. Well, most of us. Did you notice how Tonya physically stepped back when Zach started talking about the exercises? Tonya can't stand him, which I get, but the important part is that it was amazingly easy to tell she couldn't stand him. She's not a very accomplished actor. Not that an extortionist has to be a good liar, but it would help."

"Huh, no. I didn't see any of that. I was occupied for most of that discussion."

Yeah, he'd noticed. "I think Kyle and Olivia want a threesome with you."

The sheets rustled and the mattress wobbled on her side. "What? Why would you say that?"

Angie's voice was a lot clearer and nearer. Ryan had a quick debate with himself as to the wisdom of turning to look at her. So far, watching the clock had worked pretty well, but the clock wasn't going anywhere, and he wanted to see her reaction to his observation. He turned. "How did you not notice?"

"We weren't talking about anything. Restaurants in L.A. There was no mention of beds or sex or anything like that."

He could make out her features thanks to the augmented moonlight. She'd taken off her makeup leaving her skin soft and not quite as pale as was recommended by the AMA. He probably wouldn't have known that fact if he hadn't seen her come out of the bathroom, but now, half in shadow, he wanted nothing more than to brush his lips over those smooth cheeks. "They were eating you alive," he said.

"I'll admit they got up into my bubble, but I would have noticed if it was anything more than that."

"Would you?"

"What, you think I have no life experience? I'm not a kid."

"Okay, okay," he said, realizing too late that mixing this discussion with the ability to see her had been a stupid move. "I take it back. I was completely mistaken."

She turned with a flounce and a punch to her pillow. He thought about what an idiot he was for bringing up the topic in the first place.

Then she turned again. "Why did you think so?"

The clock changed from 1:45 to 1:46. "It was the personal space thing. That's all."

"No, come on. That's not why."

"It is."

She huffed.

He only imagined he could feel the warmth of her breath

on the back of his neck. "I don't know. I guess I thought they were both checking you out."

A sigh this time, then some kind of movement he didn't want to know about. "They were doing that to you, too."

He turned. "Kyle was?"

Angie's mouth quirked up and so did her eyebrows. "Oh, really?"

Ryan mimicked her eye-roll. He knew she was messing with him because she'd already admitted to being oblivious, but he'd let her have her fun. "I'm wondering how I didn't catch that. They were obvious as hell when they were looking at you."

"Well, you were in no position to judge because you were bending over to pick up Tonya's napkin."

He grinned. Yeah, he'd picked up the napkin, but Angie was still full of bull. "Okay, that's good information to have. Maybe we can use it."

Again, she huffed at him, but this time it was somehow suggestive.

"Get your mind out of the gutter, woman. For the case. If the two of them are interested in some extracurricular activity, maybe I can exhibit some interest in return."

She gave up the whole back-to-back business and her shuffling made him turn around. She ended up sitting cross-legged with her sleep T pulled over her knees. It was plain blue, nothing special and Ryan figured it wasn't part of the disguise, but something she wore regularly.

"How," she asked, "would you go about doing that?"

Ryan sat up, too. They were supposed to have come home on the early side so they could get some sleep before taking their six-thirty run. "Subtly. In the presence of at least one of our suspects."

"That could potentially mean that you'd come on to Kyle

four different times. I don't care how subtle you are, that's going to make waves."

"We're supposed to make waves."

Angie shook her head. "Not the kind you're talking about." She sat straighter. "We're supposed to be working on our marriage. Not looking for orgies."

"Some would argue the added spice would keep the relationship more interesting."

"Yeah, like who?" Her head moved, just a little, and he really, really wished he could see the details of her face. "You?"

He almost lost it then, but pretended to yawn. "I won't get myself into anything I can't get out of. I promise."

"That's good," she said, lying down again under the white duvet. "Because it would blow our cover all to hell if I had to come sweeping in to save your ass."

"I see what you did there," Ryan said, grinning at her even though she couldn't see it. "Save my ass. You're a riot."

"So you've said."

"Being a riot is not the same thing as being funny."

Another punch to the pillow, observed this time, and her hair flowing over the ghostly white of the case made his smile fade and his stomach clench. It was too easy to talk with her, to lose track of how she affected him until it was too late. His cock wasn't hard, but it wasn't ignoring the circumstances, either.

"You set the alarm for six o'clock, right?" Angie asked, her voice lowered and missing the teasing he found he liked very much.

"Yeah."

"Okay. Good night."

"You, too." He took his time settling back into his safety position, thinking about the giant gap between his idea of safety and Delilah's. But Ryan also knew that a bed didn't exist that was large enough to make this deal with Angie one of the most difficult challenges he'd faced. Despite his determination, his promises to himself to stop thinking of her as anything but a coworker, there was no way.

He'd seen Kyle and Olivia scoping Angie out and he'd wanted to pull her away so fast he'd have left smoking tracks. He wasn't bothered by jealousy much. When he was younger, yeah, but in the past ten years he never put himself in a situation where there would be any competition. The women he picked had already picked him.

This, now, this was something else. And he was starting to realize how unprepared he was. The defenses he'd built up only worked in the scenarios he manipulated. This bed? This assignment? A thousand and ten miles from his comfort zone.

ANGIE CROSSED PERFECTLY manicured nails as she waited to see if Liz was there to get her call. If not, Angie would try her cell phone, but she had to be fast because Ryan was waiting for her. While she'd spoken to Liz earlier that morning, she needed another dose of best friend.

Just before Angie was about to hang up, Liz's face came into view. "What happened?"

"Nothing."

Ryan's voice, muffled, stopped Angie cold. "Are you speaking to me?"

She hadn't remembered to turn on the water. "Nope," she said, loudly. "Talking to myself." Then she turned the sink's spigot on full blast, hoping it was enough.

"Show me that dress," Liz said.

"Shh. Whisper."

"He can't hear *me,* you idiot. Now, show me the dress."

Angie did, but only because Liz wasn't going to let it go. When she whistled, Angie winced, sure Ryan had heard that. She pulled the tablet up so she was face-to-face with her friend. "Your theory about sleeping with him is ridiculous," she said, whispering, but with as much venom as she could muster.

"Okay." Liz said it with complete nonchalance.

"I'm not kidding. It's stupid. I'll have to see him in the office."

"Fine."

"Liz!"

"What? I'm not arguing with you."

"Delilah and Ira gave a class on pleasure props today."

"Pardon?"

Angie sat back down on the side of the tub. "You heard me. We had to play with everything from riding crops to gray silk ties. No one was naked or anything but the only thing worse than having Ryan Vail suck flavored lube off my finger was when I had to practice, uh, binding him while he gave me hints and smiles."

Liz took in a deep breath and let it out slowly.

Angie could see she was struggling not to laugh. "It wasn't funny."

"I can see how it wouldn't be. I'm sorry you had to go through that."

"Thank you," Angie said, the sympathy easing her discomfort hangover.

"Why are you calling me?"

She noticed that her friend was in her sports bra with her hair up. She was in her bathroom, too, and the sound of the tub filling was kind of loud. "Tonight I have to be all over him at the casino."

"Ah. Well, I guess you just do what feels right, Angie. Go with your instincts."

"He screws up my instincts."

Liz's condescending smile made Angie want to slap her. "Go take your bath."

"In all seriousness, hon, you can do this. You're the most

focused person I've ever met. When in doubt, remember the promotion. Do what's necessary to get it."

Angie nodded, knowing her friend's words were wise but unsure that she could follow the advice. "I'll try. But don't be shocked if I call you in the middle of the night."

"I have to work tomorrow," Liz said, her voice whiny and high.

"Tough. It's your fault for being a good friend. I'll talk to you later." Angie clicked off, not feeling one iota better. After she shoved the tablet in her case, she checked herself in the mirror, feeling equally hot and embarrassed. She'd never worn a dress like this, ever, and even though the material squeezed her like a giant Ace bandage, she felt more naked than she did wearing a bikini. It not only emphasized the curves she had, but created new ones. A person would think she had boobs in this Hermes concoction. Then there was the question of the length. Or the lack thereof. Her fingertips skimmed the bottom hem, for God's sake.

The shoes didn't help. The ludicrously tall heel was the same purple as the dress, but that was the only attempt at matching. The strap around her ankle was orange, the platform black patent and the peep-toe a dayglo pink. The instructions were to carry a white clutch with this mess of Crayola colors. She had no idea why.

One final look at her face, painted with far too much makeup, and she turned the knob, ready for a night at the casino.

From the back, Ryan looked great. He'd put on a jacket that fit him very well, emphasizing his broad shoulders and trim waist. When he turned around, the picture was even more alluring. She had a thing for athletic bodies, the clean lines of a ripped stomach and the masculinity of a perfectly muscled chest. The shirt he wore was white, elegantly simple and just a tad too snug. The slacks were black like the jacket. No tie. Classic shoes. Altogether stunning.

"Holy…"

Angie looked up and was taken aback to see the expression on Ryan's face. His eyes got wide and full of pupil, a slight flush tinted his cheeks, and then there was his dropped jaw. "What?" She looked down, wondering if something unfortunate had popped out.

"Wow," he said. "You continue to be very surprising."

"It's too much, isn't it?" she asked. "I have a couple of other choices in there. I look like a hooker, don't I? Oh, God. I do."

"No," he said, stepping toward her but stopping more than an arm's length away. "You look fantastic. You look like you should be on the cover of Vogue or on a red carpet, making all the actresses hate your guts."

Angie couldn't help the grin that tugged at her lips. "Really?"

"Yeah. It's perfect. Everyone in the casino is going to notice you. Actually both of us. Because they'll all be wondering what the hell you're doing with a guy like me."

"Oh, come on, Ryan. You're just fishing. You know you're gorgeous in that. It looks like it was tailor-made for you."

"It was. It cost a fortune. The best part is that because it's bespoke, I don't have to return it."

"Oh." She looked at the dress she'd suddenly come to like more than anything else she'd ever worn. "I suppose I'd better not spill any wine on this thing. I have no idea what designer dresses go for, but I can't imagine they're cheap."

"On the other hand, if you stain it carefully, it might not be returnable."

"That would be defrauding the American people."

"Only technically. I see it as doing the people a favor.

Any citizen who sees you in the dress is going to be very impressed with the FBI."

"I'm not going to wear my badge with it."

"You should. You should be on the cover of *FBI Monthly.*"

Okay, that deserved the eye-roll. "There is no *FBI Monthly.*"

He smiled. "They'd start one, if they knew you could be on the cover."

The blush that had started when he'd said, "Wow" had taken root, and while she liked the compliments, she could only deal with so many. "You know what? Give me a minute, would you? I, uh, need to brush my teeth."

Ryan's surprised look was cut off by her shutting the bathroom door.

Angie steadied herself on the sink as she tried to find the breath Ryan had stolen. She wasn't used to such extravagant attention for her looks. Yes, she understood she was attractive, but attractive hadn't counted for much in her life. Everything was about strength, athletic ability and intellectual achievement. That had been enough to contend with, and hearing Ryan talk about her that way, look at her with those eyes. It was great, and also not easy to deal with. But she needed to. Confidence was a key part of Angie Ebsen's character, and tonight, Angie would be on display.

She swiped a bit of toothpaste on her tongue, just in case, then stood up straight. Flicking her hair back, she pretended she was the woman she was playing, who wielded her sexuality the way Angie wielded her weapon.

When she stepped out of the bathroom, Ryan was standing by the bed. He gave her a long, considering look from the top down.

"Let's hit it," she said as she picked up her small bag and made a beeline for the door. "But not too fast because walking in these shoes is the most dangerous part of this assignment."

"I could argue that one," he murmured, but it was low, as if he hadn't meant for her to hear. He made it to the door first and held it open for her.

The night was chilly enough that if she'd been herself Angie would have worn a jacket. At least it wasn't a long walk to the casino, and she'd suffered through worse. She waited for Ryan to join her, picking up the pace as they moved along the well-lit pathway. Slowly, so she could get her feet under her.

She'd thought he might touch her once, but that only happened when they had to step aside for someone passing. Three times, his arm had moved behind her, but there'd been no contact. It was too close to the not-quite massage they'd suffered through all afternoon. "You know how earlier I said I could feel the energy of your body?"

Ryan slowed down even more. "Yeah?"

"I lied because that's what Delilahexpected me to say. I didn't feel anything."

"Oh. I felt yours."

They were almost at the entrance. She stopped.

"You all right?"

Angie thought about asking him if he was telling her the truth, but why would he lie? "I will be," she said. "I'm always nervous before the start of a race."

He leaned in and rested his hand carefully on her bare lower arm. "You're going to knock this out of the park. Just go with your instincts."

That was two votes for instincts, and for once, she didn't overthink it. She simply leaned forward the few inches between them and kissed him on the lips. It was meant to be a quickie, but his arm snaked around her back and he pulled her close as he licked the crease between her lips until they parted for him.

A girlish laugh and a low wolf whistle registered seconds before the glass doors to the casino slid open. It took her a second to realize Ryan had pulled back.

7

A WALL OF NOISE HIT RYAN from the casino, rock music from somewhere near the entrance, bells and dings and chimes from hundreds of slot machines, laughter, cheers from the craps tables. No wonder the doors were so heavy, not just to keep the desert heat out, but to mark the distinction between the casino and the courtyard.

Still, as he walked with Angie, the taste of her on his tongue, none of the glitz and sparkle could hope to compete with this incredibly surprising version of the woman he'd thought he'd known.

A cocktail waitress passed, forcing him to step closer to Angie and he struggled for a second against his need for more contact. He gave in, though. His hand at the small of her back, because while they were in the casino there was no question about who he was. Ryan Ebsen would feel proprietary about his wife, especially considering the hungry looks that were coming from every direction. Even the pit bosses stared as he and Angie passed the table games. The players, including those who had no chance in hell, stopped in midmotion, their hunger blatant. But then that was what a casino was all about.

"Of course, all the restaurants are at the back of the building," Ryan said, moving his mouth closer to her ear. "At least we can keep an eye out for any of the gang."

"I'm not ready to see anyone yet," Angie said, "but God, please tell me that band doesn't play all night."

"You're probably out of luck with that. Did you decide which restaurant?"

"Let's see if we can get in to Hachi first. It's still early, so I don't think we'll have too much of a wait."

Ryan nodded, then noticed that the open staring had eased up considerably. He smiled as he realized it was because they were passing the banks of video poker machines. These folks never looked up. Angie could have been stark naked and not be noticed.

Okay, perhaps he shouldn't think about Angie being naked. Especially when there was no hiding a thing in that dress of hers. Every curve was on display, perfectly wrapped like the most stunning present ever.

"Why are you slowing down when I'm so hungry?" Angie asked, tugging at his sleeve.

Somehow they'd separated. Unacceptable. But instead of the sexuality of his hand on her back, he went to the opposite end of signaling ownership and took her hand in his.

The move startled her, but she got back on track in a few seconds. "Have you seen any of the foursome?"

"Nope," he said, although to be honest he'd been distracted.

"I haven't even found any of the couples," she said as they moved closer to the perimeter, past the steakhouse and the Italian bistro. "I guess this is why the sessions start so late in the day."

"Lots of playtime. Smart to have an intimacy workshop at a casino where there's maximum stimulation of the senses and the endorphins are already swimming."

"Right now, all I care about is sushi. If we can, let's get a table by the window. Get seen."

"I'll do my best," he said as he led her into the foyer of the elegant and ultramodern Japanese restaurant. There was a small line, but the place wasn't packed. He pulled a fifty out of his wallet, reluctantly left Angie standing by the large art thing that looked strangely woodsy, then went to the tuxedo-clad maître d'.

Not five minutes later, they had their window seat, facing each other. It was going to be a long night, so he passed on having a drink and as expected; so did Angie. The food selection was huge, and if they'd had time, he would have gone for the chef's menu, but they needed to be out there, at center stage.

Instead of choosing between the spicy tuna and the sea urchin, he kept stealing glances at Angie. More than eating at the group lunches or room service, this felt like a date. He figured Ebsen would feel the same way, given his goals. As soon as they filled out their sushi orders, he reached across the table for Angie's hand. "You, my love, have been causing quite a stir."

She stared at where he touched her. "How's that?"

"That dress is probably illegal in most states. You're a stunner."

"Trust me, it's the dress more than me. It's actually uncomfortable as hell."

"Really? Too tight?"

"Too much. Too clingy. I'm not used to being so on display."

"You'd never know it. You walk like you own the place."

She looked down, differently this time; a shy move, something to hide the blush that stole up her cheeks. "Thank you," she said, but her voice was lower. Softer.

The waitress came then, and he let Angie go, but man, he didn't want to. And that scared the hell out of him.

IN HER WHOLE LIFE, ANGIE had never felt ornamental. She'd been a loner, a second fiddle, a third wheel, but never arm candy. Looks weren't the currency of worth in her family. Only achievement. Even though she wore Angie Ebsen like a costume, Angie Wolf was still inside and she wasn't sure how to feel about his compliments and the way he looked at her. Flattered, yes, but uneasy, as well.

Sipping a sour apple martini, standing slightly behind Ryan as he threw the dice at the craps table, Angie distracted herself by taking another long look past the immediate crowd to the casino floor beyond, seeking out anyone having anything to do with Intimate At Last.

A loud cheer interrupted her search, making her tense with the knowledge of what came next. Ryan, continuing his wicked winning streak, turned halfway toward her, far enough to wrap his hand around her waist and pull her into a kiss.

He tasted like whiskey and excitement as he thrust into her mouth. While it was perfectly in character, each kiss set her heart pumping as she struggled to remember that none of this was real.

When he finally pulled away, it was only long enough to reach for the dice. Thankfully he didn't ask for her to blow on them, because she couldn't have pulled that off. Besides, Angie Ebsen would never have done something so lowbrow. It was bad enough that she continued to wince each time he returned his attention to the game.

A bump to her elbow made her spill a few drops of her martini, and a quick, deep-voiced apology followed.

She smiled, a reflex more than anything. "No problem."

The man, who had to have fought his way into his slot at

the table, didn't turn immediately to the game. Instead, he tilted his head, looking concerned.

He wasn't as tall as Ryan, not quite as good-looking, although again, Ryan was unfairly handsome. The man whose shoulder brushed against hers wore a natty retro shirt and had a television smile. "Is that a sour apple martini? I'll get you another."

"Don't worry about it," she said, aware of what was going on. Just because she wasn't used to casinos and skintight dresses didn't mean she hadn't had to deal with her fair share of pickup lines.

"I insist," he said, leaning closer.

The arm around her waist surprised her, but only because it hadn't been preceded by a cheer. Ryan wasn't even looking at her. Everything about him had gone into caveman mode. He stood ramrod straight, his nostrils flared, his pupils darkened his eyes and he pulled her so close he practically bent her sideways.

"Is there something we can do for you?" he said, and hell, if she thought the stranger's voice had been deep, Ryan's was just damn dangerous.

"Nope, nope." The man stepped back, not accepting the challenge. "Sorry to have disturbed you."

Ryan didn't move. Not an inch. From her quick glance, Angie realized he was holding up the game. The interloper ceded his territory to the alpha dog and crept off. It was like something from a nature documentary.

"You okay?" he asked.

His voice was still low, but it had softened as he moved in so close she felt his breath on the shell of her ear. She wondered if he'd had one drink too many, because this didn't feel like part of the game plan.

"I'm fine," she said, frowning. "But you're supposed to be neglecting me."

"Sir," the croupier interrupted. "Would you like to pass on the dice?"

Ryan dropped his hold on Angie and turned a brilliant smile on the waiting crowd. "Do you guys want me to pass the dice?"

Like a flash mob, the entire group yelled out some version of "No way," quite a few of them with far more cuss words. Angie could only see him from an angle, but even she recognized the power he exuded, and if she hadn't believed all the stories about his legendary conquests before, she did now.

She polished off her drink and looked around for a cocktail waitress. Ryan evidently threw the ideal numbers, and his fawning audience grew even more exuberant.

She didn't find the waitress but she did discover Marcus sitting at the circular bar in the center of the room. He was alone, his back toward the bar, watching the craps table. Actually, he seemed to be watching Ryan through the space created by the dealers.

Curious that he hadn't looked her way. Also curious that for the first time, Marcus seemed tense. He was leaning forward, his weak chin jutting out, the martini glass in his hand gripped tightly enough for her to notice. Perhaps he was sizing up Ryan as a likely target. If so, tonight's performance should help nudge him in the right direction. The blackmailer had waited until after the retreat was over to send the initial text message, but the move to Cancún could be enough to change the M.O.

Ah, something else snagged his attention. He pulled a cell phone out of his pocket, put his glass down on the bar behind him and started texting.

It occurred to her that there had been at least two cheers since she'd turned her attention to getting another drink. Which meant that Ryan was ignoring her. Good. All part of the sting. Now it was her turn to react. With a pronounced pout, she left the table and headed for the bar.

As she made her way she looked past the stares and out-right leers to get a broader picture than she'd been able to while standing behind Ryan. To her left were the big glass doors to the courtyard, and to her right, the hotel lobby, which was separate from the spa lobby. They were equally flashy, but this one didn't inspire calm and relaxation. Soft mood music would never be heard in this cacophony, for one thing. Here, the front desk looked as if it was made of black oil and the uniforms of those who worked it were that much tighter on very fit bodies.

She checked back to find Marcus still texting, looking serious but less intense, but she slowed her step in a delayed reaction to something she'd seen by the front desk.

Looking again, she found what had caught her eye. Tonya Bridges, behind the desk, speaking to one of the assistant managers. Angie recognized the dark suit and the lapel pin that signified the man in charge.

Without another thought, Angie shifted her trajectory. Not in a straight line to Tonya where she stood, but where Angie estimated Tonya would be in a few minutes. Angie walked very slowly, which did nothing to discourage a couple of young men who needed to be cut off from the booze.

Ignoring their attempts to speak with any kind of coherency, Angie observed Tonya quickly scan several pages before the man pulled her into a conversation. Tonya gave off every indication that she didn't want to speak to Mr. Assistant Manager. Visibly worked up, he grabbed her just above the wrist.

Angie was no longer walking slowly. All her danger alerts had gone red at that touch. Tonya smiled, but even at this distance, which was closing by the second, Angie could see how strained it was.

Held up by a large party of tightly packed revelers, Angie didn't lose her cool. She waited the minute it took for the group to pass. There was Tonya and the man who'd touched her, and they were separate now, his hands by his side, his posture tight.

Angie was just within hearing range when the manager said, "Let me know if you need any more faxes. Anytime. At all."

Tonya looked back at him for a moment, then pressed on, right into Angie's path.

"Hi there," Tonya said, quickly folding her paperwork and sticking them in her purse. Her voice was as breezy and casual as she'd been this morning at yoga. "I saw you at the craps tables. Ryan looked like he was having a heck of a lucky streak."

"Yeah," Angie said, glancing back to the table. She wasn't able to see Ryan from this angle, but she did catch a glimpse of Marcus, still sitting at the superlong, elegant open bar that went all the way around the pit where the band continued to knock out terrible covers of Journey and Kansas. She brought her gaze back to Tonya. "He's on fire."

Tonya gave her a questioning head tilt. Angie had already thought about what her reactions should be in this situation. She'd specifically had Tonya in mind, given what they suspected about her father's gambling activities. Quick as a wink, Angie slapped on a loving smile, complete with an indulgent eye-roll that wouldn't have fooled a high school girl let alone a woman raised by two therapists.

"I gather you don't play," Tonya said. She looked great in black skinny jeans and a blue silk short-sleeved blouse. She'd gone heavier on the makeup without overdoing things, and Angie had a strong feeling she was on the hunt, but not for the fax man.

"Oh, no," Angie said, exaggerating her expression. "If I'm

going to give away my money, I want it to go to something that needs it. This casino is doing fine without me."

Tonya chuckled, but there was no humor involved. "No, the house always wins. Were you headed somewhere specific?"

Angie looked back again, this time catching a quick glimpse of Ryan and a young woman who seemed to be standing very, very close. "No," she said. "Well, I was trying to find a cocktail waitress."

"Are you all right?"

Angie turned back, lowered her eyes, avoiding the other woman's. "Peachy," she said. Then she shook her head. "I'm sorry. I didn't mean…"

"No, it's okay. Why don't we head toward the big bar. If you want to, that is."

"You're not booked?"

Tonya smiled, but the grin didn't hold. She was looking behind Angie's shoulder.

When Angie followed her gaze, she saw Ira walking past the table games, and she wondered if he was heading to the sports book. A few seconds later, Delilah followed him. There was no smile on her face, either.

"I can't believe it," Angie said, making sure she was looking at the craps table.

"Can't believe what?" Tonya asked, her voice very strained.

Angie sighed. "Nothing. Just, Ryan's having himself a time."

Tonya started walking more toward Ryan than the bar. It was interesting that being with Tonya, who was very attractive, had a sort of dampening effect on the men around them.

They didn't speak until they were midway between the still-texting Marcus and Ryan, who'd picked up not one, but two admirers. They were both young, college age, probably.

Over twenty-one, at least, but not by much. They weren't touching him, but they were clearly in his orbit. Rooting him on with a lot of hair-touching and giggling.

He couldn't have been rolling the dice this whole time, and when she moved slightly to her left, Angie saw that he'd lost a considerable number of chips. The ones he reached for were black.

"Wow, those are hundreds," Tonya said, then pressed her lips together.

"It's not the money," Angie said, stepping a few inches closer to her would-be friend. "He knows he can't go too crazy or my business manager will take away his cards. Still, I hate gambling. I've always hated it."

"Oh?"

"Ryan isn't a compulsive gambler." Angie made sure she sounded defensive.

Tonya didn't say anything, but questions were there in her eyes.

Angie bit her lip, then sighed. "It broke up my family. Among other things."

"I see," Tonya said. "Believe me."

Okay, so Tonya knew about her father's gambling problem. It was clear from her reaction, from the way she looked at Ryan. "Anyway, it's no big deal. Most of the time, he's wonderful. And we don't come to Vegas often."

"No, I'm sure you don't."

Angie smiled bravely. "What about that drink, hmm? I'm getting desperate."

Tonya returned the grin, and they headed once more toward the bar, but she stopped two steps in. So sharply, Angie had to turn around to find out what had happened. Of course, she knew it was the sight of Marcus that had stopped Tonya. It was evident there was no love lost between those two. And who was that standing next to him?

Angie put herself next to Tonya, then faced Marcus and his flashy companion. Now Angie understood the shocked expression on Tonya's face. Marcus was trying to find the woman's tonsils with his tongue. The woman was several inches taller than him, had long, curly red hair that had to be out of a bottle. And her dress made Angie's look like a tent. Especially across the bust. When the two of them came up for air, Angie was surprised again to find out the woman was legit gorgeous. A ten, at least. Marcus was a two on his best day.

"Is that Marcus's girlfriend?"

Tonya barked out a laugh.

"Oh, God." Angie turned her head, feigning acute embarrassment. "I didn't mean…"

"It's fine. Marcus has…special needs."

Looking back at Ryan, Angie guessed that he'd seen the Marcus-and-call-girl show, as well. But that didn't matter in the least because one of Ryan's young admirers had gone from looking to touching. "Damn him," she snapped. "I don't even know why we bothered."

Silence followed, and Angie didn't have to look to know that Tonya had seen Ryan's new best friend. Angie made sure she looked hurt, but not surprised. This was not new behavior she was witnessing.

Then, Ryan touched the blonde. His fingertips brushed her cheek as he swept back a loose strand of hair. Something inside Angie twisted. It was crazy because the jealousy she'd felt when Ryan had spoken to Jeannie was nothing compared to the body slam she felt now. Which she was supposed to be faking and not experiencing all the way down to her stupid polished toes. The sudden itch to pull the blonde out of his reach scared the hell out of her.

She abruptly turned away and met Tonya's sympathetic eyes. Angie swallowed hard and tried unsuccessfully to force a smile. This was good, she told herself, she was supposed to look as if the rug had just been pulled out from under her. After all, the man she loved had just broken her heart in two.

"Look," Tonya said. "Why don't we get out of here? I'm sorry I said anything at all about Marcus. He's a good guy, and he doesn't mean any harm."

Angie nodded, heading for the doors. "It's all right. Everyone's got something to hide. I hope I haven't given you the wrong impression about Ryan. He can be very sweet. He loves me. He does."

"I've seen you two together," Tonya said, keeping up with Angie's quick steps. "It's obvious he's mad about you. Casinos are just bad news, that's all."

Behind her, Ryan's voice carried over the noise of the slots, of the music, calling her name. She didn't want to stop. Not just because of the role she was playing. Seeing him with that girl rubbing up against him had been painful enough, but when *he'd* touched *her*...

She needed to leave, now. Get away from Tonya, from the job, from everything until she could clear her head. Somehow she needed to make sense of the churning in her stomach, the tightness in her chest.

But before she could make her final move, a hand gripped her arm, and a fresh cascade of unwanted emotions poured through her. When she turned to look at Ryan's stricken face, she didn't have to act at all.

8

RYAN'S HEART LURCHED in his chest as his focus narrowed to Angie and only her. The look of betrayal she'd given him hit low and hard, as if he'd done something unforgivable.

He hurried back to the craps table, and as he stuffed chips into his pockets he called out Angie's name. He didn't have to fake his desperation.

How had that one look made it stunningly clear that she wanted no part of him? Not even sure he'd picked up all the hundred-dollar chips, he darted through the crowd to the exit and chased after Angie and she was fast, even on those heels.

It was Tonya who brought some reality back to the situation, and he was damn grateful for it. He'd caught her reflection in the glass display case, and just like that he was back in the game. Shit, the past couple of minutes…

Tonya followed him with no attempt to hide what she was doing. Worried for Angie's safety? Gathering more data for possible blackmail?

He sped up for a few paces. "Angie, wait."

She didn't look back.

Fine, he could deal with that, at least until they got to their room. If he didn't have a heart attack first. His reactions were messed up. He needed to calm down, let her keep ahead of him. Make sure he gave himself time to turn off the weird and unexpected panic that made it difficult to breathe.

They'd passed the gate to their private courtyard. A few folks were using the spa pool, people from their group. None of the suspects. Ryan didn't pause but the clicking of Tonya's heels stopped. He walked more quickly now that they were a few feet away from their bungalow. Angie opened the door before he had a chance to get out his card key and he had to hustle before it closed behind her.

Once inside with the bolt locked, he let out a long breath. He almost asked her what the hell she'd been doing, but he didn't dare say a word before he checked the room for surveillance. He put his finger up to his lips. Angie's startled nod told him that she wasn't thinking clearly, either. The bug sweeper had been locked away along with his real cell phone. He took out both, put the phone in his pocket and began the scan.

Angie hadn't moved. "I'm going to get ready for bed," she said. "Do you need anything in the bathroom?"

"Yeah, give me a second," he said as he hurried to make sure the room was clean. No red lights went off as he scanned, which wasn't surprising. A moment later, he left the bathroom to Angie.

With her night things held close to her chest, she barely looked at him as she slipped past him and closed the door.

He continued the sweep, wanting to be done. He'd have preferred to use the time alone to regroup. The fact that he'd confused reality and work bothered him a hell of a lot. He'd fought hard to keep work and personal business separate but more than that, he had no need or desire for this kind of… emotion. He didn't get entangled. Not ever. Now he felt up to his ass in alligators, unable to find solid ground. It sucked.

At least there were no red lights on the sweeper as he moved it carefully through their room. This particular device could detect not only all kinds of radio frequencies but pinhole lenses of tiny cameras. Finally he was assured that no one had planted a bug, but that still left one more item to check. He went to the laptop he'd left on the dresser.

The plastic tab was no longer in place. Someone had screwed around with the laptop.

Everything extraneous left his thoughts as he replayed each word they'd said since they entered the room. Habit and discipline had insured that neither of them had misspoken. There was no camera in the dummy computer for just this reason. However, there was a microphone.

He was at the bathroom door in three strides. Of course it was locked, why wouldn't she lock it? But he had to get in there, now, because whoever had been in the room might be listening to everything, and she needed to be on her toes until their team in L.A. had a chance to check out the hard drive.

He knocked. Loudly. "Hey, sweetie. What did you lock the door for? Was I really such a bad boy?"

He leaned against the door, but got nothing. Not even the sound of the water running. When it opened, he nearly knocked her over, but he did manage to grab on to her shoulders. Her naked shoulders. A towel covered her breasts, but the naked part was far more important.

"Are you drunk?" She was stiff in his hands but allowed him to walk her backward until he could close the door.

Releasing her was more difficult than it should be, which pissed him off. This was business, dammit. "Someone's been in the room," he said, leaning in, noticing that the only clothing she had on was a red thong. He considered running out and getting her a blanket to cover herself with, but a tilt of her head stopped that thought in its tracks.

"Well?" she asked, clearly having had to wait too long for him to explain.

"Wait," he said, letting her go in order to turn on the water in the shower. He thought about dunking his head under the spray, but that would be admitting far too much. When he straightened, she was close enough to him that he could see the small gold flecks of her dark brown eyes. Still, he leaned in. "No cameras. No radio frequencies in any part of the room. It's the laptop. We need to get it scanned," he said. "Right now."

Angie's eyebrows rose and her towel lowered, but only a little.

Calling Jeannie forced him to move back. As he hit her speed dial, he made the mistake of glancing at the mirror. Christ. Angie's bare back made his cock stir. Which was nothing compared to the view of her nearly naked behind. The thong made it sexier than if she hadn't had a thing on.

"What's wrong?" Jeannie's voice was rough with sleep and annoyance.

Turning his gaze to the bathtub, he explained about the laptop.

"Any other signs of intrusion?" Jeannie asked, not pissed anymore.

"Nope, that's it."

"I'll see that it gets done. Leave your phone on. I'll have someone text with the outcome. Just keep being a happy couple until we get this sorted."

"Right," he said. "Tell them to hurry." When he hung up, he found Angie leaning against the sink, her towel still in place and her expression pensive. He should have gone back to staring at the tub, but he couldn't, despite the fact that they'd had their first real confirmation that the blackmailer was scoping them out.

"There's no camera on that computer," Angie said.

"What?"

"Whatever they loaded on to the computer isn't video."

He blinked, nodded, brought his thoughts to heel. "That's

the upside." He looked at the cell phone again, urging it to ring, despite the fact that no one could have possibly searched the hard drive yet. Like a man under a spell, he couldn't help but stare once more at Angie, at the way her dark hair swept over her shoulder, the curve of her hips. "I wonder if it was just us," he said. "Or if whoever it is will be trying to surveil everyone. That might be the approach across the board."

"Not everyone would have brought a laptop."

"True. But I imagine they have options. Anything quick. In and out, because it's a risk, breaking in like that. Maybe someone on the hotel staff working for them? Someone with a master key?" He glanced at his phone again. Focused on it as if his thoughts could make it ring. "Did you get anything useful when you left the craps table? I should have asked. Was there something else to tell Jeannie?"

Angie's inhale drew his gaze, and he just gave it up. As long as they were in the bathroom and she was undressed, he was physically incapable of not looking. Unbelievable. Thirty-two years old and this was his life.

"Tonya knows Ira's a problem gambler," she said, talking faster than normal as if she would forget if she didn't spit it out. "And Marcus likes high-priced hookers."

"I saw him with that redhead. She had to cost him a pretty penny."

"From what Tonya said, it's a regular thing with him. I also saw her leaving the front desk office. The assistant manager had faxed some pages for her. I only got a glimpse of them, not enough to see what they were, but it made me wonder. Intimate At Last has an office here, on site. There's no way on earth they don't have a fax machine. So what was she faxing so late on a Wednesday night that couldn't have waited till morning? Why not use the hotel's business office for guests if it was something she didn't want her partners to know?"

"Well, hell. The only one we haven't caught doing something hinky is Delilah."

"She's probably the mastermind. At least she's clever enough not to get caught."

"I don't know." Ryan shook his head, trying to piece together the night, what he'd want to put in his report. "Marcus was watching me like he knew something. Or maybe he was waiting to hear something back. For example, that our computer had been breached. You'd left the craps table already—"

Angie nodded, clearly clicking with the notion that Marcus had been up to no good. She pushed off from the sink. "If we can get a trace on whatever he did to the computer—" She gestured with her arm. The one holding the towel.

Her breasts were perfect. Small, pert, with hardened nipples that made his mouth water.

Her gasp made him turn away, guilt slamming him in the gut. He knew she'd covered herself again, but he wasn't sure at all what to say.

She cleared her throat. "Um, there's no camera on the laptop," she said.

Keeping his eyes low, he nodded. "We've already established that."

When she didn't respond, he dared a glance. Angie, with very wide eyes and pink cheeks, motioned to the door with her chin.

"Oh," he said. "Sorry. Sorry. I—" Now the sound of the water seemed exceedingly loud and he noticed she'd been in the middle of taking off her makeup because there were cotton balls on the counter and a bottle of something blue open. "There's no reason for me to wait in here."

"Not that I can think of," she said, looking at everything but him. When he moved, she moved, skittering around trying to keep herself as covered as she could. Only, there was a flash of her from the side, a reflection in the mirror as he took the few steps to the door.

The swell of her breast made his pace stutter and his hand slip on the knob. The nipple was hidden, but it was too late. He'd seen it, the exact shade of pink and how her areola was like a perfect halo. The modest glimpse of side breast shouldn't have knocked him for a loop, but it was the most erotic thing he'd seen tonight.

He was out the door in a flash, upset, embarrassed and more confused than ever. "Well, that happened," he said softly, not sure whether he should laugh or offer to sleep in the bathtub. In the meantime, he put on his pajamas, keeping himself away from the computer even though he couldn't imagine there was anyone watching.

Changing wasn't easy, though, because his body was clearly trying to make a point. His brain filling him with urges and memories that made it hard to breathe. His cock, on the other hand, was being a son of a bitch, already more than half-hard. Like a man obsessed, he imagined kissing her now, when he knew so much more. Wondered what it would feel like to meander up those mile-long legs of hers, first with his hands, then with his mouth.

In perfect and swift retribution, Angie walked out of the bathroom just as he pressed his palm against his now very hard and insistent erection. A second later, the cell phone rang, but the damage had already been done.

ANGIE DID HER BEST NOT TO STARE. Not that he didn't deserve to be stared at, but she was above that sort of thing. What was important now was the report from the team. She needed the distraction more than she could say, especially since she'd realized in the middle of washing her face that she could have put on her sleep shirt the moment Ryan had entered the bathroom.

"That's a relief," Ryan said into the phone. He'd turned his back on her, the chicken. Too late. She just wished there was a way to delete the image that was now burned into her brain forever. It wasn't as if those pajamas were especially thick or tight fitting. Or that his hand hadn't been *right there*.

Although he had looked amusingly like a kid caught with his hand not just in the cookie jar, but with a fistful of Oreos. Quite a fistful, in fact.

"No, okay. We'll work on it tomorrow. Maybe an email from Roxanne wouldn't be out of the question?"

Oh, so, keylogging. She imagined it would be hypervisor based, software running underneath the operating system, becoming a virtual machine that would reproduce itself on the blackmailers end. At least, that's what she'd look for first. She would have asked Ryan to put the call on speaker, but his back was still turned.

At least it wasn't just her. Angie wished it wasn't so late, as she'd love to talk to Liz about, well, everything, but that would have to wait. What Angie needed this minute was to put herself to bed. Because falling asleep was the only possible way out of the mess in her head. Unfortunately, despite being tired enough to face-plant in the middle of a run, she was also chock full of adrenaline and raging hormonal influences.

Even so, she put her clothes away and parked her bathroom case, then slid beneath the sheets. Ryan was either listening to a very long explanation of computer tech or was waiting until his hard-on deflated.

Finally he made a quick dash to the bathroom. She wanted to be snarky about that, but in truth, he was being considerate. He didn't want to make her any more uncomfortable than she'd been. God, when she'd lowered the towel…

She closed her eyes as she positioned herself on her side,

facing away from Ryan's sleep spot. Nothing needed to change. Outwardly, at least.

So much had happened since they'd gone to dinner she could barely get things straight. The way she'd reacted to Ryan in the casino was a major issue. Made more immediate than ever now that he'd seen her, and she'd seen what she did to him.

It wasn't a terribly big surprise. This thing between them had been burning like a slow fuse, and hell, maybe Liz was right and they should just bow to the inevitable. But the idea of sleeping with her partner while in the middle of a case felt fundamentally wrong.

Nothing about this case wasn't fundamentally screwed up, even without adding sex.

The bathroom door opened, and in quick order, she felt the bed dip and the covers move.

"No trace of a microphone," he said, calm as could be. "Whoever it was is key—"

"Keylogging, yeah, I figured. I assume we're going to use that to our advantage." She started to roll onto her back, but stopped short.

"The team is working on that. Getting together some scripts. A push by Roxanne to keep the affair going. Something like that."

"Good," she said, closing her eyes. A sudden and vivid picture hit her. Of Ryan in his pajama pants, pressing down on his cock. Followed immediately by the way he'd stared at her when the towel had slipped. She bit the side of her cheek to keep steady. The last thing in the world she wanted was for him to hear something weird in her voice. "Who'd you talk to?"

"Arnold. He said that a trace will take time, especially because whoever uploaded the program knew his stuff."

She nodded. "So not a game changer. We keep doing what we've been doing."

"Yep," he said.

Silence fell, and while it should have been a comfort, it was the opposite. Her nipples had hardened. Just like that. Hard like erasers and she found herself pressing her palm on her breasts, which just reminded her again of his hand and his pajamas....

Angie was reasonably sure she was going clinically insane. What the ever-loving *hell* was she doing to herself? Only a complete masochist would continue to somehow forget that Ryan was not her boyfriend, her lover, her husband, her dream man, her *anything* except her partner. Regardless of erections. Regardless of dubious advice from friends.

There just didn't seem to be anywhere for her to hide. No switch that would let her turn off the thoughts. Even during her run this morning, her last bastion of sanity had been filled with thoughts of Ryan and sex. Sex and Ryan.

Perfect. Wonderful. She should be getting the FBI Special Agent of the Year award any minute now.

"What was that sigh about?" Ryan asked.

"Frustration," she admitted, and winced at what he undoubtedly thought she meant. Great, the incredibly uncomfortable silence came back to make everything worse.

"I have to admit, it's harder than I thought it would be," Ryan said, his words soft and half-mumbled.

"What is?" Angie did roll over this time. Onto her back, so all she had to do was turn her head to see him. At least, see him in shadow. Because he couldn't mean what she thought he meant.

"Pretending."

She froze as his response derailed her. She understood the word but not what he meant. Pretending to be married? Pretending they hadn't been hot for each other for ages?

He turned until he was lying on his side facing her. Then, as if he hadn't already stolen her breath, he reached over and took her hand in his.

She wished she could see his eyes more clearly, even though she was pretty sure about his intention. The next bit would be up to her. If she slipped away from his grasp, they could hold on to their very rocky status quo. If she reciprocated…

Before she could talk herself out of it, she pulled away.

9

"I MEAN, TONIGHT," HE SAID, as if he'd never touched her. "It was weird flirting with those girls. Acting like a jackass at the table. Not my style, that's not me."

"You were very convincing. I'm sure what Tonya and Marcus saw helped the case. You looked like a man trying to puff himself up, to make himself feel more powerful. That's exactly what you were supposed to do."

"True," he said. "I think we both did really well tonight."

Except for the part where she'd completely lost touch with reality. But he didn't have to know that. "Agreed."

"So, six?"

"Yeah. Thanks."

He leaned over and did something to the clock, then ended up with his back to her once more.

She stared at him, the shape of his head, the edge of his T-shirt, his shoulder rising and falling with his breath. It was tempting to take another stab at understanding him. For all the seeing each other in compromising positions, all the touching and kissing they'd practiced, this talk right now was by far the most intimate thing that had happened since she'd arrived.

What she didn't know was if that was a good thing or a

bad thing. Keeping her distance felt like a matter of survival, but opening up to Ryan might end up being the linchpin to this whole operation. Perhaps if they became real people to each other, the mystique left over from the night that almost was would go away.

Knowing the real man would certainly change the fantasy Ryan she'd been carrying for so long. It was ridiculous to think her reaction this evening had been about Ryan himself. She didn't know him well enough to feel anything more than physical attraction, and that had never been enough for her. Her fantasies weren't built on anything but lust and fiction. Until this week, it had felt like being in lust with a character in a TV show.

STARING AT THE CLOCK wasn't in any way helping Ryan relax. At the very least it should have bored him to sleep. But the night ahead of him was destined to be uncomfortable in every possible way.

She wasn't sleeping, either. He could tell from her breathing, her small movements. What he needed was a brain wipe, but what he might be able to get was something less provocative to replace the miasma of erotica starring his bedmate that continued to plague him. "Tomorrow I'm going to sign up with Marcus for a private session. Give him an opportunity to ferret out some damning information."

"Oh, God," she said.

"I know. I haven't wanted to avoid something this badly since my old man gave me *the talk*."

"Oh, that," she said. "How old were you?"

"Twelve." He stared at the window, so aware that she was a matter of inches away from him it was hard to think. "I'll give him credit. He was creative about it."

Angie shifted. "What do you mean?"

Without looking he could tell she was on her back again.

"Books weren't his thing. Neither was a straightforward conversation. What he did tell me wasn't exactly orthodox."

"No 'When a mommy and daddy love each other very much…?'"

He laughed, the sound surprisingly bitter even to his own ears. The heat in his face made him yank on the comforter. "Why are we talking about this?"

"You brought it up."

"I really, really don't want to think about getting a massage from Marcus."

"Understood. Carry on, then. He was creative…?"

Ryan's sigh was more telling than he wanted to admit. But at this point, talking about his father, which was his least favorite topic in the world, was preferable to letting his mind have free rein. "It wasn't the mechanics that he'd gotten wrong," he admitted. "It was the entire subject of women."

"Oh?" Of course Angie sounded surprised. He never discussed his private life. Not even with Jeannie.

"He's sure as hell not anyone's idea of a model father." Ryan tried to make it sound as if he were joking but the attempt fell flat. "He lives his life as if he's in a pulp novel from the fifties."

"For example…?"

"Chauvinistic crap about a woman's place, blah blah blah. You know that old saw, 'A man wants a maid in the living room, a cook in the kitchen and a whore in the bedroom'? That was…is…his credo."

When she didn't say anything for a weirdly long time, he couldn't hold out any longer. He used rearranging his pillow as an excuse to not only settle on his back, but to look at her.

Even in shadow, he had no difficulty filling in the details. No cover would be thick enough, ever again, and wasn't that completely screwed up. He bit back a groan that would have made everything worse.

ANGIE WAS GLAD, NOW, that she was staring at the ceiling. Things had just gotten very personal. She could sense his embarrassment as if his thoughts had weight. If she didn't do something soon, this would be the last time he'd open up to her, of that she felt certain. The risk seemed worth it. She faced him, moving that much closer to the middle of the bed, but being the chicken she was, she stared at her hand instead of meeting his eyes.

"My mother gave me the talk. She had a book of some kind that explained everything in excruciating clinical detail. With pictures. It was horrifying."

"I can only imagine."

"A week later, I got to go over the entire subject again, with my father. Evidently he'd found my mom's book and thought he could do better."

The bedclothes rustled. His warm breath swept gently over her hand, and when she looked up in surprise they were only inches apart. One-quarter turn more and they'd touch.

"How long did it take you to recover?"

It took her a second to remember what he was talking about. "There is no recovery. Only shudders when the thought swims to the surface."

He did laugh then. "How old were you?"

"Still in middle school. Hadn't been kissed yet. Never really thought about boys. I was too caught up in training."

"Track and field."

"Yeah. That was our religion. Competition in general. My family is really into overachieving. In every aspect of life. Needless to say, they weren't thrilled to discover I wanted to work for the Bureau. They had me penciled in as an attorney. After all, they already had two doctors in the family. I would have rounded out their résumés." She shrugged, tempted to move her hand closer, just to feel more of his breath.

"They must be really proud of you now."

She checked to see if he was being sincere. Ryan's free hand moved scant inches across the mattress until he touched her. It was different. Surprisingly sweet. "Not yet," she said.

"What? I can't imagine any parent not being proud of you. Look what you've accomplished and you're not even thirty. You were what, in the top five at the academy? You're the highest-ranking woman in hand-to-hand in the whole damn country. Which is chicken feed next to what you can do on a computer. You've made a major contribution to forensics, Angie. That's like winning all the gold medals and a bag of chips on the side."

She laughed. Thank goodness he'd given her a reason because even though she didn't want to, her eyes had filled with tears. How was this moment even happening? Ryan was the least sentimental person she knew. Whom she thought she knew.

After she pushed her hair back, she rested her hand on Ryan's. Gave him a little squeeze to say thanks. When she went to pull away, he stopped her. Stopped her breathing, too.

He sighed and his breath warmed her neck. "This is not a good idea," he said.

Right. At least they were on the same page. "No, it's not."

"We're not…"

"God, no."

"But," he said. "We do need practice. Kissing, I mean."

"We do," she said, but the conversation was slipping away from her, the timbre of his voice and his closeness taking over.

He inhaled a long breath between his teeth. "I don't know about you, but I'm not going to sleep anytime soon."

"Maybe it'll be relaxing. Practicing, I mean." Who was she kidding? They were on a precipice with a lot hanging in the balance. Did she want to pull herself back up to the ledge, or let herself fall? With her heart pounding and her fingers crossed, she said, "Tomorrow we're going to the hot springs. We'll have to touch a lot."

"The hot springs," he echoed, his voice a gruff whisper. "Right. It'll be…hot."

The hand that wasn't holding him up took all of Angie's attention. It had moved from his side to just above her right cheek. Almost touching her. Slightly tickling as he pushed some wisps of hair back.

"Hot," she whispered, even though she didn't really know why.

It wasn't just his hand that was moving now, but his whole upper body. Achingly slowly. Giving her plenty of time to say no.

"It's just…" His voice had become even rougher, softer, making Angie strain to hear.

She had to lift her head off the pillow. To hear.

"Say yes," he whispered, inches away from her, so close to her parted lips they might have touched. "You need to say it. Say something."

Her wince wasn't planned. Neither was the hand to his chest. "Wait a minute."

She felt him stop breathing again, still completely. A lot of rapid heartbeats went by before he moved back. Not just back but away.

As she lost contact, she thought about grabbing his T-shirt, pulling him down, but she couldn't.

"I'm sorry," he said. He cleared his throat, and repeated the words twice. By the time he grew quiet, he was as far away from her as he could get on the bed. "I have no excuse. That was completely unprof—"

"Stop." She tugged at his arm, forcing him to move until she could see his profile in the moonlight. "Please, stop. I'm not…" Holding up her index finger, she closed her eyes so she could concentrate. When she opened them again, she felt calmer, although still unbelievably shaken. "I'm not saying no like that."

"What?"

"Not like, no, this is wrong or bad. More like no, this is something we'd better think about. I was kind of swept away there, and I need to be here. This isn't a minor decision."

He didn't say anything for a long time. They both were breathing as if they'd just come back after a quick jog, and she had to squeeze her legs together to ease the pressure, but finally, he said, "We really are all wrong for each other."

"Yes, we are." She felt the urge to pull the covers up to her chest, but she didn't. "That doesn't necessarily mean—"

"It's this undercover bullshit—" he said, breaking in. "I had no business—"

"I was jealous," she said, louder.

"What?"

"Of that girl at the craps table."

Silence. Then, "Huh."

"I know. Ridiculous. And you're right. This role-playing stuff and the kissing. I didn't expect... I didn't know what to expect. This is so far outside my range of experience...."

"No one on earth has experience doing what we're doing."

"I know. I do. But it's really complicated. Between us."

Ryan's hand moved halfway across the bed, as it had before. She wished he would stop doing that because she couldn't help the reaction it caused. The way it made her ache.

"For what it's worth, I think you're really brave," he said.

"What? Why?"

"You just dove into the deep end of the pool. Jumped in without a life vest, without any prep at all. For this sting? That took one hell of a lot of courage."

"The whole operation was on the line."

"Doesn't negate my point."

She smoothed down the comforter. "I'm not that altruistic. I'm going after the job in D.C. You did hear what I said about me and my family, right?"

"Yeah, I get it."

"But thank you."

She had no reason to believe he was smiling when he said, "You're welcome." Still, she was pretty sure he was. If she flipped on the light right now, she'd see it. See his strong jaw and his humor in the face of their impossible situation. Made so much worse by the months she'd spent making him into her fantasy man. Here, in the flesh, she'd seen his toes. The way he pulled on his bottom lip. How he looked when he was out of his depth and when he still had sleep in his eyes.

Her hand went out to meet his and this time their fingertips brushed. It felt startling and intimate and sweet. And if she had half a brain, she'd roll back onto her other side, roll all the way back to L.A. before it was too late. Because the only thing that had changed since that long-ago party was that she wanted the real Ryan now.

THE TOUCH OF HER FINGERS on his got his poor confused cock revving up again. Granted, it had never softened completely, not even after her "no" had penetrated past the layers of brain-fogging lust. Thank God it was dark and there were covers. Thank God they were talking and it wasn't horrible and weird and that she didn't want to leave this very minute.

It wasn't as if he'd planned on seducing her. He knew what that was like, exactly what that was like, and tonight he had not been hunting. He'd been…cast in a spell.

Yeah, that totally sounded macho. Cast in a spell. What were these stupid exercises doing to him? New-age music was dissolving his brain.

Her nails came into play, and he hissed at the sensation. For Christ's sake, a fingertip was not supposed to be a huge erogenous zone. Everything was out of proportion, and damn, he wanted to be next to her, her body pressed to his.

"Were you drunk?" Angie asked.

"When? Tonight?"

"No. Halloween."

"Oh. No. Not particularly. At least not until after."

"After the party?"

"After I realized what I'd done. How I'd come on to you. Not my finest moment."

"Hey, we didn't cross any lines."

"I crossed one of my own."

She sighed, and he closed his eyes, wishing he had that sound on tape so he could hear it over and over again. He'd like to fall asleep to that sound.

"I was very tempted."

His eyes shot open. "What's that?"

"Halloween. I wanted to."

"Seriously?"

"Yeah. But I'm glad we were interrupted. Because we work together and all."

"Which is why—"

"Exactly," she said. And then she moved closer to him, pulling the bedding with her.

He could reach much more than her fingertips now. He could feel the shift in the air, in his rapid pulse as he skimmed over her amazingly soft skin. "In a way, we are technically on vacation."

She laughed. "Technically we're not, but I do see your point. It feels as if we're on vacation. As if the rules don't apply here."

He nodded. "Exactly. I mean, we're sleeping together. Every night. Kissing each other. Our homework is to hold you in my arms and we were supposed to wash each other's hair." Then he swallowed, and willed his erection to simmer the hell down, because getting too hopeful here could end badly. For both of them. The important thing was to let her call the shots.

But hoping was acceptable. Unavoidable.

Her position had changed, her head was no longer resting on her palm. It was on her pillow, and he was about ten seconds away from turning on the light because he had no idea what she was thinking.

When her fingers trailed up his hand to his inner arm, then all the way to the crook of his elbow, he began to get a clue.

"It's late," she said.

"Yep." His voice didn't sound half as squeaky as he'd feared.

"I'll never get back to sleep now."

He could hear the quaver in her voice. She teased him with touches so light they were barely there, making his entire nervous system ache with the need to be inside her. Jesus.

As a measure of self-defense, he turned over so he was on his stomach. That he was inches away from Angie was, well, perfect.

"I'm extremely attracted to you," he said. "Just to be clear. But I'll stop this right now if you need me to. I won't touch you, or make jokes, or even insinuate anything that could make you uncomfortable. I mean it."

"You're saying what happens next is up to me."

"I am." His free hand itched to turn on the light, to know if she was smiling, or frowning, or—

"Yes," she said. "Yes."

He'd known from that first day that Angie was going to kill him, and he was damn sure this would be the moment.

10

ANGIE HELD HER BREATH, waiting. She'd said the word, but she couldn't follow through. She wanted to, God, she did, but her body was in some kind of shock or something, because—

Ryan pressed up against her, holding her gently as one hand slipped behind her neck and the other ran down her arm. His lips brushed hers. With a so-soft "Thank God" she might have missed it, he deepened the kiss.

Despite all the verbal foreplay, the tease and the tension, she was unprepared for the shock of his body. She wanted his clothes off. Hers, too. Now, right now because she needed the contact everywhere. She wanted to be wrapped up in Ryan, to do everything all at once.

Their lips and tongues were ravening, insatiable, so eager each time they parted she had to gasp in as much air as she could, only to immediately return to drowning in sensation.

He made soft noises as he kissed her, as he reached down to the bottom of her sleep shirt and snuck his hand underneath. The sounds were low, and growly and she doubted he even realized he was making them, but each time, her hips arched of their own accord.

It took her a few minutes to realize she was being equally loud and demanding, growing more impatient even as she grabbed on to his rock-hard ass as if she never planned to let it go.

The heat and hardness of his cock bled through his poor pajamas as he rocked into her. He'd better have condoms right next to him or else there would be big trouble.

He broke from their kiss, murmuring something that sounded like "Up, up, up," until her dazzled brain understood he wanted to take off her clothes.

Of course, she obliged, but as soon as her nightshirt went flying across the room, her hands were yanking on his pajamas, tugging as if wanting him naked was enough to make him so.

"Wait," he said. "Wait, I need to…" And he went too far away from her, whole inches, it wasn't fair, and then he whipped his T-shirt off. "Close your eyes."

"I want to see."

"I know," he said. "That's why you have to close your eyes."

"What the hell are you talking about?"

He growled, literally, then said, "Just close them for one second."

She did, but she wasn't happy about it until the light right above the headboard came on. "Oh."

"Exactly."

She should have waited another thirty seconds to open her eyes again, but there was entirely too much to see. His chest, of course, but seeing that wasn't the good part. Touching, playing with his sparse, dark hair and his little peaked nips, now that would be something to remember.

It occurred to her that it might be rude that she'd been staring at his chest the whole time the light had been on, but when she glanced at his face, she realized he hadn't noticed.

She did like the way his lips had parted and how his own eyes looked utterly dazed.

"You're incredible."

Her hands went to her barely-B-cup breasts, but quelled the urge to cover herself. For God's sake, he'd already seen them. His pupils were huge, he was practically drooling. So she captured her nipples, which were pretty long, between her middle and ring fingers.

Ryan groaned as if she was hurting him.

When she looked down to see the outline of his erection pressing against the soft cotton of his pj's, she arched her back. It might have been her imagination, but the wet spot over the crown of his cock seemed to get larger.

"You're killing me," he said. "I knew you would. But I never guessed. If I could move, I would have those panties off you right now. I would bury myself between your thighs for the rest of my life."

"That's sweet," she said, "but how about you take off the rest of your clothes first."

"What?"

She nodded, looking straight at his bottoms.

He exhaled as he followed her gaze. "Okay, but you have to put your hands somewhere else. Please."

Her chuckle stopped dead as Ryan got up on his knees and pushed his pajamas down. Oh, the cloth hadn't lied. He was impressive. And eager. She didn't even blink as he bared himself completely. She'd seen so much of his body but she couldn't have imagined how the sight of him like this would affect her.

Every part of her reacted with want. Between her legs, her breasts, her breathing, the very feel of her skin, the flush that spread like honey all through her body. "Condom," she said, the word breaking on the last syllable.

He had started toward her, inching across the bed on his knees, but he stopped, turned just enough for her to ogle the single most stunning bare male ass she'd ever seen, and she'd seen Michelangelo's *David*. Ryan yanked open his bedside drawer and struggled with his wallet.

His cursing got creative for a minute, and then he pulled out two packets and threw the wallet on the floor.

"That's ambitious of you."

"I was a Boy Scout. Now, please, dear God, if you have any mercy in your heart, please let me take off those panties."

She smiled as she made herself ready. Her hands, as they adjusted her pillow, actually trembled. Somehow she managed to kick the sheet and comforter down far enough. When she looked up she found Ryan gripping his thick erection, on his knees right next to her.

"You're stunning," he said, his voice husky and thick.

"What I am is impatient," she said, lifting her hips a few inches.

"Stop, stop, don't help. Not yet. Let me… Just let me."

To see him so undone, and before they'd even started made her heart pound and her flush deepen. She'd never felt more desired or more beautiful. It sent a rush through her that felt better than winning any race.

He positioned himself between her knees, gently parting them until she was spread enough for his liking. Then he ran his hands up her thighs, stopping when he reached the edge of her underwear. He slipped underneath the white cotton and his eyes closed for a moment as he brushed his fingers outward for a few inches, then back to the center, where he explored, with only his fingertips, across that exquisitely sensitive skin between thigh and labia.

Her squirming made him open his eyes, but he didn't speed up and he didn't move closer to where she wanted him, the bastard.

If he didn't pick up the pace, she was going to start flicking her nipples, which she might do, anyway, because God, they were so tight, and she was so ready. "Ryan," she said, surprised that the word came out so breathy.

He grinned wickedly, and bent down, still not removing her panties. With widely parted lips, he covered her exactly where she ached the most, and warmed her with his hot breath.

She knocked his chin with her arched hips, but he didn't seem to mind. "You need to remember something," she said, seconds away from ripping off the last of her clothes. "I'm top of the class in hand-to-hand."

He laughed as he pulled the crotch of her underwear to the left, baring her, at least partly. The growl returned, and then there was his tongue sneaking between her lips and finding her swollen clit with uncanny precision.

She cried out, pushing up into that hardened tongue, impossibly aroused. It wasn't like her. Ryan had barely touched her, and yet she could already feel the beginning of her climax building deep inside. She'd grabbed on to the sheet so tightly she was afraid it might rip, but dammit, something had to give. Now.

RYAN COULDN'T BELIEVE HOW amazing she tasted, how hard her clit was between his lips as he sucked the nub until Angie was a quivering mess beneath him. Her legs were holding him down, heels digging into his back, but he didn't care. He doubted she even realized she'd done that. Doubted she could think anymore.

He went back to flicking, fast and hard, then when her thigh muscles tensed he pushed two fingers inside her.

She came like a bottle rocket. He hoped the bungalow had thick walls because she was loud. And gripping his fingers so tightly he could scarcely imagine what it would feel like to bury his cock inside her.

He pulled back, letting her legs fall to the bed and taking

ʜer panties down at the same time. For a moment, he simply ɩooked at her. The full body blush, the way her dark hair was ᴡild on the pillow, her breasts with those gorgeous nipples ɾising and falling with her gasps. She was magnificent naked. ᴌong lines, sleek and defined, and damn how she made his ᴄock pulse as he looked at her beautiful sex. Lips thickened ᴀnd damp, pink and perfect, and all he wanted to do was give ʜer pleasure. Bring her to the brink over and over again, until ꜱhe begged him to stop. And when they were both dripping ᴡith exhaustion and wrung-out from pleasure, he'd hold her ɪn his arms just to feel her breathing.

With shaky hands, he opened the condom, and carefully ꜱheathed himself. For once, he was grateful for the barrier. He needed the dampening effect because he was one clench ᴀway from coming.

He lifted those amazing legs again, kissing her inner ᴛhighs as he brought them to his shoulders. She had another aftershock with his lips on her skin, and that was intense all by itself. He'd done that. Given her that.

He had to stretch to get hold of the free pillow, but he was able to tuck it neatly under her, planning to get a much better ᴠiew of that behind when they weren't so occupied.

She'd opened her eyes, finally. Dark as night, slightly damp eyelashes that worried him for a moment, but her smile let him know she wasn't crying. "Oh, my God," she said. "That was…"

"Only the beginning."

She rolled her eyes, but not the way she'd ever done it before. "You're going to kill me."

"I know the feeling."

Letting her hips down, he positioned himself, his whole being urging him to thrust now, now, now. "Angie. Look at me."

She did. She met his gaze, and damn if there weren't sparks.

"Keep your eyes open," he said, his voice barely recognizable. He rubbed himself between her lips, groaning at the slickness, then found where he belonged. "As long as you can," he whispered, needing to watch her right back. To see her come apart.

He pushed forward into the wet heat of her, and every part of him was there, right there where they were joined. Every part but his eyes as he watched her head go back, her mouth open in a silent cry, the perfection of her neck as she arched. For him.

When he was fully in her, he had to stop. No choice. His gasp reminded him to breathe again, his shudder was like that kick the moment before sleep.

He wanted to stay there for as long as she'd have him, but his cock needed friction.

Moving inside her became a symphony, every push building to an inevitable crescendo. Ryan wanted to see her eyes, watch her body, stare at his cock each time part of himself disappeared. As he thrust faster, his world narrowed and there, the pool of heat that signaled the start of it, his balls tightening, his muscles tensing tighter and tighter.

She spasmed around him, her climax squeezing his cock and it was as if all his atoms came apart, a supernova that made him see spots behind his eyelids and sent his heart racing so fast he thought he might just die.

Some time must have passed, though, because he could feel his burning lungs and his aching thighs, and when he looked down, there she was, the light making her skin look golden.

All he wanted to do was fall where he was and do nothing for a week, but instead, he pulled out of her, reluctant to leave then forced himself to climb out of bed to take care of business.

When he came back, she slowly moved her head so she could look at him. "You're here."

"I am."

"I'm glad."

He grinned. "Me, too." Then he pulled up the bedding, grabbed the pillow she'd pushed to the side and settled next to her.

She rolled into his arms as if she'd always known the way.

11

"ANGIE." HER SHOULDER was being tugged, and that needed to stop right now. "Angie, we're late. We slept through the alarm." She turned over so quickly she kicked Ryan. "Sorry. What time is it?"

"A quarter to ten."

"Oh, no."

Ryan, looking dazed and disheveled said, "Go shower. And leave me some hot water."

She scrambled to pull her act together, not sparing even a moment to be embarrassed about doing it naked.

Once she was under the spray, she started to relax as she soaped herself, acutely aware that Ryan had touched every inch she covered. Memories of a few hours ago filled her mind's eye like a really sexy slideshow. He'd caught her off guard so many times it left her breathless. She'd imagined him slick and dangerous, smug with his expertise as he showed her his wicked bag of tricks.

Instead, he'd been almost selfless. Oh, he'd gotten off all right, but his ego had left the building. His focus had been on her. So attuned he anticipated every desire. The memory made her shiver as the hot water cascaded down her back.

She jumped at a loud knock, then Ryan's panicked voice. "Angie, sorry but we've really got to move it."

"I'll be right out." She got busy, his tension sparking her own. They'd never been late before, she'd missed her run, yoga, coffee, dammit, her talk with Liz. And here she'd been off in the clouds daydreaming as if what had happened was one of her fantasies.

She stilled as her happy buzz abruptly went down the drain. As it hit her, exactly what she'd done. God, oh, God. She'd slept with him. She'd said yes. He'd offered to back off, but she'd just pulled him closer, and had the best sex of her life. With Ryan Vail.

Hell, she hadn't just said yes, she'd thrown away her ethics and reason, and now the memory of him inside her was so vivid she wanted to cry. How could she still want him when it was all so wrong?

Maybe that's what Liz had been getting at. Having sex with Ryan hadn't magically changed the fact that they were never going to be a couple. Not even friends with benefits. She knew she wouldn't pick things up when they went back to the office, and he certainly wouldn't want to. Maybe that's why the sex had been so unbelievably hot. Because he was taboo. She worked with him. He was completely the wrong man for her. Of course, it would probably be awkward as hell, but they both deserved that.

Well, they'd done it. Fine. Experiment over. Now she could concentrate solely on the job.

So why did her hand shake as she turned off the water, just because he was right outside the door? A part of her was glad they were late. There'd be no time for stolen glances, mumbled regrets. They had to jump into work. Which they were screwing up by being late.

As soon as she pulled her towel off the rack she realized she hadn't brought in her clothes. But she didn't want to leave the bathroom naked. It didn't matter that he'd already seen her. They were back on the clock. There was a clear line of demarcation, last night to this morning. She wrapped herself tightly in a towel.

He was waiting at the door as she opened it, clothes in his hand, his impatient gaze taking in everything. "I'll be quick."

"Should I wait? Go ahead without you?"

"Whatever." Their gazes met for an instant before he closed the door.

His single word answer made her feel both relieved and terrible. She didn't like the dip in her tummy that told her she'd been dismissed, but his cool nonchalance was exactly what they needed to find their footing again. They'd have to get into their roles damn quickly, but they each needed to get grounded in reality before that happened.

As she threw her clothes on, she reminded herself yet again that they only had one job to do. Make the suspects believe Ryan was ripe to be blackmailed. It had already begun with the break-in, but for it to stick, they needed to keep in character, keep to their routines. Be goddamn professional FBI agents.

She wouldn't put the sting at risk again.

Behind her, Ryan's shower turned off, and she pulled a brush through her hair. She didn't even have time to put on makeup, which was one of the central keys to Angie Ebsen.

Great. Just great.

THE RUSH TO GET TO THE Lavender Room had precluded much talk, for which Ryan was profoundly grateful. Turned out they missed the brief meeting, anyway. Today was their trip to the hot springs, which they'd completely forgotten, because what they'd done in that bed was enough for him to forget his own damn name. They weren't going just to soak, but to do some sweaty, physical exercises on the bank surrounding the springs, to be followed by comfort and support in the hot water.

They did get their things-to-take list and a colorful tote bag marked with the Intimate At Last logo. He didn't miss the irony, and he'd be damned if he'd carry that sucker to the bus waiting for them out front.

Sex with Angie hadn't been surprising. Normally his only concern was that he and his partner both got off, and that the woman didn't resent his quick departure after the fireworks were over. But with Angie, his orgasm had been more about her pleasure then his own.

He chalked it up to the cumulative effect of pretending to be in love with her combined with the inherent physicality of the masquerade. He'd have to be a damn sight more careful about separating his role from his life. Angie was the first woman in a hell of a long time that he had to see the day after.

With a few minutes to spare, he and Angie had settled in a comfortable bench seat on the minibus. Their thighs touched and she muttered a "sorry" and angled the other way. It made him wince. Would she have done that two days ago? Or was he reading too much into her every move?

In the fifteen minutes they'd had to change again and pack their tote, they'd managed to say perhaps a dozen awkward words. Angie had behaved like a textbook agent and had barely looked at him, and he'd gone along with it because it was hands down better than talking. But even after they'd pulled up the bedding, the room still smelled like sex, making it difficult to pretend that they hadn't taken a giant step over the line. She had the right idea, though. Play the part, forget about the rest.

He leaned his head against the window while they waited for late arrivals Luke and Erica and concentrated on his agenda for the day. He needed to get Ira and Delilah to see him as vulnerable and desperate. He'd screwed up with his wife the night before, in front of the whole casino. So today would be about kissing Angie's butt.

Not a wise thing to think about when she was sitting so close. The clean scent of her was already driving him wild, and they had a full day of togetherness to get through.

If only he could stop the quick flashes of memory, of the way she'd tasted, how it had felt to enter her for the first time. He shifted on the seat and looked around regaining his bearings. What he saw surprised him.

He leaned slightly toward Angie. "What's everyone so pissed at us for? We're not even the last ones on the bus."

She didn't make a big deal about checking out the group. "They're not pissed, they're curious."

"About...?" He coughed, trying not to choke. "You don't mean—"

"No." Her eyes narrowed, she gave him a long, drawn-out look. Feeling like an ass, he pretended his mind hadn't gone straight to the gutter.

"I'm pretty sure everyone has heard about me storming out last night after catching you with your coed," she said, finally, resettling another inch away.

"I didn't notice anyone but Tonya and Marcus," he muttered, painfully aware that he'd been overly focused on Angie in that dress.

"All it would have taken is one person. Now they're all waiting to watch you grovel."

"Yeah," he said. "I'll bet. Maybe I won't give them the satisfaction."

"Oh, you'll grovel," she whispered, then followed through by leaning back, frowning at him and turning so she was sitting sideways.

Across the aisle Hannah didn't even try to hide her interest. She gave him a quick evil eye, then smiled with theatrical flair at Angie, the picture of a sympathetic friend.

Okay, this was good. All wasn't lost. Playing the part of the guilty husband was no stretch. In fact, it was a little too real. From the moment he'd opened his eyes this morning he'd felt guilty and that was another thing he hadn't expected. Guilt about women hadn't been part of his repertoire for years.

Right there, that was the central problem. He shouldn't have ever thought of Angie as anything but a colleague. The moment he'd seen her as a woman, everything had begun to unravel. This morning, he'd seen shame in her eyes, at least when she could make herself look at him. By the time they'd arrived at the Lavender Room, she'd gotten her act together, but he knew what he'd seen. It upset him more than he cared to think about.

Last night had been an eleven for him, more memorable than any encounter he'd had in years. That scared the crap out of him, with good reason, but dammit, he also didn't want regret to overshadow everything else.

He couldn't imagine she felt anything but regret. After all, he was the player of players, his reputation built on solid evidence augmented by rumors that he never bothered to squelch. In the real world, she'd made it clear she wasn't the least bit interested in the likes of him. Maybe that's what appealed to him.

Whoa, he backed out of that thought at the speed of light.

Too much was happening at this retreat. All of it coming fast and furious. He'd said too much, relaxed his guard, let his feelings take control.

That stopped right now. This minute. Everything was at stake here, and he didn't just mean the case.

During the rest of the drive to Hoover Dam, Angie spoke and laughed with most of the women on the bus, all chummy and rolling their eyes about *men*. Ryan stared at the high desert landscape, going over his plan to ask for help once he got

Ira on his own. It didn't matter that he'd rehearsed before. He didn't dare think about anything else.

Ryan would admit to the affair, to the prenup, to his desperation to keep Angie happy. But the kicker would be an earnest confession that despite his behavior, he loved his wife· and that it would kill him to lose her.

He doubted he'd have a bit of trouble acting the part.

ANGIE HADN'T GONE IN THE hot springs yet. She was purposefully keeping back now that they'd finished their first round of tandem exercises.

The first time they'd touched—she'd fallen back into his arms and let him catch her, which was supposed to build trust. It probably would have worked if the feel of him hadn't felt like a body blow. But they'd played on. Touching with their sweaty bodies, holding each other. Staring into each other's eyes.

At least their difficulty would read like they were a couple in trouble.

The idea of taking some time alone in the hot springs was tantalizing, but this break wasn't for feeling better. It was for confiding in Delilah.

So she stared at the rock formations and the way the native plants poke out of every crag and furrow, knowing Delilah would come check on her. The last time Angie had been in Vegas it had been summer, over a hundred and ten outside. Today it was mid-seventies and the sky was ridiculously blue. She stared up at the bouncing waterfall, leaping from rock to rock on its way down the canyon. When she turned, she could almost see the entrance to Sauna Cave through the tamarisk bushes.

It was difficult not to seek out Ryan. He was on the opposite side of the big shelf of rock, huddled next to Ira. The two of them had started talking the minute the break had begun, and even though Angie knew Ryan was telling the story they'd crafted, she had to wonder if he was as distracted as she was.

He was too good an agent to let his personal issues interfere with the assignment, and she'd thought she was right on par with him. And she had been. Until she'd let down her guard, allowing her hormones to subvert her intelligence.

Seems she could only hold on to her rationalizations for so long before she reverted to a doubting mess. Mostly she felt disappointed in herself. She'd thought she was stronger. That she could handle herself in any given situation, even something as tricky as pretending to be in love.

She'd been wrong. Regardless, she had to put all her personal turmoil aside and keep her head in the game. If only she'd been able to talk to Liz.

Yes, her friend had encouraged her to go for it, but once Angie explained the very real consequences, Liz would be there to help. Liz was an agent herself, and she understood that the success of this sting was the only thing that mattered. Wasting time trying to read into what Ryan was thinking... He was completely in character, none of his issues bleeding through, and she needed to step up and do the same.

"You mind some company?"

Angie spun around at Delilah's voice. The woman exuded compassion and comfort, and for a second, Angie wished she could tell her the true story and get her counsel. Instead, she nodded, and instantly her eyes filled with tears. "Ryan's a good husband," she said. "He really is, you know."

"I believe you." Delilah took Angie's hand in her own. "Tonya told me that you seemed upset about his behavior at the casino last night."

Wiping her eyes with her free hand, Angie nodded. "It wasn't the gambling I minded."

"No?"

Delilah was so close to her that Angie had to be careful of every move. She avoided the older woman's gaze and her wince lasted but a second. "He doesn't mean anything by his flirting. He can't help it. Women come on to him all the time. But that's because he's very sweet and so good-looking. I was the one who started things with him when we first met, so I can't blame them for trying."

"If you know it's harmless, what bothered you?"

Angie sniffed. "I guess I'm just the jealous type." She laughed, but it was rueful and matched her small shrug. "I didn't know until I met Ryan that I could be jealous. I haven't had a lot of good experiences with men. Mostly because of the trust fund."

"Oh?" Delilah walked them over to an outcropping large enough for both of them to take a makeshift seat. "Your family is wealthy?"

"Very," Angie said. "We're not old money, third generation with me. But I'm an only child and my father was the one who inherited, so there wasn't a lot of practice dealing with men. I mean men who weren't with me for the money."

"Ah. Trust issues."

"Trust fund issues. After my third boyfriend turned out to be a lying bastard, yeah, you could say I came to some conclusions. But Ryan, *he* wanted the prenup. He gets nothing if we get divorced. It would be ridiculous for someone who was only after my money to do that."

"But deep down, you still think he's another fortune hunter?"

"Yeah, maybe," Angie said, after a moment, then shook her head. "I don't know. I'm probably not being fair because of my own baggage. That's why I jumped all over coming to this retreat when he suggested it. I want to believe in him and love him properly, but I'm not sure I can."

Delilah squeezed Angie's hand. "After this is over, I

can't recommend strongly enough that you consider marriage counseling. Ryan's crazy about you. I can see it as clear as day."

Angie couldn't help but smile. That conclusion proved that Delilah hadn't bothered to look past the superficial. But then, this whole sting had been predicated on the fact that the therapists would see only what the Bureau wanted them to see.

It would have ruined everything if Delilah had gotten close enough to realize that while Ryan liked sex, and he liked Angie, there was no possibility he was crazy about her.

"You flinched."

"What?" Angie straightened to attention. "I did?"

"When I mentioned that Ryan is crazy about you." Delilah genuinely looked sad. "For a minute, let's consider I can see something in each of you the other can't right now. Ryan cares, of that I am certain. But I think he has trust issues of his own. It could be very powerful for you to work on it together and that's why I want you to seriously explore counseling. But also?" Delilah waited until Angie met her gaze. "Give yourself a break. You've had some stinkers. They leave a mark."

Angie nodded, but in her head she was hearing Delilah sound certain that Ryan cared. Her ridiculous heart pounded as if the words had been true, and that was the trouble with what they'd done last night. This surging emotion was terrific for Angie Ebsen. But it nearly crippled Angie Wolf, because she would be the one returning to L.A., working in the same office as Ryan.

And there he was, heading toward the hot springs with Ira. It was eighty-five degrees in the water, and everyone splashing around looked relaxed and happy. Three couples had decided to let it all hang out, but Angie didn't care. She wanted to be done with this part of the afternoon. Return to the resort, slip into her familiar running clothes and run as far as her legs would carry her.

"Thanks," she said, as she stood. "I'm glad we spoke."

"Anytime." Delilah squeezed her shoulder. "Please think about what I said." Then the woman went to join Ira, passing Ryan with a smile.

He came straight up to Angie, took her hands in his. "You okay?"

She nodded, afraid she was close to tears. It would be okay, though, the fake Angie would—

He pulled her into his arms and kissed her. Not a peck, not a tease, but a full-on blistering kiss that stole her breath. Of course, Ira and Delilah were watching. Everyone was. But Angie's talk with Delilah had left its mark, and she wasn't sure how her character should respond to this very public declaration. She started to pull away, but the hand at the small of her back and the groan that only she could hear stilled her thoughts.

They'd gone from zero to sixty in five seconds. She felt dizzy with flashes of their night. God, she remembered his body as if she'd studied it for years, the hard planes and the soft skin. Her hand went to his thigh, the indent that had flexed when he walked naked from the bed to the bathroom.

She had to squeeze her own thighs together at the primal reaction he stirred in her. Her breasts were pressed against his chest, but with each breath she could feel how her nipples had beaded, and how they ached for more than the material of her bathing suit top.

The sound of catcalls from the hot springs hit her like a slap in the face and she jerked back, dislodging his hold as if they'd been fighting.

Ryan's lips were still wet and parted, his eyes filled with a level of hurt she couldn't understand at all. Why hurt? It couldn't be, because Delilah was wrong. Ryan was a consummate actor, that's all. That's all any of it was. Even if her heart didn't want that to be true.

She was in trouble. Her reaction to him was so not part of the charade it wasn't funny. No more. No more sex with him. Not again; not ever. It was imperative that she get herself together. Everything was at risk. Her career, this sting, her dignity.

Her job was to play this role. If not for that, she'd have never touched him, never kissed him and, by God, she'd never have been in the same bed as Ryan Vail.

Frantic to get away, she opened her mouth to tell him she was going to get in the water. Nothing came out so she just started walking, leaving Ryan behind, sure he was watching her and wondering what the hell had just happened.

IT WAS AFTER SIX WHEN THEY finally made it back to the room. Ryan had gone with the flow, acting the chastened and groveling husband, but Angie's performance had been all over the place. One second she'd been hot, the next freezing, and while he considered himself an intuitive guy, he'd been lost.

Of course, they hadn't been able to talk about it until now.

"Listen," she said as she put down her tote bag once Ryan had completed his search for bugs. "You go ahead and use the shower first. I'm going for a run before dinner."

"Right now?"

She was standing by the round table at the far end of the room, her arms crossed over her chest. Her nod and smile were equally awkward.

"Want to tell me what's going on?" he asked.

"Nothing."

"Noth—" He stopped, took a breath as he tossed his sunglasses on the dresser. "Did you have a plan for the evening? Aside from running?"

"I don't know," she said, turning to her tote and pulling

out first the towel, then her sunscreen. "Debrief. Sleep. I'm wiped out."

He almost asked her why she was going running then, but it seemed unwise. "Okay," he said. "Enjoy yourself. I'll be cleared out of the shower by the time you get back."

She abandoned her unpacking to grab her shoes, but instead of putting them on, she just waited until he was at the bathroom door.

"Would you like me to order some room service for dinner?"

"No," she said, looking anywhere but at him. "That's okay. But go ahead if you want that. I'm probably going to pick up a salad from the café."

Again, he stopped himself from asking the obvious question. But what was the point? Dammit. He didn't want her running off before they talked this thing through; he just wasn't sure how to stop her. Or even if he should. It was increasingly evident last night had been a spectacular error, but they still had a case to work here.

She'd put on one shoe, and was about to slip into the other. "Angie."

She froze. Just stopped moving at all.

"We should talk."

Her answer came after what felt like far too long. "We will. But I need to think."

"Okay. Whenever you're ready."

She kicked into gear again and in a moment she was at the door, a small backpack he'd never seen before strapped on. It was too little to carry all her clothes in case she wanted to book a separate room. She didn't look back.

He used his long, hot shower as his own time to think. The fact that she'd run was actually a good thing. She'd set the future terms of the game very clearly. In her own way, she'd said everything that needed to be said.

Rather than put her through any more discomfort, he decided to clear out for the evening. After he dressed, he wrote her a note, letting her know he was going to see if he could find Marcus, set up the massage thing. He'd catch up with her later, and they'd talk in the morning.

The words he used were straightforward, all business. Surely she'd read between the lines and realize he wouldn't bring up last night again.

He had no illusions that he wouldn't think about it. But he'd keep his thoughts, and anything that wasn't the job, to himself.

12

NOT ONLY HAD SHE RUN at least six miles, but Angie hadn't changed into her sports bra and running gear. Big mistake. Especially with the backpack. Small wonder, since mistakes were becoming something of a specialty. It was ironic that it was the bra that had done the most damage. She was so small it didn't seem possible, but the way her stride worked and the position of the material under her right arm hadn't gotten along since the half-mile mark.

She really needed to shower, to eat, to sleep. But first, she needed her friend. And perspective. She found herself a nice little corner in a building not only far away from the room, but primarily used by staff. There was a patch of green about the size of the backseat of her car, and she was still breathing heavily after her post-run stretch.

She dialed Liz, hoping very hard that she was home, because Angie didn't want to face Ryan with only her own thoughts in her head.

Liz connected, and Angie felt so grateful she nearly cried. God, she was tired.

So was Liz if her flushed face and heaving breath were any indication. "What's up?"

"You want to go shower before I hit you with my news?"

Liz walked her to her kitchen. Although the view was weird as hell, bumpy and dizzying, but Angie heard the way her sneakers squeaked on her kitchen tile, the soft *whump* of her fridge opening because the door tended to stick, and knew Liz was pulling out OJ before she saw the bottle. Liz always pulled out a bottle of OJ first, with a water chaser. She gulped a few times, then brought the tablet's camera up. "Talk to me, I missed you yesterday."

"I followed your advice. Kind of."

"What adv— Oh, do not say this unless you're telling me the absolute truth. You slept with him." Liz sat down hard enough to make the chair groan, then straightened the iPad again.

"Yes. But not because I was 'going for it.'"

"What the hell does that mean? And where are you? That's a horrible sound."

Angie looked down the path and watched as a huge cart full of sheets rolled noisily past. "I'm hiding. Near the laundry, evidently."

"Good choice. Anyway, back to the earth-shattering news. Why did you sleep with him?"

Angie closed her burning eyes. "I may have gotten three hours of sleep last night, but I'm probably off by two and a half hours. It's complicated."

"Start from the beginning."

"I have no patience for beginnings. Bottom line is that I got confused. I let down my guard. He saw me half-naked, okay? What was I supposed to do? We'd been bugged, and he came in the bathroom. And then he got hard, and he was wired, and there was all this adrenaline."

"Okay. Getting some of this. Thinking this wasn't a slam against the wall, rip your clothes off and do it on the floor kind of encounter, even with the adrenaline."

"You'd be correct. It was, however, a confess things about

your life and family and other intimate stuff, then be totally decent about it, and smell so damn good kind of encounter."

Liz's eyebrows had gotten comically high on her forehead. "That's the most perfect thing I've ever heard. I couldn't have written it better. Me? I go for against the wall, but you love all that confession crap. And men being decent. So what's your damage?"

"I. Work. With. Him."

Liz waved her hand so dismissively it was a good thing they were hundreds of miles away from each other. "You are so busy trying to meet every unrealistic expectation of that insane family of yours, you are missing the best parts of things. Last night was the marrow of life, Angie. The thing you'll remember when you're seventy. You won't give a rat's ass about this assignment by then, you know that, right?"

Maybe calling Liz wasn't the smartest move. "That's all well and good and dramatic and poetic and all that other shit, but the truth is I'm not seventy and I have a lot at stake here. I can't be this off balance. It's day three. We've still got two more to go, and I can't imagine getting in bed with him tonight."

"Why not?"

Angie wiped her face with her hand, and looked at her friend, who was calmly drinking her orange juice. "Please be here for me. Be on my side. I need you."

Liz lowered the bottle. "Sweetie, I am here for you. I have been and will continue to be here for you. However, I will also consider the fact that the broader picture is not what you're looking for at the moment. So here's what you do. Talk to him. Tell him you're confused, and you desperately need to sleep. That you don't regret what happened, but it probably won't happen again. How does that sound?"

Angie nodded. She could do that. She could say those things. They made sense. They sounded as if an adult had come up with them. And it didn't leave any room for arguments. "Thank you. Perfect. But do me a favor?"

"What?"

"Email me those exact words because I'm too tired to remember them."

"Will do. And I'll be here all night, so if you need me, call. Cell phone or Skype, whatever will work best. If not, please be in touch tomorrow, okay? I'll worry."

"I promise." She disconnected, put the iPad in the backpack and made it back to the empty room ten minutes later. Starving and wobbly, she called for a room-service dinner, then made it into the shower and stayed there for a long time.

When she was dressed again, just jeans and a T-shirt, she found Ryan standing by a room service cart signing for her dinner. He'd gone for the same look, in a pair of jeans that she hadn't seen before. They must have been his own, not part of the wardrobe, because the wear was obviously from his body, not some artificial distress. His snug T-shirt was tucked into those close-fitting Levi's, and before she could attempt to stop it, her body reacted with a hunger that had nothing to do with the scent of pasta.

Her forehead dropped with a thunk to the wood of the open door. It hurt.

"You okay?"

She stood up straight. Ryan was alone, standing by the ottoman where her meal had been laid out. "I should have called you. Asked if you wanted me to order something."

"I ate. With Marcus."

"Ouch."

"Not the most fun I've ever had. You should eat, though, if this is the first thing you've had since lunch."

Her stomach reinforced his point, and after stashing her things, she sat in the big wing chair and practically stuffed half the pasta into her mouth in ten seconds.

Forcing herself to slow down, she dared another glance at
Ryan. The jeans and T-shirt look was just as effective from
the front, although there had been a special something about
his butt and how the denim curved. It didn't help that he was
leaning against the round table across the room, staring at
her, arms and ankles crossed, and dammit, she had to stop
thinking about him as a man.

"Why don't you fill me in on Marcus?" she said, then
turned her attention to her salad.

"I gave him a very similar story to the one I told Ira. Didn't
want it to be verbatim, because I assume they talk to each
other. This time I went for more of a physical angle. Asked
him if he'd teach me how I could use nontraditional methods
of showing you how much I loved you."

Swallowing her bite carefully, she gave him a quick
glance. "Nontraditional?"

"Yeah, massage. Oils. Candles. All that crap. He was far
too eager to show me."

Angie caught the tail end of his full body shudder. "Eww."

"Hey, sometimes we have to take one for the team."

She popped a cherry tomato in her mouth, reining her
thoughts back, and then back further.

"The point is, he knows about the affair, the trust fund,
that I'm desperate. The only one who might still need more
convincing is Tonya. Thoughts?"

"I've been trying to figure out a way to find out about her
stealth faxing, but honestly, I can't. I'm guessing she's up to
speed with our situation by now."

"Yeah?" he said, and his arms came down so he could
grab the edges of the table.

Angie switched her gaze back to her salad. This was becoming a serious issue. They were having a work discussion.
There was no thinking about his body during work discus-
sions, period. "I'll try to have a friendly talk with her in the

morning, poke around, see if she was included in the conversations from the hot springs."

"Maybe talk to her about that tantric massage thing?"

Thankfully Angie hadn't been eating because she'd have spit the food straight out. She knew just enough about tantric methods to know it was done naked, with no parts left un-massaged. "And I would do that why?"

"Maybe because you want to keep me interested." He kind of shrugged one shoulder, the move casual, but the rest of him tense. "Maybe Angie Ebsen doesn't want to kick her husband to the curb just yet."

This was bad. Horrible. She couldn't read him. Even staring straight into his eyes. She had no idea which Angie and Ryan he was talking about. A flash of an image hit her, Ryan on the bed, *in her,* and she darted her gaze away, knocking her napkin to the floor. She picked it up slowly, willing the heat to dissipate from her face. So, so bad.

EVEN THOUGH LEANING against the table edge was becoming more uncomfortable by the second, Ryan didn't dare move. With his ankles crossed and bending slightly forward, his half-hard dick was hidden, and that's the way it would stay until he settled the hell down.

All she'd done was eat her dinner. Drink some water.

He'd reacted as if she'd done a pole dance wearing nothing but red high heels, but try explaining that to his cock.

They'd been discussing the case as if they were in the bullpen back in L.A., and what had he done? Brought up tantric massage. Yesterday he could've gotten away with it. She would've automatically assumed it was about the case. But after this morning?

Eventually they were going to have to sleep. Share that bed again.

That was it. Bottom line. No room for error, so they'd better get over this thing and get back on point.

She was staring at him when he looked up, her brow furrowed and her napkin dangling from her fingers. "About last—"

"Oh, hell," he said, cutting her off and pushing away from the table. "I'm two hours late checking in with Jeannie." He pulled his cell from his pocket and made a beeline for the door. "I'll be back."

He hadn't looked at her as he'd made his escape, and that, he figured, was the most chicken-shit thing he'd done in his life. Including hiding in the school library for an entire year to ditch a gang of bullies.

He didn't want to talk about last night. The note couldn't have been plainer. Of course, Angie didn't have to know that given a choice, he'd probably make that same mistake all over again.

He was pathetic. He stared at his cell as he walked down the pathway, trying to think of ways he could avoid calling Jeannie. Man, he was just racking up the points, wasn't he?

Why did he still want Angie so much? He'd been there and done that. The mystery had been solved. And yet all day, he'd wanted nothing more than to be near her. To touch her, to smell and taste her. He'd had a miserable time at the hot springs, even when he'd been allowed to touch her. To kiss her. Shit.

Jeannie was going to kill him, but she was his only hope of getting himself straightened out. When he was far enough away from the bungalow and in a good position to see if anyone was around, he pressed Jeannie's number.

She answered after the first ring. "About time. You know I have kids to put to bed."

"Yeah, well, I told you to get goldfish, but did you listen?"

"Ha. You're a scream. Tell me what's going on."

The first part was easy. He went through the night at the casino skipping the in-room entertainment, then told her about not only the field trip but his meeting with Marcus. Then, it got tricky.

"What aren't you telling me?" she asked.

"Why would you ask that? I've told you everything about the case."

"That's why," she said. "I'm not just a pretty face, you idiot, I know you. What did you do?"

"Me? Why do you always assume I've done something wrong?"

She didn't say anything. She didn't have to.

Ryan sighed. Deep down he'd probably known she'd ask, and maybe getting it out there would ease his guilt, although he doubted she'd offer absolution. "Okay, but I didn't force her. We mutually decided that—"

"You slept with her. Dammit, Ryan. You had one thing you weren't supposed to do. One thing."

"I had a lot of things I wasn't supposed to do."

"Not helping your cause."

"Fine. It was an error. We both realize that."

Jeannie went radio silent. She wasn't supposed to do that. A real friend would reassure him that this, too, would pass. "You've talked?" she asked finally.

"Not precisely."

"Meaning, no, you've been avoiding the conversation like the plague."

"I'm getting a new partner when I get back. You suck."

"Stop it," Jeannie said. Her voice had lost all humor. "This is not a minor deal, Ryan. I expected better of her, for God's sake, but it's not like you, either. Did you ignore everything we talked about?"

"There were circumstances," he said, hearing how weak that argument was, but not having anything better.

"Yeah. Your dick got hard. That's not a circumstance, honey. That's a breach of conduct. Even if it'll never be reported, it is not how two agents on assignment behave, even when the situation is as tricky as the one you're in. I have to admit, I'm disappointed."

He sighed, and if he'd been near anything, even a brick wall, he'd have smashed his hand through it. "Yeah. Me, too."

"You need to discuss this with Angie. No making jokes about it, either. Tell her you're sorry."

"But—"

"Be the bigger man, Ryan. Dammit. You are the bigger man. You've never done anything like this before. I know it's been tough. I get that. But you can't afford the luxury of letting your personal feelings get in the mix."

He didn't have an answer to that, either. Just a profound sense of his own shame. "Yeah, I screwed up. No excuses."

The silence grew, but his pacing stopped. He needed to listen to what Jeannie had to say, as hard as it was to hear. She was his friend. The first honest-to-God friend he'd ever had. She was the only person in his life who dared to tell him the absolute truth.

"I think," she said, and he had to press the phone close to his ear because her voice was so low, "that when you get back from this assignment, you and Angie need to have a different kind of conversation."

"What do you mean?"

She sighed. "I think you like her. Maybe more than that."

He squeezed his eyes shut. "What?"

"You know what I'm saying. She's not like the women you normally date. And, kiddo, unless there was something serious happening in your head about Angie, there's no way you would have put so much in jeopardy to get laid."

His heart was hammering in his chest, and he wanted to

run for the hills, but kept the phone up, and opened his eyes. "I still… Shit, Jeannie, it's like I…"

"Feel something?"

He took in a deep breath, then gave it up. "Yeah."

"Put it on the back shelf until you get home. Your first duty is to the job. You got that?"

"Oh, yeah. Big time."

"Fine. Talk to her, and let her know you want to discuss it after. Don't leave that part out."

"Are you kidding?" He was starting to sweat now. If he could gauge Angie's reaction it would be different, but he had no idea what she was thinking, outside of that one look of shame that still haunted him. "How do I know she'll even want to do that?"

"Ryan, she didn't put her career on the line on a whim, either."

"All right, but…"

"Go talk to her before you two have to crawl between the sheets. Let her know she's not going to have to worry about you doing anything else unprofessional. Then for God's sake, don't do anything else unprofessional."

"Okay." He ran a hand through his hair and thought about going to the gym to duke it out with a punching bag, but he put that aside. He owed Angie the courtesy of an apology. "Thanks. I'll give you a call tomorrow night."

"Anytime. And Ryan?"

"Yeah?"

"You made a mistake. It happens. You move on."

"Right. Go put the kids to bed."

She gave him one last goodbye and hung up.

He disconnected, put the phone back in his pocket. This next part wasn't going to be fun, but it would also be a relief. He wasn't going to let his life be run by lust. That was his old man's game, not his.

But what Jeannie had said about him and Angie needing to talk once they returned to L.A.? She was wrong. Angie was great, but they weren't the right mix. Not even for one night, let alone more.

ANGIE HAD THE TV ON HBO, to a movie she'd been wanting to see for ages. Pity she couldn't concentrate for more than a minute at a time.

Ryan had been gone for an eternity. She'd put her dinner plates outside the door, changed into her sleep shirt, washed up, brushed her teeth and crawled into bed, once again all the way at the very edge. If she thought she wouldn't look like a complete nutcase, she'd have taken every cushion and pillow and put them straight down between them like a bundling board. She'd still know he was there, but it would be so much easier if she didn't have to see him.

No matter how much he wanted to avoid her, she'd realized while he'd been gone that she needed to talk to him. It wouldn't be pretty, but one thing she'd learned over the past few days was that nothing got fixed without communication. Their impossible situation had crossed over the line last night, but that didn't mean they couldn't regroup.

Competition running had taught her that dwelling on mistakes was a waste of valuable time. Learn from them, then let go. To rehash was the gateway drug to losing, and she and Ryan were so close to the end of this assignment that to blow it now would ruin everything.

Her promotion was on the line, and if she'd been back in L.A. that would have been the only thing in her life that mattered. All her efforts would have been tailored to the furtherance of that goal. Here, just an hour's flight away, the D.C. job was an afterthought, a footnote.

She didn't want things to be weird with Ryan when they finished out the week, but that ship had probably sailed. It wasn't that big of a loss. She'd barely known him. An almost indiscretion at a party, a foolish mistake during a stressful time? The problem was the illusion that they were more to each other than was true. Forced togetherness and a couple of personal revelations did not make a relationship. It didn't even make a friendship.

Her logic was impeccable, and that should have been that. The crushing sadness that made her gut ache begged to differ.

She noticed that the action on the screen had become a steamy love scene, and as quick as her clicking finger could move, she turned to the nature channel. Shark Week seemed safe enough.

Finally, after squinting through a terrible circle-of-life moment where something cute got eaten, Ryan came back inside. He seemed subdued, but that was in comparison to his manic desperation to escape. "How's Jeannie?"

"Good," he said. "She'll pass on the info to the team in the morning."

"Great. Brad told me that Gordon and Director Leonard are pleased with our reports so far. He heard it directly from Ellen, which is as good as hearing it from the horse's mouth."

"No kidding. That's great. That's…great."

Angie closed her eyes. Her next move needed to be made with a clear head and it seemed looking at Ryan, especially wearing those jeans, clouded her judgment. "Are you going to run out again if I bring up last night?"

"No."

Surprised at his vehemence, Angie's eyes snapped open. "What does that mean?"

"It means no. I'm not going to run out again."

"Okay," she said, hitting the mute button. Maybe she should have just turned down the volume. It was really quiet. "Because it wasn't completely my fault."

The look he gave her was this close to a slap. "I never—"

"I know. I know, but dammit, this is awkward."

"And I'm sorry about that," he said, but softly. Humbly.

"We both got carried away," she said, matching his tone. Wishing she hadn't gotten in bed yet. It would have been easier to walk around.

"I'm not sorry," he said. "I don't want you to get that impression. Not about…" He waved his hand in a general way at the bed. "Just the timing. The situation."

Angie held herself still. "Tell you the truth? It wouldn't have happened if we weren't here."

He took two steps away from the table, then stopped. "So you regret the whole thing?"

"No. Not, no. I'm not sure what I feel, exactly. Confused, I guess. But not shocked."

Tilting his head slightly to the right, he closed one eye as if that would help him understand better. "Explain?"

"I find you very attractive," she said. "But even disregarding the work situation, I doubt I'd have acted on that. I'm not good with casual sex."

"And I'm not looking for anything but."

Her smile had to look as cockeyed as she was feeling. "In the interest of full disclosure, however, I will admit that it's… difficult not to think of you like that now."

"Well, we are supposed to be acting like lovers."

"But I'm not supposed to be feeling like a lover."

He inhaled, then stopped. Just held his breath and stared at her. Long enough for heat to climb up her face.

"I meant—"

"I know what you meant," he said. "At least I think so. Because I've been feeling that myself."

That was a hell of a thing to hear. Coming from anyone other than Ryan Vail, it would have been a game changer.

"But we both know our feelings aren't real," he said. "They'll be gone the minute we're out of this predicament."

"Right," she said, nodding a little too enthusiastically as she tried to ignore the fist in her chest. "Exactly. We just have to get through the next two days, then boom, all our problems will be solved."

"As long as we don't touch each other."

The moment the words came out of his mouth, she realized that was going to be impossible. Not sure what she was supposed to say to that, she just sat there and tried not to react.

"I mean, we don't touch each other unless there's someone there who's supposed to see it."

She nodded. "That works. That's good. That's the rule, then. No touching unless someone else sees it."

Ryan opened his mouth as if to say something, then closed it again. "For what it's worth, I also happen to like you. And that part's not going to disappear when this assignment is over."

Angie winced and pressed her mouth together tight. Of all the things, he had to go and say that. Just when she was making peace with the cold, hard fact that Ryan wasn't the least bit interested in anything but a casual screw. But she'd asked for honesty. "Well, dammit," she said. "I like you, too."

13

AFTER ONE OF THE MOST miserable nights of her life she had barely survived the excruciating morning with the group. She'd known massage lessons were on the program, but she hadn't realized it would be a lab situation where they learned on each other. Now, with only a few bites of lunch in her tummy, she was overdosing on caffeine. That likely wouldn't end well…unless it made her sick and she had to bow out of this afternoon's session. Not a bad idea.

"You want more coffee?" Ryan asked as the last of their plates had being cleared.

"Sure do." She smiled. "Thanks."

Giving her a suspicious look, Ryan left her, Tonya, Zach and Rachel at the table, after making sure no one else wanted anything.

Angie watched him go, glad that he wasn't wearing his own worn jeans because every minute of this morning had been torture, and she didn't need any more visual aids, thank you. He still looked fantastic. Especially with his shirt off. On a massage table. Smelling like a wicked mix of cinnamon and spices from the organic oil she'd used to rub him down.

Ryan put her fresh cup on the table. Her gaze went to his

thighs, enjoying how even the high-end jeans molded against him, and she let out a sigh.

The laughter from her tablemates sent her into a tailspin, hoping she hadn't sounded like a dopey schoolgirl.

"I can sell you guys a bottle of that massage oil at cost," Tonya said, pretty much confirming Angie was being a twit.

Ryan happily took her up on her offer, but then he'd been deeply in character all day. Angie concentrated on her caffeine input, ignoring everyone. Especially him. She should ask for hazard pay, is what she should do. Because come on. He still smelled like warm chai and sex.

Tomorrow was the final day, thank goodness. The team hadn't been able to trace who'd installed the program on their computer, but they'd managed to send a few emails from the fictitious Roxanne that would lead the blackmailer to believe Ryan was a perfect mark.

She remembered so clearly when she'd first heard about the art scam from Deputy Director Leonard. It had felt like such an intellectual exercise—setting up the sting, writing the database program. How in hell had she gotten here? Learning how to turn on her pretend lover with oil and touch hadn't been covered in any of her FBI training.

At least there were only two more sessions for sure, and Delilah had hinted that there would be something special as a farewell. Although Angie was seriously contemplating cutting things short. The idea stirred a whole pot of conflicting emotions. This morning's exercise had blurred the lines nearly to oblivion. In spite of all her logic and reasoning, her goals, her plans, the reality of everything, she'd found herself aching with desire for the stupid man. When she'd massaged his shoulders, a shower of sensual memories swamped her, making it hard to breathe, to think, to find her footing.

The professional that was still inside her knew the faster she could get out of here, the better off she'd be.

All things considered, she and Ryan had done everything they could do to establish their vulnerability. The keylogging incident was a bonus none of them could have predicted, totally in their favor. If she could come up with an exit that reinforced what they'd accomplished, she wouldn't hesitate. The longer they stayed, the more likely they were to slip up.

"What's the plan for after lunch?" Ryan asked, surprising Angie until she saw Ira standing by him.

"We're switching things up a little."

"No more massages?"

"No. Something else."

The troubled way Ira was looking at Ryan had Angie thinking that even if she didn't feel sick, she was getting to be a good actress. Ryan seemed uneasy, too. Then, Ira smiled and stepped over to Zach and Rachel. He kept the grin, though, no worried gaze in sight.

"Wow," Ryan whispered as he turned to Angie. "I can't wait for the next session to start."

"The worst has got to be over, right?" she said, referring to his earlier session with Marcus.

Ryan shuddered, and she held back her laugh because what he'd gone through was not amusing at all. The pale man with the hooker fetish had actually put his hands on Ryan's body. Above the waist, of course. Still. Eww.

"We have time to go back to the room," he said. "You gonna stay and guzzle more coffee or join me?"

She basked in his slow easy smile, annoyed that her heart actually fluttered. It had ceased to matter that she wished she felt nothing more than respect and camaraderie. Life as she knew it before making love with Ryan was already crumbling around her. Why delay it? "Let's go. I want to change shirts, and I have a proposition for you."

RYAN WASN'T LIKING THIS one bit. Especially the part where he had to go first. So far the only thing he'd liked about today was Angie's suggestion that they leave early. Even that sucked as far as propositions went, and the plan only shaved off a day. But trying to keep his hands off her made every minute matter.

They were in the Lavender Room and if he never saw the color purple again, it would be fine with him. The much-hated bean bags had been shuffled off to one corner and the massage tables from the morning session had disappeared. Now there were twelve chairs in pairs that faced each other in a broad circle. He was sitting so close to Angie that his knee was nearly touching hers. Not by choice, because being this near her was dangerous. But at least their proximity meant that unless they spoke loudly, whatever they said to each other wouldn't be overheard. It was, according to Ira and Delilah, a matter of trust.

"The first timer will be set for thirty minutes, the second for thirty-four minutes." Delilah spun slowly around as she explained the exercise. "You will remain seated for the entire time. Once the first chime goes off, everyone stops speaking. Be sure to make and keep eye contact until the second chime. For the first thirty minutes, you may speak to each other, but you must remember not to be judgmental or sarcastic or dismissive. Everyone clear?"

Ryan was barely listening. He was too busy thinking about the private instruction he and the other men had received a few moments ago. Ira had explained that the point of this psychological torture experiment was to reveal something intimate, something they'd never told anyone before, and then let the conversation take its own course. And to pay particular attention to the last four minutes of eye contact.

Ryan had about forty-five seconds to decide if he should make something up that might be true for Ebsen, or to tell

Angie about a part of his life. That would have been a no-brainer, but he knew that Ira would be paying particular attention to him during this exercise from hell.

"And so," Delilah announced. "We begin."

Silence all around him wasn't making his decision easier. His thoughts darted from topic to topic in an attempt to find some piece of business he could build into a convincing fiction. Something with heart, something that would sound true, and painful and like a secret held close to the vest, but everything seemed stupid or was from some movie he saw on TV, or had too many guns involved.

He knew Angie had no idea what to expect, except that he was supposed to speak now. From the way her eyes darted to the right, then widened at him, he knew someone was coming to help them get started.

"When I was fourteen, my father brought home a prostitute," he said. "For me."

Angie got very still. Her breathing stalled for a moment, then started again, but she hadn't blinked.

He was having some trouble on that account, himself. Of all the things in his life, why the hell had that slipped out? Could he change tracks now? Take it back?

Ira's goddamn patchouli smell hit him before the man himself crouched beside him. "You can say anything you wish to say. Remember, there are no mistakes. The only requirement is willingness."

Ryan was willing to smash the moron's face in, but he just nodded, getting the message that if Ebsen wanted to save his marriage, he'd better cut open a major vein.

"She was young," Ryan said, lowering his voice while leaning toward Angie. But he didn't say another word until Ira in his ugly aloha shirt walked away.

While he could have switched the topic, one look at Angie stopped him. He'd already said too much, and he didn't want her thinking he'd been traumatized for life. It was better to tell her the truth then leave room for her to make stuff up. "She was over eighteen, I know that, because he told me. She also looked a whole lot like my mother. Same dark hair cut blunt at the top of her neck. Green eyes like her. Same kind of body. Short, curvy. Her top was cut so low I could see her bra. It was red.

"I've never been so embarrassed about anything in my whole life as when she walked into that room. She had two glasses with her. Scotch shots. I'd had beer before, and I'd tried some booze with my friends, but this was drinking my old man's scotch with a hooker. Of course, I was horny, I was fourteen and smothered in puberty, but I was dying, too. Because my father was in the other room. He knew exactly what we were supposed to do. That she'd be naked. She'd see me naked."

He paused, not wanting to give Angie an opening but not wanting to talk, either.

"Was she nice to you?"

Of all the questions she could have asked, that's what she led with? "Huh. Yeah. She was okay. She didn't point and laugh. At that age, I wasn't exactly *Playgirl* material."

"You were a child. He'd go to jail for that now, if not then."

"Yeah. Probably. If I'd told anyone."

"You never told anyone? Not even a friend?" she asked.

He inhaled sharply, wondering why the hell he was telling *Angie?* What was he doing? His heart had been beating fast since they'd walked into the room, now he was pretty certain he was headed for a stroke. He shook his head.

"You didn't want to brag about it?"

"I wanted to forget it ever happened." He leaned back, wishing the chairs were farther apart.

"Did you?"

He shrugged his shoulders. "It was…memorable. Even the horrible parts."

"There were good parts, too?"

Leave it to Angie to keep looking for that silver lining. "One or two."

Interestingly Angie was the one mirroring his body language, even though that had been part of his instructions. She'd leaned back when he had. Her right hand was fisted to match his left. Their knees were touching now. Barely, though, mostly his pants and hers brushing against each other. He scooted forward on his chair far enough that he could feel her.

"Wow, your father sounds like a real sweetheart and a dream dad."

That made him laugh. Good for her. He had no idea how much time had passed, and he wanted the damn chime to happen so he could stop. Even though the eye contact thing was going to be a bitch. The two of them kept dancing around each other. Looking away, looking back, over and over.

"I had some difficult things happen to me when I was young," she said. "I told you about the whole sports connection, but what I didn't say was that my parents forced me into situations that were far too complicated for a child my age. But what your father did was child abuse. My God, you were so young."

The bark of a laugh that was meant to disabuse her of her dramatic notions came out way more pathetic than it should have. "Look, I wasn't scarred for life, if that's what you're thinking. It was a crappy thing to pull on your own kid, which is why, by the way, I have no plans to have children of my own, but it wasn't a deal breaker. I went on to kick ass in school. In college. Anything I ever wanted I went after hard, and here I am, so there's no use wringing my hands over my childhood issues. We all have crap happen to us, and some of us turn that into motivation. I'll never be like him. Never."

The way she looked at him told him exactly how much she believed him on that last score. His back straightened. "I'm not denying that my attitude toward women hasn't been damaged. But we play the hand we're dealt."

"I didn't say—"

"You didn't have to. It's fine. I'm not unhappy or wishing I could be something that I'm not."

"No, of course you're not." The sympathy in her eyes irritated him. "I admire you."

"Because I had a bad childhood?"

"I admired you before today."

"Even after we…?"

Her lips parted and curved up slightly. She must have licked them while he'd been talking because they glistened. If he could have, he'd have leaned over and kissed her.

"Where was your mother in all this?" she asked very gently.

He shrugged. "No idea."

"You okay with that?"

"Yeah. I think she was lucky to get out."

"She left you behind."

"She did."

Her hand went to his knee and he felt it all the way up his body. As if her touch were made of sparks. It was just her *hand*.

He covered it with his own. The flare transformed into a warm diffusion of comfort that settled right next to the steady and unceasing arousal that had taken root near his spine.

It was Angie who leaned toward him this time. He mirrored the move, guessing she might want to whisper something, just to make sure no one else could hear.

He was wrong. She moved straight on in for a kiss that caught him completely off guard. It wasn't much, compared to what they'd done before. Just lips, soft and sweet. But damn.

He barely heard the chime go off.

AFTER THE CHIME, ANGIE pulled back. Not far, though. Before she could meet Ryan's gaze, she had to clear her head. She closed her eyes, took a deep, cleansing breath and let it out slowly. When she looked again, it was straight into his unwavering gaze.

It was a revelation.

The urge to turn away was profound, not from looking, but from being seen. Of course, she'd held eye contact before. Never so intentionally and never with someone who'd just poured his secrets into her lap.

Her lips parted and she had to struggle to fill her lungs, as if the room itself were losing oxygen. Her eyes flicked down and took in his strong jaw, the gap between his lips, the first hint of stubble on his chin, but then she returned to the connection, to the pull.

The next urge was to talk, to make a joke, to hide behind words, but that wasn't allowed, and how long had it been? A minute? It had to have been at least a minute.

God, his eyes were so dark. His pupils had taken up all the room, and she knew it was an illusion that she could see herself reflected. If the old proverb had been right and she was peering into his soul, the view was less poetic than she'd been led to believe. The only thing she could read was want. Then again, perhaps that's why she thought she could see herself.

His hand moved, a slow drift to gripping her lightly around her wrist. Then his thumb went to her pulse point, and he rubbed, back and forth. Delicately. She wanted to watch, of course, but she held steady. The edges of his eyes crinkled, and she knew exactly which smile he'd put on. Could picture its every detail.

What was he seeing in her? How sad she felt for his child-hood? How brave she knew he was? He made so much more sense now. It was as if he'd handed her his Rosetta Stone, and she had a whole new view of the path he'd taken. At least, some of the path.

It was tempting to think the revelation explained all of him. Just because there was such an obvious correlation didn't mean there weren't a hundred different stories that would change the picture dramatically.

She couldn't help wondering, though, if he would ever find a way out of the fortress he'd built around himself. Now, though, she wanted to kiss him again. They were going home tomorrow morning. While she'd been in the shower during their break, Ryan had received the go-ahead from Gordon, and the team was busy setting up their departure, complete with a verifiable paper trail.

So this really would be the last time she could kiss him. She had no business being upset at the fact, but there it was. She moved in closer, with no doubt at all that he was on board.

Just as her lips brushed his, the chime rang. Ryan's hand disappeared, he jerked back as if she'd been about to slap him and before she could get her bearings, he was out of his seat and across the room.

A moment later, he was gone. The session wasn't over. Other couples were kissing, were touching. All of them deeply involved with their mates. Angie looked at Delilah, who gave her a sympathetic smile.

Ira approached, then crouched down beside her. "It happens sometimes."

"What's that?"

"Fear. That he revealed too much. That he was too truthful. People, particularly men, aren't used to that level of intimacy."

"It was extreme."

"Believe it or not, this is a good sign. Even though the session isn't over, I think you ought to go after him."

Angie nodded, still in shock, not just from Ryan's vanishing act but the thirty-four minutes that had preceded it. She collected her purse from the back of the room and slipped outside, not wanting to disturb the rest of the group. If she hadn't been so worried about Ryan, she would have breathed a tremendous sigh of relief. Instead, she hurried toward the bungalow, to their room, wondering if she should, in fact, walk in or knock, or just give Ryan some time alone.

When she walked in, Ryan had his suitcase on the bed, and a bundle of folded clothes in his arms. If she was reading him right, and she was pretty sure she was, he was leaving. Now.

14

"RYAN?"

He didn't turn around. In fact, he sped things up, shoving his belongings into the case as if they'd wronged him in some way. "There's no reason to wait until tomorrow," he said. "We're done. We might as well get back to L.A., start the paperwork."

"I'm all for leaving," she said, "but don't you think this might look a little suspicious?"

He glanced at her, then walked to the dresser. "What difference does it make? Today, tomorrow."

"Because of the session we just had."

"What does that mean?"

His words were brusque, and yeah, okay, she understood. He'd opened himself up to her in there, not something he was used to. However, they had to think this through and not let his self-consciousness mess up the finale.

"It means that we should take a minute." She walked over to her side of the bed, sat by her pillow. He'd have to look at her if he was going to continue to pack.

"It was your idea to get out of here."

"And we put the plan in motion. Gordon agreed to our leaving in the morning."

"That's just a technicality."

She closed her eyes as she gathered her equilibrium. Not even ten minutes ago, the two of them had been gazing into each other's eyes, and she'd felt a connection to Ryan that had gone so deep she'd seen that her feelings for him were more complex than just a crush. To find him like this made her all the more aware of what a mess she'd gotten herself into.

Although Ryan tried to look as if everything was normal, panic was just below the surface. Given what she knew about him now, that made a world of sense. "Can we at least take a breather?"

His chin dropped to his chest and he sighed deeply. "I can't believe how I blew it in there."

"What?"

"I have absolutely no idea if Ira or Delilah was listening." He slammed the dresser door shut and walked to the window, tension rippling through his every motion. "I couldn't get it together fast enough, and I should have been better prepared. I don't even remember half of what I told you, and for all I know I completely contradicted everything I'd told Ira at the hot springs. God dammit, I bet I said some things to Marcus this morning that put Ebsen's mother in the picture. If they put two and two together—"

Angie joined him at the window and put her hand on his shoulder.

He jerked as if she'd shocked him.

"You didn't blow anything," she said. "Ira and Delilah weren't near us."

"How do you know? We were too busy staring at each other—"

"I know. You know it, too. Both of us have been trained to always be somewhat aware of our surroundings."

He shook his head, his jaw tensing, and that little vein on his forehead had made an appearance.

"You were amazing," she said, squeezing his shoulder. He must have felt it even through his tension. "What those two saw were two people deeply engrossed in each other. We couldn't have done a more convincing job if we'd rehearsed for months. They would never doubt that we were exactly who we said we were, that you are deeply frightened of losing everything that matters to you. And that I would be devastated if I discovered you'd been with someone else."

"That's the voodoo talking," he said. "I don't know what it was about that exercise, but come on. That was like hypnosis or something."

She couldn't disagree, truth be told. It had felt as if they'd been mesmerized. "It doesn't matter. What happened in that room was the icing on the cake." She dropped her hand, but she didn't step away. "You were great."

His eyes slammed shut so tightly it was painful to watch, and the urge to hold him filled her.

He spun around and before she could even understand what was happening, she was in his arms and his lips were on hers, the kiss so desperate it made her gasp. He took advantage and used his tongue while his hands ran down her back pulling her tight against his body. She hung on to his sides as if her life depended on it. As if his did, too.

"It's over," he said, his lips brushing hers. "We aren't breaking the rules." He kissed her again, grasping the back of her head with his broad hand and tilting her just enough that their mouths locked together like pieces of a puzzle.

It was impossible to think when he kissed her like that, when her body wanted so badly to let him in.

When he reached underneath her blouse to caress her skin, she jerked her head back, the sensation dizzying. Ryan didn't give her a second to adjust. His mouth moved down her neck, licking, nipping, his low moan a rumble that was felt more than heard.

"Wait, Ryan, wait. We can't."

"No, shhh, no. We can. It's over, and we're done and I can't stop thinking about you, haven't stopped since I was inside you." He lifted her blouse, the silk slipping up her back and her bra, until it was over her head.

She could stop things right now. If she didn't let go of her grip on him, he wouldn't be able to finish undressing her. Not without a struggle, and there was no way in hell he would do that to her, no matter how frantic he seemed.

When he straightened, when he finally met her gaze, his desperation was written on his face and in the tension that strained his muscles. He'd been through so much. Not just what had happened all those years ago, but today. He'd laid himself bare in front of her, the most private confession she'd ever heard.

She wanted him so much her body ached, even as she understood what a risk it was. If she gave in… No, if she chose to be with him one more time. This was her heart she was playing with. He'd be fine, he'd go home and everything would go back to normal. She couldn't say the same.

It was just turning dark outside, the room filled with shadows and quiet, except for their heated breathing. All she had to do was say no.

Instead, she released his polo shirt, and his shoulders sagged with relief. When he lifted her blouse off, he moved carefully and he never turned his gaze away.

She was the one to reach behind and unhook her bra, letting it fall to the floor.

"Oh, Christ," he whispered right before baring his own chest and pulling her close once more.

She sighed as her nipples pressed against him, as his arms tightened around her. She leaned into him, abandoning any pretense, thrilled insensibly by the small noises Ryan made as they drowned each other in kisses. He maneuvered them until her legs hit the side of the bed.

He broke away and cursed. "What idiot put a suitcase there?" Looking as if it hurt, he released her and dispatched the wretched thing, his clothes leaving a trail from the end of the bed to the wall.

When he turned back to her, he stopped, lips parted on an inhale as he studied her, starting with her naked breasts but returning to her face. "I don't want to make a mistake here," he said. He flexed most of the muscles she could see from his arms to his jaw. Her own wince surprised her, but only until he whispered, "I'll just get..." as he picked up her blouse from where she'd let it drop.

She took it back and tossed it on the seat of the leather chair. Then she put her arms around his neck and brought her mouth close to his ear. "Take me to bed, Ryan Vail."

His lips were on hers so fast it was like magic, and he was fiddling with the buttons on her slacks, not having much success. Covering his hands, she said, "Let's make this simple. Strip."

The laugh wasn't a big one and his attention stayed on her as he toed off his loafers and slipped out of his jeans.

God, he looked good in those black boxer briefs. She loved how obviously he wanted her. But then she was being pretty obvious herself with her body blush and hard nips.

She made a little show of taking off her panties. They were the palest pink, a match to the bra that was somewhere else. He finished removing his socks, and when he stood up tall and oh, so erect, she wanted to do *everything*.

THE ROOM WASN'T CHILLY, but his skin was so hot that a shiver shot down his spine. Or maybe that was from looking at Angie, so beautiful it made him throb. What had been a mad rush to have her, to lose himself inside her, had become something else. Part of him wanted to throw her down on the bed, take her hard using every trick in his large arsenal.

Instead, he pulled her close again, taking a minute to savor that stunning body rubbing against him. She felt better than anything. If he could package the sensation, he'd be the richest son of a bitch in the world.

"Oh…" She turned the breathy word into a hum while she ran her hand slowly over his chest.

"Did anyone ever tell you you've got amazingly soft skin?" he asked.

"I think you might have mentioned it. A couple of times."

He sighed before he caught her bottom lip between his teeth and gave it a little tug. After he let it go, he lapped at that tempting flesh and found himself drowning in the taste of her.

Finally she pulled back. "We gonna do this standing up?"

"We could try," he said. "But I think we'd have to be closer to the wall. Leverage."

Her laughter was as addictive as every other single thing about her. "Let's not get carried away. I'd hate for you to break something important just before we go home."

"That's a deal." He took her hand and helped her lie back, no clever moves, no showing off at all. He simply paid attention, holding back the covers even though he'd have preferred doing it on the comforter. But Angie had goose bumps and she seemed to like having the covers available.

When he settled himself beside her, they rolled together so easily it shocked him. He wasn't sure what was happening here. He should be putting as much distance between them as possible, racing for home and his real life. If not that, then applying his go-to recipe for fixing what ailed him by burying himself in someone new, a mystery to be solved in the span of an evening.

He'd broken every rule with Angie. He'd let her in where

no one was allowed. Thank God this was it. That they were going back to where things made sense. But for now, for the few hours they had left together, he wanted to stop thinking so damn much. Let it be.

"This is…"

"What?" he asked.

She shrugged, then kissed his shoulder. "Nothing." She looked up at him. The room was filled with the gold of the sinking sun, making her look tanned and sexier, if that was even possible.

After a kiss that made his cock harder than it had any right to be this early in the game, he started a systematic, highly detailed deconstruction of one Angie Wolf. By the time he reached his destination, he wanted her to be a quivering mess, begging for release. Which he would give her, all in good time.

If he made it that far, himself.

It was her long, graceful neck that lured him in to start. Using his lips, tongue and a hint of teeth, he got the party in gear. She tasted like honey and smelled like the beach. By the time he was nibbling his way across the divide between neck and shoulder, she'd bucked her hips twice as she squeezed his flesh wherever she could grab. It was her soft whimpers that made his cock jerk, though, that and knowing he was safe for the rest of the night.

ANGIE MOANED AS RYAN'S fingers entered her, a prelude, but delicious on its own. He was all over her and she'd never dreamed she'd ever actually feel ravished, but she did, as if he was taking her apart and putting her back together piece by piece.

The desperate noises she couldn't hold back were the same for pleasure as want, and how did that even work?

His finger pumped, which had her lifting her hips even as

he pinned down her back. His lips were on her right nipple, sucking and flicking to beat the band, and then his thumb came into play right *there,* steady as he pushed and licked and made her thighs tremble.

In one shocking moment, he abandoned her completely but before she could do more than cry out, he'd flung the comforter back. "I need to see," he said, then he went straight back to killing her with wicked bliss.

Her hand was in his hair, mostly running through it, but when he did something noteworthy, which was about every other second, she tugged. The first time it happened, she'd felt terrible about it, but the second time the way his body jerked and his low moan told her he not only didn't mind, but that he liked it.

Ryan switched his attention to her other breast and the sweet torment made her moan. Gorgeous, too much, and not nearly enough. His thumb, though, had most of her attention. It was the slow circle with the perfect pressure that was doing her in.

She tugged again, actually lifting his head back until their eyes met. "My thighs are two seconds away from meltdown, and I'm going to come and you won't be in me."

His slow grin was as full of mischief as his dark eyes. "I won't be in you yet."

"I can't hold on. You'll be sorry, because I'll be worn out."

"You're a long distance runner, sweetheart. I know what you can do."

Her legs gave out. Dislodging his hand just as she was starting the wind up. "I warned you."

"I think," he said, easing his head and hair away from her relaxed fingers, "that I'm going to make you come three ways tonight."

"Huh?" she said, eloquent as ever.

"First," he whispered, after a quick kiss goodbye to her right nipple, "with my mouth."

She watched him slide over, all strong limbs and flexing muscles, until he was between her legs.

"Then, with my fingers." He paused for a hello kiss to the very top of her sex before he maneuvered her legs over his shoulders.

"After that—" he met her gaze again, more predator than mischief maker "—with my cock."

She let her head drop to the pillow. There was no response to what he'd said. None. She thought about laughing, but she didn't want to waste the energy. If his objective was to wring her out like a wet cloth, well, he was going about it the right way.

"Fine," she said, her hands flopping up near her head. "Do to me what you will."

His chuckle was the kind that sent all kinds of shivers directly to the good parts. "I intend to."

It was some ungodly hour, and she was tapioca and overly sensitized at the same time. She couldn't move and could barely catch her breath. He was beside her, gasping away. Where his hip touched hers felt as if they were melting.

He'd done it. All three. In that order. Like a magic trick because she wasn't one of those multiorgasmic women the magazines were so impressed with. *Three times.* Holy crap. Shouldn't there be an award or something? At the very least one of those parchment paper certificates, signed by the Commissioner of Amazing Sex.

Her head was only half on the pillow, there were at least two spots she didn't want to sleep on and, if she'd had the wherewithal, she'd turn on the air conditioner.

It occurred to her that while this part of the sting had certainly ended with a bang, tomorrow would begin a very different operation. They were heading back to normal. To being on the same team. Sleeping in different places. Acting like FBI agents.

Which would all look much simpler once they were dressed. Especially in her own clothes. With her sturdy, two-inch heels and her slightly baggy work suits. She'd get back to running her regular routes, dive into the post-assignment paperwork which was an achingly familiar slice of boring that felt like home.

Ryan and her? She turned her head far enough to see his eyes were closed and his body seemed completely relaxed. He deserved a rest. Not just from the sex, but for stepping so far outside his comfort zone. All week, actually.

No, the two of them wouldn't pick up where they left off. Not possible, not after what they'd been through. If it had just been sex, that would have been one thing, but they'd been intimate. She'd been closer to Ryan than she'd been with any other man in her life.

You didn't just walk away from that with a tip of the hat.

She couldn't imagine what it might be like, because of their jobs, because of so many things, not the least of which was working in the same office on the same team.

But then, one of them would probably be shipping out to Washington, D.C. If the blackmail text came through. If there wasn't someone more qualified, or more on the Deputy Director's radar. If it wasn't her, she was going to put in for a transfer to cyber crimes, so that would help.

She'd miss him. More than she could have imagined. It might have been a lot of role-playing and spy stuff, but he'd been incredibly open with her. She knew him now, seeing with such clarity that it wasn't the length of time that mattered, but what was shared that made people...close. He must know her, as well. Somewhere in this long, strange week, he'd changed from being an occasional fantasy to a man she cared for. Deeply.

RYAN OPENED HIS EYES AND stared straight up into the dark. He wanted to wake her again, bury himself in her body, in her pleasure and his own.

What he didn't want was the twisting sick feeling that was eating him alive. The memory of what he'd said to her burned inside him like a flare before the flash.

What the hell had he done?

15

A SHAFT OF SUNLIGHT brought Angie from dream to foggy awareness. Memories of the night came first. She wallowed in how it had felt to have Ryan's arms wrapped around her, the way he'd kissed her insensible, how her muscles had tightened in those last few seconds before release. Stretching her legs now brought an unexpected ache to her calves and thighs. She was in damn good shape but she was tempted to skip her run and soak in that sadly unused whirlpool tub.

Ryan wasn't next to her, which was a shame, but she knew he was in the bathroom. Must have heard something during the foggy part. Ah, there was a gurgling message from her stomach, angry at her for not eating dinner last night. God, she was starving.

The hell with yogurt and bran, she wanted something decadent. Eggs Benedict or French toast. *Hash browns*.

Where was he? Opening her eyes, finally, she got her watch from the bedside table, shocked that it was 8:20. So late she'd probably have to choose between the soak and the meal, and a run was out of the question.

The bathroom door opened. Ryan was already dressed in jeans, although not the worn ones, and a slate-gray short-sleeved shirt. His hair wasn't even wet, so he must have show-

ered a while ago. He was staring at his cell phone until she
cleared her throat. She grinned, looking forward to his good
morning, wondering what he had in store for her.

"Hey," he said, giving her a glance and a smile that felt
like an absent pat on the head.

She must have interrupted something important for him to
act so dismissively. It shouldn't have disappointed her. Certainly not this much. They weren't on vacation, and if he'd
gotten a message from Gordon or Jeannie, his behavior was
entirely appropriate.

"You hungry?" she asked, watching him scroll through
messages on his smartphone.

"Sure," he said, not even giving her a glance this time.
"Go ahead and call room service. I'm trying to book the
soonest flight out."

"What's the rush? Let's have something wonderful for
breakfast." She grabbed her sleep shirt from the floor and
slipped it over her head.

Ryan looked her way, but didn't meet her eyes. "I just
want coffee."

"Did something happen?"

He lowered the phone and went to the patio window to
stare outside.

With every step her insides tightened. What the hell was
going on?

"I just want to get back to L.A.," he said, his voice as ex-
pressionless as the glimpse she'd had of his face. "Get started
on the next part of the case."

"Okay," she said, not meaning it at all. She wanted him
to look at her, to have the man she'd slept with look back at
her. Things had happened between them that couldn't just
vanish into nothing.

The only thing she could think of was that he was having
a delayed reaction to the intimacy exercise yesterday. She'd

known at the time that it was way out of his comfort zone, so, yeah, it was understandable that he was freaking out a bit, but to treat her like a one-night stand? No, that was just…no.

If that was the case, and she honestly couldn't come up with anything else, then he was probably embarrassed, which made her ache inside. Did he think she was going to tell anyone about what he'd said? That she would mock him for revealing so much of himself?

She walked over to him, even though he'd gone back to hiding behind his cell phone while keeping his back to her. She rubbed his arm, gently, the way she'd touched him yesterday. He'd found comfort in her then, and she hoped he'd feel it now.

Instead, he tensed.

"Hey," she said softly. "If this is about the thirty-four minutes, don't worry about it, okay? I consider what you told me privileged information. I'll never say a word about any of it. I'm just really honored that you trusted me enough to open up." She laughed a little, feeling her face heat. "For what it's worth, I thought you were amazingly brave."

Ryan took a step away from her, glancing at her once more, but only for a moment, and she couldn't tell if he was angry or embarrassed or what. "Look, nothing I said yesterday was about me. It was the job. That was all made up bullshit designed to make it look like I'd do anything to keep you. My personal life is just that. Personal. Sorry if you got confused." He paused, keeping his eyes averted. "About any of it."

Angie stood very still, trying to calm the surge of emotions so she could think. No way he'd made all that up yesterday. No way. The best actor on the planet couldn't have pulled that off.

And what the hell did he mean by any of it? Was he dismissing that they'd had amazing sex, that they'd made a real connection? Good God, she knew they wouldn't be strolling into the office holding hands.

But for heaven's sake, he couldn't even look at her. That body language in a suspect would signal guilt from a mile away. He was deflecting, that's all. He'd crossed every boundary he had for himself, and now he was trying to reclaim control the best way he knew how.

It was sad, and it was a lie, but it made her feel like an utter fool. She'd done it again. Let herself believe that he was someone other than the notorious Ryan Vail. God, she was an idiot.

But she couldn't deny that the overwhelming sensation right now was hurt. Deep, stabbed-in-the-back hurt. He had a right to his feelings, including shame and anger and whatever, but she felt slapped in the face, which she didn't deserve.

"If you haven't already, you should let the team know about the change of plans. Call Delilah and tell her whatever the hell you want, just don't blow everything we've managed to accomplish so far." She headed toward the bathroom. "You know what? I'll call Delilah. You just get us out of here."

Ryan looked her in the eyes for the first time that morning, and instead of making things better, the cool *nothing* she saw there made everything a hundred times worse.

DESPITE THE EXPENSE, ONCE they'd landed in Los Angeles, Ryan took a taxi to his apartment in the arts district downtown. Not that he used the place for anything to do with art. He kept meaning to tackle the bare wall situation but he'd never found sufficient motivation. Frankly, all he gave a damn about was his bed and the shower. He'd shelled out a hell of a lot on both of them, and considered it money well spent.

His place was on the fifth floor, and as always the elevator smelled like pine-scented chemicals. He'd lived with much worse. One of the reasons he'd moved into this high-tech, overpriced high-rise was the twenty-four-hour security. Also the weekly maid service. But mostly the security.

Unlocking the door relaxed his shoulders and he felt as if he could breathe for the first time since this morning. He left his suitcase by the couch, dropped his armful of mail on the counter, then headed back to his bedroom.

It was seven-thirty. He'd hoped to be back from Vegas earlier, but there'd been one mess up after another. The whole damn day had been a nightmare. He fell across his bed, the big old navy-blue comforter and the unbelievably great mattress made things somewhat better. If he thought he could sleep through the night he would have just let go, but it was too early and he was too wound up.

Being alone for a while would do him a lot of good. Christ, what an assignment. He'd better get that D.C. job, that's all. Then he wouldn't have to see Angie in the bullpen, in the elevators, in his head. He winced at how he'd been such a royal bastard to her. But it had been the right decision, even though it had killed him to see how hurt she was. He couldn't afford to regret it. But he couldn't help it. Every time he'd looked at her. Or thought about her. Or remembered how it had felt to be inside her.

His actions this morning had been in both their best interest. They were in the real world now and he had to work with Angie until he got the new job, so what was he supposed to do? Pretend he had feelings for her? That would have been much crueler. At least now, they both knew what was what, and they could return to the slightly uncomfortable but workable situation they'd had before Intimate At Last.

Ryan rolled over, spreading himself across the California King. *This* was precisely why he never went after a woman who was in any way connected to work. He'd broken his own rule and now he was paying the price. So he liked her.

So what? He'd liked a lot of women and somehow he'd managed to separate work and pleasure.

Jeannie was going to crucify him. If she found out he'd screwed up a second time. Who was he kidding? She'd find out. Somehow. He wouldn't tell her and he knew without any question that Angie wouldn't, either, but Jeannie had a kind of radar with him that by rights should creep him the hell out.

If that didn't make him want to leave the country on the first plane out, he didn't know what would. But since he couldn't get out of town, at least he could stop obsessing and get back to living his own life. Shower first, then go.

Zero Sum sounded right. It was the kind of club where it didn't matter what night of the week it was or who was behind the bar. He'd find himself a friendly woman who wanted nothing more from him than a few drinks and a couple of decent orgasms.

By ten-fifteen, he had his scotch rocks in hand, and three women in sight that were contenders. There was a petite brunette with a sexy overbite. Unfortunately she was with a friend, so that could be a problem. But he set his sights, made his plan and went for it.

ANGIE SHIFTED ON HER COUCH. It should have felt fabulous to be home. It didn't. There was nothing edible in the fridge, but she couldn't bring herself to look through her take-out menus. Her iPad sat next to her, turned off.

Three hours she'd been home. Showered, done laundry. Put on a nightgown, not a sleep shirt. She'd meant to call Liz, but she didn't think she could handle anything her friend had to say. Sympathy might just kill her.

The thing was, she'd done it to herself. Ryan had been nothing but Ryan. She'd known it, and she'd known the outcome, and she'd still opened herself to him. Opened her feelings. Opened her heart. Stupid. So stupid.

The only thing she'd done right all day was that she hadn't cried. She wouldn't. Not over him.

RYAN PAID HIS BAR TAB, NOT really surprised he hadn't scored. He'd stepped back into the real world too abruptly, that's all. Give him a day or two, a trip to the gym, and he'd be back to himself. He had to be back to himself because this was nuts.

The whole time he'd been talking to the short brunette, he'd been thinking about Angie. He wanted her. There was a physical ache inside him that one touch from her could cure. Or maybe that was hunger. He'd stop and get something on the way home, because his fridge was empty. Even his mustard had gone bad.

Despite it being out of the way, he stopped by a Korean place that was open late and ordered some bulgogi and cha dal with a side of kimchee then ended up eating it in his Mustang.

It wasn't hunger.

"SO WHAT WAS IT LIKE?" Paula asked, scooting her chair over to Angie's desk, bringing a skinny hazelnut venti latte as her bribe. "Sleeping with Ryan?"

"Awkward," Angie said, as rehearsed. She'd stood in front of her mirror for far too long making certain her expressions gave away nothing. "Very, very awkward. The whole time was. And I owe whoever picked out my clothes a giant slap upside the head."

"Come on. Don't be like that. I know you guys had to kiss and stuff."

Angie hadn't even put her purse in her bottom drawer yet, and already she wanted the day to be over. The month to be over. She'd had a horrible night's sleep, and coming back to the office had been almost as hard as telling her parents she wasn't going to go to law school. Wearing her own clothes had been difficult, which pissed her off. Not thinking about Ryan had been impossible.

"He's a good kisser, isn't he?"

"Paula, I swear to God, you have got to let up on this. We weren't away filming a reality show. It wasn't at all like that. It was weird, and I'm grateful it's over."

"Okay, jeez, I'm sorry. I mean you guys were sharing a room. I looked up tantric massage. What was I supposed to think?" Paula had the decency to blush, for about two seconds, then she said, "Tonya Bridges isn't going with the gang to Cancún."

"What?" For the first time since the casino night, Angie felt herself come down to earth. "She never said a word."

"Well, according to public records in the state of Nevada, she's applied for a massage license in Clark County. The paperwork was registered the day before yesterday."

"Hmm. That explains the furtive faxes. I wonder why she wants it so hush-hush? What kind of business is she planning to establish?"

"We're working on it. Now apologize with something juicy, would you? We can't talk about it when Jeannie gets here because she thinks we're perverts."

"We are perverts." Sally who was practically running to join them, stole Brad's chair to horn in on the prime desktop territory next to Paula. Why did all the women in this team have to come to work so early?

"She claims nothing happened," Paula said in her second snottiest voice. "That it was awkward."

"Because it was true, you troublemaker. I said it was awkward but we got through it. We planted all the right information, now we just have to wait for the right response. And fill out reams of paperwork." Angie finally stowed her purse in the drawer. "So if you would act like the professional, well-trained agents that you are, tell me what else has happened since I left."

"Joanna Tighe from ERT is getting married to Ken Westerly, you know, the guy from SWAT."

"Good for them, but I was asking about the actual work we do. In our office."

"Boy," Sally said, "did you have to sign up to get that stick up your ass or was it included in the workshop?"

Angie closed her eyes. It was a losing battle, and she had to either give them something or come up with a legit excuse quickly. Terrified of giving anything away, she went with an excuse.

"I'm sorry. I'm exhausted. I had a bad night after a rough week. I promise we'll all talk another time, okay? We'll do lunch soon, I promise."

Sally and Paula, both looking as if she'd betrayed some unwritten but important female coworker code, moped back to their own desks and Angie took comfort from her still-hot coffee.

Too bad nothing seemed to warm her up. Not the late night shower that had turned her pink from the heat, not huddling under her thick duvet. It was as if she'd been hollowed out, left empty and confused.

The thing was, she'd been *so wrong*. Missed the mark by a light-year. It had felt special. Magical. Real. Where had she gotten lost? Yes, she got it that the thirty-four-minute exercise had sealed her fate, but that wouldn't have been enough on its own.

Probably, it had begun with the very first kiss. Or maybe it had started at the Halloween party, and she hadn't realized the depth of the problem. She never should have agreed to the assignment.

Something had told her it would be dangerous. God, if she'd only known.

She took another sip while she turned on her computer. It was still twenty minutes from the opening bell, but her team consisted of overachievers and rabid gossips, so it wasn't at all surprising that the only two still missing were Jeannie and Ryan.

The thought that he'd truly be here, in person, in a matter of minutes, stole her breath. Tendrils of panic were snaking around her chest, and she used every trick her coaches had ever taught her about calming down.

She had to get her act together, that's all there was to it. This was the office. She was, despite her behavior in the past few days, a professional. This would not break her.

As she logged in her user name and password, she remembered how it had been right after that stupid party. The truth of him had been so much clearer back then.

Then she'd started letting him into her fantasies, and that had been the beginning of the end. It probably wouldn't have done lasting damage if Jeannie hadn't been held up in court. Angie could have gotten along with him up until the day she got the job with the Deputy Director.

Now, she didn't even deserve that job. Not after the fiasco that had been the Las Vegas sting. She just prayed that Ryan would be the chosen one, because at least he'd be across the country. Out of her sight, and eventually, out of her head. She'd gotten in bed with a viper and been shocked that she'd been bitten. Who's fault was that?

Knowing all that, it should have been a simple thing to shake it off. Like a side stitch or shin splints. It shouldn't make her want to curl up into a ball and hide from the world. She shouldn't feel worse than when she'd broken up with Steve.

Her sigh was too loud, her posture slumped, and if anyone looked at her right now they'd see she was on the verge of tears. All the effort she'd put into practicing to appear cool and calm had gone down the drain even before work had officially begun.

If she had any self-preservation instincts, she'd pack up and go home before it was too late.

Turning to pick up her cup, she froze. It was already too late. Ryan had arrived, and he couldn't have looked more carefree and happy.

16

RYAN KEPT HIS SMILE IN PLACE, made sure his movements weren't tense and that he didn't shy away from meeting anyone's eyes. Especially Angie's, although that lasted about five seconds.

On the inside, he wasn't handling things, as well.

He masked the ache in his chest by making the rounds, going from desk to desk in the bullpen, being his typical smartass self. Slyly inappropriate innuendoes were traded with the men, completely different more politically correct innuendoes with the women. Angie was last, and by that time he'd found his rhythm. He probably should have gone into acting instead of the Bureau. The money was better and the women hotter.

Well, no one was hotter than Angie.

It was all he could do not to let his gaze sweep over her. To linger on her neck as her remembered scent blossomed in his mind, nearly as real as when he'd had his nose buried in the soft spot right behind her ear. Other recollections hit him in a jumble. How her fingers felt on his arms, the way she squeezed his hips with those strong legs, pulling him closer even though they'd been as close as two people could be. God, the way she'd tasted.

"...at four."

Ryan blinked, a splash of panic bringing him to the present. He thought briefly about nodding, then somehow unraveling what Angie had just said, but gave that up as a losing battle. "I'm sorry. I was miles away. Could you repeat that?"

"Which part?"

He could feel heat rise to his cheeks and he wondered again what earthly good had ever come from the act of embarrassed blushing. "All of it."

"Late night?" she asked. She didn't look angry or particularly invested in his answer. Kind of indifferent. Which was good. So why did it sting?

He nodded, and this time the truth wasn't at all hard to admit. He'd tossed and turned doing everything he could to think of anything but her and failing miserably. How she'd managed to completely upend his well-ordered life. He might've gotten three hours.

"We have to write up the week," she said, sorting through papers on her desk, probably so she didn't have to look at him. "Separately, then go over our conclusions together. Palmer wants the team in his office at four."

"So much for getting out of here early."

"Well, life is tough all over."

Her clipped response was only slightly more obvious than the underlying weariness she was trying to hide. Before last week, he wouldn't have noticed. Wouldn't have cared.

Clearly, she hadn't had a peaceful night, either, although it had taken him some time to see her as she was, rather than how he pictured her. The glow had dimmed, her skin looked pale.

"Was there something else?"

He shook his head. "Let me know when you're ready for the wrap-up."

She nodded then turned to her computer. In profile the

tension in her shoulders was obvious, as was her desire to have him leave.

He obliged. It was only when he'd booted up his own computer that he let himself think about the past few minutes. She'd barely looked at him. Granted, they hadn't spoken for long, but her gaze had darted all over the place, most often landing on the bridge of his nose or his right ear. He hadn't realized how accustomed he'd become to reading her through her eyes. Sometimes they were so expressive it was as if she'd given him the key to her thoughts.

Complete avoidance said even more.

At least before when they'd danced around each other it had involved a little teasing, some heat, but always, there'd been respect.

He'd certainly managed to screw that up. She'd probably never really look at him again, and she certainly wouldn't want to laugh with him, or ask his opinion about work. About anything.

It shouldn't matter so much. It did, though, because he honestly liked her. Admired her. She didn't use her looks to get ahead, to manipulate anyone, as a crutch. He knew that because he did all of those things. The statistics were there, and he'd decided early to go with them, exploit every advantage he had.

Playing the handsome card wasn't evil or even unethical, but it was the easy way out. Also, it was something his father had done. Still did. His old man had been a model when he was younger. He still reminded people of Clooney, at least until he had a few. Then he got ugly. The kind of ugly that had nothing to do with mirrors. But by then, it was usually too late for whatever hapless woman had been deceived by his packaging.

The horrible thing was, Ryan was sure his own behavior wasn't going to change anytime soon. And yet, in retrospect,

he should have handled yesterday morning with more tact.
But that was the only part he regretted. As for the rest? He'd
done Angie a favor.

THANKFULLY ANGIE WAS sitting across from Gordon Palmer
with Ryan to her right. Jeannie sat next to him, and the rest
of the team fanned out around the large conference table.
The pretence of normalcy was easier in a group.

The private wrap-up had been accomplished in record
time, but at least they'd had the comfort of FBI-speak to hide
behind, paperwork and notes to focus on. Not that she'd gotten through it scot-free. Despite her efforts, the worst kinds
of memories kept breaking through. All the different ways
he'd looked at her. The way he smiled as if she were someone extraordinary. Most often, what she'd seen during those
thirty-four minutes.

The pitchers of water were a big clue that the meeting was
going to be a long one. Angie sat up straight, prepared to
focus solely on the business at hand. She hadn't gone through
that sting only to lose it when they were so close to the finish line. Now that everyone was settled, Gordon leaned forward to begin.

"We've received two interesting pieces of information this
morning from the Vegas bureau. They've got hard evidence
now that Ira's bookie has been dipping his pen into illegal
ink. The only thing that matters in our case is that they were
able to seize the operation's books. Ira lost well over fifty
thousand dollars in the past few months. There's sure to be
more as the Vegas team digs deeper. It's possible the amount
of money he's lost this month alone is responsible for the
second piece of data. The suspects have moved their flights
up. They'll be out of the country at the end of this week."

Angie looked at Ryan, just as he looked at her. He seemed
as surprised as she was.

"Was there a ticket for Tonya?" Ryan asked, jerking his gaze back to Palmer.

"Yes."

"So she still hasn't broken the news," Angie said. "Do we have any more intel on that business of hers? Is it a real thing, or a ruse or what?"

"Vegas has tails on all four of them." Gordon looked point-edly at Angie and Ryan. "We're all waiting on the text, which has to be coming soon. They're not going to want to leave without their nest egg. I'd expect to hear from them no later than the weekend."

Ryan leaned back in his chair. "Since Ebsen doesn't have access to multimillion-dollar art, we know they're going to ask for cash. So how do they expect to get the money out of the country?"

"If the blackmailer is Ira working alone, he may need to clear up his debts." Jeannie's gaze went to Ryan, then turned to Angie.

Brian leaned in. "If it's Tonya's game, she could be keeping the cash to help open up her business here, but that could also mean we won't necessarily hear so quickly."

Ryan nodded. "Marcus has some tricks up his sleeve. I'm not sure what, but he has some power issues. That milquetoast persona he's got going doesn't quite cover the rage. It wouldn't shock me to find out he's behind everything."

"Marcus?" Jeannie asked. "He's probably too busy with his call girls."

"Expensive call girls." Angie glanced quickly at Jeannie, but switched over to focus on Brian instead. Jeannie had looked…off. But Angie couldn't think about that right now. "This woman must have charged a couple of grand. We have no idea how often Marcus indulges. It could be nightly, for all we know."

"Yeah, but according to Tonya the family knows about

his hooker hobby. Which could mean they're all involved with the blackmail."

Angie shook her head. "Maybe everything comes down to Delilah, and she's just so good at blackmail and manipulation that she didn't leave us any breadcrumbs. She looks squeaky clean and that could mean she's smarter than all of them put together. Which could explain why Tonya changed her ticket. A last-minute escape attempt."

That set up a few minutes of chatter around the table. Not Angie, though. She was still caught up in trying to figure out what was going on with Jeannie. Had Ryan told her what had happened? Did Jeannie blame her for having sex while on the case?

Angie thought about her conversation with Liz. They'd talked for over two hours the night before. Liz had been furious at Ryan on Angie's behalf, which was nice, even though none of it was Ryan's fault. Liz had tried to convince Angie to talk to Ryan, to clear the air, but there was nothing to clear. He'd made his stand, and she'd known from the start that this was the most likely outcome. What was she supposed to say, "No fair, you were supposed to have changed for me?"

The thought swamped her with shame, but thankfully, Gordon brought the meeting to order again.

"Everyone got copies of the reports from Angie and Ryan? I want to go over the conclusions, see if we've missed anything. Then I want each of you to get the two of them caught up. Paula, why don't you start us off reading page one."

Perversely Angie found herself turning to Ryan instead of Paula. He was looking down at the papers in front of him, and he seemed unnaturally still. Also, his chair was upright. Ryan liked to swagger even when he sat, well, leaned back. His hands weren't moving at all. Normally he was a fiddler. No nearby pen was safe from his fingers, rubber bands were particular favorites and he'd bent more paperclips per meeting than anyone she'd ever seen. But there he was, head bowed, motionless, as if his vitality had flown the coop and left his body behind.

Watching him made her uneasy, and if she'd been sitting next to him she might have touched the back of his hand or rubbed his shoulder with her own. Despite everything. It was too much like looking at an imposter, and she didn't care for it. The squeeze of tension in her chest swelled as she tried again to understand how things had fallen apart so drastically in such a short period of time.

She should have looked away. She meant nothing to him, and in return, she should do herself a favor and feel nothing for him.

His eyes closed. Slowly, as if he had to think about what he was going to do. Then his head swiveled toward her until he was staring right at her. The expression on his face was neutral. Almost. Because his gaze made her stop breathing, made her lean back in her chair. Made everyone else in the room seem to disappear.

She couldn't guess what he was thinking. Only that it wasn't about their report, or even about the case. All she knew for sure was that he'd lied to her. Whatever was going on between them, the thirty-four minutes and their night together hadn't all been an act.

MIDWAY THROUGH SALLY's overview of the Intimate At Last financials, Ryan's phone rang. The sound brought everything to a standstill even though it wasn't particularly loud. Everyone present knew that particular ring tone was Ebsen's.

He pulled it out of his pocket. It was too soon for a blackmail text. But then nothing about this case had gone as expected. The blocked number told him it was the text they'd been waiting for. He knew from the interviews with the victims that they wouldn't be able to trace the call, that it would be routed and rerouted in a convoluted trail that ended some-where in Romania. He clicked View Now.

Dear Mr. Ebsen: If you wish to continue your very pleasant life with your beautiful wife, with your expensive car and your many elegant vacations, you will be at Du Par's on Ventura Boulevard tomorrow night at 12:00 a.m. You will be alone, you will not be wearing a wire, and you will have with you $500,000.00 in cash, in hundreds, in unmarked bills with no dye pack and no tracers and no bugs and no hint that any-one, including the police, has been alerted. You will sit at the counter with a suitcase beside you. You will order coffee and you will not look around. If you do, your wife will receive every photo and every text and every email that is on your cell phone and computer. The suitcase will be taken. You will remain at the diner until 1:30 a.m. You may then return to your delightful life.

He nodded, so that the room understood this was the text. This was the ball in play. But there were still photo attach-ments to be looked at.

He began the slideshow. There was Ebsen's ex-mistress. Next was a photo of breasts. Nice ones that hadn't actually belonged to the woman who was pictured as his lover. She was a Special Agent out of the San Diego office, matter of fact.

Then came a series of pictures of emails and texts. From Ebsen to Roxanne, from her to Ebsen, deleted emails and deleted texts. He looked up, met Gordon's eye. "Well, we were right about them cloning the SIM card and the laptop."

"Let's hear it," Palmer said.

Ryan clicked back on the original message and as he read, half the people in the room took every word down.

"That's awfully smug," Jeannie said.

Angie nodded. "Sure. They've already gotten away with

it. We have no idea how many times. This transaction is a done deal. It could be from any one of them or all of them."

"All right," Palmer said, looking his version of pleased. "We know the timeline. We'll have the money ready. This is going precisely to plan."

"Whoever's running the pickup can't get back to Vegas by plane that late." Ryan looked over at Angie, a reflex, but one he'd have to curb if he didn't want to get jolted out of his thoughts. "I doubt there are any trains. So, they'll be driving. Unless the blackmailers are also in L.A."

"We're following the money," Angie said, but Ryan kept his gaze on Palmer. "They don't have the tech to discover our bugs, so we can wait it out until it changes hands."

"Are we absolutely sure the Vegas team has to take the bust?" Ryan had been okay with the deal up until about two minutes ago. "We did do all the heavy lifting."

Palmer's pleased smile disappeared. "It will show up in your files as a joint operation. Don't sweat it. We all know what everyone did for this sting." He looked right at Ryan as he spoke, then at Angie.

Ryan hoped to God that Palmer didn't know everything that happened, but he nodded at his boss, anyway. At least the hand-off would be up to him. He couldn't wait to see who was going to show up to take the cash.

"WHAT'S GOING ON?"

Angie wasn't using Skype, so she couldn't see Liz's face, but she could picture her friend perfectly. Worried, mostly because of how wrecked Angie had been last night. Probably because Angie couldn't keep up any kind of facade with Liz even over the phone. "I'm sorry. It's been insane. I'm on a stakeout. Well, actually, I'm a block and a half away from the surveillance van in my car at the moment. I just wanted to touch base."

"I wish you'd reconsider talking to Ryan."

"I'm thinking about it. He's been gone all day, acting out a day in the life of Ryan Ebsen. Being at work without him felt weird."

"In what way?"

"Damn it, I missed him. I can't stop thinking about him. I don't believe it was all an act. We connected, I'm sure of it. The thing is, I'm positive that he knows all that, too. He just doesn't like that he'd gotten involved. Especially with someone at work. So this feeling, this boulder in my chest, it's all my problem, not Ryan's. It hurts like fire, Liz. It just gets worse and worse."

"Oh, boy." Liz's voice was softer, careful. "Angie, honey. I think you went and fell in love with the guy."

Angie closed her eyes and willed herself not to let the sudden hot tears fall. "I didn't."

"Right." Liz sighed. "The good news is, it won't actually kill you. The bad news is, you'll kind of wish it would."

It took a minute of the heel of her palms pressed against her closed eyes, but Angie won the fight. No tear dropped. Only the penny. But if this was love, she wanted nothing to do with it.

"I've got to get back to the van. Ryan should be coming soon."

"Good luck," Liz said. "You know I think you should still talk to him. Outside of work."

"Goodbye, Liz. Thank you." Angie put her cell in her jacket pocket, locked up the car and walked back to the surveillance van, which had been parked down the street from DuPar's diner. It smelled like a men's locker room. Which wasn't the bad part. There were four other people in the van with her that all had very defined tasks. She was a guest, and therefore, she wasn't allowed to complain that she couldn't see, couldn't hear and technically shouldn't even speak.

So she tucked herself into the corner and waited till Ryan Ebsen's red Ferrari came into view. Their team was in place, with backups and hidden cameras using new stealth tech, and the wired money and cars that would physically follow the cash to see where it ended up.

She refused to think of anything but the stakeout and the money transfer. Every time something personal popped up, she squashed it like a cockroach. This moment would justify everything that had happened to her since they'd been assigned this case. It would make up for being in the most awkward and ultimately painful situation of her life. She'd be damned if she was going to miss a second of it on some insane emotional idiocy.

"He's on the Boulevard," Max said. He was their electronics guy, the one who'd come up with the nontraceable cash tag. "Everyone stand by."

Angie took him at his word and stood, as cramped as it was. All she wanted was for this night to be over. For the case to be turned over to the Vegas office. And for Ryan to be safe. Even though he wasn't the kind of man for her. Despite the fact that it was likely that she'd become more attached than was wise to the part he'd played instead of the man himself.

The truth was, he didn't love her. *He didn't love her*.

There was nothing to be gained by talking it out with him. She still stood by the decision she'd made this morning to put in for a transfer to Cyber Crimes. Just in case the D.C. job fell through, of course. She'd covered her bases, given herself a backup exit strategy. No matter what happened, she wasn't going to spend any more time working in the same office as Ryan. Not if she could help it.

"He's here." Max's voice was calm and low, but the words constricted Angie's chest, and she maneuvered herself so she could see one of the monitors.

That car was captivating, but it couldn't hold a candle to

Ryan himself. God, he looked nervous. Of course. He was a consummate actor deep in his character.

He carried the suitcase with him into the brightly lit diner. The cameras they'd put in place an hour after the text showed every seat in the house. Particularly at the counter. But no one turned to look at him.

He ended up taking a stool to the far right, where there were the fewest customers. He put the case next to his feet, as ordered. An agonizing twelve minutes later, a tall blonde walked through the front door.

"I'll be damned," Angie muttered.

Everyone in the van looked at her.

"It's Marcus," she said, her gaze glued to the woman. "I mean, he's in on it. She's got to be one of his call girls. Clever."

The blonde didn't even bother to sit down. She just picked up the suitcase and walked straight through to the back entrance, where the exterior camera showed her getting behind the wheel of a white Chrysler. A moment later, she took off into the night.

By the time Ryan left the building at exactly one-thirty, the Ferrari was gone.

17

IT TOOK FOREVER TO GET HOME. He'd had to go to the house they'd set up as belonging to the Ebsen's first, then sneak off super-spy style in Jeannie's minivan. By the time she dropped Ryan back at his apartment, he was more exhausted than he could ever remember. It felt as if he hadn't slept in years, not days, and now that the adrenaline had worked through his system, he was running on fumes.

That didn't seem to matter to his beleaguered brain. As he stripped for bed, letting his clothes drop at his feet, he replayed every word Jeannie had said to him on the longest drive of his life. He'd confessed his sins, and she'd put him through hell for it. Truth was, he didn't mind. It wasn't half of what he deserved. The only thing he took exception to was Jeannie's advice to talk it out with Angie.

What Jeannie didn't know was that he'd already thought of that. The number of imagined conversations he'd attempted must have been in the dozens, each one falling flat or worse, making him want to wring his own neck.

They all began with, "I'm sorry. I messed up."

The bed beckoned, but there was still one thing he had to do. Booting up his laptop took forever and made him very aware that it was damn cold wearing just his boxers on his metal desk chair, but doing anything about it was out of the question. One click opened a new document and he started typing. Once he got going he realized the short message he'd envisioned wouldn't be sufficient so he kept on until he'd said everything he'd needed to. Literally dizzy with fatigue, he copied the text and found the two, no three, contacts for his email. Then he pasted his note, saved everything, shut off the machine and somehow made it back to the bed. And sleep.

DEPUTY DIRECTOR LEONARD had arrived at ten that morning, although Angie hadn't seen him. She supposed he was being personally filled in on the success of their mission by A.D. Palmer. Rumor had it Leonard was going to stay on for a while, probably to conduct interviews.

Angie wasn't fussed. The only thing worrying her was that it was almost noon and Ryan hadn't made it in to the office. She wasn't pining away for him. The opposite was true, in fact. She needed to prepare herself to see him. To get her thoughts in order as she ruthlessly shoved her feelings to a dark, small box in the back of her mind.

Not knowing when to expect him was messing with her timing. The last thing she needed today was that kind of distraction.

The Vegas team had taken over once the white Chrysler had crossed into Nevada. The go-between had gone to a very expensive high-rise condo just off the Strip, which was immediately put under surveillance. She hadn't left again.

Despite Angie's realization that the woman had to be one of Marcus's call girls, all the staff of Intimate At Last were being watched. Each of them had been seen at least once during the morning, but no one had left their homes.

Her office phone rang, and it was the Deputy Director's assistant, asking her to come to the third floor temporary office. She popped a mint as she went to the elevator, amazed at how calm she felt. At least about this.

On three, the elevator doors opened. Ryan stood directly in front of her. It took her so by surprise that Ryan had to block the doors from closing.

"You've been here all morning?" she asked.

"An hour." They traded places, but he kept the elevator stalled.

She had questions, but the director was waiting, so… "It went great last night."

"I heard you were in the van."

She nodded, then motioned with her chin toward the director's temporary office down the hall. "I have to…"

"Yeah," he said, looking as if he wanted to say more. Instead, he moved back in the car, letting the doors close.

The walk to Leonard's office wasn't nearly long enough. But she managed to settle, to get back some of her calm before she tapped on the door.

She took the offered cup of tea just to have something to hold on to. Of course, she'd met Leonard before, but she doubted he remembered her.

"Congratulations on a job very well done," he said, gesturing for her to sit in the guest chair.

"Thank you, sir."

"Not just for your software program, but for stepping into a very delicate situation."

She nodded, smiled, took a sip of tea that really needed some sugar. "Thank you," she repeated. God, how she hated interviews.

"I received an interesting email this morning," he said, rising from his chair to walk around his desk. He leaned back against the dark wood, and Angie remembered Ryan standing just that way in their hotel room.

"Oh?" she said, in another stunning moment of grace and intelligence.

"Special Agent Vail had a lot to say about you."

That took her so by surprise that she had to put the tea down on the console table. Luckily she didn't have to respond verbally, because she wouldn't have known how to begin.

"He was quite impressed with how you handled yourself in such a potentially awkward situation. The Bureau doesn't make it a habit of asking our agents to go as far as you had to. I can't imagine that it was easy."

"It wasn't. But I assure you, Agent Vail made all the difference. He was deeply committed to making sure the sting was successful. The lion's share of the responsibility rested on his shoulders."

Leonard's smile was brief, but knowing. "He warned me you would say that." After a strangely intense stare, the director leaned forward a couple of inches. "I'll be frank with you, Agent Wolf. I asked Vail to meet me earlier to offer him the position in my office."

"Good choice, sir," she said, hoping he understood that those weren't idle words.

"He turned me down. Said you'd be the right person for the job. That with your computer skills and your adaptability and skill as an agent, you'd be an unbeatable asset."

Angie's mouth opened, but nothing, not even a breath escaped as she tried to make sense of what she'd just heard. He'd turned down the job? That was crazy. Absolutely nuts. She knew he wanted it. That he'd be great at it. Hell, even the Deputy Director knew he was the right man for the position. "I'm flattered," she said, finally, "and confused, to be honest with you."

"That's probably because I haven't asked." He smiled again, this time it was more open. "Which I'm doing right now. I think both you and Agent Vail would make excellent additions to my staff, but I only have the budget for one of you. The job is yours if you want it."

She should have been jumping on the offer without a second thought. Last week, she would have. Her family would have been so proud. A lot had changed since then. "Thank you, sir. I appreciate the vote of confidence. But I'm afraid I'm not going to be able to accept."

To say he looked surprised was an understatement. "Excuse me?"

"I submitted a withdrawal of my application this morning. I've decided to apply for a transfer to Cyber Crimes, here in Los Angeles. I believe it's where I can do the most good, and frankly, working in programming suits me."

Now it was the director's turn to appear a little shell-shocked. He was a distinguished-looking man in his elegant navy suit, and she'd never seen him ruffled. Until now.

She almost apologized again, but decided against it. "Agent Vail had no idea about my decision, sir. For what it's worth, I think your first choice was the right one. He's the most impressive agent I've ever worked with."

"Thank you for your candor, Agent Wolf." He studied her for a long, uncomfortable moment, then continued with a short speech about what the move to D.C. would do for her career. The professional pep talk was eerily close to too many she'd heard from her parents.

It was her reaction that was different. She didn't feel as if she were sitting on the hot seat destined to disappoint someone. No, she'd weighed the pros and cons and took responsibility for the choice she'd made. From this point forward, the only person she could disappoint was herself, but only if she didn't try her best.

She sipped, nodded when it was appropriate, but it was obvious when the director recognized that she'd already made up her mind. With a faint smile of defeat, he straightened.

She stood, held out her hand.

He shook it with a certain gravity, which she understood. "I'm regretting my budget restrictions even more after speaking to you both. But I agree you will make a considerable contribution to the Bureau working in Cyber Crimes."

She smiled as he let her go and took a huge breath once she was back out in the hall. It was only with great determination that she started walking again, because *Ryan had turned down the job. For her.*

Okay, so maybe Liz had a point about the whole talking thing.

AFTER A TERRIBLE NIGHT, Ryan had gotten to work a few minutes late. He hadn't seen Angie at all after her interview with Leonard yesterday. He'd even stuck around for a while after hours, but she'd been locked up in meetings with the tech heads from Cyber Crimes. He'd spent his night at home, staring at his cell phone, debating between calling her, showing up at her place or trying one more time to make something happen at one of his night spots.

In the end, he'd fallen asleep on the couch, and woken late with a stiff neck and the lingering memory of a dream. About her. About them.

The 9:00 a.m. call from the Supervisory Special Agent in Las Vegas came directly to Ryan, and his two-finger whistle brought everything to a halt in the bullpen. He put the phone on speaker. "You've got our attention," he said.

"At 7:22 a.m. we arrested Marcus Aldrich for extortion under Penal Codes 518-527 inclusive. We've obtained full warrants for all material including computers, cell phones and any and all electronic devices belonging to or rented by the Intimate At Last staff. Delilah Bridges, Ira Bridges and Tonya Bridges are officially persons of interest in the case and won't be leaving the country anytime soon. Well done, Los Angeles."

The team burst into applause with more than a few members whooping it up. Ryan found Angie's gaze and held it. Whatever else had happened, this was their victory. They'd come through for the team and for the Bureau. He hadn't always believed they would, so this was a good thing. A damn good thing.

She smiled. Picked up her phone. He watched her type a text from about fifteen feet away. It wasn't a surprise that his cell rang.

I would like to speak to you. Tonight. At your apartment. After work.

Despite his desire to speak to her, it took him a minute to respond. He wasn't sure he wanted to hear what she had to say. Most likely that she'd accepted the D.C. job. He figured she'd heard about his letter to the Deputy Director, but that didn't excuse his behavior last week. No matter what, there was no happy ever after ahead, not for the two of them. It was surprising enough that he found he wanted one, even though he wasn't sure he had what it took to make Angie happy.

He'd like to try, though.

Next life, he'd know better. This life, he texted her a quick You bet. She'd have her say, and then he'd figure out what was next for him. He'd stick around in White Collar and milk this victory for all it was worth, then take a look at what was available. He was free to go anywhere, maybe take on Major Crimes or tackle Terrorism. The only place he wouldn't look was Washington, D.C. He couldn't bear the idea of working in the same office with her again.

He put his cell away as Gordon Palmer walked into the room, causing yet another swell of celebration.

"Great job, everyone," he said. "We'll continue to support the Las Vegas team as we head toward convictions and restitution. You all deserve a raise. You're not going to get them, but you deserve them."

He got a laugh, even though it wasn't all that amusing.

"Now get back to work. We've let too many of cases slide these last few months. It's time to play catch-up."

The transition back to work mode was smooth, but unsettling. Ryan wanted the assignment to be over. To get back to normal. But normal had left the building.

Somehow, he was able to read an entire brief without thinking of what would happen after work at his place. But he kept sneaking glances at Angie. Surprisingly, she kept sneaking glances back.

ANGIE STOOD OUTSIDE RYAN'S door, unable to bring her hand up to knock. He knew she was standing there. She'd told him she was coming, and he'd buzzed her in, but that didn't matter. She was scared to death and there was still time to make an escape. He wouldn't press her about it. They were already riding a tidal wave of awkward. But if she knocked and he let her inside, and she did what she'd come to do, there was every chance that wave might drown her.

But not doing the thing that needed to be done? She would regret it forever. It was all about choices. Especially the hard ones. So she knocked, and he must have been standing right there, probably looking at her through the peephole, and wondering if she'd lost her mind.

The answer was clearly yes.

She hadn't been in his apartment before, although she'd been to the building. Once, a long time ago. He'd met her in the lobby and she'd driven the two of them to a weapons seminar. She'd expected the white walls, but she hadn't been prepared for the emptiness. It was as if no one lived there.

More like a home used by undercover agents than anyone with a real life.

It made her sad and scared for him, although she wasn't sure why about that last part.

"You want something? I've got coffee. Uh. Coffee. Oh, water. Tap water."

"I'm good, thanks."

They hadn't moved from next to the door. He'd closed it, done up the dead bolt. Some things became a habit when you worked in law enforcement.

The silence stretched between them, and Angie knew that because she'd called this meeting, she'd need to be the one to speak first. If only she'd thought of that before right this second.

"Want to sit?"

His couch was masculine and leather, dark brown, big. There was a coffee table that was some other kind of wood, and while she was no decorator, she could tell the two didn't go together. But she didn't want to sit there. In the kitchen, a small table had four utilitarian chairs. Those would do.

She took off her jacket and put it, along with her purse, on the coffee table. Then she arranged two of the chairs in the plentiful empty space, facing each other. A few feet apart.

Of course, he recognized the setup as the one they'd used in the thirty-four-minute exercise. The look of dread on his face wasn't surprising. She'd blindsided him on purpose. "You can say no," she said. "But I'd appreciate it if you didn't."

He stood still for a really long time. He was in his work clothes, sans jacket. He'd rolled up the sleeves of his white Oxford shirt and removed his tie. He bore a striking resemblance to Ryan Ebsen. Both of them were as masculine as that huge couch, but thankfully much better-looking.

"If this is to yell at me, couldn't we just do that standing up?"

"I'm not here to yell at you," she said. That he thought so surprised her.

"Why not?"

"Because you didn't do anything wrong. Well, maybe you could have been nicer, but no. I won't be yelling."

He moved, stepping closer so abruptly it startled her. "I was a jackass. Of all the people in the world, you did not deserve me being such an unmitigated prick."

"True."

He snorted, as if she had to be nuts. "That's it?"

She nodded. "You were just being yourself. I knew what we were doing there was an act. You could have softened the blow, but I suppose I needed the wake-up call."

He met her gaze. She didn't shy away, just let him look. Her visit was more about her than him in the long run, but it was also about them. About clearing the air; and while he'd started that ball rolling, she wanted to steer it in the right direction.

Stepping over to the chair, she didn't sit, just waited, prepared for him to bow out. God knew, Ryan was nothing if not averse to emotions of any kind. But maybe, perhaps, hopefully, their days at the workshop had opened a tiny crack in the giant fortress he'd built to protect himself.

With a rueful shake of his head, he sat down in the awful chair. That's when her heart started pounding double time. She figured she could get through this as long as she didn't stop to think. No crying, either. Under any circumstances.

She sat across from him. Judged the distance, then scooted in an inch. Then she set her watch alarm for thirty minutes.

"When I was ten, I had won a race at a district-wide meet. It was nothing, really, but it was held at a high school that had a proper track and there were ribbons and too much screaming from parents. I won my race, and my team also won the relay. So I came home with two ribbons, which my parents put up on a really large poster board in the family room.

"Anyway, they had some company over, I don't remember who. It was late, but I needed to use the bathroom, and had to walk down the hallway to get there. I passed the family room on the way, and I heard my father talking. I slowed down when he said my name.

"He said that I was built like a thoroughbred. That he'd always known that I was going to be a champion, and today was just the beginning. He'd bet everything he owned that I'd end up in the Olympics, and that I'd be a gold medalist. He planned on building a special display case for those medals.

"Then my mother started. About how I was a natural, how coaches were lining up, wanting to take me under their wings. They were being very picky, and if it meant moving to another state, they'd move. Because I was going to finally bring home the gold."

Ryan had leaned forward. But he hadn't looked away from her, not at all. "Sounds like a lot of pressure."

"I was utterly terrified," she said. "I shook so hard I had an accident in the hallway. Luckily it was a hardwood floor, so I was able to clean it up, but I ended up throwing my pajama pants out my bedroom window, then tossing them in a trash bin the next day. I was humiliated, but more than that, I knew without any doubt whatsoever that I was not going to be an Olympic champion. Not only was I not that fast, but I didn't care about it. I mean, competing was okay, but I didn't want to get up hours before school to train, dedicate my life to the sport.

"I wanted to go on sleepovers and playdates and I had it bad for horses, but I knew in that moment that I would forevermore have to do everything I could to make them proud of me, but in every way, not just on the track. I've lived my whole life trying to be that perfect person. Let me tell you. It's exhausting."

He sighed, finally looked down, but only for a moment. "I'm sorry you had to go through that."

"I don't think they meant any harm. They wanted what they saw as an ideal life for me. They had no way of knowing that conversation was going to set the direction of my life. That it would become the foundation of who I believed I was. How I was destined to fail."

"But you studied computer tech in college."

"My scholarship was in track and my major was pre-law. It nearly killed them when they realized I truly didn't have the talent for either. It's never been the same between us. Never."

"Do parents ever get it right?"

"Some more than others," she said.

He nodded, and she knew he was thinking about his father. About the way his mother had discarded him.

"But at some point," she said, "I realized I had to let go of what they wanted from me, and become the person I wanted to be." Angie cleared her throat, because this was coming up on the hard part. The part where she put her heart in her palm and let the chips fall.

"I'm not sorry I went to Vegas," she said, and he had to lean in a little closer because her voice wasn't coming out very loud. "But especially, I want you to know that I'm not even a little sorry about what happened to us personally. I've been attracted to you for a long time, and while I understand you aren't interested, I'm okay with that. What I don't want is for us to be weird with each other. Besides realizing how amazing sex could be, I found out so many other more important things. You were careful with me. You were creative and clever, and you always had my back…every minute and—"

"Stop," he said, and Angie gasped because she hadn't noticed that his eyes had changed, that he wasn't commiserating with her any more, he was in pain.

"What? I'm sorry. I—"

"Don't apologize, for God's sake, don't. And don't you dare say that I was careful with you. I was reckless. I thought you were just another…"

He stood. He walked all the way into the kitchen, opened up a cupboard and pulled out a bottle of Johnnie Walker. He poured himself a shot, and then brought down a different kind of glass and poured another shot for her. But he downed his standing by the counter, then just stood there, staring at the white cupboard.

Finally he walked back to her. Offered her the drink. She shook her head.

He sat again. Swallowed hard, put the drink on the floor, reached over and took her hands in his. When he met her gaze, she wouldn't have looked away for all the money on earth. "I'm so sorry, Angie," he said. "I was a complete bastard to you. I took advantage of the situation. I was unprofessional, and it was unforgivable. I just wanted you so damn badly.

"And then, that last night in our room, I got scared. Truly terrified, like you standing in that hallway. You aren't like any woman I've ever been with. I didn't want to let you go, and that was…unprecedented. You're the most amazing person I've ever met, and you've kind of messed everything up. I've tried to slide back into my life, but I can't. You're everything I didn't know I was missing."

"What?" The rug had not only been pulled out from under her, but she'd lost the ability to put two words together.

"If I were any other man, I'd never let you go again. I'd move heaven and earth to make you happy."

That helped her find her voice. "If you were any other man, I wouldn't want you."

The way he smiled broke her heart. "You don't know. You couldn't know."

"You don't, either," she said. "God, if you weren't going to Washington… And hey, that letter—"

"If I wasn't going to… What?"

"Oh. Leonard hasn't contacted you yet?"

"I'm seeing him tomorrow afternoon, but I wasn't told the agenda."

"He's going to restate his offer. I'd already decided I wanted to stay in L.A. and transfer to Cyber Crimes."

"But working with the Deputy Director is a huge opportunity. It'll open doors, put you in the center of the action."

"I know. But it's not what I want. Although, hearing you'd turned him down, that you'd written a letter on my behalf…"

"That letter was only the truth."

"Thanks. But now you can take the job with no regrets."

He stood up again, paced his sterile living room. When he ended up at the window, he turned to her again. "It's three thousand miles away."

"Yeah."

"You wouldn't be there."

The way he was looking at her and the tone of his voice kicked up her heart rate to the power of ten. She wasn't even sure why. "I know."

"I'd rather stay here. Near you. Which is a problem. Because I am not the kind of man who sticks around."

She stood up, weak knees and all. "Ryan."

"I hated that you were going to leave. I can't stop thinking about you. But, Jesus, I'm such an incredibly bad risk, I have no right to even be telling you this."

She met him at the window, aching for him, for them. This was the crossroads. Decisions made now would echo for a lifetime. "I would hate it if you didn't take the job, then found out you'd made a mistake."

"I'd hate it worse if I missed the one chance I had to be with you. There'll be other promotions."

The alarm went off, making both of them jump. She silenced it quickly. "I don't think I want to do the four minutes of silence."

"No?"

She shook her head. "I think we could find something better to do."

He pulled her into a kiss that stole her breath but not her reason. This unlikely man was the one for her. She'd want to kiss him for the rest of time.

He pulled back, but didn't let her go. "You're risking a lot here."

"I know. Remember that whole 'I learned to choose who I wanted to be' part?"

"And that includes me?"

"We've already been married, so dating should be a piece of cake, don't you think?"

His grin was slow in coming, but when it hit, it lit her up inside. "I never dreamed I would say this in my lifetime. Angie Wolf, I'm in love with you. And I will do everything in my power to make you proud and happy you're choosing me. But only if you understand, I have no experience when it comes to love or relationships."

"You're off to a great start," she said. "Besides, I already know you're a quick learner."

"I am one lucky son of a bitch," he said, seconds before he pulled her into the kiss of a lifetime.

* * * * *

COMING NEXT MONTH FROM
HARLEQUIN® BLAZE™

Available January 22, 2012

#735 THE ARRANGEMENT
by Stephanie Bond

Ben Winter and Carrie Cassidy have known each other forever. And they like each other—a lot! But when those feelings start to run deeper, Ben thinks he's doing the right thing when he ends the "Friends with Benefits" arrangement he has with Carrie. After all, he wants more from her than just great sex. It seems like a good plan...until Carrie makes him agree to find his replacement!

#736 YOU'RE STILL THE ONE • *Made in Montana*
by Debbi Rawlins

Reluctant dude-ranch manager Rachel McAllister hasn't seen Matt Gunderson since he left town and broke her teenage heart ten years ago. Now the bull-riding rodeo star is back and she's ready to show him *everything* he missed. All she wants is his body, but if there's one thing Matt learned in the rodeo, it's how to hang on tight.

#737 NIGHT DRIVING • *Stop the Wedding!*
by Lori Wilde

Former G.I. Boone Toliver has a new mission: prevent his kid sister's whirlwind wedding in Miami. The challenge: Boone can't fly, so he agrees to a road trip with his ditzy neighbor, Tara Duvall. She's shaking the Montana dust from her boots and leaving it all behind for a new start on Florida's sunny beaches. It's one speed bump after another as they deal with clashing personalities and frustrating obstacles, until romantic pit stops and minor mishaps suddenly start to look a whole lot like destiny.

#738 A SEAL'S SEDUCTION • *Uniformly Hot!*
by Tawny Weber

Admiral's daughter Alexia Pierce had no intention of ever letting another military man in her life, even if he was hot! But that was before she met Blake—and learned all the things a navy SEAL was good for....

YOU CAN FIND MORE INFORMATION ON UPCOMING HARLEQUIN© TITLES, FREE EXCERPTS AND MORE AT WWW.HARLEQUIN.COM.

HB0113CNMENHB

Navy SEAL Blake Landon joins this year's
parade of *Uniformly Hot!* military heroes in
Tawny Weber's

A SEAL's Seduction

Blake's lips brushed over Alexia's and she forgot that they were
on a public beach. His breath was warm, his lips soft.

The fingertips he traced over her shoulder were like a gentle
whisper. It was sweetness personified. She felt like a fairy-tale
princess being kissed for the first time by her prince.

And he was delicious.

Mouthwatering, heart-stopping delicious. And clearly he
had no problem going after what he wanted, she realized as he
slid the tips of his fingers over the bare skin of her shoulder.
Alexia shivered at the contrast of his hard fingertips against
her skin. Her breath caught as his hand shifted, sliding lower,
hinting at but not actually caressing the upper swell of her
breast.

Her heart pounded so hard against her throat, she was surprised it didn't jump right out into his hand.

She wanted him. As she'd never wanted another man in
her life. For years, she'd behaved. She'd carefully considered
her actions, making sure she didn't hurt others. She'd poured
herself into her career, into making sure her life was one she
was proud of.

HBEXP0113R

And she already had a man who wanted her in his life. A nice, sweet man she could talk through the night with and never run out of things to say.

But she wanted more.

She wanted a man who'd keep her up all night. Who'd drive her wild, sending her body to places she'd never even dreamed of.

Even if it was only for one night.

And that, she realized, was the key. One night of crazy. One night of delicious, empowered, indulge-her-every-desire sex, with a man who made her melt.

One night would be incredible.

One night would *have* to be enough.

Pick up *A SEAL's Seduction* by Tawny Weber, on sale January 22.

Evangeline is surprised when her past lover
turns out to be her fiancé's brother. How will she
manage the one she loved and the one
she has made a deal with?

Follow her path to love January 22, 2013, with

THE ONE THAT GOT AWAY

by Kelly Hunter

"The trouble with memories like ours," he said roughly, "is that you think you've buried them, dealt with them, right up until they reach up and rip out your throat."

Some memories were like that. But not all. Sometimes memories could be finessed into something slightly more palatable.

"Maybe we could try replacing the bad with something a little less intense," she suggested tentatively. "You could try treating me as your future sister-in-law. We could do polite and civil. We could come to like it that way."

"Watching you hang off my brother's arm doesn't make me feel civilized, Evangeline. It makes me want to break things."

Ah.

"Call off the engagement." He wasn't looking at her. And it wasn't a request. "Turn this mess around."

"We need Max's trust fund money."

"I'll cover Max for the money. I'll buy you out."

"What?" Anger slid through her, hot and biting. She could feel her composure slipping away but there was nothing else for it. Not in the face of the hot mess that was Logan. "No," she said as steadily as she could. "No one's buying me out of anything, least of all MEP. That company is *mine,* just as much as it is Max's. I've put six years into it, eighty-hour weeks of blood, sweat, tears and fears into making it the success it is. Prepping it for bigger opportunities, and one of those opportunities is just around the corner. Why on earth would I let you buy me out?"

He meant to use his big body to intimidate her. Closer, and closer still, until the jacket of his suit brushed the silk of her dress, but he didn't touch her, just let the heat build. His lips had that hard sensual curve about them that had haunted her dreams for years. She couldn't stop staring at them.

She needed to stop staring at them.

"You can't be in my life, Lena. Not even on the periphery. I discovered that the hard way ten years ago. So either you leave willingly…or I make you leave."

Find out what Evangeline decides to do by picking up THE ONE THAT GOT AWAY by Kelly Hunter. Available January 22, 2013, wherever Harlequin books are sold.

VM

HKEXP0213

"That's twice you saved my life today," Lori told Nick.

"I'd better be careful," he said with a grin. "This could become habit-forming."

"Well—" Once again, Lori was at a loss for a brilliant phrase to roll off her lips. "I'd better get going."

"Okay, then—see you." With a warm smile, Nick jammed his hands into his navy blue wool jacket with white leather sleeves and walked off in the opposite direction.

Wait a minute! she cried silently as he disappeared from view. *Where are you going? You haven't even asked for my phone number!*

Merivale Mall

TWO FOR ONE

by Jana Ellis

Troll Associates

Library of Congress Cataloging-in-Publication Data

Ellis, Jana.
    Two for one / by Jana Ellis.
        p.   cm.—(Merivale mall; #1)
    Summary: Although sixteen-year-old Lori is accustomed to competing
with her beautiful but spoiled cousin Danielle, she fears that her
romance with football star Nick Hobart is doomed when Danielle
decides to take him for herself.
    ISBN 0-8167-1354-5 (pbk.)
    [1. Cousins—Fiction.]   I. Title.   II. Series: Ellis, Jana.
Merivale mall; #1.
PZ7.E472Tw   1989
[Fic]—dc19   88-12384

A TROLL BOOK, published by Troll Associates,
Mahwah, NJ 07430

TWO FOR ONE

CHAPTER ONE

"Hey! Watch out!"

Sixteen-year-old Lori Randall, who had been gazing into Merivale Mall's wishing fountain, looked up just in time to see a boy on a skateboard heading in her direction. Her cornflower blue eyes widened in horror. He was about to run right into her!

But he didn't. At the last possible moment two strong hands grabbed Lori from behind and yanked her out of the way. The boy whizzed past and out of sight down the ground floor promenade of the mall. Just the breeze from his passing sent Lori's straight blond hair flying in every direction. The book she had been carrying went flying too—right into the fountain.

"Oh, no! My book!" Lori gazed in horror as the paperback sank to the bottom.

"Sorry about that," said a soft, deep voice behind her. Startled, she turned and looked at her rescuer for the first time. In that instant Lori Randall's life changed forever.

She was looking up at a boy about six feet tall, with aquamarine eyes, slightly tousled golden brown hair, and muscles that wouldn't quit. He was so handsome that it was hard for Lori to look him in the eye.

"Are you all right?"

"I guess so," Lori answered hesitantly.

"Someone ought to let that kid know this isn't an interstate," he said with a smile.

"Oh, he's just a little boy," Lori replied, finding her equilibrium again. "I have a couple of little brothers at home who are just as crazy."

"Sounds like you like them. Are you sure you're all right?" His masculine voice was full of concern, and his eyes searched hers for an honest answer.

"Yes, I'm sure—thanks to you. I didn't even see him coming till the last second. By the way, I'm Lori. Lori Randall."

"Hi, Lori. My name is Nick. Nick Hobart."

Bong! A bell went off in Lori's head. *Nick Hobart!* Only the star quarterback of Atwood Academy's football team, the Cougars. Only the best athlete in the most prestigious private school in the country. Only the boy every girl in Merivale was dying a thousand deaths to meet. And there he was, talking to *her!*

Lori searched frantically for something to say, but she was totally tongue-tied.

"I work at the mall," she finally said. Why, oh why couldn't she have come out with something brilliant?

"I kind of thought so. It's a little hard to miss. 'Tio's Tacos! Muchos Buenos!' " Nick chuckled as he read Lori's fluorescent yellow apron. The black letters screamed their message.

Lori winced. When she wore her Tio's uniform she had nightmares about ending up as a fashion Don't in a magazine. The situation was doubly insulting since she had taken the job to save money for college—to study design!

"Guess I'm a walking advertisement," Lori said shyly, smoothing down her apron.

"Well, you sure caught my eye," Nick replied with just a hint of a smile. "I work here too. At my dad's electronics store—you know, Hobart's, *High* Tech at *Low* Prices."

Hobart's Electronics, of course! It was directly across the mall from Tio's. On slow nights at Tio's—which meant most nights—Lori and everyone else who worked at Tio's could watch shoppers streaming in and out of the busy shop.

But Lori didn't remember seeing Nick before. She would have remembered him if she had.

"Well," Nick said, clearing his throat and breaking another awkward moment. "Maybe I can fish your book out for you."

Rolling up the sleeve of his blue- and white-striped rugby shirt, Nick reached into the water and picked out the sopping paperback. *"The Old Man and the Sea.* How appropriate," he remarked dryly.

"Yep. Looks like the old man drowned." Lori took the book and tossed it into a nearby trash bin with a mournful laugh. "I have a big test on Monday too. Oh, well, so much for an A in English—"

Just then a clock chimed nearby. "Yikes! I'm supposed to be at work!" Lori cried.

"Well, I'm going that way. Why don't I walk you?" Nick said. "You know, I think both Book-O-Rama and Gold Book Shop are closed on Sunday. What are you going to do about your test?"

"Oh, I'll just have to think of something," Lori answered wistfully. At that moment English class was the furthest thing from her mind.

Hurrying down the mall with Nick, Lori felt a brand-new tingling sensation up and down her spine. For a guy so incredibly good-looking and talented, Nick Hobart was totally down to earth and really sweet.

And she couldn't help but notice the little glances that he kept stealing at her. Was it possible that he liked her—just a little bit? Or was his kindness only a good deed, the kind of thing a guy like him would do for anybody?

With a push of his muscular arm, Nick opened the door of Tio's for her. "Here you go, Lori. Well, watch out for wild skateboarders."

"I will." They stood staring at each other silently for a long, long delicious moment.

"And, uh—well, I'll see you."

"Okay. Thanks again."

Watching him walk off across the mall, Lori couldn't shake the feeling that her knight-in-shining-armor had finally arrived.

Even the odor of overcooked burritos and tasteless tacos couldn't drive the thought of Nick from Lori's mind that evening. Spooning up hot sauce from plastic containers, Lori relived every moment of her rescue again and again. Nick's hands had been so sure, his eyes so caring. And all the while they were together she couldn't help feeling that he liked her.

"Do you realize we had a grand total of ten customers in here tonight?" Ernie Goldbloom, the owner of Tio's, was helping himself to another cup of coffee. He didn't look happy.

"Cheer up, Ernie." Lori began straightening up the storage cabinets under the counter. "It's just the slow season."

"Humph. That's what you said last summer."

Business never did pick up, and anybody who ate Ernie's food knew why. His "authentic" Mexican cuisine was about as authentic as fake fur, and it tasted about as good too.

Still, Lori felt loyal to Ernie and she liked the other people who worked there. It would be a catastrophe if Tio's went bust: Ernie would never be the same, and Lori would have to find another job—far from Hobart's Electronics and the most wonderful boy in the world!

Lori rinsed out the lettuce shredder with a tender smile. Everything about her near-accident had turned out to be fantastic—everything, that is, except her drowned book.

By the end of the evening hard reality had set in. How was she going to pass her English test the next day? Borrowing a book from a classmate was out of the question. Her friends all needed their copies as much as she did. She'd have to do something—but what?

When Tio's finally closed for the night, Lori headed up the corridor to meet Ann Larson and Patsy Donovan, her two best friends at Merivale High.

Both girls also worked at the mall. Ann, a beauty with her long brown hair and startling gray eyes, worked as an aerobics instructor at the Body Shoppe, the mall's exclusive health club.

Patsy, on the other hand, held a less prestigious job. She worked at the Cookie Connection. It was an unfortunate job for Patsy, who had a hard time not eating her wares.

Dashing out into the mall, Lori couldn't stop smiling. Looking around her, she took in the grandeur of the mall as if for the first time. Merivale Mall was brand-new and completely modern. With its four levels, sleek chrome elevators, stone benches, and big leafy trees, the mall was like a clean, restful park.

"Hey, Lori!"

Lori jumped when she heard that wonderful voice behind her. Spinning around, she found herself face to face with Nick Hobart once again. This time, he was holding a copy of *The Old Man and the Sea.* Just looking at him, Lori almost forgot to breathe.

"I thought you might be able to use this," he said, handing her the book.

"Gosh, thanks!" Lori replied gratefully. "Where did you get it?"

"That's my secret."

"You know, that's twice you've saved my life today," Lori told him.

"I'd better be careful," said Nick with a grin. "This could become habit-forming."

"Well—" Once again, Lori was at a loss for a brilliant phrase to roll off her lips. "I guess I'd better get going. I'm meeting my friends."

"Okay, then—see you," he said. With a warm smile, Nick jammed his hands into his navy blue wool Cougars jacket with white leather sleeves and walked off in the opposite direction.

Wait a minute! she cried silently as he disappeared from view. *Where are you going? You haven't even asked for my phone number!*

"Let's face it," said Lori, two weeks later over ice-cream sundaes at The Big Scoop. "He's never going to ask me out."

"Of course he is!" Ann Larson said, her lively gray eyes challenging Lori. "I know Nick Hobart from the Body Shoppe. He works out there in the summer, and he happens to be a terrific guy—but he's just not a wolf, know what I mean? He's probably just slow about these things. Some guys are, you know."

"Right!" freckle-faced Patsy Donovan said, agreeing. "He may be the silent, romantic type. Maybe he's waiting for that one magic moment—" Patsy smiled mischievously and spooned up another mouthful of Death By Chocolate. It was a treat she certainly didn't need. Patsy was pretty, but she was a good twenty pounds overweight.

"Oh, yeah, right, you guys—" Lori ran a hand through her silky pale blond hair. "*Nick Hobart* is waiting for the 'magic moment' to ask *me* out. What a laugh."

But Lori wasn't laughing.

Ann and Patsy exchanged a concerned look. The three girls had been good friends since their freshman year at Merivale High. Now that they were juniors, helping one another out had become a way of life.

"Just because he goes to private school doesn't mean he won't ask you out!" Patsy exclaimed. "And besides, you're pretty gorgeous yourself, Lori, in case you haven't noticed."

"Oh, sure," replied Lori, tearing at her napkin nervously.

"You know, Lori, I was just reading that sixty-five percent of boys polled actually like it when a girl asks them out." Ann Larson tucked a loose strand of chestnut hair back into her french braid. She always seemed to have a million facts at her fingertips. "Maybe *you* should ask *him* out."

"No way, José. What if Nick is in the other thirty-five percent? If he said no, I'd die. I just don't have that kind of courage."

"There is only one girl I know who does," Patsy threw in, with a meaningful look toward Lori. "Your cousin Danielle. She never has a problem asking for what she wants."

"Danielle? She doesn't have to call boys up, Patsy—they're always after her in droves."

"Hey!" Ann said, interrupting. "I've got a super idea. Danielle could ask Nick out *for* you!"

"What?" Lori was incredulous.

"It's brilliant!" Ann insisted. "She goes to Atwood, right? They probably run into each other all the time! And, you know, a little hint here, and a subtle suggestion there. . ."

Patsy wrinkled her nose. "When was Danielle Sharp ever subtle?"

"I think she would help me out, if she could . . ." Lori's mind was ticking.

"Danielle? Help somebody out? Are you two talking about the same Danielle Sharp I know?" Patsy said, amazed.

"Oh, come on, Patsy," Lori countered, "Danielle isn't so bad. She's just—"

"Self-centered? Selfish? A little wrapped up in herself? Do any of those definitions ring a bell?" Patsy asked.

Lori shifted uncomfortably in her seat. "I've known her a lot longer than you have, Patsy, and honestly, Danielle has a sweet side."

Shaking her head, Patsy shoved her spoon into her chocolate ice cream again. "You always think the best of people, Lori."

"But it's true, Pats," Lori explained. "Danielle and I practically grew up together. She taught me how to dive and how to put on eye shadow. It's only since she moved to Wood Hollow Hills and my uncle Mike made all that money developing Merivale Mall that she's been a little— Well, just because she has a lot doesn't mean her life is easy."

"Oh, poor Danielle. She's so-o rich, the poor thing. It must be hard for her, driving that white BMW, going to Atwood, having that gorgeous red hair—"

Lori stood up. "There's just more than one side to Danielle. That's all I'm saying."

"Right," Patsy said, agreeing. "There's the snobby side and the sneaky side. She'd probably use the chance to go after Nick herself!"

"Oh, come on, Patsy. I don't think Danielle needs anybody else in her collection. I would never ask anyone to ask a boy out for me. But if I did ask Dani, I know she would never betray me like that." Would she?

Ann glanced at her watch. "It's almost six!" she announced, standing up and reaching for her jacket. "See you later, guys!"

"I'd better go too, Lori," said Patsy. "Yuck. This huge chocolate-chip cookie I have to wear for a hat has got to be the stupidest thing on earth. And you think *you* have problems?"

"If he would only ask me out," Lori murmured to her friends, only half joking, "my life would be complete."

"Don't give up, Lori!" Ann said before she got on the up escalator on her way to the third floor. "I think he likes you."

"Yeah," said Patsy. "I saw him looking at you the other day as if he were a starving man and you were a hot fudge sundae."

"Oh, you guys," said Lori with a laugh. "You say the silliest things!" But inside, she was wondering if it were true. Oh, if only he liked her—she'd be the happiest girl on earth!

CHAPTER TWO

The pace at Tio's was unusually brisk late that next Thursday afternoon. Soon Lori had no time to think of Danielle, or Nick, or anything except enchiladas and tacos, Cokes, and 7-Ups. After the rush, Ernie was so happy he gave everyone behind the counter a ten-minute break.

Her history book in her hand, Lori planted herself on the bench outside Tio's directly across from Hobart's. But she barely saw the words in her textbook because she kept looking up, hoping to catch a glimpse of Nick.

"Hey, Lori! What's up?" Lori glanced to her right and saw her cousin Danielle. Danielle looked fabulous in an electric blue jumpsuit, covered with zippers. It was perfect with her soft, black leather boots. Lori became miserably conscious of her ugly uniform.

As if she had read Lori's mind, Danielle announced, "I spotted you a mile away. What a color! Do you glow in the dark?"

"Not yet." Lori laughed. "You look great, Dani!"

"Honestly, I don't know how you put up with it," said Danielle. "Too bad you couldn't get a job someplace more interesting."

"Yes, like at one of the boutiques?" Lori mused, imagining herself surrounded by racks of elegant fashions from Facades or even Snazzz.

"If I had to work, I'd think more about an electronics store. You know, like Hobart's." Danielle's gaze was fixed on Hobart's window.

A pang went through Lori. "I didn't know you were interested in electronics, Danielle," she said carefully.

"Oh, well, not electronics, really—" Danielle said, inspecting her long, tapered nails. "Oh, what's the difference? I guess I can tell you. There's this great-looking Atwood guy who works there. His father owns the store."

"Nick Hobart?" Lori replied numbly.

Danielle shot Lori a look of annoyance. "*You* know Nick Hobart?"

"Well, uh, he works right across the way. It would be hard to avoid him." Lori's instincts were shouting at her that it could be dangerous to reveal her true feelings.

"He sits next to me in French," Danielle confided with a dreamy look. "We fool around so much that the teacher threatened to detain us. I wish she'd do it too. I'd love to spend another hour every day with Nick."

It was the worst news Lori had ever heard. No boy could possibly resist Danielle once she set her sights on him. Danielle was fantastic looking, rich, and fun.

"He hasn't said anything, but I think he likes me too," Danielle said, rubbing the bad news in deeper. "The way things are going, I think we'll be the next 'junior class couple.' "

"Wow—" Lori replied tonelessly, her spirits on a crash dive.

Suddenly a voice boomed out at them across the mall. "Danielle! What are you doing!" Danielle's father sounded irritated as he edged his way to the girls through a group of shoppers.

Mike Sharp, older brother to Lori's mother, was the very image of a successful businessman. He was always impeccably dressed and groomed, and the touch of gray in his thick dark hair gave him a distinguished air. His flashing dark eyes helped to reveal his intelligence— and added to his handsomeness. But right then he seemed more frantic than anything else.

"Thank goodness I found you! I waited in the parking lot for half an hour."

"But, Daddy, you said five-thirty." Danielle held up her gold-and-diamond watch. "It's only five."

"I said four-thirty, Danielle, but let's not argue. Did you bring the papers I need for my meeting?"

"Don't worry, Dad." She rummaged around

her calfskin bag and finally pulled out an envelope.

"Great! Next time I mention a time, try to listen. Okay, honey?" He sighed and turned to Lori, wearing his familiar, friendly smile. "How's it going, Lori? Working hard?"

Lori smiled. "Oh, Ernie talks tough, but he's pretty easy on us. Don't tell him I said so."

Her uncle Mike laughed. "Well, I think it's great the way you're learning responsibility and saving for college." He glanced at Danielle with a tolerant smile. "Saving money has never been Danielle's strong point. Maybe your good example will rub off on her."

"Oh, Daddy." Danielle sighed, rolling her emerald green eyes skyward.

"Gee, Uncle Mike, it's just a job," Lori said.

"No need to be shy with us, Lori. We're all family. And we're all very proud of you. As a matter of fact, I've been thinking about you and your situation, and I have a proposition for you—whatever is in your savings account by your birthday, I'll double for you as your present. But you've got to put in at least two hundred dollars before then. How does that sound?" He spoke to Lori, but he was looking at Danielle, whose eyes were wide with disbelief.

"Oh, Uncle Mike, I can't let you do that. That's too big a gift!"

"Don't think of it as a gift, Lori," said her uncle Mike. "I won't. It's an investment in the

future of my family, and you're going to be a
living example of the value of honest hard work.
What do you say?" He grinned at Danielle.

"Sounds fantastic!" Lori didn't know what
else to say. *Double my savings!* Her mind raced
ahead to the extra hours she'd have to put in
before her birthday so she could earn as much
as possible. All of a sudden, college was close.

"So—it's a deal!" Mike Sharp thrust out his
hand and they shook on it.

Danielle glared angrily at her father, her
green eyes narrowed dangerously. "Aren't you
late for your meeting, Dad?" she asked icily.

He glanced down at his watch. "Right you
are. I had better be going. See you girls," he
said, winking as he headed for the escalator.

"Bye, Lori," Danielle said frostily. "Don't
work *too* hard." She walked into Hobart's.

Back at Tio's, Lori rushed to Ernie's office
to sign up for extra hours. Fortunately, one of
the crew was taking the next weekend off, so
she hurriedly signed on for her hours.

Business was slow during the dinner hour,
so Ernie asked Lori to help Stu Henderson, the
cook, take inventory. Lori was glad for the break
in her routine, even if it meant counting tomatoes in the huge, walk-in refrigerator. After only
a few minutes, however, she began to shiver.

Stu looked up from his clipboard. "Wait a
second. I hear tap dancing," he said.

"Um, I think it's my teeth chattering," Lori
said. With that, she sneezed.

"Gesundheit." Stu looked at her with concern. "Why don't you grab a cup of tea and take a break? I'll tell Ernie. I'm sure he wouldn't want you to get frostbite."

"Thanks, Stu." The last thing she needed was to get sick—not now when she had those extra hours to put in.

Her Styrofoam cup of tea in hand, Lori walked out into the mall. Moving quickly past the storefronts, she came to an unmarked door that most shoppers would never even notice. She pulled it open just enough to slip in. The door opened onto a stairway that led down to what Lori thought of as the secret, underground world of Merivale Mall. It was a great place to sit and think.

On that lowest level were the underground passageways and loading docks where trucks made their deliveries. Lori often felt as if she were backstage at a theater when she went down there. It was a shadowy, mysterious place that the public never saw, but without which the mall couldn't function. She walked over to a stack of wooden crates and sat down.

"Hey, lady! What do you think you're doing?" a gruff voice demanded behind her. "That crate ain't no lounge chair. There's some very expensive electronic stuff in there."

Lori jumped up, expecting to see a security guard, until she focused on Nick's grinning face.

"Oh, it's you!" Lori laughed, relieved and

happy to see him. "I wasn't really sitting on anything important, was I?"

Nick shook his head, smiling. "They're empty." He strolled over and sat down on one, gesturing for her to sit next to him.

"Taking a break?" he asked.

"I was counting tomatoes in the walk-in refrigerator and all of a sudden, I just—" Without warning, Lori was overtaken by another huge sneeze.

"Gee, that doesn't sound good," Nick said. "Here, why don't you wear my jacket for a while, until you warm up?"

"I'm okay, honest." It was true. The tender look in Nick's eyes made Lori feel ten degrees warmer.

"Sure you are." Nick pulled off the jacket and slipped it around her shoulders. "That's why your arms are covered with goose bumps. There—doesn't that feel better?"

Lori nodded. Nick's jacket was still warm and it smelled faintly of spicy after-shave. "Thanks." She held her cup of tea with both hands, suddenly shy again. *Why is it that in my daydreams Nick and I have such great conversations, but when we're actually face to face my mind goes totally blank?*

"How's the Atwood football team doing?" she asked, searching for a topic of conversation, even though she always checked the newspaper for the score after an Atwood game and knew exactly how well Nick's team was doing.

"Fairly well," Nick said modestly. "But our toughest game of the season is a week from Saturday. If we win that one, we have a good chance of taking the title."

"Well—good luck," said Lori. She didn't know much about football, but since she had met Nick she'd been taking a crash course from her brothers and her father. "You'll just have to keep scrambling, Nick," she said.

Nick grinned and cocked an eyebrow. "Whatever you say, coach," he said, teasing her. "When we beat the Vikings next week, I'll tell everyone that I was just 'scrambling' like Coach Randall told me."

Lori laughed. "Oh, I really don't know the first thing about football," she admitted shyly.

"That's okay. Maybe I can explain it to you sometime." He was sitting very close to her on the crate, looking into her eyes in a way that made her catch her breath. The silence grew, and she wondered if Nick was waiting for her to say something.

Lori rushed to fill the silence. "By the way, you know my cousin—Danielle Sharp."

"Danielle is your cousin? She's in my French class." He threw her an unreadable look, and for a second he looked as if he were about to say something else. Then, instead, he glanced at his watch.

"Lori," he said. "I've got to get back to work in a minute, but there's something I've been wanting to ask you. Are you busy this Saturday night? I mean, I was wondering if you'd like to go to the movies, or something."

This was it! This was the moment she'd been waiting for! He finally had asked her out! Lori's heart started beating so fast that she thought she'd fly right off the crate.

Sitting up a little straighter, she held the jacket around her shoulders and smiled. *Wait until Patsy and Ann hear about this!*

"Oh, Nick. I'd *love* to see you Saturday night," Lori answered happily. Then a little black gremlin crawled into her brain. She had just volunteered to work extra hours on Saturday night! There was no way to get out of it.

Her heart in her mouth, Lori turned to Nick. "Oh, this is terrible. I just remembered I have to work on Saturday night."

"Really?" Nick sounded disappointed.

"I'd change it if I could," Lori said quickly. "But I really can't."

Nick shrugged. "Well, don't worry. I understand. How about— "

"Hey, Nick! Your dad wants you upstairs, pronto," a Hobart stock clerk called from the top of the stairway.

"Tell him I'll be right there," Nick called. He turned to Lori and sighed. "Guess I'd better be heading back up. Maybe I'll see you later," he said, lightly hopping down off the crate.

If only we hadn't been interrupted! Lori had

hoped Nick would suggest another time for their date. But it was too late now. "Don't forget this." She jumped down beside him and slipped the jacket off her shoulders.

"You can borrow it for a while if you want."

Lori was tempted. *What would Danielle do if she saw me waltzing around in Nick's Cougars jacket?* she asked herself. *Probably murder me,* she thought with a wry smile. But it might be worth it, just to see the expression on her face. "No, you'd better take it back now. I don't know when I'll see you again," she said truthfully.

Nick looked at her for a long moment. "Well, we'll have to do something about that," he said.

He took back his jacket and waved briefly, then leapt up the stairs two steps at a time. Lori watched him disappear into the darkness. She felt suddenly chilled again, but it wasn't because his jacket was no longer around her shoulders. A new thought had entered her mind.

Now that she had turned Nick down for Saturday night, would it become Danielle's big chance? Would Nick ask Danielle out?

There was nothing Lori could do but wait. Wait, and hope that Nick would ask her out again before he fell for the beautiful and charming Danielle.

CHAPTER THREE

"What do you think?" Danielle asked, just to be polite. She knew she looked great as she twirled in front of the three-way mirror at Facades. The fawn-colored skirt and blousy, belted top were stunning, and the soft suede showed off her figure to perfection. Danielle's dazzling smile grew even wider when she saw the envious look on Teresa Woods's face.

"There's something about suede," Teresa was murmuring. "You get this irresistible urge to touch it."

"Which is *exactly* the idea," Danielle said with a wicked grin.

"Okay, Danielle, what's the story?" Teresa raised an eyebrow as they walked back to the changing room. "You've been on a shopping spree since last Thursday night. Don't tell me it's because you're still mad at your father."

Teresa took out a comb and began working

on her thick, shoulder-length brown hair. Her long swoopy bangs seemed to highlight her chocolate brown eyes. A smattering of freckles dotted her upturned nose; Danielle loved to tease her about them. Even though Danielle was a redhead, she didn't have a single freckle, which really annoyed Teresa.

"Oh, that tiff with my dad was nothing," Danielle replied. "I was annoyed so I got some new clothes to put me in a better mood." Danielle still cringed inside to think of how her father had totally humiliated her in front of Lori. Why did he always hold her cousin up to her as a paragon of virtue? After all, Lori *had* to work, and Danielle didn't. It was that simple. *He* was the one who made the money, after all.

Ever since the day she ran into her cousin, Danielle couldn't help suspecting that little Lori was more interested in Nick Hobart than she had let on. What girl wouldn't be? Not that Danielle was worried. After all, she was Danielle Sharp—who always looked great, acted outrageous, and got any guy she wanted. Nick Hobart just happened to be next on her list. That was why she had spent the weekend shopping. She was stockpiling an arsenal of great-looking outfits. And suede was the best ammunition of all.

"Come on, Danielle. Who's the lucky guy?" Teresa demanded. "You can't fool me. I've seen you in action too many times."

"Well, I'll give you a hint—he's a real hunk, and the best player on the Cougars."

"Ben Frye?" Teresa asked, alarmed. Ben played wide receiver for the Cougars, and Teresa had had a crush on him for ages. "If it is, you've just lost yourself a friend."

"Oh, calm down, Teresa," said Danielle with a laugh, pulling on her own black knit pants and aqua, angora sweater. "I'm not going to tread on your turf."

When Danielle had transferred to Atwood from public school, Teresa Woods and Heather Barron were the first girls of the in-group who had accepted her. There was no way she would cross either of them. They could freeze her right out of Atwood society if they wanted.

"Besides, I said the *best* player on the Cougars. *Everyone* knows it's the quarterback."

"Since when did you become an expert on football, Danielle?" Teresa asked. "No, let me guess. Since you decided to go after Nick Hobart?" The relief in Teresa's voice was obvious.

"Touchdown, Ms. Woods." Danielle gave Teresa an innocent, wide-eyed stare as she brushed out her hair. "You know, you're really not as dumb as you look," she said teasingly.

"And you're not as smart as you think," Teresa said back in a voice dripping with honey. "I wonder if you're smart enough to get Nick Hobart."

*   *   *

"Lori? Didn't you hear me?" George Randall looked at his daughter with an amused smile. "I said, 'please pass the potatoes.' "

Looking up with a start, Lori passed the bowl down to the other end of the table. "Uh, sorry, Dad."

"Nice to have you back. You looked like you were in another world there," her father teased. He managed to maintain a sense of humor with his children even though he was the principal at Merivale Elementary School.

"Lori's in the ozone again," eleven-year-old Theodore, the family clown, said. "Another case of taco fallout!"

"Now, Teddy." Lori's mother stopped him with a warning smile. Cynthia Hobart, who was a registered nurse, had the same blond hair and good looks as Lori. She rarely used makeup, but her bright gray blue eyes projected sparkle and energy nevertheless.

"Your sister has a lot of responsibilities these days," Lori's mother said, continuing. "School and a job, and now this offer from Uncle Mike. It's a lot to think about, right, Lori?"

"You talking to me, Mom?" Lori was having trouble thinking about anything these days—anything but Nick Hobart. She couldn't stop wondering if he would ask her out again, and worrying about Danielle going after him while Lori was helplessly ringing up tacos. Orange

polyester couldn't compete with Danielle's vast
wardrobe, and her charm, and her BMW—

Up in her room after dinner, Lori put a
record on the stereo and set up her drawing
table. If anything could take her mind off Nick,
it was her artwork. She was designing an album cover for her graphic arts course at Merivale
High, and it was almost finished.

She inspected her work with pride. Ms.
Cavanaugh, her teacher, always loved her projects and said that Lori had a natural flair for
design since she was sensitive to color and perspective and had an orderly mind. Lori also
was a talented seamstress. She could whip up
her own designs so well that even Danielle would
ask enviously, "Where did you get that dress?"

Lori knew that she didn't impress most
people as the artistic type. Only her close friends,
family, and teachers knew about her dream—to
be a fashion designer. When she was sketch-
ing a dress design or creating a new piece of
jewelry in the metal shop, she was lost in a
very special, private world that she wouldn't
reveal to just anyone. She could escape her
concerns about school, about work—about everything.

Well, almost everything, she thought as she
looked more closely at the album cover. The
lead singer in her pastel drawing bore an amazing resemblance to someone. It seemed that
there was no escaping Nick Hobart.

*   *   *

The same thought echoed in her mind the next day at lunch with Ann and Patsy. "I haven't seen him or heard from him for a whole week. He's probably not used to being turned down. Maybe he ran straight into Danielle's arms. With her in the picture, I don't know what's going to happen." Lori sighed and pushed a forkful of macaroni and cheese across her plate.

"He'll ask you out again." Ann tried to assure her. "It sounds like he really likes you."

"For a guy who likes me so much, he sure has a funny way of showing it. Why hasn't he even peeked into Tio's once? Maybe he's too busy helping Danielle *parler francais*."

"Hey, wait a minute," Patsy piped up. "Just because your cousin has the advantage of going to Atwood doesn't mean you have to hand Nick over to her on a silver platter."

"Patsy's right, Lori. Remember, he asked *you* out—not Danielle," Ann said, reminding her.

"But that was last Thursday. What am I supposed to do now?" Lori moaned. "I never even see him unless we run into each other at the mall. Which isn't very often. The next time I see him, he and Danielle will probably walk hand in hand into Tio's and order twin tostadas. It's enough to make you lose your appetite." Lori dropped her fork on her plate with a sigh.

"Speak for yourself, Lori," said Patsy, crunching a handful of potato chips. "Maybe you could arrange to run into him, you know, accidentally on purpose? What does he like to do? Where does he like to hang out when he's not at school or at work?"

"He's on a football field, practicing. Thank goodness it's too late for Danielle to join the cheerleading squad," Lori replied.

Ann's gray eyes lit up with inspiration. "But it's not too late for *you* to be a cheerleader, Lori—for one particular Cougar quarterback, I mean. The Cougars are playing the Vikings Saturday at Atwood. It's the perfect chance to see Nick."

"Hmmm—you're right," Lori murmured thoughtfully. "I know it's an important game. Maybe if he sees me there, he'll know I like him."

"You'll have to talk to him after the game too, silly," Patsy said. "That's the whole idea. You've got to dazzle him. Think of what Danielle would do. Fight fire with fire."

"Hey—wait a minute! Don't I have any say in this at all?" Lori asked, laughing.

"No!" Patsy said firmly. "Don't worry. You'll thank us later."

"Are you both planning on coming with me?"

"Of course we are. We wouldn't want you to chicken out at the last minute," Ann said.

"We'll be over tomorrow afternoon to help you pick out something to wear."

"Nothing too obvious," Ann said cautiously. "I don't think Nick goes for that type. Let Danielle overdo it. You just be yourself. We could fool around with my new makeup though. Just to bring out your eyes. And maybe a little peach blush."

"Hey, wait a second! I thought I was supposed to be myself," Lori said.

"Relax." Patsy patted her hand. "When we're finished, you'll just be yourself—but utterly irresistible."

CHAPTER FOUR

"I don't understand it! How can he resist me?" Danielle slammed down on the brake and pulled her car into the Atwood Academy student parking lot. She, Teresa, and Heather had sneaked off the school grounds for lunch and were just returning for the afternoon classes.

"Look at this dress." Danielle tugged at the apricot cashmere creation, which had cost a small fortune and looked as if it had been designed for her. "Todd Schaeffer was practically *drooling* on my desk in homeroom. If the neckline were any lower, I'd be sitting in the dean's office right now."

"It's pretty hot all right," said Heather.

"Well, as far as Nick Hobart is concerned, it might as well be a burlap sack." Danielle pouted.

All through lunch, Heather and Teresa had listened to Danielle pour out her heart about

Nick. It seemed she had finally met a guy she couldn't twist around her little finger. Her friends listened patiently to her problems, but one or two times she thought she saw them smirking at her. *Well*, Danielle had thought, *I'll just have to show them.*

"Too bad there aren't any parties coming up this weekend," Heather said, fingering one of her dangling silver earrings. "You can't really get Nick's attention at school. You need to get him alone, in a more relaxed, romantic atmosphere. You know, low lights, slow dancing."

Danielle glanced at Heather, a wicked smile slowly replacing her frown. "That's it! A party! Flirting in French class is kid stuff," she said, scoffing at herself. "But at a party things could *really* heat up."

"Well, maybe," Teresa said. "But there's one small problem. No one we know is having a party any time soon."

"Oh, yes, someone is," Danielle retorted quickly. "The most popular hostess at Atwood Academy is going to throw the *bash* of the season this Saturday after the football game. The Cougars will definitely beat the Vikings, and Nick will be ready to celebrate—at my house."

"And what guy in his right mind could resist a beautiful girl, ready, willing, and able to help him?" Heather added in her whispery, sophisticated voice.

"Exactly. Saturday morning's the game. Saturday afternoon's the party, and Saturday night, who knows?"

"By Monday morning, it will be all over school that you and Nick are going out," Teresa said gleefully. "By the way, I hope you invite Ben Frye too."

"Yeah, and Rob Matthews!" Heather said. Heather had a crush on Rob, who had transferred to Atwood in September. His family had moved to Merivale from California and he spent a lot of time complaining about Merivale, which he considered a "hick" town. His goal in life was to be a movie star and to live in Beverly Hills. Of course, those things made him perfect for Heather. With her long, glossy black hair and blue eyes, Heather was the richest and the most sophisticated of the three friends.

"*First* on my invite list is Nick," Danielle said. "I'll see him in my next class."

"I *hate* to bring it up, Danielle, but what if Mr. Wonderful turns you down? What if he's busy or something?" Teresa asked.

Danielle frowned. Teresa could be such a bore sometimes. "Oh, he'll be there," she said confidently, smoothing her long, thick hair. "You'll see."

The three girls emptied out of Danielle's car and walked up to the stately brick school. The nineteenth-century structure had white columns in front of its ivy-covered walls and tall, arched windows. Atwood reeked of status and prestige, and Danielle adored every detail.

Time for some serious flirting! In French, Danielle grabbed a seat next to the one that Nick usually took. To her horror, he came in late and took the first empty seat he saw. Madame DuChamps stood at the front babbling about a verb tense or something while Danielle looked at Nick. He was too far from Danielle for her even to pass a note.

When class ended, Danielle quickly maneuvered herself into Nick's path. "Hi, Nick. Too bad you got to class late. I saved a seat for you. Did you have a problem?"

"Oh, hi, Danielle," he answered in a distracted tone. "As a matter of fact, I've got a big problem. My car died this morning just as I pulled into the lot, and it still won't run after I worked on it all through lunch. Now I've got to call my father and let him know I'll be late for work. Check out these hands!" He laughed. "I look like a real grease monkey."

"That's too bad," Danielle said sympathetically. "Cars can be such a pain. But I'm going to drive to the mall later. I'd be happy to give you a lift."

"That'd be super. If it's no trouble."

"No trouble at all, Nicky." With that, she flashed him her sexiest smile. *If only you knew,* she thought. "Just meet me in the parking lot after school. Do you know my car?"

"A white BMW with a license plate that says SHARP 1?"

"That's right." Danielle smiled, pleased that he had noticed. "See you later."

As usual, history class dragged for her. Who cared about the past when the present was so exciting! When the bell rang, Danielle dashed out and went straight into the restroom. She brushed her hair to its wild best, retouched her eyeliner and lip gloss and spritzed her wrists and neck with the Fallen Angel in her purse atomizer. Her father had hit the roof when she bought it, but obviously he didn't know a good investment when he sniffed it!

Nick was already leaning on her car, his arms folded loosely across his chest, when Danielle strolled out of the school. He waved, and she made her way down the steps. Fantastic! Now everybody would know that they were leaving together. That thought alone was thrilling.

"Hi! Hop in—the door is open," said Danielle, easing into the driver's seat. "How was chemistry?"

"The usual." Nick laughed, folding his long, lean body so it would fit into the passenger's seat. "Rob Matthews tipped over a Bunsen burner and nearly set the place on fire."

So Heather's true love was a total klutz. "And I'll bet Mr. California didn't even blink an eye," Danielle said sarcastically, starting up the engine. "Rob is so *totally* mellow. Nothing short of a forest fire could get him excited."

"Oh, he'll get over that act," Nick said. "It's not easy being the new guy in town. He probably misses San Diego."

How sweet! Leave it to Nick to be nice even to that jerk. "Oh, of course. I know," she said, agreeing. "But he does tend to act sort of above it all, and I just have no patience for snobs."

Nick glanced at Danielle with a curious look in his eyes, but it quickly disappeared. "Thanks for the lift. If it weren't for you, I would've ended up taking the bus."

"Horrors! We couldn't let you do that!" Danielle couldn't remember the last time she had taken public transportation. It had certainly been a long time, before her dad had made all his money. Now, she could hardly imagine a worse fate—except maybe *being seen* taking public transportation.

"Would you believe my cousin Lori doesn't even *have* a car. She takes the bus every day. I don't know how she can stand it."

"I don't think she'd let it bother her," Nick said, his eyes wandering out the window.

Danielle gritted her teeth. Why had she ever brought up stupid Lori? What a dumb thing to do! "So, Nick," she said, changing the subject, "what are you going to do with all your free time once football season is over?"

"I guess the Christmas crunch will be starting up, and I'll be working more at the store. It really gets wild. I'm lucky my dad is so understanding about all the time I have to practice now. He's a real Cougars fan, I guess."

"Isn't everybody?" Danielle asked him with her most sincere, wide-eyed look. "Speaking of which, I'm going to throw the biggest victory celebration Atwood's ever seen after the game on Saturday. I'm inviting the whole team!"

Nick looked surprised at Danielle's sudden outpouring of school spirit. "That's great."

"Can I count on the star player being there?" Danielle graced him with another thousand-watt smile.

Nick looked embarrassed by her lavish praise. "Everyone on the team plays hard."

"Oh, don't be so modest, Nick," Danielle said, scolding him with a smile. "Just say you'll come. It will be a great party. I promise."

"Okay. How could I let down such a big fan? Now, let's just hope we win."

"How could the Cougars lose with Nick Hobart calling the plays?" Danielle asked with a dazzling smile. "Here we are! I'll drop you off here so you won't be late and then I'll go park."

Nick shook his head shyly and reached for the door. "Thanks again for the lift, Danielle."

"Anytime," she said brightly. "See you tomorrow." With a wink and a wave, Danielle pulled away from the curb. In the rearview mirror she noticed that he stood a long time on the sidewalk, watching as she went to park. That made her victory even sweeter.

CHAPTER FIVE

"Oh, no! I can't look," Lori said, covering her eyes. "Somebody tell me what's happening."

The crisp, fall day was perfect for football, and the bleachers at Atwood Academy were filled. With a roar, the crowd came to its feet, faithfully cheering the Cougars, who were down five points with two minutes left in the game.

"Nick has the ball," Patsy said. "He's moving back. He can't find anyone to pass it to. Oh, no. He's going to be tackled again."

"Not again!" Lori moaned. Her eyes flew open and she searched the field. When he came into view, she sighed with relief. "Look, he got away! He's making a pass!"

"What a beauty," Patsy yelled as the football moved in a long, graceful arc down the field. The ball met its mark with breathtaking precision. The receiver carried it quickly over the goal line to score a touchdown, and the crowd went wild.

"I can't believe it!" Ann yelled above the noise as the extra point was kicked. "Nick just won the game!"

The three girls jumped up and down in the bleachers, cheering until their voices were hoarse. Lori scanned the field for a glimpse of the star player. There he was, jumping up and down on the field, being hugged and playfully swatted by the other Cougar players.

"Way to go, Hobart!" Lori screamed, but she knew Nick couldn't hear her.

Within seconds the final gun sounded. Everyone poured onto the field and ran toward the Cougar bench to congratulate the team.

Lori wore a pink-and-white-striped cotton sweater, brand-new pink knit pants, and a lavender jacket. She had looped a lavender-and-pink scarf around her neck and had hot pink sunglasses perched on top of her head. "You look just like the quarterback's favorite girl," Patsy told her as they stepped off the bleachers.

"There he is!" Ann said, running out onto the field. "Now's your chance, Lori."

"Better hurry," Patsy said, urging her forward. "Those Atwood girls are swarming around him like hungry piranhas."

It was true. Nick *was* surrounded by fans. Most of whom, Lori noticed with a sinking heart, were beautiful girls from Atwood. Danielle was first in line, clinging to Nick and planting a kiss on his cheek. Lori couldn't bear it. She turned away, her spirits sinking low.

"I don't think I could get within twenty feet of Nick right now—not with all those female bodyguards around him," she told her friends. "Maybe I'll see him around the mall later this weekend. I can congratulate him there."

Ann and Patsy exchanged a look. "Hey, you didn't come all this way so you could talk to him at the mall," Patsy whispered frantically.

"Listen, I know you guys went to a lot of trouble, and I know you think I'm chickening out—"

Ann wasn't listening. Suddenly she pushed Lori backward, directly into someone.

"Sorry—" Lori apologized before she saw the person she had collided into.

"Lori," said Nick with a smile, holding his arm out to steady her. "What are you doing at a Cougars game?" His hair was damp and curly, and his skin flushed from exertion.

Lori shot a glance at Ann when she realized what had happened. Then she tried to collect herself. "I, uh, came with some friends—"

But when she turned again, Patsy and Ann were out of sight. Lori turned back to Nick and swallowed hard.

He was still holding on to her arm and gazing down at her with a tender smile. "Thanks for coming, Lori," he murmured. "This means a lot—" Suddenly she couldn't breathe. *This is sheer heaven*, said a voice inside her head.

"You were wonderful today," she said finally, floating back to earth. "That last pass was spectacular."

Nick broke out in a shy smile. "Just a lucky toss," he said modestly. "I missed being sacked by an inch—until I remembered what you told me."

"What *I* told you?" she said with a surprised smile. "What was that?"

"You know," he said. "About 'scrambling'?"

Lori blushed. That was the last time she'd try to throw around words she didn't understand just to impress somebody! "Is that what you were doing?" she asked. "The only kind of scrambling I really know about is with eggs."

"Well, the Vikings' defensive line is known for turning quarterbacks into mashed potatoes," he said with a laugh. "That team hits pretty hard."

"Yes, I noticed," replied Lori carefully. "You didn't get hurt out there, did you?"

He looked at her warmly, touched by her concern. "Not a bump. I've got more padding on me than a grizzly bear." With that, he gave his shoulder guards a resounding *thwack*. "As a matter of fact, it takes me almost an hour to get in and out of this get-up."

Glancing around, Lori could see that they were practically the only ones left on the field. "I don't want to keep you, Nick. I mean, I'm sure you want to get cleaned up and everything."

Nick gestured at the streaks of mud and

the grass stains on his torn jersey. "What's the matter? You embarrassed to be seen with me?"

Lori couldn't tell him that no guy had ever looked better to her than the Cougars' battered, but victorious, quarterback did at that moment. So she reached out and picked a clump of sod off his jersey instead. "I just hate it when guys are so fussy about their clothes."

Nick laughed. "Well, would you dare to be seen with this walking mud puddle at a party this afternoon?"

"A party?" Lori's sky blue eyes lit up with delight. Nick was really asking her out again! She hadn't missed her chance. "Oh, I'd love it!" she answered, offering a silent thanks to Patsy and Ann.

"Great, I'll just shower and change. Wait right here for me." He took both of her hands in his. "Okay!"

Lori couldn't think straight for a second. Everything was happening so fast. And it was all so wonderful. "I'll be right here," she said. Too soon, he let her hands go and headed for the locker room.

"Wait! Where is this party?" she called out to him as he trotted toward the door.

Nick turned back to her with a quizzical look. "Don't you know?" he asked. "At your cousin Danielle's!" He waved and turned away.

At Danielle's! Lori bit her lip. Danielle was not going to be pleased.

Just then Patsy and Ann magically reappeared at her side. "What happened?" Patsy asked eagerly. "You were talking to him for such a long time."

"He asked me to go to a party with him," said a dazed Lori.

"Fantastic!" Ann shouted.

"At *Danielle's* house," Lori said.

"Whoa!" exclaimed Ann. "I hope you can handle a wild tigress!"

Patsy shrugged. "She can't do anything too horrible in front of Nick." *Or could she?*

"Oh, hi, Nick! Great game!" Ann said a little too loudly. Lori turned to see Nick right behind them. He had changed into a pair of faded jeans, a red flannel shirt, and a denim jacket. He looked more handsome than ever.

"Hi, Ann. Glad you could come down for the game."

"It was terrific. And I'm Patsy Donovan— Lori's friend," Patsy said. Nick smiled and nodded. "Merivale better watch out next month." The Merivale High and Atwood football teams had a long-standing rivalry.

"Can't say we didn't warn them," Nick said pointedly. "Meanwhile, I'm going to steal your friend from you for a few hours." He glanced at Lori with a grin. She met his gaze, then looked away quickly.

"She's all yours," Patsy said in a tone that

caused Lori's peaches-and-cream complexion to turn bright pink.

"Well, we have to go," Ann said, tugging at Patsy's sleeve. "See you."

"Yeah—so long," Patsy said, taking Ann's not-so-subtle cue.

As the two girls walked away, Nick took Lori's hand. "Let's go," he said. "The party can't start without us."

Walking hand in hand with Nick, Lori couldn't help but smile. The fall breeze blew her hair back as she hurried to keep up with Nick's long strides. His hand clasped hers so firmly—nothing had ever felt so safe or so perfect to her before.

Now I really do feel like the quarterback's girl, Lori told herself happily.

But on the way to Danielle's, Lori got a few fluttery butterflies in her stomach at the thought of facing her cousin. Danielle could be impossible to handle when she was crossed.

"The entrance on the left," she said, directing Nick as he drove to the end of the quiet street where Danielle lived. The houses in Wood Hollow Hills couldn't be seen from the street but a sign on the wrought-iron gate where Lori was pointing announced, THE SHARPS.

Nick turned up the long shady drive, and soon the gigantic house came into view. The modern design featured light, natural wood with glass windows over its entire three-story height.

A wide deck stretched across the front of the house.

When he pulled into the circular driveway, Nick let out a low whistle. "Wow! Some house. Looks like something in a magazine."

"It was," Lori said lightly. "It was in *Beautiful Houses* last year. My uncle is so proud of the place. There's a double-level deck in back, which leads down to a terraced garden, an in-ground pool, and tennis courts."

"I can see why he's proud," said Nick, obviously impressed.

What if seeing Danielle on her own fantastic "turf" would win Nick over? Lori worried. After all, Nick did go to Atwood. He was probably a lot more comfortable in a place like this than he ever would be at Lori's modest ranch home.

"Looks like we're late," Nick said, taking her hand and walking toward the house. "Hope you don't mind making an entrance."

"I don't know—" Lori replied, doing her best to smile confidently at him. "I've never made one before. But I guess there's always a first time for everything. . . ."

CHAPTER SIX

"Hi, everybody. This is Lori Randall," Nick announced to his teammates as he and Lori stepped onto the deck. "I figured with you guys around I'd get desperate for some intelligent conversation, so I kidnapped Lori."

"Hi, Lori." A chorus of rough voices answered.

"Nice to meet you, Lori," said Ben Frye, a stocky, dark-haired boy. "Listen, when you get tired of this guy's bad jokes, just holler."

Lori laughed. Maybe not everyone at Atwood was like Danielle's crowd, after all. "Oh, I don't know—his jokes aren't *that* bad." Lori glanced up at Nick with a teasing glint in her eye.

With that Nick put his arm loosely around her shoulders. Its warm strength began to melt away her fears, although she couldn't help but peek around to see where Danielle was. *Please don't let go, Nick,* she silently pleaded.

"Looks like you've got the good stuff right here, Lori," said a snide whisper behind her.

Startled, Lori whirled around to face Heather Barron's catty smile. *Who else would have the nerve to say something like that to me,* thought Lori.

"Excuse me?" Lori asked sweetly.

"Oh, no excuses necessary," Heather said in a drawl. "But you'd better live it up while you can. Here comes our hostess, and she's going to be very surprised to see you with her date."

Danielle had just emerged from the wide sliding glass doors. Her outfit was absolutely fabulous—a suede top and skirt that fit like a second skin. Lori had seen it in the window at Facades, and knew it cost a small fortune.

With her luxurious red hair cascading in waves over her shoulders, Danielle was undeniably beautiful. And the spark in her emerald eyes only heightened her attractiveness.

Lori stared straight ahead while her stomach turned to jelly. Nick was chatting nonchalantly with Heather about the game, and Lori watched Danielle approach as if she were waiting for a bomb to drop.

"There you are, Nicky!" She greeted Nick with a bright smile, ignoring Lori completely. "I almost thought you weren't coming. After you promised me you would, and everything." Her tone implied that it wasn't all he had promised.

"Well, here I am," Nick said with an innocent shrug. Lori noticed that although he still stood close by her, Nick had taken his arm from her shoulders the moment Danielle appeared. "I brought along somebody you know too."

"Yes— Hello, Lori," Danielle replied, her voice dripping with honey. "I thought you'd have to work today. Isn't that matching fund good only until your birthday? My father is helping Lori save for college," Danielle told Nick.

Lori felt heat and color rising in her cheeks. She hadn't told Nick about the deal with her uncle. And the way Danielle was putting it, Lori suddenly felt like a poor relation!

But when Lori looked at him, Nick was smiling proudly at her. "Your uncle offered to double your savings? That's great! He must have a lot of confidence in you!"

Almost imperceptibly, Danielle's eyes rolled upward. "Oh, he does!" she said. "He's very proud of her. She practically holds that tortilla stand together singlehandedly, you know."

Lori tried to laugh off her cousin's sly insults. "Don't worry, Danielle. Tio's won't fall apart if I'm not there for a few hours. As amazing as that might seem to some people."

"Oh, Lori." Danielle's laugh was high and hollow. "You always have such a great sense of humor. Doesn't she, Nick?"

"I think so," Nick said.

"Well, I guess you have to, in order to

work in Taco-land." Danielle sighed. "Even the food there is a joke. By the way, I ordered some stuff from Rio Grande," she said, mentioning an expensive restaurant near Wood Hollow Hills. "There's guacamole and shrimp tamales. You really should try some, Lori. Maybe you can give poor Ernie some helpful hints."

"Sounds great. Maybe I will."

Danielle seemed to be backing off, Lori thought with relief.

"All the food is inside. And while Lori's eating, I want to introduce you to a few friends of mine, Nick." Danielle twined her arm through his and began to lead him away. "They were all in the group I traveled through Europe with last summer. They're dying to meet you."

"Sure, I'd like to meet your friends, Danielle," Nick said, and Lori's heart fell. "But I'm kind of hungry too. I think I'll grab something to eat first with Lori." He glanced backover his shoulder at Lori, who was determined not to act as possessive as Danielle had.

"Oh, that's okay—I'll be fine. I want to take my jacket off anyway," Lori said, forcing a smile as Danielle tugged Nick away. Then Lori quickly turned and walked inside, her heart pounding. Maybe it was best to give up right then, before everything got messy.

The buffet table was filled with delicious things to eat, but none of it looked very appetizing to Lori.

Maybe she had been wrong to run away from Nick like that. But what was she supposed to do? Grab his *other* arm and pull? She wouldn't exactly have gotten a lot of help from the other Atwood girls. It was clear from the looks on their faces which girl they thought should be on Nick's arm. *And they've all known him a lot longer than I have,* she reflected.

Lori walked out on the deck and surveyed the scene. Danielle was standing at the center of a circle of her friends, her arm still linked through Nick's. Her guests were hanging on her every word—Nick included, it seemed.

And Danielle was loving it. She was laughing and tossing her wild mane of hair from side to side, with all the grace of a model in a shampoo commercial.

I don't belong here, thought Lori. *Nick does—he fits right in—but I don't.* She was about to leave for a walk in the garden when she felt a tap on her shoulder.

"Hi, Steve!" said Lori enthusiastically after she turned around. Steve Freeman worked in the mall at Shoe Hut. Although she barely knew him, she was glad to see a friendly face.

"Lori, there you are. Hi, Steve." Nick walked up beside her just as she was about to say, "How are you." "I've been looking for you. I guess you've eaten already, huh?"

"I wasn't really hungry," she said, avoiding his eyes.

"Well, I am. Let's go see what's left," he said, leading her away from Steve with a friendly nod. "Then we'll find someplace nice and quiet to sit—someplace where no one will bother us."

"I see two empty chairs over there," Lori replied.

So, he thought Danielle had been bothering them! That was certainly a good sign. Her mood lighter, Lori even smiled at Heather, who walked toward her carrying a huge tray of barbecued spareribs. But Heather seemed to be looking the other way—

"Oh, my gosh! I'm so-o sorry!" Heather squealed as the two girls collided. For a moment Lori stood as still as a statue, unable to believe what had happened to her. Looking down, she saw that her worst fears had come true. A slow, sticky river of barbecue sauce ran down her clothes and her skin. A chorus of snickers and giggles surrounded her.

"Lori! Are you all right?" Nick stared at her, wide-eyed with shock.

The pity in his voice was almost more than she could bear. "I'll be all right," she muttered, futilely wiping at her shirt with a sticky napkin.

"So clumsy of me," Heather cooed, pressing her hand to her forehead.

"I'll say," Nick replied through gritted teeth. "*Unbelievably* clumsy, if you ask me."

"Oh, dear, looks like someone had an accident!" Teresa Woods cheerfully strolled up and stopped beside Heather with a smirk. "Heather, you bad girl! That's what you get for cutting ballet class."

"I'll get something for you to clean up with, Lori," Nick said, glaring at the two Atwood girls as he stalked toward the house.

"Bring a bathtub, Nick," Teresa snickered.

Heather giggled. "Or an order of fries."

"Very funny!" Lori said, looking down at her new pants. Suddenly she felt a flood of tears rising in her eyes. She quickly turned and ran down the steps. A path through the trees led down to the pool and cabana. As Lori ran down the gravel walkway, the sounds of the party began to fade. Finally she reached the cabana, which her aunt and uncle kept as a guest apartment. The door was unlocked, and Lori went inside. She used some towels and wiped off her slacks.

Her new sweater was a total disaster. Lori took it off and wiped at the sticky mess, but the stains only grew larger. Her eyes were now brimming with tears, and she finally gave up cleaning her shirt and stuffed it in her bag. There were always clean sweatshirts in the changing room: Lori found one and put it on.

Then she picked up the phone and dialed Ann Larson. She was in luck—Ann and Patsy were both there.

"I'm at Danielle's. Do you think you could come get me?"

"Lori, what's wrong? Are you hurt? Is Nick all right?"

Lori took a deep breath and fought back a sob. "I'm okay—it's just—oh, Ann, I don't belong here. I want to go home."

"Hang on," Ann said. "We'll be right over. Should we meet you there?"

"No!" Lori gasped at the thought of the entire crowd watching her leave in shame. "I'll meet you at the corner where Danielle's street meets Wood Hollow Road."

"We're on our way!" Ann said.

Lori left the cabana with the sweater still tucked inside her bag. She cut through the wooded part of the yard, staying as far from the house as possible, wiping the stinging tears from her cheeks.

How had it happened? How had the very best day of her life so suddenly turned into the very worst?

CHAPTER SEVEN

"Stretch! Twist! Kick! And again! Come on, ladies, I want you to *really* work!" Ann urged on her class of leotard-clad girls and women. The music on the portable tape player urged them to jump to its lively beat.

"Okay, last time. Stretch! Twist! Kick! Very good!" Ann walked over to the tape player and turned it off to a chorus of grateful groans.

"Next week we're going to move to the advanced routine, so fasten your seat belts."

"It's about time. I get more of a workout shopping than you've given us so far," Danielle complained as the class filed out of the studio.

"My grandmother could lead a better work-out than the one we just had," Teresa said.

"Well," Ann told them, hiding her annoy-ance, "if you want to work out some more, I'm willing."

After what they had done to Lori at the

Cougar victory celebration, Ann was more than willing to give them a workout. "Should we start with your *hips*? That seems to be a trouble spot for all of you," she murmured sweetly.

While Danielle, Teresa, and Heather frantically inspected their bodies in the mirror, Ann strolled over to the tape case and picked out a cassette labeled "Level V, Intensive Jazz."

As she bent over to load the cassette, she felt a tap on her shoulder and turned to look into the face of Isabel Vasquez.

Also a junior at Merivale High, Isabel had transferred from Texas at the end of her sophomore year. Her big brown eyes were framed by long, thick lashes. She wore her long black hair in a ponytail that hung straight down her back. Isabel had won free classes for a year at the Body Shoppe in a promotional contest.

"Excuse me, Ann," she said in a soft voice, marked with just a hint of an accent. "Do you mind if I stay too?"

"Sure, Isabel," Ann said. She lowered her voice. "You can show these guys just how out of shape they really are."

"Thanks. I've got lots of frustration to work off today. I've been all around the mall looking for a job, but *nobody* has an opening."

"Gee," Ann said thoughtfully, "I might have three aerobics students I'd be willing to turn over to you."

"No, thanks!" Isabel said as she turned to find a place on the exercise floor.

"Ready?" Ann asked, standing in front of the group and winking at Isabel. The music built quickly in tempo and volume. "Just watch me and do *exactly* what I do."

For the next ten minutes Ann gave her special students a workout they would never forget. Her lithe body jumped, kicked, and twisted at top speed, finishing one exercise and moving straight on to the next.

Danielle was the first to give up. Dressed in a white leotard and pink leggings, she lay back on the carpet like a broken doll. "Enough!" she gasped. Heather and Teresa nodded.

"Are you sure you want to stop so soon?" Ann asked innocently. "I wouldn't want you girls to think we don't give a good workout at the Body Shoppe."

"It was great," Danielle said. "But I don't want to get too muscular, you know?"

Ann rolled her eyes. Danielle had an answer for everything.

"Besides, I want to save a little energy for other things today," Danielle said, continuing. "Like the Nautilus equipment. Right, Heather?"

Heather looked across the room. Ron Taylor, the handsome Nautilus instructor, was adjusting the weight on the leg-curl machine.

"Oh, no, we can't miss the Nautilus today, can we, girls?" Heather asked, checking her hair and makeup in the mirrored walls.

"I'm first in line for the leg-curl machine,"

Teresa said. Making a miraculous recovery, she bounded up from the floor and headed for Ron.

"Good riddance," Ann muttered.

Isabel laughed as she walked away. "Glad I could help," she said as she headed for the locker room.

"Hi, Ron," Teresa cooed to the dark-haired, muscular instructor. "Could you hold my ankles down while I do some sit ups?"

"If you want to work on your abdominals," Ron replied without smiling, "I've got just the machine for you. That one right there." He pointed to one of the stations that was empty. "Get started, and I'll be over in a few minutes to see how you're doing."

"Maybe you could come with me right now. I'm not sure how to set the weights."

"Just like the other machines." He was marking a chart on a clipboard. But Teresa noticed that his attention wandered to the aerobics area. Another session was starting with Ann as the instructor.

"I just took one of Ann's advanced classes," Teresa said, bragging.

Suddenly Ron took some interest in the conversation. "She really makes you work, doesn't she?"

"Oh—uh, sure," Teresa said unenthusiastically.

"But you know, if you just took an aerobics

class, maybe you shouldn't work on the machines. It might be too much."

Just then, Heather strolled over. "I've seen Ann Larson use the Nautilus after she's given two or three classes in a row," she said.

"Ann's different," Ron said, glancing again at the chestnut-haired instructor. "You just can't compare yourself with her. She's got the greatest—uh, muscle tone." Blushing, he looked back at Heather and Teresa. "It's better not to overdo it when you're a beginner."

The two girls exchanged furious glares. "Looks like it's time to hit the showers," Teresa said to Heather, grabbing her towel.

"Beginners! Can you believe it?" Heather said as they walked into the locker room.

"Oh, let's just get out of here and head for Cookie Connection," Danielle said. "I need some sugar-shock."

The girls sat at one of the umbrella-covered tables clustered in front of Cookie Connection to make it look like an outdoor café. Opposite Cookie Connection stood the Video Arcade, and next to it was Merivale Drugs. But most important, from their table the girls had a clear view of Hobart's, diagonally across the mall.

"Truly the place to see and *be seen*," Heather said as they dropped their tote bags and sat down.

At a table in the back of Cookie Connection, Lori watched Patsy munch her way through a pile of chocolate-chip cookies on her break. If she kept eating that way, Lori feared Patsy would soon be as wide as she was tall!

"Let me get this straight. You haven't seen him or heard from him since the party on Saturday?" Patsy inquired between mouthfuls.

"He did call my house a few times," Lori said. "But I just couldn't bear to talk to him." She still felt mortified every time she thought of herself covered with sticky sauce while Nick stared at her with pity. "I embarrassed him in front of all his friends, Patsy. I'm sure he's just calling to make sure I didn't die of humiliation. He must have seen just as clearly as I did that I didn't belong at that party with him."

"You think that's why he's calling? Because he doesn't want to be seen with you?"

"He just feels sorry for me, Patsy. That's all." Lori swished the ice at the bottom of her glass around with a straw. "Besides, I'm sure Danielle didn't leave his side for the rest of the party. You should have seen the two of them together, even when I was there." Lori shook her head. "I'm like a square peg in a round hole with his friends. Danielle is perfect for him."

"Oh, come on, Lori. It couldn't have been that bad." Patsy tried to console her.

"It couldn't, huh? Let's put it this way, if somebody had captured the events on film, my first and *last* date with Nick Hobart would have made a great disaster movie."

Patsy suddenly looked as if she had seen a ghost. "I can't believe who just walked in," she said, staring at the front of the store.

"Who?" Lori started to turn her head to look, but Patsy stopped her.

"No! Don't let him see us! It's Steve Freeman. You know, the Atwood guy who works up at Shoe Hut." Patsy sighed. "Don't you think he looks like a model?"

"To tell you the truth, Pats, I never really thought about it."

"I think it's his eyes," Patsy said, getting a dreamy look in her own. "Oh, forget I said anything." Her tone changed abruptly as she threw down a cookie. "A guy like Steve wouldn't look twice at me."

"Come on, Patsy. Don't put yourself down." Patsy did have to take off some weight, it was true. But Lori loved her bright, funny, straight-talking friend, and hated to hear Patsy criticize herself that way.

"No, you're right," Patsy said, joking. "He'd *have* to look twice—just to see all of me!"

"Well, maybe you should try to change that," Lori gently suggested. "You have such pretty curly hair, and such gorgeous hazel eyes. With your personality, guys could be falling all over themselves to ask you out."

For once, Patsy didn't have a clever come-back. "Really think so?" she murmured. "I don't know. I've tried dieting before."

"Maybe you never had a good enough reason to stick to it before."

"Well, Steve Freeman may be the perfect reason to get skinny," Patsy announced, pushing the plate of cookies away from her side of the table. "That's it. I'm *psyched*. From now on, no chips pass these lips."

Oh, never mind the ladies' room, Teresa thought. *This news is far more important.* She raced back through Cookie Connection to the table outside.

"You'll never believe what I just heard," she told Heather and Danielle as she slipped back into her seat. "That tub!" She burst out laughing. "It's just so painfully ridiculous."

"What tub? What are you laughing at?" Danielle asked.

Finally Teresa got control of herself. "Someone was in the ladies' room when I went back there, so I had to wait," she explained. "I was standing by those big plants, and I overheard two girls talking about Steve Freeman."

"Who were they?" Heather asked. A slow smile spread across Teresa's pretty face.

Moments later the three girls were rocking with laughter. "Can't you just see it?" Heather said. "If Patsy Donovan ever tried to kiss him, he'd be crushed!"

"He'll ask her out if she loses some weight." Teresa snorted. "That'll be the day!"

"Anything's possible," Danielle said seriously. "How long do you think it would take a person to lose a thousand pounds?"

"I just got the greatest idea," Heather announced wickedly, her silver bangles rattling against the table. "Why don't we play cupid for poor, lovelorn Fatsy-Patsy? We can set her up with Steve. Wouldn't that be fun?"

"But Steve wouldn't go out with her in a million years," Danielle said.

"Of course not." Heather agreed. "But he might go on a blind date if he thought it was with someone he really liked."

"Oh, Heather, you're brilliant," Teresa said, gushing. "Can you imagine the look on his face when he finds out he's stuck with Patsy Donovan for the night? What a laugh!"

Danielle never would have admitted it, but she didn't think Heather's humiliating idea was so wonderful. It was embarrassing to have your cousin have a tacky friend like Fatsy-Patsy, but there was no point in making Patsy's life even more horrible than it already was.

"What if Steve doesn't agree to the blind date? We don't even know who he likes," Danielle said.

"I know who he likes," Teresa piped up. "But you're not going to like it. I overheard him talking to some guys at your party, and he said he thought your cousin Lori was cute."

Lori again. Danielle couldn't figure out what boys saw in those everyday looks and that sticky-sweet personality. Somehow, boys seemed to find Lori attractive in spite of all that.

Danielle had hoped for smooth sailing with Nick after Lori disappeared so suddenly on Saturday. Except that Heather's scheme had backfired, and minutes after Lori took off Nick went after her. But Danielle had heard from a couple of guys on the football team that Nick hadn't talked to Lori since then, so the plan had been at least partly successful.

But still, as she thought about Nick speeding away to rescue his pitiful sweetheart, Danielle's anger bubbled to the surface. *So, he likes good old cousin Lori, eh?*

She thought of what Steve Freeman's face would look like when he realized his date was not with Lori Randall, but with Patsy Donovan. It made Danielle giggle with pleasure. "So where do you think our two lovebirds should begin this romantic evening?" she asked.

CHAPTER EIGHT

"Kids, the bottom line is, I'm going broke."

Ernie Goldbloom leaned back in his chair and ran his hand nervously over what was left of his thinning hair. "If business doesn't pick up soon, I may have to lay off a few of you."

Everyone was silent. "How soon?" asked Judy Barnes, another part-time employee who went to Merivale Community College.

Ernie glanced down at the pile of ledgers on his desk. "I'm not sure. Tio's Tacos might not even make it to Thanksgiving if things keep going the way they are now." He sighed. "And I had the big turkey taco promotion planned too. It would have been a beauty—"

Ernie shut his eyes, no doubt imagining some lucky employee, dressed as a turkey in a sombrero, gobbling his way around the mall.

Lori's heart sank. She knew business was bad, but she had no idea that Tio's was in such desperate trouble. She really needed her job. She hadn't noticed many Help Wanted signs in the mall lately. And even if she found another mall job, it was so huge that she might not ever see Nick again. Not that it mattered now. It might just be better to be far away from him, where she'd never have to be reminded of Danielle's party or worry about seeing Nick and Danielle together.

During her break Lori went down to the mall's lower level. She walked past the place where she had met Nick to a spot on the far side of the loading dock. No one would be able to find her here—except perhaps Nick. Not that he'd look for her.

But Nick did find her.

"There you are," he said breathlessly. "Lori, I've been trying to speak to you for days! What's going on?"

I'm trying not to think about you, she answered silently. "I've got a big exam this week, I've had to cram every spare minute," she said out loud.

"Lori—I want to know why you ran away from the party on Saturday," he said. "Why didn't you wait for me?"

"I was a mess. I couldn't stay, not looking like that." Her chest tightened. She knew she'd start crying if he stayed much longer and made her continue talking about that afternoon. "Anyway, it doesn't matter now."

"It matters to me. I wanted to take you home."

"I didn't want to make you miss the rest of the party because of me." *Or embarrass you any more than I already had in front of your friends and Danielle*, she thought. "Danielle gave the party for the Cougars."

"I missed it anyway. I left to look for you." His look changed abruptly. "If you bothered to answer my calls you'd have known that."

"I'm sorry." Lori looked up at him. Her heart was going to break into a million pieces. Why couldn't he just leave her alone? She and Nick just weren't meant to be. Danielle was perfect for him, and he was the only person who didn't see it.

"Lori, I just don't understand." Nick took a step closer. "You're mad at me, aren't you?"

"No! Of course not," Lori replied quickly. "It's just that—I have a lot on my mind right now. Ernie is thinking about laying off some people."

"That's terrible, Lori. I had no idea. If I can do anything, please let me know," Nick said.

"There's nothing any of us can do," Lori said glumly. "But, Nick, I really *do* have to study."

There was no point in trying to explain what was really bothering her. Better to let him think she was cold-hearted. Maybe it would speed up things between him and Danielle. Then Lori could get back to her friends and school and her job and forget she had ever met Nick Hobart.

"Okay, Lori, I won't bother you anymore." He walked away, pain and confusion in his eyes.

When Lori was sure he was far away, she covered her face with her hands and cried.

Shoe Hut was just about to close when Danielle, Heather, and Teresa strolled in. Danielle picked up a pair of pale pink ballet flats, then put them down before Heather and Teresa thought she would actually shop there. They bought all their shoes at The Bootery, a shop on the third level that carried more expensive brands.

"Do you ladies need some help?" Steve Freeman approached them in his most professional manner.

"We just dropped in to say hello," Danielle replied. She gave him her hundred-watt smile. She didn't really like him, but he was good-looking, and it was always smart to keep in practice.

"Oh, Steve," Teresa cut in. "I probably shouldn't be telling you this, but I know someone who is dying to go out with you."

"Really? Anyone I know?" Steve asked casually as if that sort of thing happened to him every day.

What a joke, Danielle thought. He really was an arrogant creep. Glancing in a mirror, he straightened his gray knit tie. He wore a tweed sports jacket and a deep blue shirt that brought out his dark eyes. His dirty blond hair shone to perfection. *Very good-looking, but still a creep.*

"Well, you kind of know her. She's pretty hard to overlook."

Heather started to snicker, but winced as Teresa elbowed her.

The fish was nibbling at the hook. "Hard to overlook, huh? Does she work at the mall?"

"Uh-huh. But I'm really not allowed to say who it is." Teresa gave Steve her most sincere pained look. "Please don't try to make me tell. I never should have said anything."

"You don't have to tell me her name. Just let me ask a few questions," Steve pleaded. "Maybe I can guess. Does she go to Merivale High or Atwood?"

"Merivale. Oh, please don't ask me any more questions."

Steve grabbed hold of her arm. "Hey, wait a second. How about just giving me an initial?" he begged. "What about L? Does her name begin with an L?"

"You mean Ann Larson?" Teresa replied, thinking quickly.

"No, I meant Lo—"

"Please!" Teresa covered Steve's mouth with her hand. "I *promised* not to say who it is!"

"Okay. Calm down. I think I already know who it is anyway," he said smugly.

"Listen. All I can say is that she works in the mall, she goes to Merivale, and she is very good friends with Ann Larson. But it is not Ann Larson," Teresa said, dangling more bait.

"No, it's Lori Randall!" Steve said with a huge grin on his face.

Teresa covered her ears with her hands. "I didn't hear that, Steve," she said in a stern voice. "I told you, I'm not allowed to tell you if you're right or not. But, if you want to go out with—this person, I can arrange it."

"Forget it," Steve said eagerly. "I'll ask her myself."

"Oh, no! Don't do that," Teresa said insistently. "Just leave it all to me. This person is very, uh, shy. I don't even think you should talk to her between now and the date."

"Not even talk to her?" Steve said. "I don't get it."

"Trust me." Teresa laid her hand on his shoulder and gave him a confidential look. "If you come on too strong, she won't go through with this."

"All right, whatever you say," Steve said, agreeing eagerly. "But let's make this date soon. How about Friday night? Ask Lo—"

"Steve!" Teresa interrupted, scowling. "Don't breathe a word of this to anybody. Don't even say her name out loud. She wants this to be secret and romantic. Just between you two."

"Just between us two, huh?" Steve had an eager gleam in his eyes. "Okay, whatever she wants. Tell her I'll meet her in the mall at O'Burgers on Friday at six o'clock."

Amazingly, Teresa kept a straight face. "You just leave everything to me," she said.

"Hi, Patsy. What's up?" asked Lori, flopping down on her bed with the phone cradled in her shoulder.

"Are you sitting down?" Patsy asked breathlessly. "You're not going to believe this! Teresa Woods called and said Steve Freeman wants to go out with me!"

"Steve Freeman what?" Lori couldn't hide the shock in her voice. "He wants to go out with *you*, and he asked *Teresa* to call?"

"Teresa said Steve's shy. They're good friends, see," Patsy explained. "It's for Friday night. We're meeting at O'Burgers. Teresa said he wants it to be secret and romantic. Just between the two of us. I shouldn't even be telling you or Ann. Teresa made me promise."

After what had happened on Saturday, Lori didn't trust Teresa or anyone else in the Atwood crowd. She was still suspicious, but Patsy was ecstatic. She couldn't bear to be the one to poke a hole in Patsy's dream balloon.

"You've got to help me, Lori. Picking out clothes and makeup—all that stuff. I've got to look perfect. I have to go now. I'm going to work out tonight with an exercise tape Ann lent me. I only have till Friday, and every day counts."

After Lori hung up, she wondered if she should call Teresa and find out what was going on. But what if the whole thing were true? She might end up ruining everything by prying. Patsy would never forgive her.

Maybe Steve really did like Patsy, but he just didn't want his friends to know because they would tease him about her looks. Maybe. But she couldn't shake the feeling that Patsy was headed for big trouble.

By Friday Patsy had managed to lose three pounds. On Thursday night she had gone shopping with Ann in Benson's, the largest department store in the mall. On Ann's advice, she had picked out a blue green dress in a silky fabric that highlighted her pretty hazel eyes and drew attention away from her figure problems.

After school Ann and Lori went to Patsy's house to help Patsy get ready for her date. They did her eyes in a smoky blue shadow and brought out her cheekbones with a pale blush. Her reddish brown natural curls glowed with golden highlights, brought out with the help of a special shampoo. With a dab of styling mousse and the blow dryer, Lori tamed Patsy's flyaways and gave her a more polished look.

"And to think," Patsy said, examining her new look, "the only kind of mousse I used to think I needed was chocolate."

"We're not done yet. Go put on your dress so we can pick out the right lipstick," Ann said.

"I'll be back in a second." Patsy took the dress into the bathroom.

While Patsy was changing, Lori sat on the edge of the bed and paged through a magazine. "You're so quiet today, Lori. I thought you'd be happier for Patsy," Ann said.

"I am happy for her. It's just that I have this funny feeling." Lori tossed the magazine aside. "I don't trust Teresa and her secrets."

"Don't let Patsy hear you say that," Ann warned her in a tense whisper. "You'll really hurt her feelings."

Lori was just about to say something more when Patsy twirled into the room. "Well, what do you think?"

She looked wonderful. Whether the date was a trick or not, maybe once Steve saw her, things would work out anyway.

"You guys aren't saying anything." Patsy

was strolling around the room as if she were a runway model. "Is that good or bad?"

"You've left us speechless, Patsy Donovan." Ann leaned over and gave her a hug. "You're a knockout."

Taking a deep breath, Patsy entered O'Burgers. She made her way through the maze of tables shakily; she wasn't used to wearing high heels. Finally she spotted Steve at a table next to the salad bar.

"Hi, Steve," Patsy said brightly. She cleared her throat and took a seat. "Sorry if I'm late."

"Late?" Steve looked at her with a puzzled, annoyed expression. "I think you've got the wrong table or something. I'm waiting for a date." He pulled up his sleeve to check his watch. "She'll be here any minute."

Patsy gulped. A horrible, icy fear was rising in her. She prayed that she had heard wrong. "Excuse me?" she said quietly.

Steve sneered and began speaking slowly, as if Patsy didn't understand English. "I said my date will be here soon. So please take off." Patsy could only stare. Steve grunted. "Do I have to draw a picture?"

Patsy struggled for breath. "Is this some kind of joke?" she managed to ask.

"I was about to ask you the same thing."

"What about our date?" Patsy said, her voice trembling.

"A date? With *you*?" Steve's voice got so loud that people at other tables were turning to look at them. "This is a joke! Come on, tell the truth," he said nastily. "Did Teresa and her friends put you up to this?"

"N-nobody put me up to anything," Patsy stammered. "Teresa called me and said you wanted to—" She broke off. Why explain? It was obvious Teresa had played a terrible joke on both of them. "Oh, never mind." She pushed her chair back from the table and picked up her purse. "I thought you were different," she said. Her eyes burned with tears. "But you really are disgusting, Steve Freeman!"

"Hey, who do you think you're talking to?" Steve demanded. "I can't believe this—"

She heard him muttering as she turned and hurried away, her vision blurred by tears.

Lori's night at Tio's was pretty routine. The mall was crowded with shoppers, but few of them stopped for Mexican food.

Tio's employees normally took advantage of a slow night to fool around and gossip. That night, though, everyone was quiet; Ernie had just laid off Judy Barnes, and they were all wondering who would be next.

"Lori, I have to talk to you." Lori looked up and saw Patsy, dripping wet, at the counter.

"Patsy! What happened? Look at you. You're soaked!"

"It's raining outside. I just didn't want anyone to see me after—after I left O'Burgers," Patsy sobbed. "So I went for a walk."

One look at Patsy was enough to make Lori forget about her problems. Her hair was plastered to her head in damp ringlets. Her eye shadow and mascara had melted to blue and black smudges that streaked her cheeks. And her new dress was splotched with rain.

"Come with me." Lori stepped out from behind the counter and pulled her friend through the swinging doors and into the kitchen. She opened her locker and gave Patsy a sweatshirt. "Wasn't Steve there?" she asked, expecting the worst.

"The creep was there all right. Looking as good as ever. But he wasn't expecting me, and he didn't waste any time saying so. It was all a joke. A mean joke. Can you believe it?"

"Oh, Patsy, don't cry." Lori put her arm around her friend's shoulder. "Steve Freeman is a conceited jerk. He isn't worth it, honest."

"I told him he was disgusting," Patsy said and sniffed. "But if I weren't such a hopeless mess, he wouldn't have acted that way."

"How could you possibly blame yourself? It's Teresa's fault. I'm sure Heather was in on this too. They've got to be the meanest people alive—with the possible exception of Steve."

"Those two Barbie dolls aren't going to get

away with this. I'll get back at them if it takes me years," Patsy said.

Lori knew how heartbroken Patsy was. She had been so thrilled, so determined to change her image and make it work with Steve Freeman. She only hoped all that determination wouldn't turn in a dangerous direction.

"Hello?"

Nick's voice sounded impatient and out of breath—as if he had had to run to answer the phone. For a moment Lori lost her nerve.

"Hi. It's me, Lori. I'm—uh, my mom told me you called?"

"Oh, Lori, great! I didn't expect to hear from you. Your mother said you were working until ten."

"I got home early. Not too many people were in the mood for tacos tonight. The mall was pretty quiet."

"Really? I haven't been over there in a few days. It's inventory time, so my dad asked me to work at the warehouse on Route Thirty-two. What a drag."

Lori breathed a sigh of relief. So he hadn't been avoiding her. He had just been busy.

"That's too bad," she said sympathetically. "Will it take very long?"

"About another week. It's not so bad. I get to drive the fork lift around all night. That's kind of fun."

Lori laughed. Then there was an awkward silence.

"So how did you do on the test?"

"Test?" Lori didn't know what he was talking about.

"You know, the one you were so worried about when I saw you."

"Oh, that. It went okay," Lori said, recalling the thin excuse she had given for not wanting to talk to him.

"Listen, Lori," he said in a more serious tone. "I just wanted a chance to say that I was sorry the party was such a drag for you. But I was really glad you came to see the game."

"I'm glad I went too," she said.

"Maybe you'd like to come to an Atwood game again sometime?"

No! an inner voice told Lori. *Leave things as they are. It's better for everyone.* But another voice answered Nick. "That would be great," she heard herself say.

"We're playing at other schools for the next few weeks," he told her. "But I'll let you know when we'll be at Atwood again."

"Okay. I just need enough notice to get the day off from work."

After she hung up the phone, Lori changed into her robe and floated into the shower.

Nick still liked her after all! After everything that had happened at the party, after everything she had said to him the other day.

Maybe the differences between them didn't have to keep them apart after all.

Earlier that evening Lori had heard two girls talking about Atwood's Harvest Ball. It was the first dance of the year at Atwood, held at the Wood Hollow Hills Country Club.

As she rubbed shampoo into her hair, Lori imagined herself in an elegant silk gown, her hair arranged in a striking, upswept style as she walked into the Harvest Ball on Nick's arm.

"Oh, *please* let it come true," she said out loud with her eyes squeezed shut. If only she weren't so sure that Danielle was making the exact same wish.

CHAPTER NINE

"Can you imagine the look on her face? If only there had been a hidden camera someplace!" It was already Tuesday, and Teresa hadn't shut up since Friday night.

Thank heavens there wasn't, Danielle thought darkly. *We'd be watching a video right now.*

"Are you sure Steve Freeman's not looking for a way to get back at you?" Danielle asked as she steered her BMW around a tight corner. "He doesn't seem like he'd take kindly to being made a fool of."

"Oh, Steve isn't mad at me. Not anymore, anyway," Teresa said airily. "We had a long talk, and he really thinks it was a great joke."

"What about Patsy Donovan?" Danielle asked with an edge to her voice. "Did you have a long, chummy heart-to-heart with her too?"

"Of course not. Don't be ridiculous."

Danielle pulled her car into the fast lane.

Teresa was such a bore at times. Danielle wondered why so many girls were dying for her just to say hello to them. And Danielle had a weird feeling that nobody had heard the last of this trick. Least of all Teresa.

"Gee, Danielle. You're driving a little fast, don't you think?" Teresa asked nervously.

"Here's a red light," Danielle said, squealing slightly to a quick stop. "Get out and take a bus if you want."

Teresa's laugh was forced. "Very funny. You weren't really going that fast," she said hastily.

"Thanks, *Mom*," Danielle replied. The light changed, and she put the car into gear, easing off the gas pedal a little.

"So, anything new with you and Nick Hobart?" Teresa asked. "I saw you talking to him in the hall today."

Danielle frowned and pressed the pedal a little harder. Mentioning Nick was not the way to get back on her good side. Danielle was the one who had been doing most of the talking. Nick was showing no sign of being interested in her. Nothing like this had ever happened to her before.

"Things are coming along according to schedule," she told Teresa.

"So you're sure he'll be asking you to the Harvest Ball?"

"Without a doubt." Danielle sounded far

surer than she actually felt. "I'm already shopping for a dress."

"Tickets have been on sale for a week, you know." Teresa glanced out the window.

"I know," Danielle said sharply. "I go to the same school as you, remember?"

Teresa just laughed. "Don't get all bent out of shape, Danielle. When do you think he's going to ask you?"

"Probably by the end of the week. Maybe even sooner. We're supposed to talk tonight."

"Maybe even tonight, huh? Well, make sure you call me first," Teresa said. "I always said he liked you better than that nerdy Lori."

"Lori's not a nerd," Danielle snapped. "She's just—kind of wimpy. Oh, I don't know—" Everything seemed to be rubbing her the wrong way that day.

They pulled into the mall parking lot, but instead of parking the car, Danielle drove to a spot by the entrance.

"You can't park the car here. It'll get towed."

"I'm not parking. I'm just letting you off. I don't feel like hanging out today. Heather's working out at the Body Shoppe this afternoon. She'll take you home."

Teresa knew Danielle's moods, and she knew better than to argue with her. She didn't know what had put the volatile redhead in such a wicked state of mind, but she was happy to stay out of her way. Grabbing her purse, she opened the door and got out. Danielle put the car in gear and raced out of the lot.

Driving around aimlessly for a while, she would have even settled for Christine's company. Christine was her nineteen-year-old sister who was away at college. Danielle thought of how gorgeous her sister was and decided she didn't really need her around then.

Finally she decided she was hungry, so she pulled up to a fast-food joint and placed an order at the drive-through window. A few minutes later she was parked in front of the restaurant, unwrapping the sandwich.

Just as Danielle bit into her hamburger, she got the feeling someone was watching her. She picked her head up and looked around, but no other cars were parked nearby. When she went to take another bite, she suddenly found herself inches from a pair of big, brown eyes that gazed longingly through her window. When the dog realized it had finally gotten Danielle's attention, it began to whimper, shifting its weight from paw to paw.

"Go away," she said through the glass. "You're not getting any of this, so forget it."

As if she had understood her completely, the dog threw back its head and began to yowl, which sent its ears flopping crazily in all directions.

"Oh, give me a break!" Danielle put her hands over her ears.

Suddenly a man was knocking on the passenger side window. Danielle pressed a button and lowered the glass. "Hey, miss, you want to put your dog back in the car there? My little girl is scared of dogs, and we've got to get back to our car."

"It's not my dog," Danielle told him.

"What?" The man cupped a hand around his ear. "I can't hear with that barking. Listen, it's not me. I'm not afraid of dogs. It's my little girl. She's terrified of them."

"Hey, that is not my dog!" Danielle shouted at him.

"Daddy! Make her take it away!" the little girl holding the man's hand started wailing. Danielle couldn't even hear herself think anymore.

She flung open her door and stood looking down at the dog with her hands on her hips. "Hey! Knock it off!" she told the dog.

The dog stopped barking instantly. It stood and wagged its long, scruffy tail. Then, before she knew what was happening, it scooted past her and jumped into her car. "Hey! Wait a second!" Danielle spun around, nearly knocked off her feet.

"Thank you." The man picked up his daughter in his arms and carried her over to his car.

Danielle got back in the BMW and looked at the dog. It stared back at her alertly, perched in the passenger seat. The dog's face was the friendliest one she had seen all day.

"You're pretty pleased with yourself, aren't you?"

The dog gave a quick, whimpering yawn.

Danielle shook her head. She had always wanted a dog, but her mother had absolutely forbidden it. She was convinced that a pet would turn her spotless house into a barnyard.

But Danielle still *imagined* having a dog—a Russian wolfhound, or an Afghan with long silvery fur, or even a big white standard poodle. She glanced over and took a good look at her present canine companion. It wasn't exactly what she had had in mind. Its golden brown fur was matted and dull. It looked about three-quarters golden retriever—the other quarter, anybody's guess. From the way it behaved, it must have been somebody's pet once. But it obviously had been lost or abandoned for a while. It wore no tags, or collar.

Danielle broke her burger into pieces and put it on the foil wrapper. The dog gulped it down hungrily, and Danielle had to take the paper away from her before she ate that too.

"You're still hungry, aren't you?" Danielle asked, patting her head. The dog lay down on the seat and gave Danielle's hand a timid lick. Then she wiggled herself over the gear shift and rested her head in Danielle's lap.

"Oh, boy," Danielle said. "Okay, you can come with me. But this isn't going to be easy. You'd better promise to do everything I say."

Danielle started the car and pulled out of the parking lot. "So, what are we going to call you—dog?" she asked cheerfully. If the mutt had been even half-decent looking, she could have thought of a hundred names.

Oh, what was the difference? She could call it whatever she wanted. In fact, she recalled, she had just seen a Garbo classic. Hmmm— It might be kind of funny to call her Garbo. Maybe the elegant name would encourage the scruffy, starved-looking stray to improve her style a little.

"We're almost home, Garbo," Danielle said, trying out the name. It did have a certain ring to it. "Now remember, Garbo, we have to sneak up to my room without a sound. If anybody catches us, it's all over."

Danielle drove her car up the long driveway, passing a blue van that said Premier Caterer on the side in gold lettering. Her mother used Premier for all her dinner parties—Danielle wondered who was coming that night.

She could hear her mother's voice in the kitchen, directing traffic. At least the caterers would provide a diversion, so she could sneak Garbo into the house.

Quietly, she hustled the dog in through the front door and up the stairs to her room, then coaxed her into the adjoining bathroom and closed the door. Until she got Garbo cleaned up, Danielle didn't want the mangy beast sprawling on her sofa or on her white down quilt. But she wanted to get the dog some more food before she gave her a bath.

Now was the perfect time to snoop around the kitchen to swipe hors d'oeuvres. She quietly slipped out the front door again, then went around to the kitchen entrance as if she had just gotten home.

"Hi, Mom. I'm home," she announced over the racket.

"Oh, hello, dear," her mother quickly replied. She turned her attention back to the caterers. "It's nearly four o'clock, and nothing is set up yet." Mrs. Sharp sighed with exasperation, running her perfectly manicured fingertips through her short, styled hair. "If only we lived in a big city, life would be so much easier."

Ever since her husband's business had grown and she had begun to travel more, Mrs. Sharp had become convinced that Merivale was just too small a town for them.

It was only a matter of time, Danielle thought, before her father gave in and moved his business to a place her mother considered "civilized."

"Do I have to eat dinner with the company tonight?" Danielle asked. "I have a ton of homework." She opened the refrigerator to search for goodies for Garbo.

"Yes, you do. And I want you to wear the pink knit dress we bought in New York. None of that leather stuff. Your father left instructions to make sure you dress—appropriately."

When Danielle was forced to show up at dinner against her will, she had been known to retaliate by appearing dressed like a punk rocker, or something from another planet.

"I hate that dress, Mom. I told you that when you forced me to buy it. Pink is not my color." Danielle pulled out a chair and sat down to sulk. "And the people Daddy invites are always so boring."

"Oh, come on now, sweetie. They're not so bad. These people have a son your age and are bringing him along. Maybe you know him. He goes to Atwood."

"Really? Who?"

"It's the Hobarts—Richard and Marge, and their son, Nick. Excuse me for a minute, will you, dear? These delivery people are impossible." She disappeared out the back door.

Nick Hobart is coming here for dinner! Danielle jumped out of her seat and let out a whoop of joy. Of all the unbelievable luck! Grabbing hors d'oeuvres for Garbo from the carefully arranged platters, she bounded up the stairs to her room.

The day had gone from rotten to perfect in an instant. Maybe that dumb dog was good luck! *If only I didn't have to wear that prissy pink dress*, Danielle thought. I wonder how it would look turned into a mini, with my big black leather belt and those great lace stockings? Dad will have a fit! But who cares? Nick is going to die when he sees me in that outfit!

She let Garbo eat her fill of salmon eggs and foie gras, then coaxed her into a tub of warm water filled with bubble bath. Within moments, Danielle was soaked too, and beginning to wonder why she had ever felt sorry for this silly dog. But once Garbo was dry, her fluffy golden coat shone. Sprawled across the middle of the white sofa, with her head on her paws, she was awfully cute, even if she lacked the style of a Russian wolfhound.

After her own shower, Danielle sprayed a little Fallen Angel on her wrists and in her hair. *He'll ask me to the Harvest Ball tonight*, she vowed. *Or my name isn't Danielle Sharp.*

Suddenly there was a knock on the door. "Sweetie?" she heard her father say. "Can I come in?"

"Uh, I, just a minute." Danielle grabbed Garbo by the scruff of her neck and pushed her into the bathroom before she could protest. She kicked the food and water dishes into her closet and yanked the door shut.

"Gee, Dad, you're home early tonight," Danielle said breathlessly as she opened her bedroom door.

"I wanted to shower and change before the Hobarts came. You look very pretty tonight, honey. I always like you in pink."

"Thanks, Dad." He didn't even seem to notice that she'd changed the dress into a mini.

"I think you'll like the Hobarts. Their son, Nick, goes to your school."

Danielle smiled back. "I *know* I will."

"That's my girl." Her father leaned over and gave her a quick hug. "I'd better get in the shower." With his arm still around her shoulder, he sniffed the air in her bedroom. "Why do I smell chopped liver?"

"Uh, I got hungry before, so I snitched a little pâté from the hors d'oeuvres tray."

Her father laughed. "Well, you'd better open a window or something. It smells like a delicatessen in here."

"Yeah, I guess I'd better." Danielle agreed with him as she shut the door behind him. Then she dashed over to the bathroom door and let Garbo out.

"I sure hope you're figuring out how we're going to keep this up," Danielle told her. "Because even I'm not used to being this sneaky."

Danielle's place was next to Nick's at dinner. He looked so handsome that she felt her breath catch in her throat. As they sat down she moved her chair close to his so that their arms brushed each time one of them reached for a dish or lifted a utensil. More than once, she noticed Nick blushing when she leaned close and asked in a low, whispery voice for him to pass something. By the end of the meal the salt and pepper, bread, butter, and salad were all collected around Danielle's plate. When it came to flirting, Nick was a real challenge.

After dinner her mother suggested that Danielle take Nick into the den, while the adults went to the living room for coffee and after-dinner drinks. Danielle, for once, was happy to obey.

She put a compact disc in the CD player, turned the volume down, then settled herself in the opposite corner of the sofa from Nick.

"That was a great dinner. Your mom is some cook," Nick said. Danielle could see that he found the sofa uncomfortable. It was small and so pillowy and plush that it was almost impossible for him to sit on it without having to lean very close to her.

"Here's a secret for you," Danielle said in a hushed voice as she moved closer to him. "But you have to promise not to tell anyone—not even your folks."

"Okay," Nick said hesitantly. "As long as it's not going to get anyone into trouble."

"The entire meal was catered," Danielle confessed. "My mother is a walking disaster in the kitchen. She can't even boil water."

Nick laughed. "You're kidding! No wonder she kept changing the subject when my mother asked how she made the chocolate mousse. Why didn't she just tell the truth? My folks wouldn't have cared."

She shrugged. "I guess she wants people to think she's a good cook. She tried cooking lessons once, but the school gave her a refund after the third lesson. They said she burned so much food that she was a fire hazard."

Laughing, Nick finally relaxed and let his long legs stretch out in front of him. He folded his arms behind his head. "Come on. You made that up, Danielle." He chuckled. "That couldn't possibly be true."

"It is. I swear it," Danielle said sweetly, edging closer. "Cross my heart."

When Nick pushed himself up and rested his arm along the sofa back, he found himself practically embracing Danielle. He looked into her eyes a moment, and then looked away. There was no place for him to go—which was exactly what Danielle had planned. After a moment's silence she tilted her head prettily and caught his eye.

"Is something the matter, Nick?"

"Uh, no," he said, looking up at her.

Danielle ran the tip of her tongue over her lips. "You just got so quiet all of a sudden," she whispered. "It's your turn now, you know."

Nick coughed a little to clear his throat. "My turn?"

"Sure, I told you a secret. Now you have to tell me one."

"A secret? I really don't have any."

"Oh, come on, Nick. Everybody has secrets," Danielle said. "Can't you even think of one little tiny one? It's not really fair. I told you one," she reminded him.

"Oh, well. How about this? I heard that Tio's Tacos might go out of business."

"So what?" Danielle was beginning to lose her patience. "The food is awful anyway."

"True, but your cousin will be out of a job."

Danielle's anger rose by the second. She finally had Nick alone, cornered on the sofa with soft music playing in the background, and he had to bring up Lori!

"That would be too bad for poor Lori, but let's not talk about such bad news now. Besides, that wasn't really a secret, Nick." She reached over and picked a loose thread off his sweater. "I meant something about you, silly." She gazed into his eyes. "Like who you're going to ask to the Harvest Ball—"

"The Harvest Ball! I really haven't thought about it."

"But it's barely two weeks away. You want to go, don't you?" Danielle said persistently.

"Uh, sure. I want to go—" Nick squirmed. "But I haven't asked anyone yet."

"A few guys have hinted around about asking me," Danielle said, in a breathy, confidential voice. "But it's not just any dance. I want to go with someone I *really* like—someone I think is *really* special—"

"Yeah, me too," Nick said. He turned toward her. They were so close that if Danielle moved another inch, he would have to kiss her.

Danielle looked at him from under lowered lids, her lips slightly parted. She held her breath. Was he going to kiss her? If he kissed her at that moment he'd be *forced* to ask her to the ball. A guy like Nick would naturally want to do the honorable thing.

Danielle closed her eyes, willing it to happen. She waited, imagining his face drawing near to her own.

"Nick? We're leaving, dear. Come up and say good night to the Sharps," Mrs. Hobart called down the short flight of stairs.

At the sound of his mother's voice, Nick leapt to his feet. "I'll be right up," he called. "Don't worry, Danielle. I happen to know a lot of guys who would like to ask you to the dance."

Rats! Danielle cursed to herself. *Just five more minutes alone and I would have had him!*

"I'll walk you to the door, Nick," she said sweetly. "It's been fun having you here."

"Sure. It's been, um, interesting talking with you, Danielle," he said, allowing her to go up the stairs ahead of him.

There were some framed photographs hanging on the stairwell wall. Nick stopped to look at one. "This is pretty. Was it taken at Barstow Lake?"

"Oh, that was taken years ago," Danielle said, embarrassed to have Nick see her in the old family photograph. Her hair was in pigtails and she had braces on her teeth. "I was about ten years old. That's my sister, Christine, on the left. She's away at college now."

"That must be Lori on the right," Nick said with a smile. "You two look real cute in braces."

Danielle cringed. She and Lori had their arms linked and were giving the photographer twin metallic grins. Her family hadn't moved to Wood Hollow Hills then, and they were still best friends. It was hard to recall ever having been that close to anyone.

"Yeah, we were an adorable pair, weren't we?" she said dryly.

Garbo greeted Danielle with a sloppy lick as she flopped down on her bed. A few minutes later she heard her parents coming upstairs. She worried for a second that they might knock on her door to say good night. Then she realized that they were having another argument.

"Hardware!" She heard her mother complaining. "We just spent the entire evening listening to those two bores go on about the joys of hardware!"

"Electronics, actually," her father said, correcting her mother. "Hobart is going to have stores all over the country eventually."

"I don't care if he's going to have stores on five continents. He'll still be selling heaps of metal and wire. Do you think people at big city parties sit around talking about the booming answering-machine market? No! They talk about travel and fashion and culture. And we would, too, if we ever moved out of of this sorry little backwater town."

"You know, you put on a lot of airs for a girl from Sandusky, Ohio."

Danielle heard their door slam. But she could still hear every ugly word through the walls. She put her hands over her ears, then tried a pillow on her head. It finally became unbearable. She grabbed her purse, jacket, and car keys. "Come on, Garbo," she said. "We're going for a drive."

CHAPTER TEN

Danielle drove her car to Barstow Lake. The place was deserted, but she didn't feel scared. Barstow Lake brought back happy memories of her family—when they still were a family—when they still *talked* to one another.

She parked the BMW and began to walk toward the water, Garbo bounding after her.

It was a chilly evening. Danielle zipped up her suede jacket and turned up the collar. Water lapped gently against the sandy shoreline. The breeze held a scent of pine. She closed her eyes and took a deep breath.

Suddenly Garbo hunched down in front of her, growling low in her throat. Danielle's eyes flew open, and she peered into the darkness. At first she didn't see anything. Then she heard footsteps in the dry leaves, and a tall, broad-shouldered figure appeared from the woods.

"Hey, calm down, dog. What's your problem?" a husky voice asked. Whoever it was, she thought, Garbo hadn't frightened him in the least. He sounded almost amused by the dog's show of ferocity.

"Well, if it isn't Danielle Sharp and her guard dog."

The figure stepped into the light, and Danielle recognized Don James's striking features. Don was known as a troublemaker, wild and rough. He was a senior at Merivale High School and worked part-time as a mechanic somewhere in town.

A taunting smile flickered across Don's lips. "You can let go of the dog. I'm not here to scare anybody."

"What are you doing here then?"

Don laughed and came closer. "You tell me first, Sharp." He stared at Danielle with the bold attitude that had made him famous. "I didn't think nice girls like you were allowed out so late at night."

Danielle sniffed and tossed her head. "My parents don't tell me what to do. I come and go when I want."

He laughed at her again. "I'll bet." He leaned down and let Garbo sniff his hand. "Nice dog. How old is she?"

"I don't know. I just found her today. She's a stray."

He looked surprised. "A stray, huh? I would have taken you for the pedigree-with-papers type. But then, I never thought I'd see you here at night either."

"I like to come here sometimes—to think."

"That's why I come here too," Don said. "It's peaceful, and there's no one around to bug you. What do you think about?"

"Just—things," she said, taken aback by his blunt question.

Don sat down on a big rock and folded his arms across his broad chest. "So, how does it feel to be Danielle Sharp? I'm curious."

"What do you mean?"

"Well, you're a good looker. You can get any guy you want, and your parents buy you everything else—"

"That's not true," Danielle said back angrily.

"And you have a temper. I've got one too. We're a lot alike, you and I. Maybe that's why I've always liked you, Red."

"You don't know the first thing about me."

"Oh, yes, I do." He looked out at the water. "More than you think. Hey, just because you never noticed I was alive, doesn't mean I never noticed you."

Danielle knew the smart, safe thing to do would be to turn around, get in the car, and go home—but she decided to stay. She wasn't about to let Don James think he scared her.

"I've noticed you," she said. "I mean, I knew you were alive."

"Not like you notice Nick Hobart."

"What does Nick have to do with this?"

Don shrugged. "Come on, Danielle. I know you like him. But things aren't going too great with Mr. Quarterback, are they?"

"That's none of your business," she said sharply.

Don gave a harsh laugh. "Whoa—sounds like I struck a nerve. Listen," he said in a gentler tone, "Nick's not really your type."

"Oh, really? And *you* are, I suppose?" Danielle said.

"Maybe I am, but you've got to figure that out for yourself."

They were both silent for a moment, staring each other down in the shadowy moonlight. Danielle had a sudden, shocking impulse to climb up next to Don on the big rock. But she held herself back. Something about Don made her want to do outrageous things. It was both exciting and a little scary to be close to him.

"So—what else is on your mind? Trouble with your folks?"

How did he guess that? "Have you been spying on my house?"

Don chuckled. "Red, you don't have to spy if you're an observant person. If you just sit back and watch, you see a lot of things that most people are too busy to notice." He paused a moment and looked straight into her eyes.

"Take our families, for example. I started coming here 'just to think' around the time my parents started fighting—just like you did."

It was almost as if he could read her mind!

"My mother wants to move away from here," Danielle said. Without knowing exactly how it happened, she was sitting beside Don and telling him everything. She even told him about Garbo. She really loved the silly dog, but she couldn't keep her hidden much longer in her room.

"Hey! That's a simple one to solve." Don hopped off the rock, then took Danielle's hand to help her down. "I'll take her home with me. She seems to like me. You could visit her whenever you wanted."

"You would take her? Just like that?"

"Sure, why not? We have lots of room at our place. My buddies won't mind. Besides, I've always wanted a dog."

Danielle knew that Don lived far outside of town in a rundown farmhouse he shared with a bunch of friends. The driveway was always filled with motorcycles, and it was rumored that their parties lasted for days. Danielle knew that she could never go visit Garbo there. But she also thought that Don would take good care of her.

"You want to come with me, don't you?" Don asked the dog. He patted his chest, and Garbo jumped up on him, licking his face. "See? No woman can resist me when I really turn on the charm. So—what do you say?"

"Okay," Danielle said finally. "She's all yours. She'll be a lot happier in your place than locked in my bedroom. Thanks, Don."

"It's nothing," he said as they strolled toward Danielle's car with Garbo between them.

This had been the strangest, most unpredictable day of Danielle's life. She was suddenly exhausted as she thought of all she had been through.

Danielle gave the dog's head a gentle pat. She was going to miss that funny furry face.

"Don't worry. I'll take good care of her," Don said as a promise.

"I know you will," Danielle said, looking up at him.

He smiled, and two deep dimples softened his intense gaze. Danielle had never noticed before how handsome he really was. Or maybe she'd never really seen him smile like that before. "See you around sometime, Red."

He walked off toward the lake with Garbo at his heels, her tail wagging. Danielle watched them until they disappeared into the shadows. Then she headed for home.

CHAPTER ELEVEN

All the stores in the mall were packed with late-Saturday-morning shoppers—all, that is, except Tio's Tacos. Lori watched anxiously as shoppers glanced into Tio's, debated about entering, then passed on. She didn't know how much longer Ernie could stay open. And if Tio's closed, she wouldn't be able to add much more to her savings account. At this rate she could say goodbye to her uncle's generous offer.

"Hi, Lori. I didn't know you worked here."

Lori's gloomy thoughts were interrupted by the cheerful voice of Isabel Vasquez. "Oh, hi, Isabel. I don't usually work this shift, but I'm working extra to try to save a little more right now. Doing some shopping?"

Isabel nodded. "I was just looking for a present to send to my grandmother. It's her birthday in a few weeks. Thinking about her and San Antonio made me homesick for tacos."

Lori took Isabel's order and then served it to her on a plastic tray. "Hmmm, well, it looks good." Isabel took a small bite of the taco while the tray was still on the counter. Her expression changed instantly. She looked as if she were a poison victim.

"Lori," she finally said, "you don't have to be Mexican to know this food is terrible." She looked around. "No wonder there aren't any customers."

Lori leaned across the counter. "I think we're about to close for good, to tell you the truth."

"No wonder," Isabel said, sliding the tray back toward Lori.

"I'd be happy to get you something else," Lori offered. "How about some french fries?"

"What's wrong here?" Ernie appeared at the counter beside Lori.

"Are you the owner?" Isabel asked.

"Is there some problem with your order, miss?" Ernie nervously ran his hand over his head.

Isabel looked Ernie over carefully. "No problem," she said. "Other than the fact that this is not a taco. And that whatever it is, it's inedible."

"Now, hold on just a second, young lady." Ernie glanced around nervously to see if other customers were listening. "Why don't you come back into the kitchen to discuss this, Miss—"

"Vasquez," Lori said, cutting in. "Isabel Vasquez."

"Miss Vasquez. You just come right back here, and we will discuss this privately. I'll be happy to get you a refund—"

"I don't want a refund," Isabel said as she went through the swinging doors into the kitchen. "I just want a good taco. And Tio's is the only Mexican place in the mall."

Lori turned to take the next customer's order. "Uh, I think I'll just have some french fries and a cola," the boy said, glancing nervously at Isabel's taco, which still lay on the counter. Lori quickly threw it away.

Soon it was time for her break. When she went back into the kitchen, she found Isabel in an apron, standing behind the long butcher-block cooking table and ordering Ernie around the room. "Here, taste this." Isabel deftly lifted some of her tortilla-wrapped concoction onto Ernie's plate. "Now that's real Mexican food!"

Ernie took a bite. "Delicious!" he exclaimed. "Absolutely fantastic! How did you make this? You're a genius! If I could put this on my menu, I'd be a millionaire."

"So, you like it, huh?" Isabel smiled with satisfaction. She untied her apron and tossed it on the table. "Back home, we call that a taco. So long, Ernie. I hope you learned something."

"Wait! You can't leave yet!" Ernie jumped out of his chair. "You have to stay. I'll pay you anything you want. Will you be my new cook?"

"Your new cook?" Isabel looked stunned for a minute. "Gee, I don't know."

"Please say yes." Ernie was practically begging. "You tasted my tacos. I'll go out of business if you don't start working here."

Isabel nodded. "Okay. I always loved to cook anyway. Who knows? It might be fun."

Ernie clapped his hands and practically danced around the kitchen. "What luck! We're back in business! Can you start now?"

"I'd better call home." Isabel smiled.

Ernie gleefully rubbed his hands together. Lori had never seen him so happy. "We're going to feature a whole new menu, starting this afternoon," he cried, disappearing into the office.

Lori looked over at Isabel, and the dark-haired girl gave her a wink. "I came in for a taco and ended up with a job. You never know what's going to happen when you wake up in the morning, do you?"

A few minutes after Ernie posted the new menu, Tio's actually began getting more customers. For the first time all week, Lori was really busy—people were coming back to the counter for seconds!

Lori was so busy, she didn't even notice Nick until he was standing right in front of her.

"Hi, Lori? What's going on in here? Is Ernie giving away free food?"

"Nick!" She smiled brightly. She hadn't heard from him since their phone call, almost a week before, and it was the first time she had seen him since that awful conversation at the loading dock. She pushed back a stray wisp of hair that had escaped from her ponytail. Of course he had to wait to stop by until she was an absolute wreck.

"Can you believe the crowd in here?" She laughed. "Ernie hired a new cook late this morning. It's kind of a long story, but she just whipped up some fantastic new dishes, and now Ernie has more business than he can handle. If things keep up at this pace, I don't think I'll have to worry about losing my job."

"Congratulations," Nick said, surveying the line behind him. "To tell you the truth, I was hoping it would be slow in here right now. I wanted to talk to you about something."

Although his voice was low and serious, he was smiling and looking shyly down at the counter. Lori's heart skipped a beat. Was he going to ask her to the Harvest Ball? She hadn't exactly dreamed it would happen that way—with Mexican food flying around them and Ernie barking orders as background music. But right then Lori gladly would have danced on Tio's tabletops to hear what Nick had to say.

"Lori!" Ernie called. "I need you a minute." He sounded frantic. "Hurry!"

"You better go," Nick said hurriedly. "I don't want to get you in trouble."

"But there was something you wanted to talk about," she said, prompting him. A lecture from Ernie was a small price to pay for an invitation to the Harvest Ball.

"Oh, it'll keep." Nick smiled at her. "I'll stop by later—when the crowd thins out."

"Lori, I'm waiting," Ernie called impatiently.

"I'll be right there, Ernie," Lori called back, turning around. But when she pivoted around again, Nick had disappeared.

She ambled back to Ernie, determined to pour a thick, frosty strawberry shake all over his head. She just couldn't get rid of the uneasy feeling that she had missed her big chance to be asked to the Harvest Ball.

Ann Larson ran into Nick sitting on a bench outside Tio's. She took it as a good sign. "Hi, Nick," she said. "What in the world is going on in there?"

"Ernie's got some new cook or something," Nick muttered. "If you're stopping by to see Lori, don't bother. She's too busy to talk to anyone right now."

"Oh! You sound pretty disappointed. Was there something you wanted to tell her? I'll see her later. We're taking the bus home together."

Nick glanced up at Ann. "I've been trying to ask Lori to the Harvest Ball, but she's never at home. I keep missing her."

Ann wanted to scream with happiness for Lori, but she did her best to keep a straight face. "Oh, please don't give up, Nick—" She stopped herself. She didn't want to make Lori sound desperate. "I mean, I know she's busy, but today she finishes at five-thirty. Why don't you try her then?"

"Good idea. Thanks, Ann," Nick said with a broad grin. "Ernie can't keep her locked up in there forever." He looked down at his watch. "Got to get back to the store." He waved as he walked toward Hobart's. "If you see Lori, tell her I'll be waiting for her later."

"Will do!" As soon as Nick had gone she dashed to Tio's entrance. The lines were still long, and Lori was dashing back and forth behind the counter.

What do I do now? Ann wondered. She had to teach a class at the Body Shoppe in five minutes. Lori was going to be busy at least that long. *I know, I'll send her a note!* Ann took a scrap of paper and a pencil from her purse and scribbled a hasty message to Lori as she walked toward the escalator.

But who can I get to deliver it? she wondered as she walked into the studio. Just then she spotted Charlie, the cute seven-year-old son of Donna Baxter, who owned the Body Shoppe.

"Charlie," Ann called to him. "Would you like a yummy chocolate bar?" she asked. Lori and Patsy teased Ann, because no matter how much she cared about fitness, she couldn't cure her weakness for chocolate. She always had

candy in her purse. Now she took out a chocolate bar and handed it to Charlie.

"Uh-huh." Charlie nodded, reaching for the
candy. "But don't tell my mommy, okay?"

"I won't," Ann said, crouching down beside him. "But I need you to do something for
me. Take this note," she said slowly, folding
his already sticky hand around it. "Don't let go
of it until you get to Tio's Tacos. Do you know
where that is?"

"Uh-huh." Charlie nodded.

"Go inside and give the note to a girl named
Lori—the pretty girl with long yellow hair. Can
you remember all that?"

"Uh-huh." Charlie nodded. "Lori with the
yellow hair."

"That's right." Ann stared down at him.
She wasn't totally convinced he understood everything she had just said. But Charlie did know
his way around the mall. Ann decided to take a
chance. The worst that could happen was that
she wouldn't get the note. Nick would still ask
her out later, even if she didn't have any ad-
vance warning.

"Okay, Charlie, you've got yourself a job."

Charlie went down the escalator and started
through the first level to Tio's Tacos. He stopped
for just a second to watch the big kids play
games at the Video Arcade. He reached into his
pocket to see if he had a quarter to play a game.

All he found was one dime and a folded-up baseball card he had been looking for all week.

Charlie kept walking to Tio's. Tio's was really crowded. For a minute he forgot what he was supposed to do. Then he remembered—the note for Lori. He reached into his pocket, but it wasn't there. He checked all his pockets, but he couldn't find it. It was a long way from Tio's to the Body Shoppe. He'd have to go back upstairs and tell Ann he lost the note. He hoped she wouldn't want him to give back the candy bar because he'd already finished it.

Heather Barron strolled past the Video Arcade very slowly, trying to see if anyone interesting was inside. Just as she was about to move on a scrap of folded paper on the ground caught her eye. It looked like the kind of note she and her friends passed around in school, so she bent over to pick it up. She was right. Oh, but this was too much! Suddenly the day had become a lot more interesting. "Lori—" the note began. "Guess what? Nick is going to ask you to the dance! Ann."

Heather laughed wickedly to herself. She had a feeling Lori had never seen the note. Now, if she could mess things up between Nick and Lori, Danielle would really owe her. Especially since Danielle had informed practically the entire school that she and Nick were going to the dance together.

She thought fast. Then she wrote a note, folded it, and took it up to the Body Shoppe. More luck. No one was watching the front desk. Heather wrote Ann's name on the note and left it there. Then she sneaked out before anyone saw her. Next she rode the escalator up to the fourth level and walked toward To The Manor Born, the salon where she and her friends always had their hair and nails done.

"Hello, Miss Barron," the receptionist chirped.

"Hi, Sheree. Tell me, is Danielle coming in today?" Heather knew pefectly well that Danielle was planning on having a manicure.

"Miss Sharp is due in half an hour," Sheree said.

"Please give this to her when she comes in." Heather handed Sheree the note addressed to Lori that she found in the front of the arcade.

"Of course, Miss Barron."

"I wouldn't go out with Nick Hobart if he was the last guy on earth—Lori."

Ann was shocked. It just didn't make sense. What was wrong with Lori? Ann looked at the note again, and saw it wasn't even Lori's handwriting! Something crummy was going on. Somebody was trying to mess things up.

Hadn't Danielle and her slimy friends done enough damage recently? It was time to give them a dose of their own medicine. Ann considered the possibilities for a few seconds. Then she took out a pencil, erased the signature on the note, and wrote, "I wouldn't go out with Nick Hobart if he was the last guy on earth—Danielle." *That should fix her*, Ann thought.

As she admired her handiwork, she felt a timid tug at the sleeve of her sweater. Charlie stood beside her, his mouth bent down in a chocolate-edged pout. It was easy to guess what he had come to tell her.

"Ann, something bad happened," he said beginning. "I lost the note you gave me—"

"I know. Don't worry, Charlie," Ann said sympathetically. "If I give you another note, do you think you can deliver it without losing it this time?"

Charlie nodded eagerly. "Sure I can."

"Okay. I want you to take this to Hobart's Electronics store, right across from Tio's Tacos. Do you know where that is?"

Charlie nodded. "Sometimes I watch the TVs in there."

"Give the note to *Nick*. He's tall and has light brown hair. Just ask for Nick, okay?"

"Okay," Charlie said. He took the note. "I won't lose it. I promise."

Ann smiled as she watched him leave. In just a few minutes Danielle and her friends would be sorry for every rotten trick they had played in their evil little lives. Very sorry.

CHAPTER TWELVE

Charlie ran through the mall toward the electronics store. He didn't want to mess things up this time. All of a sudden he slammed into a pair of long denim-clad legs. A strong hand reached out and held him before he could tumble to the ground.

"Hey! What's your rush, speed demon?" Don James set the boy back on his feet.

"Sorry, mister," said Charlie, backing away. "I'm in a hurry."

"Okay, but I think you'd better walk if you want to get there in one piece."

Charlie had disappeared into the crowd again when Don looked down at his feet and noticed a note. The little boy must have dropped it, he realized and bent over to pick it up.

Don opened the note and read it. What unbelievable luck! "I wouldn't go out with Nick Hobart if he was the last guy on earth—Danielle."

Don broke into a big smile. This was the best news he had had all week! Whipping out a pen and a scrap of paper, Don scrawled, "Now that you're through with Nick, how about giving the James charm a chance? I'll be waiting at the lake next Saturday, the night of the Harvest Ball. Eleven sharp. Don."

With a laugh, he tossed Danielle's crumpled note about Nick Hobart toward the trash can. The paper hit the rim and bounced back onto the floor, but Don didn't bother to pick it up. Instead, he turned to see who was pulling at the sleeve of his jacket. "Hey, mister," Charlie asked, pleading with him. "Did you see a folded-up piece of paper on the floor?" His voice was trembling.

Don crouched down and ruffled Charlie's hair. "Listen, little guy," he said. "Don't worry about that note you lost. If you bring this to somebody for me," he said, holding out his note to Danielle, "I'll buy you a big ice-cream cone from that stand over there."

Charlie looked over at The Big Scoop and drooled. "How about the cone first and *then* the note?"

They walked over to the ice-cream stand, and Don bought Charlie his cone. "Now, here's the deal," Don said to Charlie. "Take this note and give it to a real pretty girl with long, red hair. Her name is Danielle. She's going to the beauty salon upstairs on the fourth level to have her nails done. All you have to do is go up there, give the note to the lady at the desk, and say it's for Danielle. Think you can do that?"

Charlie nodded. "I just say—it's for Danielle," he said between licks of his cone.

"That's right, pal." Don nodded. "Up at the beauty salon on the top level."

At To The Manor Born, Sandy Peters was taking over as receptionist. Sheree was away from the desk. Sandy walked over to take a look at the red-leather appointment book. It was going to be a hectic afternoon. Then she noticed a folded note that had Lori Randall's name written on it. Sandy was puzzled. There had to be some mistake. She went to Merivale with Lori and knew Lori never came to Manor. She also knew that Lori worked at Tio's.

Sandy looked at her watch. She had five minutes before she had to work. She rushed down to the mall's first level and into Tio's.

"Here, this is for you," Sandy said, handing the note over the counter to Lori. "I don't know how it got to the salon."

"Thanks, Sandy." Lori unfolded the note.

It said, "Guess what? Nick is going to ask you to the dance! Ann."

"Good news?" Sandy asked.

"The greatest!" Lori replied, with a dazzling smile. She had been right. Nick *did* want to take her to the ball. She felt like jumping across the counter to hug Sandy.

"Well, I'm glad I stopped by then," Sandy said.

"Hey—on your way back, could you drop this note off for Patsy Donovan at Cookie Connection?" Lori asked as she hastily scribbled a message for Patsy.

"Sure," Sandy said. "It's right on my way."

Danielle pulled into the mall and parked. Since she was a few minutes early for her manicure, she decided to stroll through the mall to see who was around.

She was standing in front of the Video Arcade when her car keys fell out of her pocket, right near the trash basket. As she bent down to pick them up, a scrap of paper caught her eye. It seemed to be a note—and she thought she saw her name on it! She unfolded the crumpled wad of paper and read: "I wouldn't go out with Nick Hobart if he was the last guy on earth—Danielle."

Danielle was infuriated. Obviously, Lori and her friends were trying to make trouble for her with Nick. Well, they weren't going to get away with it!

Working quickly, Danielle threw out this note and rewrote it signing Lori's name. *That should fix her*, Danielle thought. With the revised note in her pocket, she started up the escalator for the salon. Why hadn't she thought of something that simple earlier? Once Nick got this note, he'd be done with Lori for good.

Maybe he'd even be looking for someone to help him forget her completely.

Charlie had finally figured out where the entrance to the beauty salon was. As he looked up at the door, a pretty lady with long, red hair reached out to open it. She looked just like the lady the guy downstairs had told him about. But he couldn't remember her name.

"Hi, sweetie," the lady said, patting his head. "Are you lost? Are you looking for your mommy?"

Charlie shook his head. "I'm not lost. My mommy's down in the Body Shoppe. I think I forgot your name," he explained.

The Body Shoppe? Danielle thought. *How perfect!*

"Aren't you cute? How would you even know my name, honey?" Danielle opened up her purse and took out a dollar bill. "Look, when you go down to the Video Arcade, you pass a big store with the TV sets in the window, don't you? Do you know where that is?"

Charlie nodded. "Sure I do!"

"Well, here's a dollar for you to play games or to buy whatever you want. Just take this note into the TV store. I want you to give the note to someone named Nick. Think you can remember that?"

"Nick? Sure. I can remember that."

"Good." Danielle smiled. "Remember, the store with the TV sets," she said sending him on his way.

She read the note Charlie had handed her. It was from Don! How did he know about any of this? She hurriedly crumpled the note and stuck it into her pocket. She couldn't have anything more to do with Don James. If Teresa or Heather ever found out she had been at the lake with him, she'd never hear the end of it.

Charlie got back on the escalator and headed down to the first level. He passed by the Cookie Connection and decided to buy himself a big chocolate-chip cookie with the money Danielle had given him. He stepped up to Patsy's counter.

"I want a giant chocolate-chip cookie, please."

Patsy eyed him suspiciously. He was alone, and she was used to little kids ordering things without any money to pay for them. Her manager had told her to ask to see their money before she filled any orders. "Do you have enough money for it?" she asked him gently.

Charlie nodded. "See, right here," he said, pulling the dollar bill from his pocket. "This pretty girl with the red hair gave it to me for bringing this note to the store with the TV sets in the window." He waved Danielle's note in the air for Patsy to see.

"The store with the TV sets in the window, huh?" Whatever Danielle had to say to Nick, it couldn't be anything good for Lori. Maybe this was her chance to pay Danielle, Heather, and Teresa back for Friday night. "Listen, I'll give you another cookie—any kind you want—if you give me that note," Patsy said. He hesitated. "I'm going over there in a minute, so I'll deliver it for you."

Charlie considered this for a moment. "Oatmeal," he said, handing the note to Patsy.

"Oatmeal it is." Patsy quickly gave Charlie the cookie, then picked up the note. It read: "I wouldn't go out with Nick Hobart if he was the last guy on earth! Lori."

Patsy was stunned. She understood why Danielle would want Nick to see the note. But why would Lori write it in the first place?

"Thanks for the extra one," Charlie said as he wandered away.

"Anytime," she answered, still puzzling over the note in her hand. It was just about time for her break anyway, Patsy noticed. She could walk over to Tio's and ask Lori to explain it all.

A few minutes later Patsy headed to Tio's two doors down. Catching sight of her reflection in a store window, she realized she was still wearing her Cookie Connection apron. She immediately stopped and took it off, winding it through the strap of her shoulder bag. She rushed toward Tio's and was bumped and jostled by the Saturday-afternoon crowd.

"So, what do you mean, you don't want to go out with Nick Hobart?" Patsy asked Lori as soon as she reached the counter at Tio's.

"What are you talking about?" Lori asked.

"Didn't you get my note? Ann said Nick is going to ask me to the dance."

"I got that one," Patsy replied. "But then this little kid came by for a cookie, and he was carrying another note that said, 'I wouldn't go out with Nick Hobart if he was the last guy on earth!' "

"I never wrote a note like that! Where is it?" Lori exclaimed.

"Don't worry, I have it right here," Patsy said, reaching into her pocket. "In my—uh—one of these pockets—" She frantically searched through all her pockets, then realized she had put the note in the pocket of her apron. "It's right here," she said. She reached for her handbag, where the apron had been hanging. It was gone. "Oh, no! I must have dropped it on my way here!"

"You've got to find it! If Nick finds that note, he'll think I really wrote it!"

Nick stepped out of Hobart's to see if the crowd at Tio's had thinned out any. It was still very busy. *Oh, well, I guess I can stand to wait until tonight to ask her,* he decided.

As he started to walk away from Tio's, he noticed a heap of crumbled fabric at his feet. Store owners got fined for litter in front of their shops, whether it came from them or not. At first Nick thought it was a rag. Then he saw that it was an apron. He picked it up and saw the Cookie Connection stencil on the front.

Nick felt in the pockets. If he could figure out who had lost it, he could return it to the owner and save somebody a little trouble with the boss. He found a slip of paper in a pocket. He took it out and read, "I wouldn't go out with Nick Hobart if he was the last guy on earth! Lori."

Nick was stunned. He sat down on a bench and read it again. He couldn't misunderstand the message if he tried.

In spite of how polite she had been to him lately, she really did mean what she had told him the week before—she didn't want to have anything to do with him. Ann must have told her that he wanted to ask her to the dance. And this was her response? Boy, was he ever dumb! He had thought she liked him. But why had she been so friendly then? Was she setting him up for something because she blamed him for what had happened at the party?

He crumpled the note in his hand. *Well, at least I didn't make a total fool of myself by asking her out*, he thought. Nick walked over to Cookie Connection and handed the apron to the guy behind the counter without a word. He had never felt so rotten in his whole life.

Patsy slowly retraced her steps from Tio's back to the Cookie Connection. Step by step, she grew more anxious. She didn't see the apron anywhere. Finally she was back at Cookie Connection.

"Hey, Patsy! Is this your apron?" Jonathan called from behind the counter.

Patsy ran to the counter. Thank heavens! Somebody had found it and brought it back! "Oh, great!" she said, taking it from him. She reached into the pocket—no note! Her spirits plunged. "There wasn't a note in this pocket when they brought it back, was there? Is it back there on the floor or something?"

"I didn't notice any note," the boy said, emptying a tray of cookies into a big bin. "That guy Nick who works at the electronics store turned it in. Why don't you ask him? Maybe he found the note."

Patsy thought she might faint right there. It was too horrible to think about: Nick had found the apron—and the note. How was she ever going to tell Lori? "This has been the worst week," Patsy groaned. "First I ruin my own life, then I ruin my best friend's." Her shoulders sagging, she walked back toward Tio's to deliver the dreadful news.

When Danielle's manicure was dry, she decided to go down to Hobart's to see how Nick was taking the good news about Lori. *Of course, I guess it's bad news from Lori's point of view,* Danielle thought cheerily as she glided down on the escalator. She held her freshly polished nails out to admire the color she had chosen that afternoon. Scarlet Revenge it was called— how utterly appropriate. Danielle couldn't keep a small giggle from escaping her lips.

She spotted Nick as soon as she walked into Hobart's. He was standing beside a shelf of video cameras, explaining the differences to a customer. Danielle noticed that he wasn't wearing his usual grin. In fact, he looked utterly dejected, Danielle observed with pleasure. Everything seemed to have worked perfectly.

"Working hard, Nick?" Danielle asked as soon as the customer left.

Startled, he whipped around to see who was behind him. "Oh, hi, Danielle," he said.

She picked up a portable phone and played with the buttons. "I just came by to say 'hello.' I had a good time when you came over with your parents Tuesday. Did you have fun?"

Nick looked down. "Oh—yeah, sure. I had a good time too."

Danielle paused, then ran her fingertips through her glossy mane. "We should get together again sometime, Nick. I mean, just you and me, without our *parents*."

Something she had said caused Nick to look up at her as if he were noticing her there for the first time. He hesitated for a moment, then spoke. "Listen," he said, "would you like to go to the Harvest Ball with me? I mean, if you don't already have a date. I bought the tickets and I wanted to ask someone—uh, I mean, I knew I wanted to ask someone who would really have a good time at a big fancy dance like that." He concluded his speech with an almost bitter laugh.

Danielle knew that he had almost slipped and admitted that he had really wanted to ask someone *else*. But she was willing to put up with Nick's little goof. After all, she finally had what she had been after all these weeks.

"Nick, that's so sweet," she cooed. "You're the guy I was really hoping to go with," she told him coyly.

Nick felt a twinge of guilt. Danielle wasn't the girl he had been hoping to go with. She was his distant second choice. *But your first choice doesn't want anything to do with you,* he reminded himself. And Danielle really was sweet when you got to know her.

"Great. It's settled then." Nick forced a smile.

He sounded determined but not exactly thrilled. *He still feels bad about Lori. Big deal. By the end of our evening together, he'll forget he ever knew Lori's name!*

CHAPTER THIRTEEN

"Nick can't be going to the ball with Danielle! It's a mistake! It has to be," Lori moaned. "I feel so awful, I could die." She threw herself face down on her bed, soaking her pillow with tears. Ann and Patsy exchanged glances.

By the time Lori had left Tio's, the news had spread all over the mall. Nick Hobart, the Cougars' star quarterback, had invited Danielle Sharp to the Harvest Ball.

Nearly everyone agreed that Nick and Danielle were the perfect match. They would be the most perfect couple at the Harvest Ball for sure. Nobody from Atwood was really surprised at the news. Lori and her friends, however, were in shock.

Lori lifted her head and blew her nose. "Danielle—or one of her *horrible* friends—wrote that note, and Nick believed it! It certainly didn't take him long to ask her," she said angrily, choking back a sob. "He couldn't have wanted to go with me that much."

"Come on, Lori. Danielle just tricked him into it," Ann said, cutting in.

"He was awfully upset when I told him the note was a phony," Patsy said.

"But not upset *enough* to change his plans," Lori said and then burst into fresh tears. "Well, I hope he's happy. He got what he wanted. And so did Danielle. From now on, I'm not interested in hearing another word about *Nick Hobart*," Lori said. "Or my darling first cousin."

"You're sure this will work?" Patsy asked Irving Zalaznick as the bell sounded at the end of chem class.

"Oh, absolutely," Irving replied, pushing his glasses up on his nose and trying to stand a little taller than his five feet four inches. "It takes only half an hour to an hour to start to work. But it takes several shampoos to get it out."

"Perfect!" Patsy said. "Thanks a million, Irv. Did I ever tell you you're a genius?" And with that, she gave him a peck on the cheek.

Irving blushed to the roots of his flyaway hair and smiled shyly at his lab partner. "It was nothing."

Oh, but it wasn't "nothing." Not at all.

*   *   *

After school Patsy removed the bottle from the bag and held it up to the light with a devilish grin. The liquid in it sparkled a pretty shade of emerald green. Sort of like the color of Danielle Sharp's eyes. The vial of goop in her hand was the crucial ingredient to Patsy's plan.

Ever since Heather and Teresa had humiliated her with Steve Freeman, Patsy had planned to get back at them. The pieces began to fall into place when Ann overheard Teresa and Heather gabbing in the Body Shoppe locker room. They had a double date with Ben Frye and Rob Matthews. The guys had invited them to have pizza at Aunti Pasta's Italian restaurant on the first level of the mall after their aerobics class. Ann had reported that the girls were frantic about how to impress them.

Well, Irving's little concoction was *sure* to impress them. *If only I could give Danielle the same treatment*, she thought as she slipped the bottle into her purse. *She deserves it as much as anybody for what she did to Lori!*

But Danielle hadn't been hanging out at the mall much the past couple days. Ever since she had snagged a date for the ball with Nick, she was making herself scarce. Rumor had it that she was devoting every spare minute to shopping for a dress. *She's just lucky this time*, Patsy thought.

Arriving at the mall, Patsy went with Ann

to the Body Shoppe and hid in a shower stall. Peeking through the curtains, she had a full view of the locker room. Right on schedule, Teresa and Heather appeared and changed for their class, blabbing nonstop about their dates with Ben and Rob.

When the coast was clear and she had heard the class begin, Patsy sneaked out of the showers and headed straight for Teresa and Heather's lockers. She took out their shampoo bottles, poured a little of the goop into each one, then carefully replaced them. The hard part was done.

Patsy slipped out of the locker room the back way, so she wouldn't have to go through the exercise studio. She wanted to get a good seat at Aunti Pasta's, so she wouldn't miss a second of the afternoon's entertainment.

An hour later Patsy spotted Heather and Teresa entering the restaurant. Rob and Ben were waiting at a table up front. She shielded herself with an open menu as the girls walked past. But Teresa and Heather were so excited, they wouldn't have noticed Patsy if she was their waitress.

"I know I must look like a wreck," Teresa was saying as she approached the boys' table. "After I work out, I just throw on any old thing." Patsy thought she was going to be sick. "Any old thing" was a brand-new pair of black leather pants and a red cashmere sweater.

"It must be the light in here," Rob said. "But it's the most peculiar thing, Heather. Your hair looks kind of green."

Two points, big boy! Patsy chortled to herself with secret glee.

"Green?" A mirror ran along the wall over the table booths and Heather peered at her reflection.

"It really *does* look green, Heather," Teresa hastily said. "It's getting greener by the second!"

Heather glared at Teresa. "I wouldn't laugh, gorgeous. Take a look at yourself!"

"I can't believe this!" Ben looked from one girl to the other and back again. "It's like watching one of those time-lapse nature movies we always see in biology. You know, when the leaves pop out of the trees and get greener and greener. This is really wild. You girls have some sense of humor."

"This is no joke, bison brain! We didn't do this on purpose!" Teresa shrieked as she jumped up out of her chair. Clutching her hair, she ran to the mirror.

Heather followed right behind her. "What a nightmare! What if it doesn't wash out?"

"But it has to wash out!" Teresa said. She was almost in tears.

"Don't count on it, sweetie pie," Patsy whispered to herself from behind her menu.

Rob, who was known for his wicked sense

of humor, added, "Let's just hope it doesn't *fall* out. Can you imagine how they'd look bald?" he asked Ben.

The two boys burst out laughing. "Somebody played the prank of the year on you two." Ben roared. "Just look at your hair!"

"How can you be so mean! Both of you!" Heather screamed. Every head in Aunti Pasta's turned to watch as she rushed to the ladies' room.

Teresa took one last look at herself in the mirror, then burst into tears. With her hands over her hair, she chased after Heather.

"Misery loves company." Patsy chortled to herself.

Patsy watched the two boys leave without Heather and Teresa. She had gotten her revenge—in spades! Not even Danielle Sharp could have plotted things more perfectly. *Thank you, Irving, wherever you are!* she thought happily. *You're the best lab partner a girl ever had!*

News traveled fast about Teresa and Heather's new hairstyles. Lori was working at Tio's when she heard all about it from Ann. The story provided the only bright spot in her otherwise gloomy week.

She couldn't stop thinking about Nick and Danielle, no matter how hard she tried. *It just wasn't meant to be*, she told herself. *I have to forget about him and get on with my life—if I can!*

But Nick wouldn't let her. He had called her the last two nights, but she refused to speak to him. There was nothing for him to explain. He had asked Danielle to be his date for the dance, and nothing could change it. After the Harvest Ball, Nick and Danielle would be inseparable. Lori just knew it. She wanted nothing else to do with him. The sooner she put him out of her mind, the better.

But Nick refused to give up. On the Wednesday night before the ball, when Lori left work, she found him standing outside Tio's, waiting for her. She pretended not to see him and walked quickly in the opposite direction.

"Lori! Wait!" he called out, walking after her. "I want to talk to you."

He caught up to her and grabbed the sleeve of her jacket. Lori stopped walking, but she wouldn't look at him.

"We have nothing to talk about, Nick," she said quietly. "Please just let me go."

Nick let go of her sleeve but stepped directly into her path so she couldn't pass him. "I think we have plenty to say to each other, Lori. I've been calling you all week. Why won't you talk to me?"

Lori glared at him. "Does Danielle know you've been calling me? She might not like that. In fact, I'm sure she wouldn't like it at all."

"Who said I need Danielle's permission to do anything? She has nothing to do with this, Lori. With us, I mean—"

"Oh, Nick, she has *everything* to do with it! Can't you see that? There is no *us*, Nick, and there never will be. There's only you and Danielle." Lori felt the tears sting her eyes.

"Lori, please, don't walk away again." Nick gently held her shoulders as she tried to move past him. "Please listen to me. I didn't want to ask her. I wanted to ask you. It was all a big, stupid mistake. You know that, and you also know I can't get out of it now. Please try to understand."

For a moment Lori's anger and heartache melted away as she met Nick's desperate, pleading gaze. She wanted to forgive him. She wanted to let him pull her close and promise that everything would be okay from then on.

But it wasn't going to happen that way. He was still going to the Harvest Ball with Danielle. Once he had spent the evening with the most beautiful girl in Merivale, once he had seen how people treated Danielle Sharp and Nick Hobart, Atwood's most glamorous couple, he would never be able to settle for Lori Randall.

"Lori," Nick whispered. "Can't we go someplace and talk?"

She let herself look briefly into his eyes, then she pulled away. "No, I'm sorry. We don't have anything to talk about. See you around."

She began to walk away from him, then broke into a run as she headed for the glass-and-chrome elevator that would take her straight up to the Body Shoppe. Her vision was blurred by tears. She was so tired of crying over Nick Hobart. Was it ever going to stop hurting?

Nick drove aimlessly around town for almost an hour before he was calm enough to go home. When he finally did go in, he went straight up to his bedroom.

He paced around his room, tossed books from one side of his desk to the other, and punched his fist into his pillow again and again. Why wouldn't Lori just hear him out? For a moment it had looked as if she was going to give him a break. Then she just turned on him again. She couldn't have felt the same way about him as he felt about her, or she would have given him a chance to explain.

Why couldn't he be really happy about going to the ball with Danielle? She was the prettiest girl at Atwood. Most guys at school would love a date with her.

Nick sighed and flopped down on his bed. *Guess I'm just crazy then*, he thought. *Crazy about Lori. She can be so funny and sweet and special. What will I do if she really never speaks to me again?*

An idea came to Nick! Lori wouldn't listen to him, but maybe Danielle would. If he was honest with her about the whole mess, maybe she'd be a sport and let him off the hook. She had a reputation for being self-centered. But now that he had gotten to know her better, Nick thought she was probably a lot more understanding than most people realized. After all, Lori was her cousin. Didn't that count for something?

Nick dialed Danielle's number. "Hi, Danielle. It's Nick," he said.

"Nick," Danielle said in a dreamy voice. "I was just thinking of you."

"You were?"

"Uh-huh. I was trying on the gown I bought for the ball and was wondering if you'll like it."

"Uh, I'm sure it's very pretty, Danielle. You—you always look great," Nick stammered. Rats! She had already bought her dress. How could he break the date with her now? Nick swallowed hard. "You know, Danielle, the real reason I called was—well, something important has been on my mind."

"Mine too," she said purring. "I've been wanting to tell you that I'm just so proud to be your date for the ball, Nick. Maybe I shouldn't tell you this, but that night when you were at my house with your parents, I was hoping really hard that you'd ask me to the dance. And my wish came true!"

There was no easy way to say it, Nick decided. He just had to be honest and come right out with it.

"I have to tell the truth, Danielle," he said in a firm tone. "When I bought the tickets for the dance, I honestly didn't plan on asking you."

"I understand," Danielle said sweetly. "You just felt funny about your car." Danielle had a sneaking suspicion he wanted to talk about Lori. But she just wouldn't let him. No way was he wriggling out of this date and humiliating her. "Don't worry, Nick. I really do understand."

"Understand what? What about my car?"

"Well, I understand that you might feel a little awkward taking a date to the ball in your car," Danielle said in her most sincere and sensitive voice. "I mean, it's perfectly safe, I'm sure, but it's not much to look at, is it?"

Nick's ancient Camaro was so tacky. Danielle did not plan to arrive at the dance in that heap! It just wasn't her style, and Nick had just given her the perfect chance to mention it. So what if she hurt his feelings a little?

"It's only three years old," Nick said, defending the Camaro. "No one will notice that dent on the back fender at night."

"Nick, you don't have to be proud with

me. It's okay. We can take my car. As a matter of fact, I just had it washed and waxed. It looks brand new," she said sweetly.

"That's because it *is* brand new," Nick replied with a sigh. He wasn't going to get out of this date! Oh, well, at least Danielle really liked him.

"We'll take your car, Danielle. That's okay with me," he said finally.

"Oh, Nick. You're going to look *great* behind the wheel of my car. Wait till you drive it. It's a dream."

"Do you really think so?"

"Oh, I *do*! And, Nick—that's only the beginning."

CHAPTER FOURTEEN

"Lori? Are you getting ready for work, dear?" her mother called up the stairs.

"I'll be down in a few minutes, Mom."

That night was the Harvest Ball. Danielle was probably at To The Manor Born, getting her hair done, and Nick— Lori's hand shook, and she dropped an open bottle of skin lotion on the bathroom counter. It splattered over the sink and ran down the front of the cabinet. *That's what you get for thinking about Nick Hobart. Another mess to clean up.*

Think about the future, she told herself. *Think about designing beautiful clothes and jewelry, maybe even moving to New York or Paris. Think about college.* Her savings account wasn't far from her goal. She was going to make it by her uncle's deadline—that was some consolation. *Someday I won't even remember what Nick Hobart looks like,* she told herself.

"Lori, five minutes," her mother called.

Lori dashed back into her bedroom and pulled open her closet. That night, she wasn't going to wear the despised orange uniform. But the outfit she had to wear made her orange double-knit look like a positive fashion statement.

All week long Ernie had been thinking about a special way to advertise his new menu. The day before, he had announced his plan. What better way to catch everyone's eye than to dress a pretty girl in an "authentic" Mexican costume? She could hand out free samples of Isabel's delicious cooking around the mall. To Ernie, it was a stroke of genius. And it was Lori who would be the lucky lady to wear Ernie's "stroke of genius."

She regarded herself in the mirror. This outfit was going to singlehandedly put fashion, advertising, women's liberation, and Mexican cuisine back at least twenty years. It was a flashy, formfitting red dress that hugged Lori's waist, hips, and thighs, then flared out in a riot of taffeta ruffles. Big puff sleeves accented a low, scoop neckline, which was narrowly saved from being indecent by a gaudy pink flower pinned in the middle of the dress.

As if the dress weren't bad enough, Lori had to wear big hoop earrings and a crazy red turban from which dangled artificial bananas, oranges, grapes, and mangoes. For once she was glad to be working on a Saturday night.

Nobody much would be hanging around the mall, especially with the Harvest Ball on.

"I'm ready," Lori called to her mother as she walked into the kitchen.

Teddy and Mark were playing checkers in the living room. When Teddy looked up, he burst into laughter.

"Hey! It's Miss Hot Tamale herself!"

"Very funny," Lori said, tilting her head back to try to look a little dignified. Her turban wobbled and tipped forward, almost covering her eyes. She slipped it off her head and smoothed back her hair.

Teddy jumped up, grabbed the turban, and put it on.

"Give me that, you little monster!" Lori chased him into the kitchen, her high black heels clacking against the tile. Teddy scooted out of her grasp and back into the living room where he grabbed Mark, Lori's eight-year-old brother. Together they formed a two-man dance line, and they did the cha-cha around the coffee table, with Lori close behind them.

"I mean it, Teddy—give it back!" But her threats were pointless.

"Uh-oh! Zee pretty señorita is getting steamed!" Teddy said, teasing her.

"So is zee señorita's mother." Mrs. Randall appeared in the doorway in her nurse's uniform, a very stern expression on her face.

"We were just having a little fun." Teddy

meekly took the turban off and handed it back to Lori. "I like the fruit, Lori. Nice touch."

"Thanks." Lori smashed the turban back on her head. With as much dignity as she could muster, she slipped on her jacket and stalked out of the house.

Though she was miserably self-conscious at first, after a couple of hours of handing out free samples, all Lori could think about was how much her feet hurt. But there was a bright side to it—with all her attention focused on her aching toes, she had no time to think about Nick and Danielle at the dance. Well, almost no time anyway.

Danielle kicked off her shoes under the table. Her feet were killing her. Nick Hobart was the worst dancer in the world. He had stomped on every single one of her toes at least once. Most he'd gotten twice. He just didn't seem to be paying any attention to what he was doing.

In fact, that was the problem with the whole crummy evening. Nick Hobart looked good, but he wasn't paying a bit of attention to her. Every other guy in the place nearly fainted when she had appeared in her dazzling, strapless black gown. A few boys even left their dates to ask Danielle for a dance. But did Nick care? He didn't even notice.

Danielle drummed her fingers on the table. So far, the Harvest Ball was a disaster, and

Danielle could tell a lot of people were beginning to notice.

"Would you like more soda or anything?" Nick asked.

Danielle was going to scream. Asking her if she wanted to drink or eat or dance was the extent of Nick's conversation for the night.

"No more soda, thanks. Or anything to eat. And, no, I don't feel like dancing," she snapped.

"Oh, okay." Her sarcasm was wasted on him. He sat back in his seat and folded his arms over his chest. That distracted look came into his eyes again.

"Listen, Nick—I hate to say it, but I'm getting bored," Danielle announced.

"So am I," Nick quickly said. "Do you want me to take you home?"

"Home?" Danielle couldn't believe her ears. It was barely ten o'clock. She couldn't go home yet. It would make her the laughingstock of Atwood Academy. "I want to leave, but I don't want to go home. Let's just get out of here. We'll get some ideas once we're on the road," said Danielle, slipping into her shoes again.

"Okay." Nick shrugged listlessly.

A few minutes later he and Danielle had left the country club and were cruising down the back roads of Wood Hollow Hills.

"Well, what shall we do now?" Danielle asked brightly, looking at his handsome profile.

"It's such a beautiful night—perfect for looking at the stars."

Nick seemed to perk up. "My folks have a telescope set up in the den. Their bridge club is over tonight, but I'm sure they wouldn't mind if we went back to my house to use it."

"I don't think we need a telescope, Nick," she replied quickly.

What was the matter with him? If any other guy had been in the car with her, she'd have been fighting him off.

"How about something to eat?" Nick suggested.

"But we just had dinner at the club, Nick."

Nick shrugged. "Maybe it was all that dancing, but I'm starved."

"Oh, all right." Danielle sighed. She could have screamed. This was turning out to be the most boring night of her life!

"How about some pizza!" Nick turned the car onto the highway.

"I've got a better idea." Danielle's eyes lit up as a wicked plan came into her head. "Let's try Tio's. Everyone's been raving about the new menu."

"Tio's?" Nick asked, surprised. "You're sure you want to go there?"

"Positive," Danielle said lightly. "I have a sudden craving for nachos." When Nick saw the two girls side by side, he'd finally figure out just how lucky he was to have ended up with

Danielle. *You'd just better turn out to be worth it, Nick Hobart,* she told him silently. *I've never worked so hard on a guy in my life.*

Lori was just tottering through the swinging doors, carrying a trayful of food, when she practically slammed into Nick. Wobbling on her insanely high heels, she caught herself just in time. "Nick," she gasped. "What are you doing here?" Her eyes were wide with horror, and her face turned as red as her dress.

"Lori?" Nick stared at her as though he couldn't believe his eyes. "What are you doing dressed like that?" The way Nick said it, Danielle thought he actually liked the hideous, red dress. But it didn't matter. Lori reacted exactly as Danielle had hoped she would.

"Oh, I can't believe this!" Lori moaned. She turned and ran through the doors into the kitchen.

Danielle couldn't have been happier.

"I don't get it. What did I say?" Nick asked as he set their tray down.

"Don't worry about it, Nick." Danielle patted his hand. "Why don't we just take this stuff out to the car with us? I'll drive," she said.

Nick nodded and wrapped up the food. He was obviously upset and would have done anything she told him. But Danielle decided to save a few things for later.

*   *   *

Lori yanked the turban off her head and sat on a chair in the back of the kitchen. She covered her face with her hands and started to cry.

For weeks she had tried to forget about Nick Hobart. But it was impossible! She was still crazy about him and she always would be.

The hardest part was that it was so clear what a perfect couple Danielle and Nick made. Side by side, dressed for the dance, they looked as if they had stepped out of a magazine. And Lori looked like a creature from another planet! In a way, though, Lori was glad for what had happened, because it had snipped the last slender thread of hope to which she had been desperately clinging. After that night there was no hope at all.

As soon as Danielle pulled into the Overlook and turned off the motor, Nick jumped out of the car as if he'd been bitten by a snake. "I'd better throw out this trash," he explained.

When he got back, he discovered that Danielle had tilted the seats back slightly. Soft music was playing on the tape deck. Nick stared straight out the windshield, tapping on the dashboard with his fingertips. Soon he felt Danielle's fingertips tickling the back of his neck.

"Isn't it a beautiful night?" Danielle whispered. "Isn't this the most romantic spot you ever saw?"

Nick felt himself getting warm under the

collar and grabbed at his bow tie. "Oh let me do that for you, Nick," Danielle said, reaching over to loosen his collar.

"Thanks," he said hoarsely. He'd never been with a girl as aggressive as Danielle. He didn't quite know how to handle it. Her perfume filled the air with wildflowers. It was even in her beautiful red hair. And when she sat close to him, with her warm, soft hands pressed against his face, she was hard to resist.

Nick turned to her, to try to explain. Those emerald green eyes were just inches from his. *Why should I resist her?* he asked himself. *I like Danielle—and she likes me.* He found himself leaning closer to kiss her.

But Nick couldn't go through with it. He pulled back. Danielle's eyes flew open and her eyes flashed with fury. "What's the matter now?" she demanded.

"I'm sorry, Danielle," Nick said. "Don't take it personally. It's nothing! Please don't be angry." He just couldn't get Lori off his mind.

"Don't take it personally?" Danielle shrieked. "How else am I supposed to take it? I'll be angry if I *want*. Don't you *dare* tell me how to act, Mr. Boring! You want to know the truth? This has been the worst night of my life. I could have had a better time staying home and picking lint off my sweaters!"

"I'm sorry you had such a rotten time. I tried to explain the other night—"

"Sorry! You're *sorry*? You haven't talked to me—or even looked at me—the whole night! I spent a fortune on this outfit, not to mention my hair and makeup. I gave up a chance to be with any one of a dozen guys who would have done anything to be where you are right now. You're sorry all right! You're—you're—" Danielle couldn't think of a name bad enough to call him.

Reaching deftly behind him, Danielle opened the door latch. With one hard push, Nick tumbled backward out of the car. "Take a hike, Nick!"

"What the—" she heard him exclaim as he disappeared off the edge of the seat.

Danielle slammed the door shut, put the car into gear, and left Nick in a cloud of dust. What a fool she had been! Nick Hobart was stupid, self-centered, boring, and obviously blind! She never wanted to see him again. Nobody treated Danielle Sharp that way and got away with it! Nobody!

CHAPTER FIFTEEN

It was closing time at Tio's Tacos. Ernie tallied the night's receipts, then looked up.

"Lori and Isabel—will you come into my office, please! I want to speak to you—in private."

Isabel shot Lori a questioning look. "I told you I overdid it with the garlic in that last batch of burritos," she whispered.

"Don't be silly," Lori said as they followed Ernie through the kitchen to his office. "Ernie said they were delicious."

But what had they done wrong? Ernie must have seen Lori hiding out in the kitchen before, waiting for Nick and Danielle to leave.

"I know you're both in a hurry to get home," Ernie said once they entered his office. "But I wanted to give you both something."

Leaning across his desk, he handed each

girl a check. "Just a little bonus to show my appreciation. You've both done a great job."

"Wow! Thanks Ernie!" Isabel squealed.

"Gosh, Ernie," Lori said, staring down at her check. "You really didn't have to do this. But I'm sure glad you did. Thanks!" With that in her account, she would make the additional two hundred dollars so her uncle would double her money.

"Hey—you both deserve it. Isabel, for her great cooking. And Lori, for sticking with Tio's when everybody else was giving up. And, hey, even a guy with *notoriously* bad taste like me can see that it was no picnic trotting around the mall in that outfit all night long."

"Ernie," Lori said, "I'm going to save this money to pay my tuition at design school. And the first thing I'm going to do when I get there is design brand-new uniforms for Tio's staff!" Laughing, she took the turban off and dropped it onto his desk.

Ernie laughed uproariously. "I accept! And thanks again, both of you."

"I'm going to clean up a little," Isabel said as she strolled out of the office. "Then I'm going home. What a night!"

"Wait a second, Isabel. I'll help you." Lori walked past her and pushed open the swinging doors. When she stepped into the dining room, she froze. Seated at one of the tiny orange tables was Nick Hobart!

*   *   *

Danielle screeched to a stop in the driveway, turned off the engine and searched for her house key in the glove compartment. As she fumbled for it, her hand touched a piece of crumpled paper.

Don's note! She hadn't even thought about it since that day at the mall. He had said he'd be waiting for her that very night—but had he really meant it?

There was only one way to find out. Danielle started the car and sped out of the driveway, heading for Barstow Lake. He had probably written that note just to tease her—no way would he be hanging around at eleven just waiting for her to show up. But she kept driving anyway. It was too early to go home.

As she pulled into the parking lot by the lake, Danielle's heart sank. There were no other cars in sight. But as she braked to a stop, she heard a familiar enthusiastic barking. Garbo came bounding out of the woods. And right behind her followed Don James, wearing his trademark black leather jacket and a wide smile.

Nick's tuxedo was rumpled, his red bow tie hung loose around his neck, his shoes were covered with dust. He had never looked so handsome before, Lori thought. Nick just smiled. "I thought I'd wait for you," he said quietly.

Lori took a few careful steps toward him. "What happened to Danielle?"

A grin twitched at the corners of Nick's mouth. "She—uh—dropped me off in such a hurry, I didn't get a chance to ask where she was going." Nick put his hands in his trouser pockets and shook his head. "Can't really say I blame her too much. I was a pretty rotten date."

"You were?" Still puzzled, Lori walked closer. "I don't understand," she said, meeting his gaze.

"If a guy took you out and spent the whole night imagining how it would have been with some other girl, that would be pretty awful. Don't you agree?"

Lori nodded. She didn't know what to say. Her heart began to fill with hope again, but she tried to ignore it. She just couldn't stand to be disappointed again.

"Lori," Nick said, "I know you're probably still mad at me. But I just came here to tell you that I couldn't stop thinking about you tonight. Danielle and I—well, it was a big mistake for us to go out together. I should have explained to her that it just wasn't going to work out."

Stepping closer to her, Nick wrapped one arm around Lori's waist. With his free hand, he gently tilted her chin toward his face. Stroking her silky, pale gold hair, he looked deep into Lori's eyes. "Oh, Lori," he said, his voice soft as a caress. "You're the only one I wanted to be with tonight. Can't you believe me?"

Lori looked up at him with a soaring heart. This one perfect moment was worth all the heartache, all the uncertainty. No one would ever come between them again. "Yes, Nick. I believe you," she whispered.

Nick stared at her for a long, breathless moment. Then he leaned slowly toward her, and their lips met in a gentle kiss. His strong, warm arms came around her and hugged her close. She had dreamed of that moment so many times before. But this time, it was for real. Dream kisses were never this warm or tender or soft. Reality was far better than her fantasies could ever be, she thought, winding her arms around his broad shoulders. She never wanted to let go of him again.

"*Caramba!*" Isabel exclaimed, standing behind the counter.

Nick and Lori hastily pulled apart. Lori blushed furiously. "You're beautiful when you blush," Nick told her, his arms still looped around her waist. "Your face almost matches your dress."

"Oh! This ridiculous dress!" Lori gasped, blushing even darker.

"Oh, it's not so bad, Lori." Nick tried to soothe her.

"You're just saying that to make me feel good. It's horrible!"

Nick leaned back and gazed at her appraisingly. "It's really not bad at all. I'll tell you a secret," he said. "When I saw you in it before, I felt pretty jealous."

"Jealous?"

Nick nodded. "You really looked sexy in it. I was afraid some other guy would steal you away before we could straighten things out." He smiled and took her hand. "I wish I could drive you home. But I don't have my car."

"That's okay. We can walk."

Nick winced and glanced down at his feet. "How about the bus? I walked most of the way here from the Overlook."

"The Overlook? But that's almost five miles away—"

"It's a long story," Nick said with a charming, lopsided grin. "Sure you want to hear it?"

"Don't worry. I'll let you know if I'm getting bored," Lori replied with a glint in her eye. She wouldn't miss hearing this for *anything*.